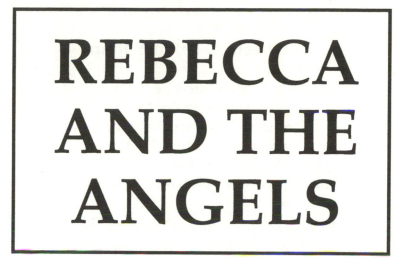

REBECCA AND THE ANGELS

Part Four
of the
Angel Mountain Saga

Brian John

Greencroft Books

2004

First Impression 2004
Reprinted 2006

Published by
Greencroft Books
Trefelin, Cilgwyn, Newport,
Pembrokeshire SA42 0QN
Tel 01239-820470. Fax 01239-821245
Email: greencroft@macunlimited.net

*All characters in this story other than those clearly
in the public domain are fictitious and any
resemblance to real persons, living or dead,
is purely coincidental*

ISBN 0 905559 83 5

Typeset by the author in Palatino 10 pt and designed on
Apple iMac computer using Appleworks 5

Printed and bound in Great Britain by The Bath Press,
Lower Bristol Road, Bath BA2 3BL

CONTENTS

North

Pen Dinas

Newport Bay

Pwllgwaelod

Sea Quarries

Dinas

Turnpike Road

Werndew

To
Fishguard
and
Pen Caer

The
Common

Mountain Track

Bedd
Morris

⇐ = Roads
···· Tracks
ᔑ Cliffs
ᨆᨆ Crags

Dinas
Mountain

One Mile

Cwm Gwaun

Pontfaen

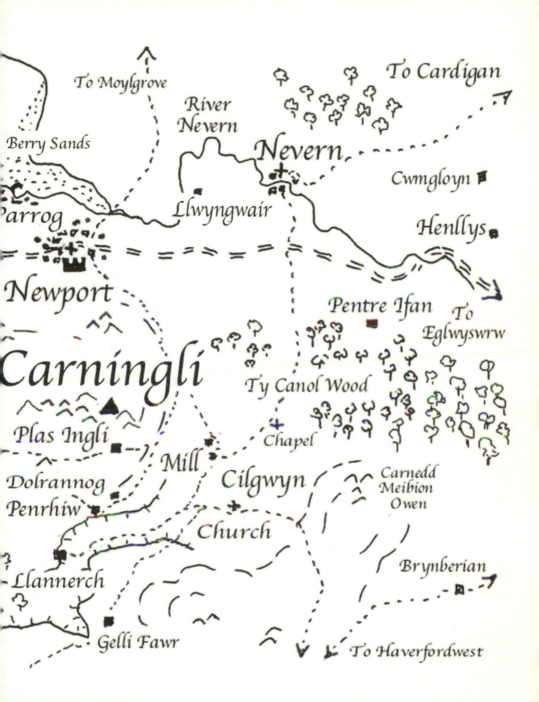

To the angels
who inhabit the Burns Unit
at Morriston Hospital,
Swansea

KEY CHARACTERS IN THE STORY

The Morgan family of Plas Ingli

Martha, b as Martha Howell on 12 May 1778 at Brawdy. Married to David Morgan on 21 August 1796, widowed 1805. Betrothed to Owain Laugharne 1807 and to Ceredig ap Tomos 1822, but never remarried. Died 27 Feb 1855, aged 76.

Betsi, b 1798, married Ioan Rhys of Cenarth 1818. Three sons, Benjamin (b 1821), Abel (b 1823) and Owain (b 1829).

Daisy, b 1801, left home for London 1821, and not heard of since.

Dewi, b 1803, died at sea 1820.

Sara, b 1805, died 1830.

Brynach (adopted), b 7 April 1807, m Anne Edwards 1830, inherited Llanychaer estate 1832. Two children, Rose (b 1831), David (b 1834).

The Howell family of Brawdy

Betsi (Martha's mother), b 1748, m 1765, d 1841.

Morys (older brother), b 1770, was Baptist minister in Haverfordwest, married Nansi 1797. Three children, Edward (b 1799), Jane (b 1802) and Robert (b 1805). Took over as Squire of Brawdy 1817.

Elen (oldest sister), b 1773, emigrated to USA 1807, m Tom Bradshaw 1810, children Susanna (b 1812), George (b 1815).

Catrin (sister), b 1776, moved to Castlebythe as tutor 1797, m James Bowen 1800. Two children, John (b 1803) and Mark (b 1806).

Plas Ingli staff

Bessie Walter, b 1776. Maid. Worked at the Plas in 1795-1799. Moved back after death of husband and son. Housekeeper from 1812.

Billy Ifans, b 1763. Carter and senior man. Started at the Plas when he was 14. Died 1829.

Shemi Jenkins, b 1782. Farm labourer and later head man. Started work 1797, aged 15. From Blaenwaun. Married Sian Williams 1810. Three children, b 1811, 1812 and 1816. Left 1836.

Gomer Jenkins, b 1812. Son of Shemi and Sian. Started at the Plas 1827.

Will Owen, b 1780, started at the Plas 1806, head man after 1836. Married Tegwen Gruffydd 1823, three children, b 1824, 1828, 1831.

Liza Philpin, Martha's personal maid, b 1784, m to Tomos 1806, two children, b 1807 and 1810. Came to the Plas 1807 as wet nurse for Brynach.

Gwenno Philpin, b 1810, daughter of Liza and Tomos, housemaid, started at the Plas in 1827.

Bryn Williams, b 1803. Cousin of Will. Farm-hand after 1833.

Other Key Characters

Skiff Abraham, respectable smuggler, waggoner and merchant after 1807. Married 1812, three children b 1814, 1816 and 1820.

Thomas Bullin, toll-farmer under contract to various turnpike trusts.

Dai Darjeeling, tea merchant, long-time suitor of Bessie Walter.

David Davies (Dai'r Cantwr), key member of the Stag and Pheasant Gang.

Lloyd Davies, Glynsaithmaen, farmer, cousin of Will.

Nathaniel Evans, tenant farmer on Bayvil estate.

Henry Eynon, Newport bailiff and then Clerk to the Justices 1843-44.

Thomas Campbell Foster, b 1813, *Times* reporter 1843-44.

Mostyn Gittins, b 1780, son of Squire of Tredrissi.

Gethin Griffiths and wife Liza. Tenant farmers at Dolrannog Isaf 1800-1835. Three children.

Aeron Griffiths, b 1773, took over Dolrannog Isaf in 1835.

Joseph Harries of Werndew, known as "the wizard", born 1761, died in 1826. Doctor, herbalist, sleuth, and Martha's friend and mentor.

George Havard Medical, the local doctor. Son of William Havard.

Mark Higgon, magistrate and Squire of Tredafydd.

Madoc Huws, Squire of Bayvil, b 1780. Took over estate 1823.

Dafydd Ifan, Gamallt, once a tenant of Martha, leader of *Ceffyl Pren* gang.

James Jobbins, Squire of Holmws and local magistrate

Hettie Jones, b 1770. Lodging house keeper on Parrog. Widowed 1801, four children, d 1835.

John Jones (Shoni Sgubor Fawr), leader of the Stag and Pheasant Gang.

James Laugharne, b 1773, took over Pontfaen estate in 1810.

Mary Jane Laugharne, b 1775, Owain's oldest sister. Married Dafydd Stokes of Trecwn 1800. Three children. Martha's best friend.

Owain Laugharne, b 28 Dec 1780. Took over Llannerch in 1802. "Lost" for fifteen years, 1807-1822. Died 1825.

George Lewis Legal, family lawyer from Fishguard, b 1740, d 1828.

Meredith Lloyd, b 1770, Squire of Cwmgloyn to 1833. Married Jane 1794, children Nicholas (b 1797) and Mabel (b 1800). Died 1833.

Nicholas Lloyd, took over as Squire of Cwmgloyn in 1833.

Richard Lord, Steward of Bayvil estate, later Clerk to the Justices 1844.

James Frederick Love, Colonel, Commander of armed forces in Wales.

Bobby Morris, farm labourer, later coachman on the Llwyngwair estate.

Robert Morris Legal, solicitor from Fishguard 1830-44.

Patty Nicholas, Martha's friend, living on Parrog. Married fisherman Jake in 1807. Two sons and two daughters.

John Owen, Squire of Gelli Fawr after 1822.

Jac Ovens (Jac Blossom), occasional gardener at Plas Ingli, d 1840.

William Parlby, Major in 4th Light Dragoons.

Eleanor (Ellie) Phillips, b 1776, oldest daughter of John Bowen, Squire of Llwyngwair. Martha's friend. Married Walter Phillips 1808. Three children, b 1810, 1812, 1815.

George Price, Squire of Llanychaer, b. 1742, m Susan 1768, d 1832 aged 90.

Iestyn Price, b 1771, d 1822, son of George Price and father of Brynach, who became Martha's adopted son.

Owen Pritchard, b 1780, and wife Sally, tenants at Dolrannog Uchaf.

William Probert (Will Final Testament), family lawyer from Newport, b 1755, d 1833.

Barti Richards, one of the Stag and Pheasant Gang.

Richard John Rice, b 1815, distant cousin of Joseph Rice. Officer in 4th Light Dragoons 1840.

Samuel Stokes, b 1811, son of Mary Jane and Dafydd Stokes.

Daniel Thomas, several times Mayor of Newport (also Coroner).

Llewelyn Thomas, Rector of Newport 1824-1875.

Zeke Tomos, Pencrugiau, b 1800, tenant on Bayvil estate.

Charlie Toms, church warden and Overseer of the Poor.

Thomas Tucker, b 1760, wife Mary and three children, tenants at Penrhiw.

Waldo Tucker, b 1790, took over Penrhiw in 1825.

Aaron Voyle, b 1780, tenant at Llystyn.

John Wilkins, young Newport lawyer in 1843.

Alexander Williams, b 1794, was tutor for Martha's children, m 1819, squire of Langton after 1820.

Caradoc Williams, b 1771, and wife Bethan. Tenant farmer at Gelli; also manager of the Sea Quarry at Aberrhigian.

Gwyn Williams, b 1782, oldest son, took over Gelli 1818.

Hugh Williams, b 1796, solicitor based in Carmarthen. Involved in radical politics, and a reputation as a Don Juan. Died 1874.

John Wilson, cooper, from Newport, most experienced constable.

Samson Wilson, John's son, also a Newport constable.

GLOSSARY OF WELSH TERMS

Aber: river mouth, estuary
Bach: "little one" (used as a term of endearment)
Cantwr: singer
Canwyll gorff: corpse candle, appearing as a death omen
Cariad: darling
Carn: heap of stones, rocky hill summit
Ceffyl Pren: wooden horse (used in folk traditions including mock trials)
Cnapan: old ball game, thought to be a forerunner of rugby football
Coed: wood or trees
Cwm: valley or hollow in the hillside
Diawl, Diawch: devil
Duw: God
Dyn hysbys: literally "knowing man", wise man or wizard
Ffynnon: spring or water source
Foel: bare hill summit
Gambo: a flat two-wheeled cart with no sides
Gwlad y Tylwyth Teg: fairy land, under the sea in Cardigan Bay
Gwylnos: wake night or vigil, before the funeral
Haidd: barley. **Parc Haidd** means "barley field"
Hen Galan: the old New Year, January 12th
Hiraeth: longing or belonging, nostalgia. Refers to a special piece of land
Hwyl: fervour, passion, mood
Ingli: uncertain, but probably an old Welsh word meaning "angels"
Mam-gu: (pronounced "mamgee) grandmother, grandma
Parrog: flat land along a shore or estuary (Newport's seaside community)
Plas: big house or palace
Plygain: candle-lit Christmas service ending at dawn
Pwnc: chapel festival associated with recitation of the scriptures
Simnai fawr: big chimney, large open fireplace
Toili: phantom funeral, interpreted as an omen of a death to come
Tolaeth: a death omen, usually heard as the sound of coffin making
Ty unnos: "one night house". A hovel built on common land
Twmpath: jolly evening of song and dance (literally tump)
Wrach: witch or hag (**y wrach** is the name given to the last tuft of corn cut during the harvest)
Ysgubor (abbreviated to Sgubor): barn

The Angel Mountain Saga

The Story so far........

In *On Angel Mountain* (Part One) eighteen-year-old Martha Morgan arrives at Plas Ingli, a small and vulnerable estate on the flank of Carningli (Angel Mountain) in North Pembrokeshire. The year is 1796. She is pregnant and suicidal, having just been forced by her family into a shotgun wedding. She is saved from harming herself or her unborn child by Joseph Harries the Wizard, who later becomes her mentor and friend. Joseph realizes that Martha has special powers, and she is very frightened when she experiences a number of visions and premonitions. She loves her husband David, and as she settles into the Plas she also learns to love the house and its extended family. But then she loses her baby and suffers from deep depression, and her resolve is further tested when there is a short-lived invasion by the French in 1797. She is increasingly concerned by the activities of a strange and sinister manservant called Moses Lloyd, and she becomes convinced that he is intent upon the destruction of the estate. After a number of misdemeanours he is sent packing, but Martha knows that he is not far away. Three local squires become increasingly antagonistic towards her and the estate, and matters come to a head when one of them, Alban Watkins, claims that the estate is rightfully his. David and his grandfather Isaac have to rush off to London to fight this claim in court. While they are away, Martha, who is pregnant again, has to face a trumped-up charge of theft. She is found guilty, and whipped through the streets of Newport. Then she is incarcerated in Haverfordwest Gaol. At last she manages to obtain her release through the good offices of Lord Cawdor. She returns home and receives a message to the effect that the court case is won, and that the estate is safe. Two of the villains are sentenced to transportation, and the other commits suicide. Martha needs space and peace in order to recover from her ordeal. She goes up to her secret cave on the mountain, and is captured by Moses Lloyd, who knew that she would eventually come. He is intent upon raping Martha and then killing her, but in a frantic struggle she kills him. She disposes of his body in a deep crevice and crawls home, more dead than alive.

In *House of Angels* (Part Two) Martha learns much about the brutality of the world, and about the devastating effect that her beauty has on the men with whom she comes in contact. She also learns a good deal about her own strength in the face of adversity. In the year 1805, her husband David is killed in the annual *cnapan* contest on Newport Sands, leaving her with three young children to bring up alone. She is also pregnant. She is helped through the crisis by her servants and friends, and her fourth child is born. Joseph is convinced that David's death was not an accident, and his investigations lead him to the conclusion that four men -- Matthew Lloyd, Joseph Rice, John Howell and Ifan Beynon -- are guilty of murder. The four villains, together with two strange Londoners and a squire's son named John Fenton, are intent upon the destruction of the estate because they are convinced that there is a treasure hidden on Plas Ingli land. Indeed there is, but only Martha knows where it is. As the story proceeds, Martha falls in love with Owain, the younger son of a local squire, and their love affair is anything but smooth. Alban Watkins, the dastardly squire who claimed the estate in 1797, suddenly returns from the colonies, also intent upon finding the Plas Ingli treasure. Martha orchestrates a treasure hunt, which results in the capture of all of the villains. In the court cases that follow, David's murderers are all sentenced to hang, and the other treasure hunters to transportation. But two of the villains manage to escape. One of them, Alban Watkins, is murdered by an Irishman in revenge for atrocities committed in the penal colonies. The other, John Fenton, abducts little Sara, and entices Martha to a lonely cottage where she hopes to obtain her daughter's release. Fenton has always lusted after Martha, and he attempts to rape her; but Owain intervenes in the nick of time, and following a ferocious struggle Fenton escapes, only to be sucked to his death in a nearby bog.

In *Dark Angel* (Part Three) the story starts in 1807 with Martha and Owain deeply in love, and engaged to be married. Martha has premonitions of dark and tragic events to come, and her unease is increased by sightings of a mysterious figure in black on the mountain. He appears to be watching her, and when others see the figure as well he is given the name of "The Nightwalker." Martha is uncertain whether he is a man, or a ghost, or the Devil himself. She becomes quite paranoid, but her attention is diverted when a small baby is left on the front doorstep of the Plas. Martha names the child Brynach, and arranges to adopt him. Plans are made for the wedding, but then Owain goes out on a fishing trip and disappears without trace. Joseph investigates, and deduces that a squire called George Price has arranged for the sabotage of Owain's boat. Again Martha becomes depressed and paranoid, and very possessive about the baby. She gets some straight talking from her nearest and dearest. Over the years that follow the Nightwalker appears over and again, and Martha suspects that Joseph Harries the wizard, and even her servants, know more about the creature than she does. Her daughter Daisy goes off to London and breaks off all contact with the family, and her son Dewi is drowned at sea. In 1822, under pressure from family and friends, Martha agrees to marry again. Squire Ceredig ap Tomos proposes, and she accepts. On the night of the wedding Owain returns from the dead, and Martha has no option but to choose him over Ceredig. She is horrified when the man she has rejected commits suicide. Owain is also ill, having experienced appalling hardship in North Africa and Spain, and she tries to nurse him back to good health. Exhausted by all this emotional turmoil, Martha goes to her cave for silence and contemplation, but comes face to face with the Nightwalker. He is terribly disfigured and injured as a result of an accident in the Napoleonic Wars, and he proves to be Iestyn Price, the son of Squire Price and the father of the child left on the doorstep of the Plas fifteen years earlier. Iestyn is reconciled with his father, but he dies within a few days of his encounter with Martha, and is buried secretly in his father's walled garden.

Note. All of the stories are told by Martha herself, in her own diaries which are written in the archaic Welsh Dimetian dialect. This dialect was once spoken widely in parts of North Pembrokeshire, but has now entirely died out.

Postscript

1. A Merry Dance

The mountain and its resident spirits were calling me. There was little point in resisting the summons, so I pulled on my boots, wrapped up well against the November chill, and started climbing. Less than an hour later I was on the summit, bracing myself against the wind and watching thick black clouds streaming overhead. The cloud base dropped, and for a moment I was embraced by gloom. Then the sun came out, and I could see all the way to heaven. A black speck appeared two thousand feet up, and I knew that I would be blessed by a visit from the old raven. She wheeled and spiralled downwards with no particular haste, enjoying her mastery of the wind. After ten minutes I could make out the essential features of her beauty -- broad black wings with ragged-fingered tips, wedge-shaped tail, plumage as black as anthracite and rainbows, short neck and heavy beak. She pulled up into the wind and settled effortlessly onto the highest crag which was crusted with lichens and bird droppings. It was her throne, the place from which she could survey her domain. She was ten feet away from me, as nonchalant as ever, perfectly happy to share her mountain with me and the angels.

I knew at once that I had to commence the search for the next episode of Martha Morgan's diaries. For a few days, with no flashes of inspiration to light my way, I stumbled over the twin problems of what to do and where to look. Gradually, a plan of action took shape. At the end of her last diary, in September 1822, Martha was 44 years old. She was in the prime of life, a grandmother and a very desirable widow. She managed a successful estate. It was clear, not from her own words but from the actions of those around her, that her beauty was still such that it sent men mad. But after the death of her husband David she never married again, for on the Morgan memorial plaque in Cilgwyn Churchyard she is referred to simply as "Martha, Mistress of Plas Ingli, released from her shackles 27th February 1855." Had she taken another name that would have been recorded, and there are no parish records of a further marriage.

A Merry Dance

Whatever happened in Martha's personal life between 1822 and 1855, she must have observed -- and participated in -- a period of tremendous social change in West Wales, culminating in the Rebecca Riots which rocked the British political establishment to its foundations in the period 1839-1844. At that time, across much of the three counties of Pembrokeshire, Carmarthenshire and Cardiganshire, groups of small farmers and labourers blackened their faces, donned women's clothes, and rode out to confront injustice. They were always led by somebody referred to as "Rebecca". They smashed down toll-gates, burned gatekeepers' houses and hay-ricks, and destroyed fishing weirs and other symbols of gentry affluence and control. They used the *Ceffyl Pren* to dispense rough justice and to intimidate their enemies. Hardly any of the leaders were captured and punished, and the rioters led the army and the constables on many a wild goose chase across a troubled countryside. Given Martha's social conscience and her inability to act as a bystander when she came across abuses of power, surely she must have had some views on the turbulent events of the time, and possibly even had some direct experience of the Riots?

There was no point in searching for more diaries within Pembrokeshire, for I had done that before and had turned up nothing. So I started to hunt for clues in the next most obvious place -- in the National Library of Wales, among the Price family papers relating to Plas Llanychaer. I knew already that there was a family link between Martha's adopted son Brynach and Squire George Price of Llanychaer, and it was reasonable to suppose that after 1822 the bond between the two families must have been strengthened. It was among those Price Family papers that the last volumes of Martha's diaries (published in the book *Dark Angel*) had been discovered. So I travelled to Aberystwyth, and searched through all the documents in the collection. The original diary, in Martha's hand and in the almost indecipherable Dimetian dialect, was still there, as was the fastidious translation by my friend and neighbour Abraham Jenkins. There were no clues in the translated manuscript or in any other papers. But there was a George Price will dated 1828, in which he left the whole of the Llanychaer estate unreservedly to Brynach Morgan of Plas Ingli in the parish of Newport. He also left six milking cows to his daughter Susanna and another six milking cows to his other daughter Mary, "on condition that they come personally to Plas

Llanychaer to collect them and drive them away." This must have been a deliberate snub to his two estranged daughters, who had not even bothered to attend the funerals of their own mother and sister. There were certain documents signed by Brynach Morgan Esq, confirming that he and his family had moved in during the year 1832, following the death of Squire George Price. At some stage, I speculated that Martha must have given her third diary to Brynach for safe keeping -- or did he acquire it and take it away from the Plas when Martha died in 1855? Questions, and more questions, and no answers...........

Catrin Mathias, the curator who had found the diary, confirmed that many of the Plas Llanychaer documents had been damaged by damp, or had been removed. There were a few estate documents dating from the 1860's and signed by "William Gwynne." After that, all of the papers in the collection were signed by members of the Gwynne family and their attorneys. When had Brynach left Plas Llanychaer, or Cwrt, as it was later called? And what had happened to him and his family after that? I was tempted to follow a trail off in that direction, but I knew that I had to concentrate on Martha.

Next, I hunted among the Plas Cenarth papers, relating to the place where Martha's oldest daughter Betsi had settled with her husband Ioan Rhys in the year 1818. Again, I was frustrated, for those papers went no further back than 1830, when a family called Gethin had taken possession and moved in. Did that mean that Betsi and Ioan and their family had moved out in that year? Where had they gone? Back to Plas Ingli? Again, I speculated but refused to be diverted from my chosen route.

After weeks of searching, I could find nothing relating to Martha after 1822. But people do not often disappear without any trace from the nineteenth-century historical record, and I felt sure that Martha Morgan would never have settled back into a cosy and disengaged retirement at the age of 44. That was not her style, I thought, and there must be something, somewhere, which would lead us to her later adventures. At last, there was nothing for it but to discuss the problem with the one man who knew Martha better than I did -- Abraham Jenkins of Waun Isaf, scholar, pacifist, bard and inheritor of esoteric wisdom. It was he who had translated the first three volumes of Martha's diaries, and I envied the extent to which he had developed an empathy and even a sort of love for the long-dead Mistress of Plas Ingli. If anybody could see into her mind and her heart at a distance of more than 180 years, it was he.

We chatted at length, over several cups of tea. We walked on the mountain, seeking inspiration beneath a bright and clean December sky. Then he said "Have you noticed, my friend, that each one of Martha's diaries has come to our attention in a different way? The first was found in an old chest, which was fun but which did not require much planning on Martha's part.........."

"Or much intelligence on ours."

"Correct. The second was hidden by Martha in the library of the Laugharne family in Pontfaen, sandwiched between the two favourite Shakespeare plays of her second great love, Owain Laugharne. It was more by chance than perseverance that we were led to it, although we had to get the better of a riddle in order to find it. That must have given Martha some amusement. Then the third volume was secreted away among the papers of another estate, and lay there under a pile of damp documents until it was removed and re-buried in the basement of the National Library, sixty miles away. I never did handle the real thing, and had to make do with lots of gadgetry, working on this thing they call a microfilm."

"I am sorry, Abraham," I said with a frown upon my brow, "but I do not quite follow your drift."

"Mistress Martha always did enjoy leading the men in her life in a merry dance across rocky terrain, and her pleasure in this respect obviously extended into the matter of hiding diaries. Very simple at first, and getting more complicated with the passing of the years. If she ever did write a fourth, it will probably require both intelligence and modern technology to find it. You are a technical sort of fellow. Have you thought of hunting on this thing they call the internet? Something to do with computers, so I hear, but my nephew Matthew tells me that you can find out almost everything on it. Well, why not try?"

I mumbled and grumbled, and searched for reasons why this would not work, but in the end I could think of nothing better. I agreed to try.

That evening I got myself thoroughly tangled up in the web. I used one search engine after another, and delved into all of the home pages and web sites I could find which provided information on family names, family trees, old estates, wills and diaries. I tried searching for internet leads to "Martha Morgan". I found hundreds of Marthas and thousands of Morgans, but not one of them was in the right place or at the right time. So I tried typing in "Rebecca Riots" in the hope that that might give me a lead. Again, there were thousands of entries. Where on earth should I look? I tried opening a few sites at random, down in the depths of the Google list. Suddenly my eye was dragged from the computer screen in front of me by a shadow on the wall of my study, caught initially in the corner of my eye. It stayed there for a few seconds, long enough for me to recognize it as the shadow of a raven, moving as if in slow motion. Strange, I thought, for there is no sun outside. I felt the hairs on the back of my neck rise. I looked back at the screen, and there in front of me, beneath an irrelevant entry relating to the home page of a certain Rebecca Jones of Philadelphia, I saw something much more to my liking. Lost in the middle of a jumble of keywords was the following: *"The language of the Rebecca Riots" by William Foster. A small pamphlet privately published in Melbourne in 1894. City Archives, Melbourne Public Library, State of Victoria."*

I knew at once that this was the lead I had been waiting for. I had never heard of William Foster, and nor had I ever seen a citation of this pamphlet. That was not particularly surprising, since it was buried in the archives of a library on the far side of the planet. But it was now newly available in full on the web, courtesy of modern technology. With a couple of clicks of my mouse it was open on the screen in front of me. I downloaded it and printed it. There were twelve pages of turgid text. At first I was disappointed, for it was all very innocuous and contained nothing new, at least for a Welsh reader. There was an analysis of the Biblical sources used by the Rebecca Rioters, a description of their charades enacted in front of the toll gates, and the language used in the letters sent to magistrates, spies and those who were deemed guilty of misdemeanours. There were many references to *"mam"* (mother) and to *"merched"* (daughters) in the conversations between the black-faced and female-garbed rioters. But then I spotted this sentence: "On the occasion of the destruction of the Boncath toll-gate on 28th January 1844, a number of the rioters referred to one of their number as *"Mam-gu."* This was attested to my father by both the toll-gate keeper and his wife, and the testimony is recorded in his notebooks."

Suddenly two things came into my mind. With rising excitement I realized that William Foster must have been the son of Thomas Campbell Foster, the *Times* reporter who had played a crucial role in bringing the

Rebecca Riots to the attention of the British public and the Government. And I also realized that I had never before seen the use of the word *"Mamgu"* or "Grandma" in the course of years of research into the social history of the riots. Was an elderly female involved during the later stages of the disturbances? And could that person have possibly been Martha Morgan? Surely not -- could she really have been so involved or irresponsible?

The pamphlet gave me no more clues. I mulled things over for several days. Then I went once again to talk to Abraham. I told him everything, including my encounter with the shadow on my wall on a grey and overcast day. When he heard about that, he raised his eyebrow, understood everything and said nothing. He advised me that nothing was to be lost by following up the Thomas Campbell Foster connection. Over the next few days we both read everything we could find on the reporting of the Riots. Foster had been in West Wales for only about a year in 1843-44, but it was clear that he had been a remarkably effective and fearless investigative journalist. Without his outspoken (and opinionated) press reports in the *Times,* the riots may well have taken a different course, and they would certainly have been much more protracted and bloody. He must have had many "underground" contacts. He even managed to attend one of the secret meetings of the Rebeccaites. And he never betrayed his sources. Could Martha Morgan of Plas Ingli, a "mere woman" but a fearless campaigner for justice, have been one of his contacts?

Next, I contacted his old newspaper, and discovered that Thomas Campbell Foster had almost been forgotten. All that the paper's records section could tell me was that he had died in 1882, almost 40 years after his time in West Wales. I dug deeper, and found that he had abandoned his journalistic career in 1846, after reporting on the Irish famine, and thereafter had become a barrister and QC. The *Times* had no record of what had happened to him or his notebooks. So I turned my attention to the Foster family, who had settled in Warwick. I found precious little in the County Records office, but did discover that there had been two sons, William (born in 1849) and George (born in 1852). George had died young, and I discovered that William had emigrated to Australia in 1877. So now I had my pamphlet author, and a verified link with Australia. But I could find nothing apart from a record that he and his wife and three children had landed in Port Philip from the emigrant vessel *Providence* in January 1878.

A Merry Dance

The trail appeared to have gone cold, and I have to admit to feeling more than a little dejected. I spoke again to Abraham, and he urged me not to give up. So I persisted. I did more web surfing, and sent off a multitude of Email messages. Eventually I established contact with the City Archives and the Melbourne Public Library. Had they by any chance got a record of a certain William Foster? A Welshman called Aston Jones picked up the case and ran with it. After a week, I found a message on my computer. Yes, wrote Aston -- William Foster and his wife Emily and three sons were registered settlers, and were recorded on the electoral rolls of 1885. He continued to hunt among the records. Days passed, and he found nothing new. At last, he had to tell me that there were many Fosters in the Melbourne telephone directory. There was really very little chance, he wrote, of establishing a link, after the passage of 120 years, between any of them and Thomas Campbell Foster, or the *Times*, or West Wales. I pleaded with him to try. "Oh, very well. Leave it with me," he said, and the lines went cold again.

A week later, I received a new Email from Aston: "Ring this number, and talk to Frank Foster. He lives in Yarra Glen, and you might be interested to know that his house is called "Efailwen". Good luck! Aston."

Early next morning, when it was evening in Victoria, I dialled the number which he had given me. The phone was answered by an elderly gentleman with the right name. I introduced myself, and as we chatted I discovered that Aston had written a piece in the Melbourne newspaper *The Age*, and had asked for any person with family connections with Thomas Campbell Foster, one-time *Times* reporter, to get in touch. Frank had seen the piece and replied. "So he was an ancestor of yours?" I asked.

"Oh yes," said Frank. "I am not a great one for family history and such things, but I do know that Thomas Campbell Foster was my great-great-grandfather. His son William was not a very nice chap by all accounts, and he came to Australia to escape from some scandal, but at least he was not a convict."

At last, after a multitude of frustrations, I felt a surge of optimism coursing through my veins. I knew that Martha was out there somewhere, grinning at me. "Do you have any family records?" I asked, hardly daring to hope for a positive reply.

"Indeed I do. An old box of stuff which great-grandfather William brought out with him in 1878. Mostly rubbish, some very old photographs, and some bundles and bulky envelopes."

"When last was this material examined?"

"Oh, God knows. I have never looked at it properly, but I recall my father John going through the box once to see if there was anything interesting or valuable."

"And was there?"

"Not a thing, as I recall," said Frank.

"Would you do me a great favour?"

"Well yes, if it is not too laborious. I am not in the best of health."

"Would you please open up the box for me and make a rough list of what it contains? You have my assurance that this could be very important indeed."

"OK, if I can find the time, what with the golf club, Rotary dinner and cutting the lawn. Leave it to me. I'll get back to you."

Three days later, there was a phone call from Australia. "Now then," said Frank, sounding, for an Australian, quite excited. "I have a little list."

"Can you read it out to me?"

"No problem, mate. Here we go -- one envelope containing notebooks and with *"Wales 1843-44"* written on it. Another with notebooks, labelled *"Norfolk 1844."* Another with notebooks labelled *"Ireland 1845: Potato Famine."* A bundle of documents that look like testimonials. A pile of papers relating to the prosecution of Charlie Peace in 1878. Some letters from somebody called Martha, written between 1845 and 1855. A cardboard box tied up with red ribbon and with *"Mam-gu, strictly confidential......."*

"Good God! Have you opened and looked inside the box?"

"No, but my father must have done, since I can see the words *"Diary left with Father for safekeeping?"* written on the side in his handwriting. I suppose that the question mark shows that he was not quite sure."

"Have you got the box next to you as we speak?"

"Indeed I do. It is right here."

"Could I ask you to open it and see what is inside?"

"You could ask, but I am not sure that I should, since it is strictly confidential......."

"Come now, Frank! You are just winding me up. I think that *Mam-gu* would probably wish it, after all these years."

A Merry Dance

"Oh, very well, if you think it is all right. Hang on a minute." Over the telephone, I picked up an assortment of rustling and wheezing noises. At last he said, somewhat breathlessly: "Here we are. There are four slim volumes, all filled with handwriting. Lots of crossings out. God knows what the language is -- Welsh or Gaelic?"

"Welsh, if I can hazard a guess. And might it by any chance be a diary?"

"Let me see..... Yes, could well be, mate. There are dates at the beginning of each entry."

"Let me hazard another guess. Around 1843-45?"

"Earlier than that. The entries start in volume one at 1832." There was a long pause. "And they seem to end in 1844 -- yes, here we are. Last entry, dated August 10th 1844."

"And any clue as to the identity of the writer?"

"Something embossed on the front of each volume -- looks like the initials MM. Then after the final entry some words -- in English, I think. Yes, I can make them out: *"To Tom from Mam-gu, with respect and affection. In trust, for your safekeeping until I am with the angels."*

I knew that between us, with a good deal of international cooperation and not a little serendipity, we had found the fourth part of Martha's diaries. I tried to control my excitement, since fate, or my guardian angels, appeared to be leading me once again towards the writings of the Mistress of Plas Ingli. So I said to Frank: "Can I call in and see the diaries some time next week?"

"Forgive me, my friend, but you are up above and I am down under. Do you mean that you are going to jump on a plane for Australia simply in order to see these diaries written back in the time of my great-great grandfather?"

"Well, yes and no. Providence has already decreed that I will be on a long-haul flight in three days' time, heading for Christmas with my son and his family near Melbourne. They live less than one hour's drive from Yarra Glen, as I recall........"

My wife and I met up with Frank and his family on a hot Australian summer's day, shortly before Christmas. We spent several jovial hours together, and I inspected the diaries. Sure enough, they were in Martha's inimitable hand, and once again they were written in her secret code, Dimetian Welsh. I was able to tell him all about Martha Morgan and

21

some things about Thomas Campbell Foster that he did not know. He had not realized, for example, that his great-great grandfather had been one of the foremost journalists of his age, having set a standard in investigative journalism which would not be surpassed for decades. But as a young man Tom Foster appears to have struck up a friendship with Martha, who was old enough to be his mother. What, I pondered out loud, could have lain behind this friendship?

Having convinced Frank and his family that the "lost" diaries might turn out to be key documents in our understanding of the Rebecca Riots and of the social conditions which prevailed in nineteenth century Wales, they agreed to present them not to me but to the City Archives. The Head Archivist agreed in turn to let me have a microfilm copy of the four manuscript volumes. In exchange, I promised to send a full translation of the document. Christmas came and went. Then, in the middle of a January heat wave my wife and I set out for home, with a microfilm in our hand baggage.

I needed a day or two to recover from my jet lag. Then I knocked on Abraham's front door. He invited me in, and over a cup of tea we talked about Australia and families. Then I said "You will not believe this, Abraham, but I have here a small box with something strange inside it. I wonder if you can guess what it is?" His face registered disbelief. "Not another microfilm? And not another episode in the adventurous life of Mistress Martha?"

"Quite correct, Abraham. Do you think you can borrow that microfilm reader from the National Library once again?"

So it was that in August Abraham delivered to me another translation, and so it was that this book came into being. I have one copy of his translation, and another now resides in the City Archives of Melbourne, deep in the bowels of the city's Public Library. In the same collection there are the papers relating to Joseph Jenkins, the famous Welsh swagman who worked, wandered and squandered his talents in Victoria for twenty-five years, between 1869 and 1894. His diary contains the most effective and accurate record ever published of the cruel social and economic conditions that prevailed in the colony around the time of Ned Kelly. And on another shelf, not far away, are the Ned Kelly papers themselves, recording the life and misadventures of another victim who was forced by corruption, injustice and prejudice into an ultimately tragic conflict with authority. Ned Kelly lived his short and brutal life between 1855 and 1880. He was born in the year of Martha's death, and died 35 years after the climax of the Rebecca Riots. As the son of an Irish convict he inherited some of the "social protest" traditions of Wales and Ireland, including the use of face blackening and female dress as a means of avoiding recognition by the forces of law and order.

Ned Kelly, Joseph Jenkins and Rebecca are now cheek by jowl in the archives, each one an icon, each one a symbol of the human struggle for self-respect, freedom and justice in an age when privilege counted for everything. "A very fitting thing indeed," said Abraham. "Can't be sure whether we should put this down to the workings of fate, but Melbourne appears to be a better place than most for the safekeeping of this one, which is the most dramatic and turbulent of all Martha's diaries."

I prepared the diaries for publication under very high pressure. At the end of August, with the pressure off, I decided that I needed space around me and a wide sky over my head. So I climbed the mountain. It was a calm and bright morning, with a heavy dew melting off the turf and the bracken. I lay on my back on the grassy patch near the summit and watched jet trails forming and dissolving high overhead. Looking back on it, I was probably waiting for Martha. Then I became aware that I was being watched. I turned my head and looked at the highest bluestone crag. There she was, the old raven, the oracle, angel and guardian of the mountain. She preened her feathers for a few minutes and looked me in the eye. Then she spread her wings and without any apparent effort allowed an updraught of sun-warmed air to carry her skywards.

ΩΩΩΩΩΩΩΩΩΩ

MARTHA MORGAN'S STORY

EXTRACTS FROM THE PAGES OF HER DIARIES FOR 1832-44, TRANSLATED FROM THE DIMETIAN WELSH DIALECT BY ABRAHAM JENKINS

PART ONE: 1832

2. The Cold and the Dark

1st December 1832

On a day such as this, I should be happy. It is a winter Sunday, delicately touched by the hand of God. Yesterday there was a bitter wind from the east, and heavy skies and snow flurries; but this morning there is a perfect calm, and the mountain looks as if it has been gently dusted with chalk powder. There is not a single cloud left in the sky, and through the window of my little dressing room I can survey my domain of bare trees and bleached fields and stone walls and cottages. Out in the cwm, at least fifteen columns of smoke rise vertically from hearth to heaven, showing me exactly where Mistress Ifans and Mistress Jenkins and the rest of them are stirring their warm buttermilk or boiling their tea water or making oat porridge. A golden sun throws long shadows. There are four red kites wheeling in the sky above Tycanol Wood, and closer to home there is a single buzzard scanning the frozen ground on the common for anything dead or alive that might provide a meal.

I should be happy, for I am surrounded by love. My dear Bessie is still here, after more than thirty-five years of employment at the Plas as housemaid and then housekeeper. She is my most valued friend, and the one to whom I turn when my equilibrium is disturbed by events, or gossip, or men, or wild imaginings. I insist that she knows me better than I know myself, and without her I would be like a rudderless vessel in a storm. Liza is another who is still here, my gentle handmaiden who first came to the Plas as a wet nurse for Brynach, my foundling and adopted son. She comes and goes each day, but her daughter Gwenno entered my service some years ago as kitchen-maid, and she lives in the smallest of the servant rooms. I love her as a daughter, and I swear that I have never encountered a young lady of such high spirits. My cow-man Will works here but lives with his family in his own cottage on the edge of the common, and my head man Shemi also comes up to work at the Plas every day between dawn and dusk. His middle son Gomer lives beneath my roof, in the room that used to belong to Billy, and he looks after the gardens and the stables. He is in love with Gwenno, but she is in love with one Bobby Morris, and that makes for hilarious complications.

Nor have I any reason to feel isolated and abandoned, for Brynach and his little family are but a short drive away, at Plas Llanychaer, and I see them at least once a week. Betsi and Ioan and their three boys are in residence nearby at Brithdir, and I see them whenever I can. Their youngest one, Owain, is now three years old, and I am besotted by him, just as a grandmother should be. He is the most delightful of children, but indeed I am truly blessed by all four of the new generation.

With four adults beneath my roof at night, and with at least three more around the table at meal-times, life is as jovial and as noisy as may be, and indeed there is a sort of youthful energy about the Plas which I have missed since my own little chicks flew away from the nest. There was also a different and more sober atmosphere in the old days when Grandma Jane and Grandpa Isaac were alive, or when our magnificent and ferocious Mrs Owen kept the place in order with the aid of her iron rod. Bessie is now the oldest person in residence, having just passed her fifty-sixth birthday, but she is still pretty and petite, and is still pursued with a wonderful ardour by Dai Darjeeling. She keeps the poems and the red roses to herself, but she cannot possibly drink all the tea that comes in her direction, and I am always pleased to help her out.

Laughter and activity on all sides, even now as winter tightens its grip on the tired countryside -- but there is still a heaviness in my breast, and a sense of foreboding that I recognize only too well. I have felt it before, prior to almost every tragedy to have overtaken this beloved family since my arrival at the Plas back in 1796. Now I fear something again, not for my part but for those whom I love and those who depend upon me for their daily bread.

The Cold and the Dark

It came upon me last night, as I lay awake beneath my warm blankets, listening to the low sighing of the wind and the spattering of granules of frozen snow upon the window-panes. I was not asleep, and it was no dream. But suddenly I was on the topmost crag of the mountain. I looked seawards, and saw a wild tempest gathering out in the bay, with grey waves piling up and tumbling far offshore, and with white streamers of spume dragged out by the roaring wind. The waves piled higher and higher as they approached the coast, and as they came I knew that nothing was safe -- not the old church tower, nor the ruined castle, nor the houses, streets and cottages far inland and high above the normal level of the sea. The monstrous waves crashed and swirled among the warehouses and fishermen's cottages on the Parrog, which were then lost from sight as the sea roared inland. Berry Sands and the Burrows disappeared as I watched. Higher and higher the waves rushed, against the flanks of Carningli and up the wooded valleys of the Nevern and Clydach rivers. Trees fell and were swept along in the maelstrom, and dead cattle and sheep were caught up into a turbulent and twisted pile of broken branches and roots. The waves crashed far inland, sweeping everything before them. They roared up to the edge of the common, across the lower fields belonging to the Plas. Massive stone walls that have stood for centuries tumbled over as easily as if they had been wattle hurdles flattened by a stampede of bulls.

And then, as I watched wide-eyed and convinced myself that this was the end for the Plas and its outbuildings, the wind dropped and the fury of the waves was spent. The water made one final assault, and swept against the side of the house, smashing some windows and leaving a filthy stain upon the whitewashed walls. But then the sea drained away back towards the bay, pouring back across fields and gates and turning lanes and trackways into streams and rivers. As quickly as the disaster had struck, it was done, leaving a landscape littered with dead animals, roots and branches, uprooted furze bushes and shrubs, wooden gates and hurdles, feeding troughs and farm implements. At the high-water mark there were mounds of flotsam and jetsam twenty feet high, and where the land had been inundated everything was covered in a thick and putrid layer of silt and slime. So the land was left to recover as best it could.

I looked down in horror, and scanned the devastated landscape from horizon to horizon from north to south and east to west, but then I was amazed to realize that in the tumult of the waves not everything had been destroyed. The big houses of the gentry -- Llwyngwair, Cwmgloyn, Henllys, Gelli Fawr and others just visible far away in the haze -- were now in ruins, with smashed walls, stripped roofs, fallen barns, and stables and cowsheds reduced to rubble. But through some quirk of fate which I was at a loss to understand, the hovels and cottages of the labourers and small farmers, flimsy and crude though they were, all stood proud and unharmed after the passage of the waves. I saw the Jenkins boys in a field near the Cilgwyn road feeding their sheep in perfectly nonchalant fashion, apparently oblivious to the fact that a tidal wave had recently passed over their heads. Dai Darjeeling was riding up the lane on his chestnut pony, probably intent upon catching a sight of his beloved. Tomos Gwyther was driving a horse and cart loaded with turnips along the Brithdir farm lane. Two of the Tucker boys were laying a hedge in the field next to the Penrhiw farmyard. They were singing some jolly folk tune, and the sounds of their fine voices, one tenor and the other bass, echoed around the *cwm* and sounded as beautiful as a dawn chorus on a May morning. Then the sights and sounds faded away, and I was once again enveloped in darkness, listening to the moaning of the winter wind.

ΩΩΩΩΩΩΩΩΩΩΩ

2nd December 1832

After a full day and night of mulling over my strange vision, and talking to nobody about it, I have to admit that when I came down to breakfast this morning I was not in the best of moods. My throat was dry, and when I tried to speak I croaked like a frog. Instead of looking like the Mistress of an elegant estate, I probably looked like a battered old crone.

Liza, who had already lit my bedroom fire, put my dress out and helped me with my hair, knew that something was wrong but knew better than to press me on the matter. Bessie had no such inhibitions. As we all sat around the kitchen table and ate our breakfasts of oatmeal porridge, brown sugar and fresh cream, she raised her eyebrows in that irritating way of hers and said: "I observe that you did not sleep well, Mistress. Too much fat on the gammon we had for supper?"

Gwenno and Gomer giggled, and I had to smile myself. "No, no, Bessie," I said. "I have to admit to a strange sort of vision not last night, but the night before, and I am at a loss to understand it. I fear that it has been stuck in my mind for a day and a night, and I would be only too happy to be rid of it."

"Are you minded to share it with us?"

"I think not, Bessie. I know from experience that whatever its meaning, it might bring fortune or fear to one or more of us who are sitting around this table."

"So it was a fearsome vision, Mistress?" asked Gwenno.

"Yes and no, *cariad*. I saw disaster strike far and wide, but not at the Plas. I hope and pray that those of us who share this simple meal, and our nearest and dearest, will come through without harm. And there were intimations that those who are most vulnerable in our neighbourhood will survive, while those who might expect to survive all manner of ills will be swept away."

Shemi was sitting opposite me, and as he raised his loaded porridge spoon to his mouth I caught his eye. I realized at once that he too had seen the vision. Like others in the Jenkins family, he sees things that others do not see and knows things that are hidden -- with good reason -- from normal folk. He and I have shared visions before, and have provided support for one another. We have no understanding of the source of our power, and we are both frightened by it, since we are no more able to influence the course of events than butterflies are able to resist a screaming tempest.

"How I wish that Owain was still here, or that I could walk over the mountain and seek Joseph's help......" I whispered, and although I tried to contain my emotions, I felt tears running down my cheeks. Gwenno and Gomer did not know where to look, but the others knew me better, and Bessie got to her feet and came and stood behind me. She placed her gentle hands on my shoulders, and kissed the top of my head.

"There now, Mistress," she said. "That is all over and done with. You have already shown that you can manage without Master Owain and Master Joseph, and you have shown us over and again that when you trust your own heart, you are usually right. What say you, Shemi?"

"No doubt about it, Bessie *bach*," said he, with a little smile on his face. Then he looked me in the eye and continued. "Quite right she is, Mistress. I saw the same vision in the night, as my beloved Sian will tell you if you was to ask. At first I was greatly afeared, but then I did what Joseph taught me, and listened to the voice inside me, and it told me just what your little voice told you. Do not worry, Mistress. Be prepared for great upheavals, but be assured that all will be well. I am never wrong. You have my word for it."

There was silence for a moment as we all looked at this big man with his grizzled chin and deep blue eyes and tousled fair hair. Then he laughed a great belly laugh, and the tension flew away. Bessie resumed her seat. Gwenno served up some more porridge, and the assembled company got back to normal, with laughter and wicked banter, and reports on yesterday's gossip and today's tasks and tomorrow's weather. We will talk no more of strange visions and dark prognostications, and get on with our lives.

ΩΩΩΩΩΩΩΩΩΩ

6th December 1832

I have had three happy days, filled with good humour and activity as we all prepare for winter and start our planning for Christmas. But today winter has temporarily reverted to autumn, and the Plas is lost in the cloud. Rain is streaming down, and the wind is in the west. It is early afternoon, but so dark as I sit here in my dressing room that I need two candles on my writing desk in order to see what I am doing. I do not complain. This is typical for early December, and I am warm enough with my coal fire flickering in the grate and an easy glow within my heart.

I am glad that I have picked up my pen again after a good many years, and once again I am experiencing the pleasure of putting words and thoughts onto paper. In truth I have been bored, and more than a little lonely. But I have nothing to complain about, as long as there is still a golden sun behind the black clouds and as long as there is still an old blue mountain hidden behind the curtains of rain. Others have far greater problems than I, and I have to record that in this new phase of my life the afflictions of others have come into sharp focus. I have taken to reading newspapers and books which others might find dangerous or subversive, and I take considerable delight in leaving them in prominent positions when my gentry neighbours make social visits. I have taken out subscriptions to the weekly *Cambrian* of Swansea and to the new and very liberal newspaper called the *Welshman*, published in Carmarthen. The latter is one that I greatly enjoy, and when I settle down by the *simnai fawr* and become absorbed in its contents I elicit the same sort of looks from young Gwenno and Gomer as I gave to Grandpa Isaac many years ago, when he warmed his toes and enjoyed his weekly reading of the London *Times*.

Only a fortnight ago I had a brief visit from Squire and Mistress Lloyd of Cwmgloyn and Squire and Mistress Edwards of Trefach. I count them as dear friends, but I noticed their raised eyebrows and the slight blushes upon their cheeks when they looked at my little side table and saw there several copies of Master William Cobbett's *Political Register* and copies of his *Sermons* relating to Bribery, Oppression and Unjust Judges. I was perfectly frank about my interest in the writings of this foolhardy and very irritating gentleman, and expressed the view that he was probably, like all geniuses, quite insufferable. Master Edwards looked embarrassed, and I compounded his discomfort by saying what a fine thing it was that a man such as Master Cobbett had at last found a seat in the Reformed House of Commons where he could seek to right the multitude of injustices to which he had previously drawn attention through his seditious writings. He swallowed hard and nodded, and Master Lloyd roared with laughter. So we talked amiably of idiotic politicians and vice and corruption, and enjoyed tea and griddle cakes, and parted the best of friends.

While it is perfectly possible for civilized people to discuss serious matters in an amiable way, I cannot escape the conviction that there are grave problems in the countryside of West Wales, and that social unrest is inevitable unless the Government takes drastic action to deal with the grievances of the labourers and small farmers. I have a warm house and a well-stocked larder, but I share many of those grievances and see the effects of them at first hand. Four local children died in October from starvation and disease, and five in November. And the winter has hardly started. God knows what will happen when we reach the hungry months of April and May, when pantries are bare and when there is nothing new in gardens, fields and hedgerows apart from spring flowers and singing birds. Beauty exists only for those who have food in their stomachs and shawls upon their shoulders and time to look and listen.

I fear that the unrest, when it comes, will be instigated not by the labourers but by the small farmers. The former live in poverty, but many of them live in the houses of their employers, or in tied cottages, and while they may have neither golden sovereigns nor pound notes in their pockets or under the bed, they obtain food and fuel from their masters and are often allowed to keep a few animals of their own. The small farmers, in contrast, suffer from the privilege of occupying larger patches of land. A farm carrying a rent of £60 might provide an income of £150 in a good year. But then the farmer has an outlay on tithes of £9, then church and road rates of ten shillings, then more than one pound on poor rates. He has to find more than £8 to pay for lime and coal, and his labourers will cost him more than £35. The interest on borrowings will cost £10, and he will probably spend more than £5 on replacements and repairs. That leaves about £20 each year for the farmer and his family to live on, or not much more than seven shillings a week. In such circumstances it is not possible for a family to survive, unless wives and sons and daughters can bring in a few more shillings or pounds during the year -- and if market prices for the farmer's animals and crops fall at the time when he needs to sell, his income again falls substantially short of his expenditure. The result, as I have observed on many occasions, is resort to bank loans at exorbitant rates of interest, or petty crime, or both. If a small farmer defaults on his tithe payments or on his rates, a summons follows, and then the bailiffs arrive to take away whatever pathetic possessions they can find, which are sold at a fraction of their market value to repay the debt. Destitution almost inevitably follows.

I have tried, on my own estate, to maintain the ancient custom of giving life tenancies to those who farm Penrhiw, Dolrannog Isaf, Gelli and my other properties, since I hold to the belief that a tenant farmer with security will work to maintain his fields and his walls and buildings, and will practice good stewardship on his land, since it is in his own interest and is for the good of his son and his grandson. The rents due to me are sometimes paid and sometimes not, but then I receive help in kind, and in all honesty I have never been exploited by lazy or incompetent tenants. They work hard, keep the land in good heart, and try to keep abreast of new developments. I insist that they use new farming methods and try new crops, and if they cannot read the works of Masters Tull and Cobbett for themselves I insist that they listen to others reading the texts for them.

Sadly, my neighbours do not share my priorities. The great majority of them have moved from life leases to annual rents, and I have seen three cases in recent years where, upon the end of a life lease, the rent has gone up three-fold between one year and the next. These rents simply cannot be sustained, and this year's tenant farmer is next year's pauper. Not that the agents of the land-owning squires mind, for the demand for land is insatiable, and when one farmer falls by the wayside there are ten others competing to take his place on the road to destitution. They are blind and stupid, all of them.

Another thing which contributes to the gathering of the storm clouds is the rise and rise of Nonconformity. As the small farmers have come to hate the church rates and the tithes which are imposed upon them by greedy rectors and vicars across the region, they have become more and more inclined to join the Baptists or the Methodists. The religious societies, both old and new, are thriving; and now there are five little chapels within a few miles of the Plas. The buildings are already too small for their swelling congregations. As religious fervour sweeps across the countryside it catches up the poorest and most vulnerable members of the community and gives them support. They remain poor and vulnerable, but they are given spiritual comfort and a sense of belonging, and also education through the Sunday Schools. That is something of which I thoroughly approve, having been involved from the early days in the Circulating Schools and in the welfare of Madam Bevan's College in Newport. More important than anything is the sudden realization of power by these poor people, who can participate in the making of decisions for the first time in their lives. They learn the Welsh Bible, they sing the great Welsh hymns, they recite the *pwnc*, and they come away from their chapels on a Sunday evening with a little more self-respect than they had at breakfast time. Their leaders are eloquent and passionate, and their sermons are charged with a *hwyl* that cannot be matched in the English language expositions which echo through the empty churches of St Mary in Newport or St Brynach in Nevern. So the seeds of dissent are sown by ministers and deacons who see the way that the world works, and who do not like what they see. And I have to sympathize with them, as one who is greatly attracted by the fervour and the essential goodness of many Methodist people including the Bowens of Llwyngwair. I do not agree with all that they say and do, and I have had many tense confrontations with Nonconformists in the past, but as I get older I think that I understand them better.

Poverty and a sense of injustice among the rural poor are combining, with greater force every day, to drive the lower orders of society in one direction and the gentry in another. In spite of my own best efforts, and the efforts of a few other good squires across North Pembrokeshire, I fear that we are seeing the emergence of two nations -- one which is becoming obsessed with the righting of ancient wrongs, and the other which has always been obsessed with the retention and enforcement of its ancient authority. There is less and less understanding between the two, and while, twenty years ago, they communicated by shouting across a watery gulf, that gulf has now become an ocean so wide that contact is all but lost. On the one side are the rich, living far beyond their means. On the other side are the poor, with aspirations. They shout and plead, but the rich are too far away to hear. I suppose that I must count myself among the rich, but I have to admit in the secret pages of this diary that my heart and my head both lead me towards the poor. I do not exactly count myself as a zealous champion of the downtrodden, but I fear that my instinct for involvement might be leading me towards trouble.

ΩΩΩΩΩΩΩΩΩΩΩ

11th December 1832

Now that I have rediscovered the joys of diary keeping, I must try to refrain from further ramblings about injustice and poverty -- at least until I have forced myself to write down what is locked within my heart concerning the highs and the lows of the last decade. I now face this prospect with some trepidation. But it has to be done, and in doing it I will be obeying the instructions of my beloved daughter Betsi. She came yesterday to visit me, and while she was here I found myself talking, as on many previous occasions, of Owain, Sara and Joseph. She gave me a look which contained both tenderness and ferocity, and I stopped in mid-sentence, and blushed.

She came and put her arms around me, pulled me close and gave me a long embrace. "Now then, Mother," she said, as if she was admonishing a small child. "No tears if you please. Have I not told you before that you need to move forward? Over and again you return to the same events from the distant past, and to tell you the truth I have heard quite enough of them. You appear to be filled with guilt for events over which you could not possibly have exerted any control. Why, oh why do you do it?"

"I do not know, Betsi, but I cannot escape from thoughts of what might have been......."

"What might have been? Mam, you now have two young families who love you and who rejoice in your love freely given. And in this place you still have your angels about you. Your ravens are still on the mountain, and the rough blue rocks are still standing proud against a bright sky. You must look forward, for all of our sakes."

Then she stood back, and took my hands in hers. She looked me in the eye, and smiled. "Did you not say that you have picked up your diary again?"

"Yes, I have. And I have rediscovered the pleasure of transferring thoughts from head to hand, and from pen to paper."

"Well then. Please record what you wish to record about those two beloved men, and your lost daughter, and in writing purge yourself of guilt and self-pity. They are with the Good Lord, and all they ever wished for you was happiness. Celebrate their lives, and smile as you see their faces before you. You betray them when you wallow in remorse. Write it down, Mother, and then close the book on that chapter of your life. Shemi tells me that you have work to do."

"Oh indeed? And how does he know that?"

"He knows, Mother. Now, promise me that you will do as I ask."

So I promised my sensible and sensitive daughter that I would write things down that I have never before articulated, and in the process get rid of my demons. I will compose myself first, and tomorrow I will do it.

12th December 1832

When Owain returned from the dead on the night before my planned wedding to Ceredig ap Tomos in the year 1822, my world was turned upside down. I had to choose between the two of them, and had to choose Owain, the one whom I loved and to whom I had promised myself fifteen years earlier. For his part he had kept himself alive, through years of cruelty and deprivation across North Africa, Spain and other parts of Europe, by the ardour of his own love for me. He kept faith when I did not, and if I had rejected him on that fateful August evening in this very house, he would have been destroyed. So I made my choice, as a consequence of which Ceredig took his own life. That almost destroyed me, and if it had not been for the succour provided by Joseph, Owain, my brother Morys and my own children and servants, I fear that I too might have spiralled down into the depths of Hell. As it was, I survived, and had to come to terms with my terrible destiny -- to follow my uncertain route through the rough byways of life, closely shadowed by the Grim Reaper whose pleasure is not to take me but to satisfy himself through the taking of others. At times this knowledge has been almost too much for me, but my angels have always folded their white wings around me in the blackest hours of the night, and somehow I have come through one episode of melancholia after another. The Grim Reaper mocks me even now as he has mocked me every year since my arrival at the Plas, keeping me alive when I have often wished for death.

But he will not defeat me. Melancholia is a stepping stone in the grey river, and just one more step away is the black shore of oblivion. The Reaper stands on the other side, blocking the route to the Pearly Gates, with a sneer on his face. I am not ready to go there, for I am older and stronger, and I have work to do. I swear that I will never again sink into the slough of despond, and that I will cherish those whom I love and fight for those who suffer. I will have my tragedies and my defeats, but I will learn -- I **must** learn -- to accept them with good grace, and to take lessons from them.

My poor dear Owain lasted for two years and six months after his return from foreign parts. He lived at Pontfaen, through the kindness of his brother James. For much of the time he was not well, for he was racked by bouts of malaria, and on several occasions his fever was so severe that

The Cold and the Dark

Joseph was hard put to drag him back from the edge of death. I spent long tense hours at his bedside, listening to his delirious ramblings, mopping his brow, holding his hand, and willing him to live. And he always came back to me, with pain in his eyes and a smile upon his lips, and asking for confirmation that he was in Heaven and in the presence of a most beautiful black-haired angel. He always was a poet and a gentleman, and a master of the honeyed word........

But his injuries were so severe that he should not really have been alive at all. Not only did he have stripes across his chest, carved out with a knife by that monster named John Fenton, but he had a broken arm and a broken leg suffered during a shipwreck upon the Moorish coast and imperfectly healed. Then he had a wound beneath his ribs where a musket ball had entered his body during the wars against the French. That would have killed him but for the skill of an army surgeon who had opened him up and extracted the ball lodged near his spine. The scar from that incision was still raw and inflamed. Then across his back were the multiple wounds inflicted by the French during his time as a spy for the Duke of Wellington. Twice he had been captured and horse-whipped to within an inch of his life, and since he would never talk of it I simply had to imagine, with tears in my eyes, what his interrogators had done to him. Even now, my heart is pounding as I force myself to inscribe these words onto the clean white page of my diary.

But against all the odds he did survive, and we were able to snatch some months of happiness together. We rediscovered our love and learned, after an interval of fifteen years, to know one another again. We had changed, both of us, and I was aware of that almost from the moment of his return. But we talked endlessly, and threw away our preconceptions, and both did what we could to adapt to changed circumstances. In the intervals between his malarial attacks we walked together, rode out over the mountain together on golden summer evenings, and made many visits to our favourite places. On several occasions we revisited our special grassy bank on the cliffs near Aberrhigian, and we loved one another with a passion born of years of abstinence. In retrospect, our violent exercise probably did his fragile health no good at all, but he always said that my body was the only thing that he ever wished to possess, and that my love was the only medicine that he ever wished to taste. We loved one another many times at the Plas and at Plas Pontfaen, and beneath starry skies on mossy beds. We loved silently and furtively when it was necessary. And when we could escape from pricked ears and sharp eyes, in Ty Canol Wood or among the crusted rocks of Mynydd Preseli, we shouted in our ecstasy and sang to the soaring buzzards, and giggled like silly children, and splashed naked in crystal streams. We were truly happy. For me, it was a second time of happiness, for I had known joy before, in the years spent with David, beloved father of my children. But for Owain, as he said to me more than once, it was the happiest time of his life, and in recalling his words I know that I should not be weeping, but smiling.

All of the family, and probably all of the neighbours, knew what was going on during the times when Owain was free of the fever, and indeed we were sometimes less discreet than we might have been. More than once we left abandoned garments which spoke with eloquence to those who found them. Bessie and Sara both told me to be careful, and said that the guardians of virtue from Caersalem Chapel had their beady eyes on me, but I laughed and replied that I would make my own peace with God without any help from them. I knew that I would not conceive again, but now that I look back on those months, from a distance of eight years or more, I am ashamed of the wilfulness and the unbridled passion which must have been all too apparent to those around me. But both Owain and I were overtaken by a sort of madness, and while I blush at the thought of it, I cannot in all conscience regret what we did in the name of love.

It was assumed by all and sundry, when Owain returned, that we would marry within a few months. I was ready for it, as soon as I realized that I still loved him and that he still loved me. I pleaded with him over and again, and said that I wanted nothing in this world other than to be his wife. But he simply deferred the matter, and at first told me to be patient while we rediscovered the joys of love. Then, one day as we lay on our backs on the top of Carningli, looking up at scudding clouds and circling red kites, he was honest with me. I still remember his words. "Martha, *cariad*," he said. "I love you more than life itself, and during my fifteen years in foreign parts I have been sustained by that love. You know it well. I came home in order to remind you that I wanted your hand in marriage. It was nothing less than an obsession. But since my return I have gradually come to the realization that nothing would be gained by it. For a start, I am not sure that I am strong enough to cope with a big wedding, or a little one for that matter. And if we become man and wife, and I move into the

The Cold and the Dark

Plas and into your bed, do you realise what complications would then arise? With the laws of this land as they are, all of your property, including your seven tenanted farms, would become mine. The Morgan estate, built up over generations and then cherished and protected by yourself in a fashion that has brought universal admiration throughout West Wales, would become a Laugharne estate. If we have a son, he would in due course inherit all of it, and your own dear family would be disinherited. I know that they can be protected through marriage settlements and wills, but do we really want to spend days and weeks with attorneys, crossing out clauses and conditions and substituting others, forgetting important details and arguing over those that are insignificant, when we might otherwise be living our lives? No, *cariad*, much as I would love to be your husband, common sense tells me that I must remain a bachelor all my life." He would not be moved, and so for two and a half years he stayed at Plas Pontfaen while I lived at Plas Ingli, visiting each other as often as we dared, and skating madly on thin ice at the very edge of scandal.

Underlying all of this, but never articulated by either Owain or myself, was the knowledge that he was dying. When the time would come, neither of us knew, but I noticed that each time his fever returned it was more severe and more prolonged than the last, and that chest infections began to take a hold of him. Joseph worked his magic on him over and again, and mixed new potions with the strangest of ingredients, but one day, before Christmas in the year 1824, I noticed the despair in the wizard's eyes and I realized that he could do no more. As Owain weakened and lost weight, everybody saw what was happening.

We gave him a wonderful Christmas at the Plas, which is where he wanted to be in spite of the pleading of his brother James and his sister Mary Jane that he should celebrate with them at Plas Pontfaen. He knew it would be his last. Sara and Brynach were here, of course, as were Betsi and Ioan and their little boys Benjamin and Abel. We were joined by Joseph, as ever, and also by old Squire George Price of Llanychaer who would otherwise have been all alone in that dark cold house of his. The tenant farmers and the labourers brought their families, and Bessie and Liza conjured up a feast the like of which nobody had ever seen before. We sang, and we danced, and the side of the wintery mountain was illuminated and warmed by love.

39

The Cold and the Dark

My main memory of that evening is of an inebriated and tearful George Price on bended knee in front of Owain and an audience of a hundred, freely admitting that in the month of May in the year 1807 he had been responsible for the sabotage of the little boat which carried my beloved man away and out of my life for fifteen years. He had not meant to kill him, he sobbed, but simply to give him a shock, and for fifteen years he had carried an insufferable burden of guilt on his shoulders, convinced that Owain was dead and that the Morgan and Laugharne families were both destroyed by grief as a consequence of his jealousy and stupidity. Owain, poet and saint, pulled him to his feet and embraced him. "I knew it all along, Master Price," he replied. "You have suffered enough because of it, as have I. There is nothing to be gained from revenge, or even from recriminations. Of course I forgive you. Let us now be friends."

He lasted for just a few more weeks. He enjoyed *Hen Galan* at Plas Pontfaen, and then in the latter part of the month of January his fever returned while he was paying me a visit at the Plas. I put him into my bed and refused to allow him to be moved back to Pontfaen. He did not want it either, and James and his wife respected his wishes. I sat with him for ten days. After six days he gave me a last kiss on the lips, and squeezed my hand, and told me for the thousandth time that he loved me. Then he lapsed into unconsciousness, calmed to some degree by a sedation that Joseph poured down his throat. He breathed his last on the third day of February in the Year of our Lord 1825. I was expecting it, and yet I was unprepared. They tell me that I was on the edge of exhaustion myself, and they are probably right, for I have virtually no recollection of the events that followed, or of the funeral.

Now he rests in the Laugharne family enclosure in Pontfaen Churchyard, in a simple grave covered with snowdrops and primroses. There is an unpretentious slate headstone which is inscribed as follows: *Here lies Owain Edwin Laugharne Esquire of Plas Pontfaen and Plas Llanerch, true gentleman, soldier and poet, taken to rest on the 3rd day of February 1825, aged 44 years. He was loved by all who knew him, and was himself sustained by love.* The grave is overlooked by a white lilac tree which I planted a year after his death, and every June, on Midsummer's Eve, I pick a posy of the heavy-scented blossoms which I then arrange in a glass vase on my bedside table. Thus do I remember my gentle poet who has found his peace. There. It is done. Now I must weep.

The Cold and the Dark

13th December 1832

Today I have been up onto the mountain, and this evening I feel better. Indeed, I feel a quiet satisfaction arising out of the conquest of my emotions. Twenty years ago I would have been reduced to the status of a gibbering idiot by the act of describing the death of someone as dear to me as Owain Laugharne. But last night, as I wept into my pillow and as a flood of memories swept over me, I realized that I needed time to myself on the mountain. I determined that I would climb up to my cave straight after breakfast, and with this calming resolution fixed inside my head I drifted at last into a fitful sleep.

In the morning I woke early, while it was still pitch black outside, and Liza was surprised to find me up when she sidled in through my bedroom door with her basket of kindling and small coals for the fire. "Good morning, Mistress!" said she. "You look very sprightly this morning, if I may say so."

"I do not feel it, Liza, I can assure you," I replied. "In fact, I was up late and my sleep was somewhat disturbed. But I do feel at ease with the world today, and I am minded to climb up the mountain straight after breakfast."

Liza looked amazed. "I do not advise it, Mistress," she said. "I have just walked up from the cottage, and it is a horrid morning, with driving rain and low cloud. Even when it is light, I swear that the summit will be invisible."

"Do not try to change my course, Liza. I am set upon it, and if I spread my arms wide, I will sail up the rocky slope with a brisk following wind, and leave the rain behind."

And so, with hot porridge in my stomach and stout boots on my feet, and a felt hat strapped to my head, and Billy's old oilskins providing some little protection from the rain, I headed out into the storm. As I climbed, of course I got very wet indeed, but I felt a sort of exhilaration, and I was spurred on by the thought that ahead of me was the warm dry sanctuary of the cave. I passed St Brynach's sacred spring, and without thinking I anointed myself with a handful of its holy water, just as I always do before tackling the last steep part of the climb. Then my sombre mood gave way to laughter, as I was struck by the absurdity of an anointment in weather such as this, with water pouring out of the shredded cloud, sluicing off my sodden hat and oilskins, and filling my clothes and my boots. Thousands of gallons of it, straight from heaven. I was still in good humour as I climbed up into the mist. I passed between rock pillars and edged along rocky ledges, as I had done hundreds of times before. Then I wound my way through the last narrow crevices, passed the last fallen boulders, and saw the entrance of my secret cave. Nobody else knows about it except my daughter Daisy, and I know not if she is alive or dead. It belongs to me, as it once belonged to old Saint Brynach. He came here to commune with his angels, as do I whenever I need peace.

Soon I was inside, and out of my boots and oilskins. Some years ago, when I slept in the cave occasionally, I carried up three sheepskins and a couple of thick woollen blankets, and I made the decision to leave them behind in case I should ever need them again. They were in the back corner of the cave, perfectly dry, and soon I was cuddled up snugly, as warm as a fluffy chick beneath the wing of a mother hen. Away from the wind and the rain, I found silence, although in truth it was quite noisy with the gale buffeting the rock surfaces outside and with the sound of running water echoing around me. I stayed for maybe three hours, thinking of my dear family and of this magical mountain which is now so much a part of me that I feel pain when it is burning and shiver when it is gripped by ice. And I thought of the men who still live in my heart although they are all dead. My beloved husband David, cut down in his prime by evil men; and Iestyn, the father of my adopted son, who survived terrible injuries and deprivation simply to see him safe; and Owain, who was beautiful, and who entranced me with the magic of his eyes and the music of his words; and poor Ceredig, a gentle man whose tragedy was that he loved me too much and who could not live with the thought of me loving another; and Joseph, who saved me from myself and from others who would do me harm, whose arms enfolded me when I needed comfort, and whose shoulder was drenched with my tears on more occasions than I care to count.

As I scrambled back down the slope, slipping and sliding across sodden rock surfaces and streaming turf, I left these dear men behind me in the tender care of the angels of mercy. All except Joseph, whom I still carry in my heart. Tomorrow, if I can remain calm, I will write of his passing, and try to let him go.

The Cold and the Dark

14th December 1832

The death of Joseph Harries, wizard, sleuth and most steadfast of friends, was in some ways even more difficult for me to cope with, because it was so unexpected. And because, at the time, I was utterly confused.

A year, to the day, after Owain's death, I decided to pay a visit to his grave in Pontfaen Churchyard. It was a strange sort of day, unseasonably warm, with a damp mist rolling in off the sea. I could not see more than twenty yards in front of me, but this was no cause for concern since I knew every inch of the way between Plas Ingli and Pontfaen. I set off on my own, riding on my quietest grey pony. I rode past Dolrannog Uchaf and Penrhiw and was about to descend through the woods towards Llannerch when my pony stopped and pricked up her ears and became very agitated. She backed into a field entrance and would not move forward or back, and neither would she obey any of my instructions. I too became aware of something, and started to feel uncomfortable. Then I realized that a *Toili* or phantom funeral was coming. I had never seen one before, but I knew what it meant. I shivered, and felt very afraid. Within a minute or so I began to hear a low hum of conversation, and soon I picked up the crunch and crackle of wheels, hooves, boots and clogs upon hard ground. That was strange, I thought, because the weather was warm and the ground in the lane was soft and very muddy. Then a one-horse hearse drove past, carrying a coffin decked with oak and ivy. The horse was one of mine. Behind the hearse I recognized Master Jacob Ifans, the minister of Jabes Chapel. Then I saw myself at the head of the mourners, followed by Betsi, Ioan and Brynach. Then came my servants from the Plas. Other people began to appear -- women in black shawls and coats, with black bonnets upon their heads, and gentlemen in long black topcoats and tall hats. They drifted in and out of my vision, but I recognized many of them as my neighbours and friends. George Price of Llanychaer, James Laugharne of Pontfaen, Byron Bayles of Puncheston, John Collyer of Tredafydd and many others. There must have been two hundred people shuffling along, with grief writ large on their faces. Many were in tears. They all passed within a few feet of me, quite oblivious of my presence, and moved off down the lane. They were travelling away from the Plas and towards Pontfaen. Then, after about thirty minutes, they were gone, and in a few minutes the last sounds of conversation and sobs were swallowed by the mist.

Gradually my pony relaxed, and I tried to come to terms with what I had seen. Why was the hearse pulled by one of my horses, and why was I at the head of the mourners? Then I was overwhelmed with fear as I realized that Sara had not been walking in the procession, and that she must therefore have been inside the coffin. Sara, my youngest child, and the only one left at the Plas, to be taken from me before reaching the age of twenty? How could that be? She was always weak and in need of medical attention, but she was surely too intelligent, too innocent and too beautiful to die. And was she not the most beloved of my children, always on hand to curb my wild excesses and to banish my black moods? How could it be that she was destined to die before finding true happiness with a good man at her side and children on her knee? Sara, whose fragile beauty could illuminate the midnight hour and whose smile could melt icebergs........

Now I felt that my heart was petrified, and I could not move. I sat there for maybe twenty minutes, with my pony becoming increasingly restless beneath me. Then I remembered that I could not shift fate, and that I had no option but to get on with life. I decided to press on to Pontfaen, since the ride would give me the opportunity to think. So I continued, although I have no recollection of the journey. In the Pontfaen Churchyard I shed tears on Owain's grave, and thought of dear Sara.

I got home just as darkness was seeping into the mist. Sara was involved in some foolishness with Liza, and they were giggling uncontrollably. I could not cope with it, so after giving my dear child a long embrace I retreated to my room, missing supper, for I had no appetite. Bessie, Sara and Liza looked in and tried to comfort me, but all three concluded that I was simply upset following my visit to Owain's grave, and they decided, one after another, simply to respect my grief. So then they left me alone. I slept hardly at all, but I knew that I could share the tale of my ghostly encounter with no-one and that it was my fate to carry on for days, or weeks or even months as if there was nothing on my mind. In the darkness I cursed my special powers, and prayed that they might be taken from me. They were not gifts but burdens which were breaking my back. Strangely, I did not -- could not -- weep, and I spent the night staring at the black and invisible ceiling above my head, with my mind racing and my heart still embedded in ice.

In the morning I decided that I must put a brave face on it and that I must carry on as if it was a perfectly normal day. I knew that it would be foolish in the extreme for me to pay extra attention to Sara, or to embrace her, or to shower her with compliments or gifts, but in truth I could hardly keep my eyes off her, and I was constantly on the edge of tears. But she was happy, and energetic, and her cough seemed to be troubling her less than usual. As she went about her appointed tasks she sang, for all who would listen, with the voice of an angel. Then she took a wicker basket, wrapped up well, and went off towards Penrhiw to fetch our weekly payment of eggs and butter.

At about noon, there was a thunder of hooves in the yard outside. We all rushed to the kitchen door and saw a man whom we did not recognize dismounting from a fine black stallion. "Mistress Martha Morgan?" he asked.

I curtseyed. "Yes, sir. Martha Morgan at your service."

"Thank God. I am James Humfrey, and my Master is Squire Gittins of Tredrissi. Come quick, Mistress! Master Harries the Wizard is wounded mortal bad, and we fear that he will die. He called for you......."

"Oh, my God!" I replied, realizing in an instant that the Grim Reaper would take Joseph and not Sara. "We will be with you immediately. Liza, ring the bell and call Shemi back from the bottom meadow. I want him to come with me. We'll take the chestnut mare and the light chaise. Ask Gomer to get the horse and make ready. I'll get some warm clothes and blankets. I hope to God that we will be able to help."

At the sound of the bell Shemi came rushing back to the house, and in five minutes we were away, following Master Humfrey down the lane to Nevern and up the far hill to Tredrissi. We drove our poor mare so hard that I feared that she might die from exhaustion, or that we might lose a wheel in one of the deep water-filled pot-holes. The Squire's servant led us not to the big house but to the sordid hovel of one of his labourers. Joseph was inside, resting on a rough bed. He was barely conscious. The labourer and his wife, Arfon and Delyth Huws, had tried to make him comfortable, but they knew not the first thing about how to treat an injured man, and poor Joseph was still lying in his filthy clothes which were impregnated with mud, cow-dung and blood. They had wrapped a rough sheet around his torso, since this was clearly where the most severe of his injuries were.

I was horrified by what I saw. "Oh Joseph!" I moaned. "What on earth have you done?" He could not answer me, but he opened his eyes for a moment and gave me the slightest of smiles.

I turned to Arfon and Delyth. "We must get him cleaned up at once," I said, "and get these disgusting garments off him. Have you got some hot water in your cauldron?"

"Yes, Mistress," replied Delyth. "Always on the boil."

"Fill up a big bowl if you please, so hot that you can only just put your finger in it."

As she acted on my request, Shemi and I started to strip off his clothes. Shemi took out his knife. We had to cut his breeches and his undergarment off him, for we had no idea how many bones might be broken. Then we peeled off the blood-soaked sheet and had to cut off his jacket and waistcoat, and then his shirt. I gasped when I saw the extent of his injuries, for there was a huge open wound in his stomach, and it appeared that his chest had been crushed by a mighty weight. Shemi appreciated at once what had happened. While we worked with hot water and rags, he turned to Arfon and said "The Tredrissi bull?"

"Yes, *bach*. He was lame, and getting worse, and down in the bottom paddock. And in a bad temper. The master and his family are away in London just now, so Gwyn Cow-man took it upon himself to ask Master Harries here to come over and put him right. He came about nine o'clock. Between us we got the monster tethered, and Master Harries had a look at his foot. But then he went mad and broke the tether. He went for me and I just managed to jump over the fence. Then he got Master Harries up against the fence, and crushed up against him with all his weight. The poor fellow fell down in the mud and the dung, and then the bull went for him. I was screaming and trying to pull him off, but he got his horn into him and threw him up into the air. Then he was going for him again on the ground, but I managed to get a hold of the chain that was connected to his nose-ring, and I gave him hell and managed to pull him off......"

"That bull always was a monster," said Shemi. "I had a very close shave with him once myself. The Devil is in him, for he is the only animal that I cannot talk to."

"So how did you get Joseph out of the paddock?" I asked.

"Well, with all the commotion, a couple of the boys from next door came rushing up. Thank God for that, for I could not have held the animal myself. They got hold of the end of the tether, tied another rope onto it, and together we got the creature tied against the fence. Then we managed to pick up poor Master Harries and carry him over to the cottage."

"How long since the accident?"

"Maybe two hours, Mistress."

I realized now, as we frantically cleaned his wounds with hot water, that we could not leave Joseph where he was. The cottage was dark, filthy and smoky, and no matter how kind Delyth and Arfon might be, this was no place for the tending of serious injuries. Neither could we take Joseph to the Squire's house, for there was only one servant left in residence. There was nothing for it but to transport my dear friend back to the Plas, where we could give him proper attention. So, having cleaned his wounds as best we could, and having ascertained that none of his limbs appeared to be broken, we bandaged up the horrible open wound in his stomach, which was still bleeding profusely. He had lost a huge amount of blood. He was shivering uncontrollably. We wrapped him up in the blankets which we had brought with us, carried him gently to the chaise, and after giving our heartfelt thanks to the labourer and his wife we set off for home. I had one further request to make of the Squire's servant. "James," I said, "if you wish to do one more thing for Master Harries, will you ride directly into Newport and ask young Doctor Havard to make his way to the Plas as a matter of life and death?" He nodded. "Anything for Master Harries, Mistress, and anything for you." And he untethered his black horse and galloped off along the Newport road.

Our journey back to the Plas was dreadfully slow. Dear Joseph was unconscious, and given the extent of his injuries I thought it a miracle that he was still alive. But an hour later we arrived, to find Sara and the servants all together in the yard. Shemi and the other men carried the patient into the warmth and security of the kitchen. We cleared the great oak table and laid him out on it, and tried once again to cleanse his body and his wounds with copious quantities of hot water and infusions of medicinal herbs. When, in better lighting, I saw the extent of his wounds, I almost passed out, but Bessie was a pillar of strength, and sent me away to prepare a poultice. I did this, working frantically in the pantry where I kept my collection of herbs. Sara helped me, and as we worked I told her everything. I used comfrey, mallow, marigold and agrimony as my main constituents, and applied the poultice very hot to the wounds. Thank God that Joseph was still unconscious, and felt no additional pain.

The Cold and the Dark

About fifteen minutes later Havard Medical arrived. James had already described for him the circumstances surrounding the accident, and had given him a rough indication of the injuries. He rushed straight into the kitchen, and examined Joseph carefully. I perceived immediately from his reactions that there was no hope. He closed his eyes, sighed and shook his head. He took me to one side and whispered: "Mistress Martha, I fear that there is little I can do. The open wound in his stomach is truly terrible, for the bull's curved horn has penetrated almost through to his spine. When Master Harries was thrown up in the air his internal organs were ripped apart, and I do not know how I can prevent his whole body from being poisoned. I am sure that his lungs are punctured. Then his chest is collapsed from the animal's weight. Most of his ribs are broken........."

"Enough, Master Havard. Enough."

"It is a miracle that he is still alive. I think that all you can do is give him comfort. Keep him warm. Keep the poultice in his open wound, and give him your strongest possible sedative. Laudanum might be best. Master Harries has, I believe, told you some of his secrets. Do you know what to give him?" I nodded. "If he does wake up, his pain will be truly unbearable. But his pulse is already slow and irregular. You have a bed for him?"

"Of course," I replied. "My room is the warmest room upstairs, and my bed is the softest in the house. We will put him there."

So we did what we could for him, and then wrapped him in sheets and blankets, and Shemi and Will carried him upstairs as gently as if he had been a newborn baby, and put him into my bed. Havard Medical asked me if he should stay, but it was clear that there was nothing more that he could do, and so I thanked him and sent him on his way. Then I mixed up the strongest sedative potion that I knew, and trickled it down Joseph's throat, a few drops at a time, while he was still asleep. Liza stoked up the fire in the bedroom grate, and soon the warmth from the glowing coals spread through the room.

I asked Bessie and the other servants to leave me alone with my dear friend, and indeed there was nothing more they could do. They needed to clear up the kitchen, clean the table, boil up the filthy and bloodstained sheets and blankets, and get on with the normal tasks of a winter afternoon. Just then, I did not even want Sara to be near me. I sat with Joseph for maybe an hour, holding his hand and trying to come to terms with what had happened. As he breathed there were strange noises in his throat, and tears welled up in my eyes as I realized that there was no caring that I could provide that might ease his discomfort. I was sure that he was slipping away. Then Liza came in with a pail of steaming hot water and a soft warm towel. "Now then, Mistress," she said. "Out of those disgusting clothes if you please. You may not realise it, but you are covered with blood and cow-dung yourself, and there is nothing to be gained from remaining in that state. Take off every single thing, and I will put out clean things for you." I nodded and undressed as she poured the water into the big china bowl on my wash-stand. She put out clean undergarments and stockings, and my softest stays, and a warm woollen dress and jacket. Then as I stood naked in a sort of trance and washed myself in front of the fire, she went off downstairs with my dirty clothes which were destined for the big washing cauldron in the scullery.

I dressed myself slowly, tidied my hair and returned to my chair at Joseph's bedside. I looked at him and was astonished to see that his eyes were open. I was covered with embarrassment as I realized he had quietly observed me at my ablutions. Close as he was to death, he gave me a wicked grin. "At last I have my revenge, Mistress Martha," he whispered. "More than once you have had me at your mercy on that kitchen table of yours, observing every detail of my body. Now I have observed every detail of yours, and I find myself in your bed at your insistence. A little late in the day, but all things come to those who wait."

"Oh, Joseph, Joseph," I replied, with tears streaming down my cheeks. "How can you be so frivolous at such a time?"

"I am deadly serious, my dear Martha."

"Whatever do you mean, Joseph?" I asked, but before I had finished asking the question the truth flooded through me like some powerful narcotic. Joseph loved me, not as a father loves a daughter, or as one friend loves another, but as a man with red blood in his veins and passion in his breast. He had probably always loved me, since our first meeting shortly after my arrival at the Plas, when I went to him and asked for his advice on how to take my own life. He had never declared it or given me any intimation of his feelings, and neither had he once taken advantage of me in over thirty years of friendship, during which he had seen me at my vulnerable worst, over and over again. Now, as I was covered in confusion, a multitude of little incidents from the past came into my head, all of which, had I not been so self-obsessed, I might have interpreted as signals of love. I could not look at him, and I knew not what to do.

"Look at me, Martha."

I looked at him again, and saw that again there was a faint smile on his lips. "I perceive that, at last, you have recognized my love," he whispered. "Do not worry, *cariad*........"

"Oh, Joseph, you call me *cariad*, and you ask me not to worry?"

"I do, Martha. At times, my feelings almost got the better of me, but self-control is one of the attributes of a wizard. It will be obvious to you that I am a very poor cow-man, but I am a very good wizard. I knew that you could never love me, and I strove never to encourage it. Mistresses of fine estates do not marry disreputable wizards."

I had to smile through my tears, and for some minutes I held his hand tight, saying nothing and remembering everything. Then he coughed, and a sort of shadow passed over his face. "Is the pain very terrible?" I asked.

He shook his head. Then, after a long pause, he opened his eyes. "I am slipping into oblivion, Martha," he murmured. "I have had a truly wonderful life, due in no small measure to the joy which you and your family have given to me in abundance. Press on, Martha, and remember everything that I have taught you. You have much to do. It is your destiny to change our world for the better."

"Joseph, please, please do not leave me," I sobbed, trying not to make too much noise. "What shall I do without you?"

"You will cope perfectly well, I assure you. Now then, practical things." He stopped, as if he was fighting for a few more precious minutes of life. Then he continued. "I will be buried in Jabes Churchyard. Ask Hettie Visionist where. She saw the *Canwyll Gorff* two weeks ago. I did not know it until now, but it was for me. You will have everything from Werndew -- my big book, my library, and all my potions and mixtures. My will is in a box under the bed. Teach Shemi all you know, and then in time pass everything on to him. He will be a great wizard. Promise that you will do as I ask?"

I nodded, and as I held his hand in mine I felt the warmth draining out of it. I tried to put healing into him, but no matter how I tried, I could not give him the strength to live. He closed his eyes and whispered: "Will you kiss me, Martha, on my lips, and tell me that you love me?" So I did as he asked, and gave him through my lips all the love that was in me. Then I said "Joseph, I truly love you." Those were the last words that he heard. As his breathing faded I rested my cheek against his, and anointed him with my tears. Over the course of a minute, or an hour, his breathing became softer and softer until I could no longer hear it or feel it. And so the Wizard of Werndew passed quietly from this world.

As his spirit flew away, it carried a part of me with it. I recall that for a long time I did not move. There was a deep, deep silence, as if the whole world had stopped breathing. I felt no emotion, and no awareness of anything but a great echoing emptiness.

After that, Sara told me that I fell to pieces, and that she and the other women rushed upstairs when they heard my wailing. They knew at once that Joseph was dead. Apparently I would not let go of him, and at last they had to drag me away and give me some of the sedation which I had previously given to Joseph. Bessie and Liza took care of him. Sara put me into her bed, and there I remained during the thunderstorm that followed. All I recollect is a drowsy awareness that the world was coming to an end.

The world did not end, but never has such a storm been experienced before or after that date, the fourth day of February in the year 1826. The first crash of thunder occurred to the north-west, over Dinas and Werndew, at twenty minutes past four, the precise moment of Joseph's death. Nobody was surprised, for the deaths of wizards are always accompanied by signs and wonders, and especially by thunder and lightning. Then the storm drifted across the mountain towards Carningli and the Plas, with a cloud so vast and so heavy that the dusk of the winter afternoon was transformed to the pitch blackness of night. There was no rain at all, which many thought very strange, but fearsome winds sprang up and died down, swinging from one quarter to another with such speed that there was no sheltering from them. Sara told me that the sheets and crackling forks of lightning were more blue than white, and were accompanied instantaneously by thunder so loud that the very foundations of the house shook, and slates rattled off the roof. At the peak of the storm, Sara and the others saw a blue light dancing over the whole of the mountain, flickering and hissing, with the summit standing out in silhouette. Inside the house, fabrics and furniture glowed, and those who touched them received shocks which flung them across the room. Then with one final mighty thunder-crack it was all over. The clouds melted away, and although the sun was below the far horizon a golden light flooded in from the west, reflected on a canopy of high mackerel cloud.

Joseph's mortal remains were placed in a coffin on the following day, and he was watched over by Shemi, Will and young Gomer, and by a succession of neighbours and friends from all over north Pembrokeshire. Never was a man more greatly loved, for almost every family in the district had called upon him at some time, to treat sick children or to mend broken limbs, to heal ailing animals or to find lost items, to provide wise counsel or to admonish those who had strayed from the paths of virtue. He had visited every house and hovel over a radius of twenty miles. He had known everybody and everything. Never had I met a man so widely read and so well informed in literature, in the classics, in science, in history, in music or in anything you might care to mention. He had been doctor and apothecary, surgeon and sleuth, wise man and man of mystery. He had been respected by all and feared by those who deserved his wrath. He had been a friend of the poor and an implacable enemy of vice and corruption. He had rescued me on a hundred occasions, brought me consolation in my grief, brought to justice those who had harmed me, and brought laughter into my life over and again when I least expected it. He had been a dear friend to David and Owain, and he had been a sort of surrogate father to my children. They had all loved him dearly.

And now he was gone. To whom would I now turn when my little world threatened to collapse around me? With Werndew cold and dark, and with the peat fire extinguished, where would I now find sanctuary when pursued by my demons? And to think that he had loved me, year after year, without any recognition or acknowledgement on my part...... That fact alone brought me to the brink of despair.

Bessie, most blessed of friends, realized what was happening in my head and my heart, and came to me on the day after Joseph's death as I sat draped in misery in the chair by my bedroom window, looking out on a cold and lifeless world. She stood in front of me and took my hands. Without a word, she pulled me to my feet and embraced me, and allowed me to dissolve in tears. I wept until there was no more weeping to do. Then she said: "Now that is enough of guilt, if you please, Mistress. Grief is quite enough for you to cope with, and there is no need for extra burdens."

"But he loved me, Bessie. He said so. I never saw it myself, blind and selfish fool that I was. Did you know it?"

"Of course, Mistress. It was obvious to me from the time when he brought you back from the very edge of death, following the loss of your first baby."

"But how could I have been so insensitive to his feelings, and so cruel, over all these years? Bessie, I am so ashamed!"

"Mistress, be sensible if you will. I am quite certain that Master Joseph did not want you to know of his passion for you. As he controlled it, I firmly believe that he clouded the mirror of your mind so that you could not see it. He was a *Dyn Hysbys*, after all. He knew, and I knew, that if he had declared his love, or if you had somehow discovered it, everything would have been destroyed. Jealousy and recriminations would have bedevilled your relationships with him and with your beloved men, and with Sara and the other children. As it was, your sweet innocence allowed you two to become the greatest and most steadfast of friends, and I am sure that that brought Joseph a wonderful joy."

"Oh, Bessie," I moaned. "I hope that you are right. As I looked into his eyes for the last time, all I saw was the pain of unrequited love."

"You are wrong, Mistress. I spoke to him many times when you were elsewhere, for he was my dear friend too. Although he could not resist declaring his love at the last, I know that he had reached an accommodation with his passion, as befits a gentleman of sixty-four."

At this, I managed a smile. "Thank you, my dear friend," I said. "Your ability to keep secrets does you credit, as it did years ago in that business of the Nightwalker. But I still feel guilt that Joseph gave everything to me, and I gave nothing in return."

"Nonsense, Mistress! Utter nonsense! It is certain that he has rescued you on many occasions, but do not forget the times when you have rescued him. And you have given him, through your beauty and your wonderful generosity of spirit, a multitude of gifts without which his life would have been immeasurably poorer. He said as much to me, on many occasions."

"Did he really, Bessie?"

"I swear it, Mistress."

So we embraced again, and over the next two days I managed to keep control of my emotions and to go through with yet another *Gwylnos* at the Plas, and yet another funeral of a beloved and quite wonderful man. On the day of the funeral the temperature plummeted, and the ground was frozen solid. Sara was suffering from a chill, and I insisted that she should stay at home rather than walking in the procession to Jabes Chapel. And so the procession took place exactly as I had observed it in the *Toili* which had given me such apprehension and fear. The Chapel was crowded, with many mourners having to stand outside in the cold. Then Joseph was buried in the south-west corner of the graveyard, away from the other graves, for that was where Hettie Visionist had seen the flame. In any case, he always said that he was not a Christian and did not really deserve to sleep in hallowed ground.

After that, life returned to something like normality. Joseph left me in peace, as I knew he would, but my private demons have troubled me until this very day. I hope that my dear daughter was right in her prediction, and that they will flee now that I have put pen to paper, and in the face of my resolve to live for today and tomorrow, and to leave yesterday behind. Shemi and Joseph have said that I have work to do, and men such as they are never wrong.

ΩΩΩΩΩΩΩΩΩΩΩ

3. Outside, Looking in

21st December 1832

During the last week I have managed to put behind me the tragedies connected with the good men in my life, and I have concentrated on matters of more immediate concern. Christmas is almost upon us, and as our day-time preparations become ever more frantic I declare that it would be impossible either to wallow in grief or to think of anything other than food and drink. Only in the very rarest of circumstances have we failed to celebrate the birth of our Lord in the traditional fashion, and this year we expect seventy people to be crowded into this dear house on Christmas Day. That will represent hospitality on a modest scale, and I quake at the recollection that thirty years ago there were some Christmases on which we filled more than one hundred and twenty hungry stomachs. I was young and foolish then, and bursting with energy, and I suspect that such Christmases will never be seen again, for there are now too many people on the land, and fewer resources on which to feed them.

We have had a busy day in the kitchen, and it is now nine o'clock in the evening. Outside, it is wet and windy, but the old house is as warm and dry as ever. I refer to it as "old", and indeed it feels to me as if it has been here for ever, but in truth it was built less than forty years ago, following the terrible fire which destroyed the old Plas Ingli. The servants are installed in their usual places in the kitchen. Shemi and Will have gone home to their families, but Liza is stopping for the night and she and Bessie are perched on the settles on either side of the *simnai fawr*, putting the world to rights and knitting stockings. Their faces are aglow with the heat from the culm fire which has not gone out since the house was first occupied in the summer of 1796. Gomer and young Bobby Morris from Cilgwyn Mill are playing chess on the kitchen table. Gwenno is playing on my Celtic harp with more enthusiasm than skill, but she has talent and I am encouraging her to take it up and practise whenever she can. I am happy to give her lessons several times a week, but since she is only twenty-two years old she finds it difficult to concentrate on anything except Bobby Morris for more than fifteen minutes at a stretch. Such are the pleasures and distractions of youth.

Half and hour since, I decided to leave them to their simple pleasures in order to pursue one of mine. So here I am, with my little book before me, and with pen in hand. My bedroom fire is burning merrily in the grate, and even though my little world is dominated by the sounds of a rough winter night, I feel a great contentment. I think that as I get older I am learning to place greater value on the good things of life -- family, friends, beloved servants, and a good little estate that gives all of us most of what we need.

So I am moved to record the gentle and happy things that have blessed my life over the last decade. One of the happiest was the marriage of Will Owen, the son of our old and indomitable house-keeper Blodwen who died in 1814. Will came here in the year 1806, and I took him on originally in order to save him from a life of petty crime. I count it as one of my achievements in life to have prevented him from being transported to the colonies. For his first few years at the Plas I was not at all certain that he would settle down, and neither was his mother. But hard work, and regular food in his belly, and sufficient coppers in his pocket for a few jars of weekly ale, have made a good man of him, and he is now the best cow-man in the district. And then a few years ago, when an old tenant died and her cottage became available, he suddenly fell in love with the oldest of the Gruffydd daughters from Brynberian and asked me if he might get married. He said that at the age of 43 it was now time to settle down. I was delighted to give him both my blessing and my cottage, and he and his wife Tegwen are as cosy as may be with three little children to keep them busy. Since the littlest of the children is only one year old, he does not have a great deal of time, nor indeed any spare pennies, for carousing in the alehouses of Newport, but he maintains his contacts with the local underworld, and I am grateful for that since one cannot maintain a good estate in this day and age without an effective network of spies.

Another good thing was the arrival of young Gomer Jenkins some years ago. He is now twenty, tall and handsome, and almost as big as his father Shemi. I took him on at the age of fifteen, to help with bird scaring and stone picking, but he proved a good deal too bright for such menial tasks, and when it became apparent that he loved horses I gave him responsibility for the stables and for the garden as well. He still has a good deal to learn from his father, and it does not appear that he has inherited the family gift of speaking with animals, but he is a cheerful young fellow, and he knows how to work hard. He deserves his wages of £4 per year, but his mother Sian complains that hardly any coppers come back to the family cottage to help with the costs of food and fuel and suchlike. It was always thus, and I remind her frequently that when she worked here as nursemaid for my little children, and lived beneath my roof, and ate my food, none of her precious earnings found their way back to her parents' home at Gelli.

Liza has just popped into my room to damp down the fire for the night and to remind me that it is bed-time. She tells me that I do not sleep enough, and who am I to disagree? So I shall settle down, and sleep well, and tomorrow, if I can find the time, I will write about Brynach.

ΩΩΩΩΩΩΩΩΩΩ

22nd December 1832

When a foundling child was left on my doorstep in the year 1807, I could never have imagined what the consequences might be, or the manner in which my life would change. I already had four children of my own, and yet this little baby, whom I named Brynach, smiled his way into my affections in a manner which indicated to me that there was some special bond between us. This was from the beginning more than a bond between a helpless infant and a maternal and protective woman. For a start, there was a physical similarity between us, with our black hair, brown eyes and dark complexions marking us out from the other members of the family. And there were other things too, subtle and yet mysterious, over which I mulled endlessly during the first fifteen years of his life.

Following his adoption and the installation of Liza as wet nurse, Brynach became another member of the family, adored by the children and servants and thoroughly spoiled by me. At one time I over-indulged him, and he became a spoiled brat, but thank God he settled down at last to become a kind and dutiful son. Indeed, he was my only son, following the death of my beloved Dewi in the year 1820. As he grew up I had less time for him than I would have liked, for I was trying to cope with the disappearance of Owain and also with the mysterious appearances of a strange creature we called the Nightwalker, year after year and with no particular pattern that we could discern. But I did notice that the creature in black made a habit of appearing on Brynach's birthdays, and on a fateful day in August 1822 the mystery was solved when I came face to face with the Nightwalker in my cave. I thought at first that I had come face to face with the Devil, but then I discovered that the fearsome creature was Iestyn Price, the son of Squire George Price of Llanychaer. He was assumed to have died in the wars with the French, but he had survived, horribly injured and disfigured by the wounds of battle. What is more, he revealed to me that he was the father of the foundling left on my doorstep. He also revealed a secret which I have not passed on to this day, namely that the mother of the child was none other than my sister Elen, who lived in Bath at the time and who fled to the United States to hide from the shame of bearing a child out of wedlock.

At the end of his life Iestyn had one great friend -- Joseph Harries of Werndew, who almost lost his friendship with me in order to protect the secret of the Nightwalker and his link with Brynach. Iestyn returned from the dead into the bosom of his father, and he ended his days at Plas Llanychaer, where only one or two trusted servants knew his true identity. When he died, and when Squire Price was left alone in the world, Brynach became the heir to the Llanychaer estate, but when I discussed matters with the old man we agreed that nothing would be said about his parentage, or about his future inheritance, until he reached the age of twenty-one. That was what Iestyn wanted. At the time the young fellow was studying at the Grammar School in Haverfordwest, but then I sent him to Oxford to learn the arts and crafts of being a gentleman and to increase his knowledge of the world. He travelled to Italy and Spain in the company of three other sons of the Pembrokeshire gentry, and managed to return without getting into too much trouble. He did a small amount of work at university, and he certainly had fun, but he knew that he would in due course inherit Plas Ingli from me, and that the time would come when he would have to take on a very heavy burden of responsibility.

Two months before his twenty-first birthday, I took him out of college, on the pretext that I now needed him at the Plas and wanted to teach him agriculture. I also wished to give him the responsibilities that might otherwise have been passed to a steward. He grumbled, but since I held the purse strings and paid his fees and his allowances, he could not very well object. Besides, he confided in me that in his heart of hearts he wanted to be back in Pembrokeshire, because that is where his beloved Anne was, waiting faithfully for him year after year.

On the 7th day of April (St Brynach's Day) in the year 1828, Brynach came of age and officially became the Master of the Plas Ingli estate. We had a wonderful celebration at the Plas, with many young people from good Pembrokeshire families in attendance. There was good cheer, good food and wine, and most excellent dancing. I participated for as long as I dared, but at last I realized that I belonged to the wrong generation, and left the floor to the young bloods and the pretty young ladies. It was the closest we have ever come at the Plas to an event classed as a highlight of the "social season". I did it for Brynach and Anne, but I have to admit that deep down I disliked intensely the shallow talk and the deep pretensions of the next generation of the Pembrokeshire gentry. I had a profound feeling that as they laughed and spilled their claret and tucked into the best food that Bessie could conjure out of the pantry, they were all living on borrowed time, hidden in their self-obsessed little world from the deep rumblings which were even then beginning to shake the foundations of the establishment.

On the day after Brynach's birthday, Will Final Testament came to the Plas with a document which gave me the right to remain at the Plas until the end of my days, and to act as Mistress in all matters relating to the house and the estate. That was done at Brynach's insistence, although he could have evicted me had he wished it. He signed the document and said with a smile: "There now, Mother, you are safe in this dear place. To move you would be to sign your death warrant, and I am still far too young to cope with the mysteries of running the Plas. My time will come." And we embraced, mother and son. Then I travelled with Brynach to see George Price at Llanychaer. I did not tell him the purpose of the journey, but he was not too surprised since we have, over the years, enjoyed better relations with the old man who was once an enemy, and have indeed participated in many convivial social evenings in his company. His manner has lightened considerably, and although he is still a forbidding and lonely figure I know that he has taken as much pleasure in watching

Outside, Looking in

Brynach's progress through his years of education as any grandfather would do. Brynach still does not know it, but Master Price has also contributed to the costs of his foreign travels and his allowances.

The chaise rolled into the yard at Plas Llanychaer shortly after two of the clock on a fine spring afternoon. George Price was on the front doorstep to greet us. "Mistress Martha and Master Brynach!" he chortled. "A very good afternoon to you. Well well, this is very pleasant, is it not? And such a fine spring day, with the primroses at their best and the first bluebells already out in the Cwm Gwaun woods!" I curtseyed, and Brynach bowed, and we returned his greetings. We enjoyed tea and buttered scones in the drawing room, and then we took a walk in the garden.

"Now then, Master Brynach," said the Squire, as we meandered through his shrubbery of azaleas, "I will come straight to the point. I daresay you have deduced that there is some dark motive behind this little visit?"

"Yes sir," replied the young man. "Mother has been very secretive, but I daresay the visit may have something to do with the fact that I have only just come of age."

"Correct, young sir. And let me interrogate you further. Why do you think an old gentleman like me might wish to talk with you?"

"Could it have something to do with property and inheritance, Master Price? I have been very aware that over the years you have shown a good deal more interest in me than in my sisters Betsi and Sara. That is in my experience very unusual, given that they are both very beautiful.........."

At this, the Squire roared with laughter, and said; "Upon my word, young fellow, you are very observant. I have to admit it. Now let me press you further, while we are playing this little game. And why should I show such an interest in you?"

"Perhaps, sir, because you are my natural father?"

I blushed and the Squire spluttered, not knowing quite how to respond. So Brynach continued, quite unabashed, reminding me that he had still not acquired the diplomatic skills that come with age. "Sir, over the years since I was a little child I have often speculated about why I was left on the doorstep of the Plas, and who my natural parents might be. Mother knows more than she is prepared to admit. I hear from others that your personal life, twenty-one years ago, was filled with sadness, and at

60

such times gentlemen have been known to stray from the straight and narrow path."

"Brynach!" said I, with my eyes blazing. "That was a most improper remark. Please apologize immediately!"

"No, no," laughed the Squire. "I like to see honesty in a young man. I brought this down upon my own head, through encouraging him to speculate. There is a long tradition of Squires fathering bastard children, and we all know it. If I have strayed at certain times in my life, I think I had better keep the details to myself."

I thought it was time to come to the point. "Squire," I said, "this is getting all of us into deep water. You had better tell my son the truth."

So the Squire did just that. "Young sir," he said. "I am not your father, but your grandfather. My interest in you, and indeed my natural affection for you, has been motivated by the fact that your father was my second son Iestyn."

Brynach did not know what to say, and looked at me for confirmation. I nodded. "The Squire tells the truth," I said. "I met Iestyn before the end of his life, and he gave me some, but not all, of the details. You may take it from me that although you were born out of wedlock he loved you very much indeed."

We walked on in silence for a while, and at last Brynach said: "This does explain something that has worried me and my sisters for a very long time. May I ask you, Mother, whether that creature in black, by whom you were terrorized when I was young, was none other than my father, keeping a paternal eye on me?"

"Again you are correct, Brynach. He was as loving and as brave a father as any young gentleman could have. Indeed we all referred to him as the Nightwalker, and we were terrified by him, but our fears were misplaced." I turned to the Squire. "Master Price, if it will not distress you too much, will you explain for my son exactly what happened to Iestyn?"

The Squire swallowed hard and acted on my request, and as he spoke the ebullience and good humour drained out of him, and before our eyes he became a sad and lonely old man, with a crack in his voice and a tear in his eye. As we walked to the far end of the walled garden in the mellow April sunshine, he talked about Iestyn's military career and about the accident which left him disfigured and caused him thereafter to lurk in the shadows and to shun human contact. He told Brynach that he had been born out of wedlock as a result of a short alliance between Iestyn and an unknown young lady. He talked of Iestyn's lonely vigil over the baby whom he had given up into my tender care at the Plas. Brynach could not understand why Iestyn had left him, as a little child, at the Plas rather than taking him to his family home at Llanychaer. I did not want to answer that, but Squire Price did it for me, explaining that Plas Llanychaer at the time had been a miserable place indeed, populated by a family which Iestyn had had every reason to shun. He freely admitted that at the time he had been a pompous and bullying fellow, that his wife had been incapable of managing the most timid of servants, let alone a small baby, and that his daughter Fanny had been a strange girl whose mind had been damaged in some way at the time of her birth.

Suddenly, either by design or chance, we came to a small slate headstone in the ground, a few yards from the southern wall of the garden. It marked the grave of somebody called Thomas Price. Brynach looked at the Squire with a question in his eyes, and the old gentleman nodded. "Young sir, this is the grave of your father. He wanted to be buried here, and he wanted a false name to be placed upon his memorial stone. I was here at the burial, as were Mistress Martha, Master Joseph and Master Owain." He turned to me. "Now, my dearest Martha, you and I are the only ones left to remember him.........."

Tears welled up into his eyes, and before I could react, Brynach did a very beautiful thing. He went up to his grandfather and embraced him, which initially gave the old man a considerable shock, since he had probably not been embraced by anybody for twenty years or more. But then he sighed, and held Brynach close, and wept tears of joy. I wept too, for I knew that this was a moment which neither grandson nor grandfather would ever forget.

At last, after drying our eyes and talking at great length about Iestyn, we made our way back towards the house. Brynach and the Squire walked arm in arm, and I walked behind them, rejoicing in their happiness. The Squire explained that Brynach was his only male heir, and that although he had no proof of a relationship he had already altered his will so that the young man would, in due course, inherit the whole of the Llanychaer estate. Brynach reacted hardly at all to this news, and in truth he appears to this day to be largely impervious to the attractions of power and wealth, but I knew that the full significance of this inheritance would strike him forcefully in the fullness of time. Of much greater importance to him was the fact that he was suddenly no longer a foundling and a bastard, but a young man with a history, a family and a pedigree. Before we left the big house at Llanychaer that afternoon, the Squire asked Brynach to keep the news of their relationship to himself, on the basis that if it had become common knowledge there would have been unnecessary and malicious speculation in the community about Iestyn's life and loves. "Let all be revealed," he said, "but preferably after I have gone to my Maker." Brynach appreciated that, and of course he agreed.

On our journey back to the Plas the young fellow spent a great deal of the time in silent contemplation, and I allowed him the rare privilege of keeping quiet myself. And how I loved him! This bright, sensitive, honest young man was my son, and mine to love; but I could now celebrate the fact that a lonely old man could love him too, and express his feelings, and receive love from him in return.

ΩΩΩΩΩΩΩΩΩΩΩ

23rd December 1832

Tomorrow morning the plough will be cleaned and polished, and brought in for placing under the kitchen table, as a sign that winter is now upon us and that the fields must be left alone. Shemi and Will, helped by young Gomer, will be in charge of the ceremony, although I admit that I still miss the rough and lovely face of Billy, who died from pneumonia about nine years ago at the age of sixty. Too much hard work and too much weather, he said on his death-bed, and he was probably right. He was a dear friend and a most excellent head man, and while he had many failings they were minor ones which I was always, during his life, very happy to forgive. He was another man who rescued me from situations of my own making, and although he had little time for godly things he is now certainly with the angels. He passed everything he knew on to Shemi and Will, and as the new generation ploughs, and harrows, and sows, and harvests in our stony fields I still see them doing little things which appear illogical but which were taught to them by Billy. Maybe he picked them up from Grandpa Isaac, who in turn picked them up from some previous head man, and so on and so on, back to the earliest days of the Plas Ingli estate........

The weather is cool and bright. Shemi has been reading the clouds, and informs us that the weather we have had over the past fortnight is very similar to that of 1808, which means that there will be four weeks of sunshine and frost, but no heavy snow and hardly a drop of rain. Perfect weather, he says, for a good deal of burning on the common in the month of January, and good for keeping down the pests in the soil. I am sure that he is right in all of this, for the Jenkins family has a knowledge of the weather which stretches back over many generations.

On the matter of generations, I must record, while I am in the mood, one other event from recent years which brought me great joy. This was my fiftieth birthday, which occurred not much more than a month after Brynach's coming of age. I recall that I looked forward to it with dread rather than anticipation, for I was in the midst of my change of life, and had convinced myself that on the twelfth day of May I would leave behind youth and beauty and would be transformed into a wrinkled old hag with a lined face and twisted fingers and hanging breasts. My trepidation was increased by the irritable moods which came upon me with alarming frequency and by the fact that I was hot and bothered one minute and calm and collected the next. I recall that I slept very badly, and that on some nights I sweated so profusely that I had to change my nightdress in the early hours of the morning. Bessie and my dear old mother had both warned me what to expect, but I was surprised and angry in any case. I daresay that I must have been impossible to live with, and for the first time in my life I was actually pleased that there was no man alongside me in my feather bed. Even a celibate saint would have found me very unpleasant company.

As I remember it (and my memory may be faulty, now that I am old) I woke up on my birthday with a jolt, to find Sara and Liza shuffling about in my room. The shutters were open, and the early morning sun was pouring liquid gold in through the window and onto the polished wooden floor. "Happy birthday, Mother *bach*!" and "Happy birthday, Mistress *bach*!" they chirped, and dragged me out of bed and hugged the breath out of me.

Outside, Looking in

They had placed vases filled with spring flowers on my mantelpiece and on every other flat surface they could find, so that the room was transformed into a veritable flower garden. Then, in spite of my protests, they carried up the tin bath from the scullery and placed it within the pool of sunbeams. They made many journeys up and down the back staircase with buckets, and filled the bath with hot soapy perfumed water. Then they removed my nightdress, and insisted that I should step in and luxuriate. I am not very good at luxuriating, and indeed tin baths are too small for the purpose in any case, but I had no option but to cooperate. They washed my hair, and then dried me with warm and fluffy towels just as if I had been a helpless infant. Then they anointed me all over with sweet-smelling lotion, and dusted my feet with fragrant talcum powder as if I had been the Queen of Sheba. I played along with this charming charade, and could not resist giggling, and at last all three of us were overcome with hysterical laughter, just as if we had been three little girls.

They dressed me in my newest and prettiest dress, and put my hair up, painted my lips and put rouge upon my cheeks. Then, when all was ready, I was required to sweep magisterially down the stairs into the kitchen, where the others were all waiting -- Brynach, Bessie, Shemi and his wife Sian and their youngest child Molly, Will and his wife Tegwen and two little ones, and finally Gomer and Gwenno. As I came into the kitchen Gomer made a fearsome noise on a bugle which he had borrowed from somewhere, and almost scared the life out of me. The bugler said it was a special fanfare, and I had to believe him. The children screamed and giggled and clapped their hands. The adults laughed and cheered, and everybody sang silly rhymes. A good deal of embracing went on.

Then Will, who does not care what he says, or to whom he says it, stood on a chair and made a little speech. "Mistress Martha," he said, "if I may make so bold, indeed you do look most beautiful today. More lovely than I can recall. Like a fragrant rose in the desert you are, or like a single bright star in the dusky sky......." Guffaws and jeers greeted this unexpected foray into the realms of poetry, and indeed I could hardly keep a straight face myself. Undeterred, he held up his hand for silence, and continued. "Like a good wine, a lovely lady improves with age, and I am desired by the assembled company of good and faithful people to say, Mistress, that we love you. We wish you good fortune and inestimable

65

happiness in the years to come, and it will be our pleasure, Mistress, to serve you as best we can, come what may. There cannot be a better or more gracious lady in the whole of Wales, and therefore while others may deserve three cheers, I call for four. Yes indeed. Four cheers for Mistress Martha!" And they gave me four rousing cheers. My eyes filled with tears, but I managed to control myself, remembering that smudgy eye-shadow and streaky cheeks do nothing for the image of a lovely lady. So I asked Tegwen if I might embrace her husband, and when she gave her smiling consent I gave this rough diamond of a man a kiss on the cheek and a long embrace.

It was supposed to be breakfast time, but our normal breakfast conventions were abandoned for the day, because in the middle of the kitchen table was the largest iced birthday cake you ever did see, covered with a veritable forest of little beeswax candles. They glowed and flickered, and I had to blow them out to the accompaniment of more cheering and clapping.

We settled down around the table to our breakfast feast of iced cake and best China tea, and the convivial occasion was made even sweeter for me when the little children sang a lovely Welsh folk song and Gwenno played an old air on my Celtic harp, with a dexterity and sensitivity which delighted me. To round off the occasion they all presented me with birthday presents, all of which must have involved great sacrifices of pennies and time which my dear servants could ill afford. Liza gave me a very pretty straw bonnet which she had plaited and coloured herself; Bessie gave me a delicate blue knitted jacket; Will presented me with a willow shopping basket; Gomer had carved a baby rabbit for me out of beechwood; and so it went on, with precious gifts from all of them.

At last, with half the cake demolished, and with animals calling from the yard for their breakfasts, our morning party broke up. I never did find out who was behind it, but there had certainly been considerable planning, and I suspect that my beloved Sara was the plotter in chief. Whatever the truth of the matter, the occasion acted like a tonic and astringent combined, and transformed me from a creature of dark moods and failing confidence into something more akin to my old self. My womanhood and my femininity were reawakened, and I was reminded that I was not so old and tired after all. If Will still found me beautiful and was prepared to say so, perhaps there was still some reason to take pride in my appearance, to cultivate the desert rose and to cherish the image of the evening star.

My recollections of the rest of my happy day are hazy, because I have to admit that as well-wishers came and went we opened a few bottles of our best claret and did them justice. After our breakfast party I took a walk with Sara around the Plas Ingli lanes and hedgerows, on what was now a warm and perfect spring day. The skylarks were high and happy, and it seemed to me that the dawn chorus, instead of fading away as the sun climbed higher, increased in intensity and beauty. I asked Sara if she agreed with me on this matter, but she simply smiled and said: "Mother, perhaps you are right, but perhaps the extra beauty is in the ear of the listener." We wandered through the sheets of bluebells near the driveway and became almost intoxicated by the scent, and then climbed up onto the common, where we were overcome again by the heavy lascivious scent and the dazzling gold colour of the flowering furze. We collected little delicate posies of primroses and daisies, violets and celandines, and then I filled my wicker basket with bluebells, red campion, foxgloves and cow parsley, crab-apple and broom which we used, on our return, for larger floral arrangements in the parlour.

I daresay that for those who are familiar with such things, the house looked and smelt like a boudoir by late afternoon when my guests arrived. I had not invited them myself, but Brynach had taken the initiative and had distributed little messages across the whole of North Pembrokeshire. And so they came: Morys and Nansi and my dear mother Betsi from Brawdy, my Aunt Betty from Solva, my sister Catrin and her good man James from Castlebythe, my daughter Betsi and her husband and two children from Cenarth, and then all of my tenants and their wives. Anne Edwards from Trefach, looking more beautiful than ever, and her mother Bronwen as chaperone, to protect her from my besotted and lusty son Brynach. To my great delight, several members of Owain's family came, including his brother James and his wife Mary, and my dear friend Mary Jane and her husband Dafydd Stokes of Trecwn. And Ellie Phillips, the daughter of Master John Bowen of Llwyngwair, one of my oldest and dearest friends. She could not induce her miserable husband to come, but she was accompanied by her son Jasper, eighteen years old and so handsome that even my ancient heart experienced a little flutter.

We had a most wonderful time together, on a May evening so mellow that we were all able to walk in the garden and to eat and drink on the lawn. As dusk fell the menservants brought out candle lanterns and hung them in the trees, where they attracted a multitude of fluttering moths. The men set up a long table in the middle of the lawn, and brought out chairs and benches from the house. Gwenno and Liza brought out a succession of dishes so varied and so magnificently presented that Bessie, as head cook, had to be called from the kitchen to receive a special cheer. We ate and drank, and laughed and talked, far into the night, until at last my tenants wandered off in order to get a few hours of sleep before the morning milking, and those of greater means who lived within travelling distance set off in their illuminated carriages and chaises. Ten of my family members stayed for the night, and for them the party continued until the middle of the next day. Then, with loving hugs and cheery waves, they were gone, leaving me arm in arm with Brynach and Sara on the front doorstep.

This is true happiness, I thought, with my loved ones around me, some related by blood and others bound to me by more mysterious and invisible ties beneath the roof of this blessed house. What we have is no creation of mine, but something fashioned by many who have gone before and by some who are still here. Indeed, even those who have passed on are still in residence, for Grandpa Isaac still occupies the settle by the *simnai fawr*, and David was the one who carved the mantelpiece in the parlour, and Dewi was the one who carved the love-spoon which hangs on my bedroom wall. And Joseph is everywhere, and Owain's music still echoes in the passageway and up the staircase.........

I realized, as I stood there, that I had got through the occasion without a husband or a lover at my side, and that I had coped perfectly well. Furthermore, I had forgotten about hot flushes and hanging breasts and had been reminded that I was still a woman whom men found attractive and whose friendship other women valued.

"Is that a tear in your eye, Mother?" asked Brynach.

"Surely not," I replied. "But it may be that a little speck of dust has caused a minor irritation."

ΩΩΩΩΩΩΩΩΩΩ

28th December 1832

Christmas has come and gone, and now that I have a few moments to myself I can record that the occasion has brought me great happiness. I trust that it has brought joy to others too, for these are not easy times for those who live on the land and who feed the stony acres with their sweat and their blood. For my tenants and labourers, and their families, Christmas is at least a time for temporary amnesia, when their stomachs are filled at my table and their frost-bitten faces are warmed before my fire. Soon enough it will be time for the plough to come out from under the table, and for them to brave the freezing rain and prepare the fields for the spring planting.

As promised by Shemi, we have enjoyed a week of fine weather, which is always an extra blessing at Christmas. The candle-lit procession to the parish church in Newport in the early hours of Christmas Day passed off just as it should according to ancient tradition, with hundreds of worshippers winding their glittering way from scattered farms and hovels to participate in the *Plygain* service. It was unseasonably warm, but the air was still and the sky was bright with starlight. The service was as dull as ever, but as my eyes roamed about the crowded church I was pleased to see that the recent outbursts of religious fervour in our community have been accompanied by outbreaks of munificence, and that the holes in the roof have been repaired. Not so many years ago, I could admire the stars from my position in the family pew.

Christmas Day was as wonderful and as chaotic as ever, even though Bessie assures me that it was an occasion blessed by her impeccable planning. God only knows what an unplanned Christmas Day would be like. Forgive me, Lord, but that was uncharitable -- Bessie and her little army of helpers, in which I include myself, did achieve miracles, with all of the chickens, geese, cheeses, eggs and hams required under our tenancy agreements safely gathered in at least a week before Christmas, and converted into a mighty breakfast for the families of all our tenants and labourers and into an even mightier Christmas supper which went on far into the night. We enjoyed the traditional fare -- to start with, roasted ox and goose, jugged hare and boiled ham, potatoes by the hundredweight, cabbage and parsnips and turnips, mincemeat pie, pickles and chutneys and rich gravy; and then to follow, ten different puddings and fruit pies, stewed plums and clotted cream, five different breads and six home-made cheeses, treacle toffee and fudge, and other sweetmeats which we count as Plas Ingli specialities. Ale and cider flowed freely, and when Will was complimented on his brewing skills he was gracious enough to say that he had learnt everything from our dear departed Billy.

My own family contributed in no small fashion to the celebrations, and we were joined by Betsi and Ioan and their children, and by Brynach and Anne and their little baby Rose. They all stayed for three nights, but then they had to return to look after their own homes and their own affairs, for even the best servants in the world need direction and supervision. But while they were all here we had a blessed time together, and rejoiced in the return of some sort of stability to our family affairs.

This serves to remind me that I have not yet written of Sara or of the turbulence of the last two years. Just now I feel strong enough to do it, and if I can find the time tomorrow to settle down at my writing desk, I will breathe deeply, and calm my palpitating breast, and put down my memories.

ΩΩΩΩΩΩΩΩΩΩ

29th December 1832

Beloved Sara. The softest and sweetest of my children. The one who would not leave me, and who stayed at home because she thought that I needed her, when others of her age travelled far afield, or joined in the frivolities of the social seasons of Haverfordwest or Tenby; the one who was abducted as a small child by a monster called John Fenton, and saved only through the intervention of my beloved Owain; the one who cheered me and calmed me over and again during the years when I was haunted by the Nightwalker; the one who dragged me out of my intermittent periods of black melancholia during the years when I thought Owain was dead; the one with the voice and the temperament of an angel; the one who was so frail that a June zephyr might have blown her away.

Now she is gone. I have to write this into my diary, although I have twisted and turned thus far into my narrative in some futile attempt to avoid it. She is gone. She is dead.

It was inevitable, and I knew it just as she knew it, for she suffered from an early age with some debilitating illness which even Joseph could not identify. He gave her potions and all manner of pills and powders, but he refused to bleed her just as he refused to bleed any of his patients. He said that bleeding was the first resort of charlatans and the last resort of incompetent physicians, and insisted that the practice killed more patients than it saved. At last, shortly before he died, he had to recognize that she was suffering from consumption, and he had to tell me that he knew no cure and no appropriate magic.

Sara, blessed child that she was, never complained, and as she developed into womanhood her courage was an inspiration to all those around her. In the year 1829 she was very ill indeed, and her health was not helped by the cold winds and more or less continuous rain which afflicted the summer and destroyed the hay crop and the corn harvest. We were all cooped inside for day after day, and we were all miserable. She struggled along into the following autumn, and without Joseph to help I tried to minister to her myself, and to call upon the skills of young Doctor Havard. But he had to admit that even with the latest advances of the modern world of medical science, he had no cure for consumption, and it was a terrible thing for me to see my beautiful and intelligent daughter, who had such a power to brighten the lives of others, consumed by the disease. She became very fatigued, and was sometimes too weak even to get out of bed. Her appetite all but disappeared, and we had to force her to eat. Then she suffered from fevers, and even the remedies which I had been taught by Joseph failed to bring her relief.   And in the spring she developed a dry cough and admitted to me, as I sat at her bedside, that she was suffering from terrible chest pains. She rallied for a while, but in the month of February in the year 1830 she started to cough up blood, and I knew that the end was near. My beloved child became unconscious in the middle of March, and died in my arms on the twenty-fifth day of the month, just a few days after her twenty-fifth birthday.

Her suffering was too great to be borne by a saint, and her death was, for her, a blessed release. For me it was also a release, for no mother can watch a child in a state of permanent distress without suffering a crucifixion of motherhood. She was buried in the family enclosure in

Cilgwyn Churchyard, with her father David, her grandparents whom she never knew and her great-grandparents Isaac and Jane, whom she loved. One day, God willing, I will rest with all of them.

In putting the foregoing words onto paper, I have struggled to record but not to embellish, and to keep control of my emotions. But coldness and detachment do not come easily to me. When my *cariad* Sara died, I wept, and I am weeping now. I will stop here, and walk upon the mountain, and then, if I feel better tomorrow, I will continue.

$$\Omega\Omega\Omega\Omega\Omega\Omega\Omega\Omega\Omega\Omega$$

30th December 1832

Having climbed the mountain and having spent the evening talking of good times and bad times with Bessie, I managed to sleep well and without nightmarish disturbances. I woke feeling that I had had enough of tragedies and disasters. So in describing the further turbulent adventures of this family, I take some pleasure in recording the fact that the rest of us have actually survived. I must also record that I have learnt the difference between a setback and a disaster.

My biggest setback occurred in the summer following my fiftieth birthday. There was a great depression in farm prices, and when I was confronted by a modest hay harvest and a truly terrible corn harvest I knew that I had too many animals on my land and that my finances were stretched too far. I decided to place thirty Welsh blacks and eighty sheep in the care of Llewelyn Drover, who was collecting animals destined for Smithfield. I asked him for payment there and then -- twenty guineas per head for my prize cattle and £2 per head for the sheep -- knowing that he could still make a tidy profit when he reached London. But he pleaded with me that times were hard, and that he had no reserves which would permit him to pay cash on the nail. I was in no position to argue. He was an honest fellow, and I had dealt with him many times before. So I let the animals go. Master Llewelyn gave me a receipt for the animals, and a promissory note for £800, which he said would be good for him and good for me. I never saw him again, and I still do not know to this day whether he is alive or dead, or whether he fell victim to the vagabonds and brigands who prowl about along the droving routes of mid-Wales. As my debts mounted, I had to sell Fachongle Isaf and Llystyn for £1,000 each, the same price that I had paid for them twelve years before. I consulted with Brynach, and did it with his consent. That at least enabled me to pay off my dues, and it was no disaster since I never really thought of those two lowland farms as belonging to the estate. And the sale brought me back to five farms, which I thought I could reasonably manage.

Then there were other events in 1830 which followed hard upon the heels of Sara's death. At the end of the month of May, with continuing bad weather, and with far too many mouths to feed upon the impoverished land, I was confronted with a rash of "illegal" *ty unnos* hovels which were springing up on the fringes of the common. Some of them were actually on Plas Ingli land, and some of them were built by the sons of my own labourers. According to ancient tradition such hovels are allowed to remain if the cottager can, with the help of his friends, put up a habitable structure during the course of a single night, and if at dawn he can show to the world a fire in his hearth and smoke issuing from his chimney. Then he can take possession of all the land around the hovel which can be reached by casting an axe from the front door. It is said that this ancient right is enshrined in the Laws of King Hywel Dda. I know not if this is true, but most of the squires deny it absolutely, and most of the new hovels are flattened by estate servants within twenty-four hours of their going up. The squires, acting in their capacity as magistrates, write out arrest and demolition warrants themselves, and many of the landless labourers end up in the lock-up, to be hauled before the Petty Sessions and given fines which they cannot possibly pay. It is still going on.

In the rash of hovel-building of two years ago I knew perfectly well what was happening, for when a labourer is seeking the help of his friends and assembling even the roughest of building materials the matter becomes common knowledge. So I saw to it, through the use of my spy network, that every homeless couple that had a mind to settle on the edge of my land knew what my rules were. There was to be no thieving of my crops or animals, and no passing over my land except on the ancient footpaths and cart tracks. Further, I expected from every resident above the age of twelve the provision of labour on the Plas Ingli estate for thirty days free and thirty days at the going rate. I insisted that every man and wife should come to see me before they started building, and that I should agree the location with them. Always they came to me with fear writ large across their faces, believing that I was intent upon bringing the full weight of the law down upon them; but when they heard my terms they were, without exception, amazed. They all agreed, and they have all honoured our agreements, made not with signatures and bits of paper but with handshakes. I felt then, and I feel today, that this arrangement does something to alleviate poverty, allows the landless poor to gain just a little self-respect, and provides me with a small amount of extra labour. It has brought me into conflict with the Court Leet and the Commoners, but I can cope with that.

Less than two months after Sara's death came another appalling event -- the sudden collapse of the good little estate of Plas Cenarth which made my dear daughter Betsi, her husband Ioan and their three little boys homeless. I had no idea that it was going to happen, for Betsi had given me no intimation that there were difficulties of a financial kind, and I was convinced, from my frequent visits to Cenarth, that their estate was well run and profitable. They had three tenanted farms, and all seemed to be well. But after it had happened, Betsi admitted to me tearfully that Ioan, who is a proud and stubborn young man, had refused absolutely to turn to me for help. I had helped them enough, he said, and he would sink or swim without me. In any case, he had been aware of my own difficulties. He had seen me grieving over a dead daughter, losing my cattle and sheep to a disappearing drover, and selling farms in order to make ends meet. I could but admire his courage and his consideration for my feelings, but how I wished that he had placed the security of his own dear family above all else, and had asked me for help. If he had come to me, I would have dug up the Plas Ingli treasure which is still in the ground at the back of the house, in a location known only to me. I have left it there, with the passing of the years, so that it could be used for just such an eventuality as this.........

What is done is done. Poor Ioan, in trying to make the estate profitable in the face of harvest failures and tenants who defaulted on their rents, took out three foolish loans. Suddenly, all three of his creditors, acting together, called in their debts, and he was forced to sell. Even the animals had to go. It was too late for me to intervene. One day they were at Cenarth, living in reasonable comfort, and the next day they were destitute, turning up in the yard of Plas Ingli with their carts and gambos loaded with furniture and personal possessions. Of course I had to take them in, and in some way I was pleased to do it, for I had room, and a part of me rejoiced in the fact that I would now have three little grandsons playing around my feet and sitting on my knee.

In the following month, having pondered the matter at great length, I thought it prudent to pass the running of the Plas Ingli estate over to Ioan and Betsi. Ioan was very morose, and thought of himself as a failure after the loss of his little estate which had been in the family for five generations. I urged him to abandon guilt, and told him that estates come and go with alarming frequency in West Wales, for a wide variety of reasons. That was little consolation to him, and I knew that a man who is used to organizing servants and labourers, and buying and selling livestock, and making all the key decisions of the farming year, cannot simply be left sitting in the settle by the fireside. Neither can he be treated as another farm servant, to be instructed at the breakfast table each day as to which fields to plough or harrow and which cows to put to the bull. So I sat down with Betsi and Ioan and discussed the matter with them at great length, and told them that I was minded to work less and travel more, as befits a gentlewoman in her fifty-third year. I said that I wanted them to act as stewards of the estate and as *de facto* Master and Mistress of the house. I told them that I had discussed things with Brynach, and had obtained his consent. With relief writ large across their faces, they agreed to try this arrangement out until we could find another farm for them. I called all the servants in, and informed them that Ioan and Betsi would henceforth be in charge, and that I would retire gracefully into the background. I told them that after a month or two of transition, I was minded to travel abroad and see some of the wonders of the world. I saw shadows of apprehension passing across the faces of Bessie and Shemi, but I paid no attention since my mind was made up.

The other auspicious event of 1830 was the marriage of Brynach to his beloved Anne. It was inevitable for they had been besotted with one another since they were both fourteen years old. Their love had been strong enough to survive Brynach's prolonged absences in Haverfordwest when he was at school, in Oxford when he was at university, and on the continent when he made his Grand Educational Tour. The Edwards estate at Trefach is a small one, but it has always had close links with Plas Ingli, and I have fond memories of the days spent in the company of Anne's grandfather William, who was for a time my tutor on matters agricultural. Her parents Rhys and Bronwen are close friends who have helped me out on many occasions, as I have occasionally been able to be of assistance to them. There were few problems in devising the marriage settlement, and I was happy enough that Anne, as the youngest of three daughters, should bring into the marriage just one small farm called Gernos-fach and a cluster of cottages at Garfeth. It was a good marriage for her, to the Master of Plas Ingli. I spoke to her at the time of the betrothal, and she also knew -- without ever betraying the confidence -- that her dearly beloved man would in due course add Plas Llanychaer and its tenanted farms to his already considerable estate.

The wedding took place in the little church in Cilgwyn in July 1830, and it was a truly splendid affair. I take no credit for that, since Master and Mistress Edwards insisted that they would take full responsibility, and my offers of assistance for the great day were politely turned down. But the bride's family did allow me and Betsi the privilege of arranging a reception for all the guests at the Plas on the evening before the wedding, and that was a wonderfully happy occasion with good food, good music and dancing, blessed by many representatives from the ancient families of the county. And what a beautiful couple Brynach and Anne made! He tall and dark-skinned, with his piercing brown eyes and high cheekbones, and she blue-eyed, fair-haired and petite, with a high bosom, narrow waist and good child-bearing hips. She looked too frail to be the Mistress of a working estate, but I knew that she was a strong and determined young woman who would do well as the new Mistress Morgan. I wept, of course, at the marriage ceremony in the crowded church, but afterwards in the big house at Trefach I enjoyed myself thoroughly in the company of old friends, with my enjoyment compounded by the fact that I was the guest of honour and not the hostess. Betsi told me afterwards that I had been more than a little tipsy, but I deny that absolutely, and declare that I was simply in a very good humour.

Where should the happy couple make their nest? There was certainly no room for them at the Plas, with Betsi and Ioan and their three children newly moved in. So on the night of the wedding the new Master and Mistress Morgan moved straight into Brithdir Mawr, which I had kept for them since the death of my tenant Jeb Phipps four years earlier. I had a strong suspicion at the time that the house would be needed, and had managed to resist many requests from far and wide that I should let the property. I wanted the young couple to spend their wedding night and start their life together under their own roof rather than under mine. I had already installed a housekeeper and a head man, so the place was run as a going concern, and I was confident that Brynach now knew enough about estate management and farming to make further appointments as he saw fit. They settled in quickly, and it was a particular pleasure for me to see that old dark house suddenly filled with youthful energy.

For much of the following year the new domestic arrangements worked well. While Ioan and Betsi got on with running the Plas Ingli estate, I was able to spend many happy hours with the three boys -- Benjamin, Abel and little Owain. I gave them lessons, took them for long walks on the mountain and along the wild coastline, and gave them all the pampering which children have a right to expect from their grandmother. It was a truly blessed time for me, and so much more wonderful than the short periods of contact with them which I had experienced during their time at Plas Cenarth. I got to know them as happy and delightful little boys, and I was able to devote time to them and to give them all the affection that was in me, in a way which had been impossible when I was a young widow with five boisterous children. Then, I had a household and an estate to run, and now I had hardly a care in the world.

And I travelled whenever I had a mind to do it. I went to Brawdy for several long visits, to spend time with my mother and my brother Morys and his family. I stayed with my friend Ellie and her family at Ambleston for a week, and got on famously with her and the three children while confirming my dislike for her brutish husband. I stayed with Mary Jane and Dafydd Stokes at Trecwn and then went to London with them for a fortnight. And in the company of brother Morys and his wife Nansi I even travelled to Paris in the spring of last year. While in Paris I was wooed with great ardour by a French count. He was a truly pompous fellow who thought that he was God's gift to womankind, and he even tried to get me into his bed; but while he failed in that enterprise he did at least succeed in doing wonders for my self-esteem and in giving me a good deal of innocent entertainment. Nansi and I have never laughed so much in all our lives. Even Morys, who is a serious and godly man, was mildly amused by the Frenchman's romantic antics.

In June of last year daughter Rose was born to Brynach and Anne, and although the birth was a difficult one they were of course overjoyed. Anne's mother Bronwen and I helped at the birth, and when I delivered my first grand-daughter I was almost overcome with emotion.

I helped Anne all I could over the months that followed, when I was not visiting or travelling , but I suddenly realized that I was more comfortable at Brithdir with the love-birds and their little baby than I was at my own home. And when I sat down and gave serious thought to the matter, I realized that there were little incidents at the Plas, over and again, which were making me feel uncomfortable. Sometimes they were to do with me and the boys, and Betsi and I exchanged sharp words on more than one occasion arising out of my very special relationship with three-year-old Owain. I did not think I was spoiling him, but when he fell down and cut his knee one day, and called for me rather than for his mother, I knew that great diplomacy was called for.

Then I noticed a reduction in the little signs of tenderness between Ioan and Betsi, and occasional sharp words. There was also a certain frostiness in the relationship between Ioan and the menservants, and this came to a head when Shemi came to me one day and complained that the new Master had a manner which they found unpleasant and overbearing. They were also worried that he imposed new rules upon them, and asked them to do things that they had learnt through experience never to do at the Plas. They questioned his priorities and they questioned the timing of his key decisions regarding ploughing and planting and harvesting. "Seriously worried we are, Mistress," concluded my head man. "Master Ioan is a kind and honest gentleman, and indeed we do like him well enough, but he is used to the lowlands and he does not know about westerly winds and salt spray."

"Come now, Shemi. He is young and he has a good deal to learn. He is doing his best in difficult circumstances. But I will not brook any insolence or disobedience, especially from Will, who sometimes speaks first and thinks afterwards. I want you to mention that to him. And then, can you not gently suggest to Master Ioan, when he makes the occasional dubious decision, that maybe it would be wiser to do things this way instead of that way?"

"I do try, Mistress. But once he has made a decision the Master gets very entrenched. Will you speak to him?"

I agreed that I would, but after Shemi had gone on his way I tried to observe quite closely what was going on within the four walls of this beloved house, and I noticed that while Gomer and Gwenno were going about their tasks happily enough, there were frowns on the faces of Bessie and Liza when normally there would have been smiles. I could hardly credit it. Were they having difficulties with dear Betsi, my own oldest daughter whom they had known ever since she had been a small child and with whom they had worked and laughed for ten years or more before her marriage? I recalled that during the times when I had suffered from deep melancholia Betsi had acted as a wonderfully competent Mistress of the Plas in my stead, even at the tender age of sixteen. I knew that my oldest daughter and my oldest and most faithful servant were intimate friends, and I was mortified to see that there was friction between them.

So I sat in the parlour one evening with Betsi and Ioan. I asked them to be honest with me, and I said that I would be honest with them. We talked heart to heart, and it was instructive and uncomfortable for each one of us to appreciate the perceptions of others. It was clear that they found it difficult to establish their own routines in the Plas so long as I was hovering about, and although I tried never to interfere I had to admit, to my shame, that my occasional comments and little instructions to the servants had sometimes had the effect of undermining their authority. I had to apologize to the young couple, as they had to apologize to me for a certain insensitivity to the old routines and the ancient wisdom which determined the details of the farming year and the management of the household. Then I said: "My dear Betsi and Ioan, I love you and the boys very much indeed, and it saddens me when little things disturb the beauty of our relations one with another. The essential problem, if we are honest with each other, is that there are too many strong personalities beneath this roof. We three for a start, and then Bessie, Shemi and Will who have been here for years and who do not take kindly to anybody -- even me -- telling them what to do and how to do it. But there are now too many of us beneath this roof, and the suffocating atmosphere is affecting all of us. I do not find it easy to be either a matriarch or a grandmother. You need a place of your own, and as from today I will redouble my efforts in finding one for you. Will you give me your blessing in that enterprise?" And of course they did. We enjoyed a three-way embrace, and agreed for the time being to carry on as best we could, with our eyes open a little wider for the spotting of small seeds of discontent and our ears pricked for identifying warning whispers.

I hunted for a property for some months, but then fate intervened. Squire George Price, one-time enemy and recently-confirmed friend, and grandfather to Brynach, died very suddenly from a heart attack. He was ninety years old. I was personally very sad, for I had grown quite fond of him and his bluff and blustering mannerisms. I received a message from one of his servants on the day after his death, and since he had no other local relatives Brynach and I had to make most of the funeral arrangements. It was not a big funeral, for he did not have many friends, and in truth most of his confederates from the old days were long since dead. All of us from the Plas, and Brynach and Anne from Brithdir, stood in the rain in the churchyard at Llanllawer as his coffin was lowered into the grave already occupied by his wife Susan, who had died in the year 1817. It had rained on the occasion of her burial, I thought, and I recalled that Iestyn Price, her son and Brynach's father, had observed that sad event at a distance, dressed in the mysterious black garb of the Nightwalker. Now the old man himself was gone, and Brynach was the last of his line.

A week after the funeral Morris Legal from Fishguard came to Brithdir, and he sat with Brynach, Anne and myself and read out the will. He said there were no impediments to it, and invited the new Master and Mistress of Plas Llanychaer to take up residence at their earliest convenience. And so they did, for an old house should never be left empty for too long. They were happily installed before another week was out, leaving Brithdir empty. It was the perfect solution to our problems at Plas Ingli, and by the end of the following week Ioan, Betsi and the three boys were in residence in that good old house, looking forward to fashioning their own lives again, free of interference from me and my fierce servants. Ioan seemed instantly to be ten years younger, and I rejoiced in his pleasure.

Brynach made Brithdir over to Ioan and Betsi, having agreed with me that it should be theirs to have and to hold. They deserved a new opportunity, I thought, for they are hard workers who share my belief in the principles of sound stewardship of the land. I gave them only one short piece of advice when I handed the signed documents over to them. "Now then, Master and Mistress Rhys," I said with a smile. "No more borrowings from strange gentlemen, if you please, and no more secrets from me." Ioan grinned, embraced me and kissed me on the cheek. "You have my word, Mistress Morgan," he said. "One hard lesson is quite enough to be going on with."

Next evening I settled into my favourite chair by the fire in the kitchen of the Plas, and opened up my latest copy of the *Welshman*. Bessie and Liza were working away with their spinning wheels next to the table, and Shemi and Will had decided to stay late in order to enjoy a few jars of cider and a few puffs on their clay pipes. Gwenno was sitting opposite me, with her pretty features glowing in the firelight, knitting a pair of socks. Gomer was whittling away at a piece of wood in the corner, whistling a wistful folk tune. The world was as peaceful as may be imagined.

"Well then, my dear friends," said I, with a little tear in my eye. "This is very pleasant, is it not?"

"Indeed it is, Mistress," came the chorus in response. "Indeed it is."

ΩΩΩΩΩΩΩΩΩΩΩ

22nd January 1833

Tonight I am exceedingly angry, not because of some foolishness involving my family or my servants, but because of events that have happened far away, in the area ruled by the ironmasters around Merthyr Tydfil and Hirwaun. I passed through the area once, on a journey to Monmouth, and I recall that it was truly like passing through the fires of Hell, with flames and smoke and steam blotting out the sun above the ironworks and with hordes of workers struggling to keep their jobs and struggling even harder to survive beyond the age of thirty-five. The town of Merthyr was a strange place, with some good shops, but near the works there appeared to be people from all over the world, many of them driven from the land by poverty and war and attracted by the prospect of untold wealth. One only had to look at their tattered clothes and their emaciated bodies to know that they were deluded fools, well-paid maybe by comparison with the landless labourers of Pembrokeshire, but denied fresh air and good food

81

and denied the freedom to go where they wished and to live where they wished. I met some of them, and they appeared to me to be little better than the slaves of Master Crawshay.

Mercifully, Pembrokeshire has escaped from the fearful depredations of industry, apart from a few places where they dig coal and slate out of the ground or where small iron foundries have been set up. But at Paterchurch on the inlet of Milford Haven there is a great new dockyard where they make iron ships for the Royal Navy and royal yachts for the English king. I fear that industry, commerce and greed are insinuating themselves into our lives, and that it may be difficult for us to escape from these monsters even as far west as the Plas. I was reminded of this very forcefully today when Will brought along a cousin of his who was thirty years old but looked like sixty. His name is Bryn Williams. He was looking for work. I could not give him any since it is midwinter, but I told him to come back later, once the ploughing and sowing is under way. He was desperately disappointed, poor fellow, but to ease his pain I sat him down in the kitchen and asked Bessie to give him a cup of hot tea and some bread and butter and cheese. And as he ate and drank, we talked.

He told us all about the iron-works and the terrible conditions endured by the iron-workers as the iron-masters like William Crawshay sought to control not only their working lives but also their leisure time through the Truck Shop system. They are paid with one hand, and then the other hand takes it all back again through the truck shop keepers, rent collectors and publicans who are all under the control of the master. Some of the works, said Bryn, pay not in cash but in tokens which can only be exchanged in the company shops for goods which may be twice as expensive as in the "free" shops on the main street. Other workers are caught up in the credit system, again forced to buy high-priced goods in shops where debts are "slated" and then deducted from wage packets before the remaining few coppers are paid over. Bryn, who was brought up in Dinas, travelled to Merthyr Tydfil five years ago, intending to make enough money in the iron works to return home and set up a little business of his own; but in the end, exhausted and still uninjured except for a tight chest, he decided to get out while he could. He came home last week without a penny in his pocket, and with an old mother to support he was desperate for work.

"I have had several very close shaves, Mistress," he said to me, "and in that business at the Castle Hotel eighteen months ago I was lucky to get away with my life."

"Ah yes," said I. "I think I read about it at the time. That was the insurrection, following the failure of the Reform Bill, that led to the execution of Dic Penderyn?"

"Indeed it was, Mistress. The Reform Bill was only part of the problem, although some of the fellows who came down from Birmingham and other places made a great issue out of it. The real problem was Crawshay, that bastard -- if you will excuse my language, Mistress -- who cut our wages at a stroke without any negotiation or any thought as to the consequences. Where there was a little spending money before, suddenly it was all gone, and so the independent shops and alehouses and lodging houses suffered too. The whole region was up in arms."

"And so you decided to take on Master Crawshay and his cronies?"

"Yes and no. We called big meetings, and thousands came, Mistress. Amazing it was, and exciting for the likes of me, being used to the peace and quiet of Pembrokeshire. Lewis Lewis, the man they called Lewsyn yr Heliwr, was a great leader and a most excellent orator. Night after night we had protest meetings in the town, and torchlight processions, and Master Lewis got us organized like a sort of army. We waved the black Reform banners. We had muskets and swords and pick-axes and bill-hooks. We raided over a hundred houses, took back property that had been seized by the debtor's court, and gave things back to the poor people who had been robbed by the bailiffs and the magistrates. That felt very good. The special constables did not have a hope in Hell, Mistress. We chased them off every time they came near. In the end we smashed down the debtor's court itself."

"Well now, Master Williams. That was all very laudable, I daresay. But did you really expect the magistrates and the iron-masters to stand to one side and simply accept all of this disorder?"

"No no, Mistress. We knew that the Yeomanry would come, and possibly the Highland Regiment too, since it was common knowledge that the men in kilts were in Brecon."

"And when you and your rabble army did meet them, you ended up, of course, with blood on the streets."

"A bad business it was. In June -- I forget the precise day. We had at least ten thousand there, all shouting and yelling, and all pressing up

83

towards the Castle Hotel. Crawshay had agreed to talk to a deputation about wages and other grievances, and Master Guest was there too. There were also some magistrates. Twelve or thirteen of our fellows, including Dic Penderyn and Lewis Lewis, went in to talk to them. There were soldiers in there too, with muskets and bayonets. After an hour our fellows came out from the meeting. They had got nowhere. Lewis Lewis urged calm, but the crowd started to get angry, and pressed forward. People were shouting that we should get the soldiers and disarm them."

He paused, as if horrified by the recollection of what happened next. I poured him some more tea, and he continued. "*Diawl*, it was a bad business, Mistress. They never read out the Riot Act. There were shots, and I think it was the soldiers who fired first. People fell in the street, and there were screams behind me. There were women and children there, you see. Some of them were iron workers and dram pullers themselves, but there were also wives and families come to support the men. Then it was pandemonium, and those at the front could not escape, since the press was so great. I saw a fellow -- not Dic Penderyn -- struggling with a soldier, and trying to grab his musket from him. It was a life and death struggle, and the soldier got the bayonet in his leg and squealed like a stuck pig. There was blood everywhere. There was more firing from the upstairs windows, and the soldiers seemed to be quite out of control. They probably feared for their lives. More screaming, and more bodies on the ground, and more blood on the cobble stones. I was in the middle of it all, Mistress, and was sure I was going to die. A mate of mine got a musket ball in the leg, and I dragged him into a side street where the soldiers could not see us."

I asked Bryn whether the newspaper reports of the time were accurate in their estimate of twenty people killed. "Much more than that, Mistress. I would say closer to fifty. Twenty bodies they found in the street, mostly men but some women and children. But many more bodies were dragged away, and others who were injured were hidden in cottages all over town, and then died of their wounds for lack of medical care."

"And then it ended?"

"No, Mistress. I am no hero, but neither am I a fool, and I got as far away as I could from the Castle Hotel, dragging my mate with me. But I heard later that the crowd returned, and the soldiers in the Hotel had to retreat, together with more soldiers from the Glamorgan Yeomanry who came to rescue them. I think Master Guest and Master Crawshay were

84

smuggled away. The soldiers got to Ty Pendarren, and then the mob besieged them there for three whole days. *Three days*, mark you, Mistress. They could not get out, but at last our leaders let them go. Then the whole town was under the control of our fellows, waving our black flags and shouting for justice. Several thousand men went up into the mountains above the Brecon Road, and set up a headquarters there. The Highlanders were a hopeless lot, although you'd have thought they would be good in the mountains. The Swansea Yeomanry were sent against the camp in the hills, but they were sent packing and were chased almost all the way back to Neath. Then on the Cefn Coed side one company of soldiers trying to get arms into the town was defeated, and another hundred dragoons on horseback were driven back too. Very inspiring it was, Mistress, and when news of these great victories over the military reached us back in town there were cheering crowds everywhere."

"And so how did it all end?"

"Well, when all the ironworks from Tredegar to Ebbw Vale and Nantyglo were closed down, news came that the fellows in Hirwaun had sacrificed a calf and had dipped a flag into its blood. They raised the dripping red flag and paraded it before the crowd as a symbol of open rebellion. The magistrates and the army got to hear of it, and they decided that enough was enough. They assembled a force of about five thousand heavily-armed soldiers, and they marched into Merthyr determined on a brutal suppression. They say that half of the town fled. I fled myself, and did not come back until a month later. And the military were brutal. About fifty of their own men had been injured since the start of the insurrection. They were out for revenge. They went after anybody who had a reputation for being involved in agitation, and also after a good many who were perfectly innocent. The soldiers killed some and left others terribly injured. I know all of this, Mistress. Very bad, it was."

"And when it was all over the authorities had their pound of flesh. Or rather, they had the body of Dic Penderyn, hanging by the neck."

"Yes, he was the one they wanted, innocent or guilty. I knew him, and I know that he was at the Castle Hotel. But he did not injure that soldier. He was convicted on the false testimony of a bastard who had a personal grudge against him. Dic was a martyr, which was a strange symbolic sort of a thing in a town named after martyrs. And the judge had more flesh too, with Lewis Lewis and ten other men and two women

85

transported to the colonies. I doubt they will ever return."

So Bryn went on his way, with a little nourishment inside him. I reminded him that he should come back towards the end of March, when I am minded to give him work. He is intelligent and articulate, and too pleasant a fellow to end up collecting parish relief.

I contained myself until he had gone, but then I hammered the table in frustration. "Idiots! Fools! Simpletons!" I exploded, much to Bessie's surprise. "Bessie, how is it that men can be so stupid as to have ten thousand people rushing about in the streets, without proper leaders, as a means of righting acknowledged wrongs?"

"I am really not sure what they were thinking, Mistress," said Bessie, although I had not anticipated a reply.

"There is only one response from the authorities in such a situation, and that is the use of overwhelming military force. The insurgents were lucky that the army did not bring in field guns and that they were not forced to use them. Tragedy was inevitable from the beginning, and it was encouraged by the sheer numbers of people rushing about, by the lack of discipline, and by the presence of trade unionists from outside the area. I know they were there, because the matter was well reported in my newspaper at the time. If you have trade unionists involved in riotous behaviour, that sets them back at once in the estimation of the law-abiding public and the politicians. So although their cause may be just, they achieve nothing. The Government may set up a commission and investigate the causes of the trouble, but when they receive their bulky report they say "Splendid, splendid!" and put it on a shelf somewhere, and go back to sleep. Is that not correct, Bessie, in your experience?"

"I am sure you are perfectly correct, Mistress."

"The only way to defeat injustice, Bessie, is through subversion and smart military tactics. No huge armies of men, but small groups employing hit and run methods, like the Spaniards who harried the French in the Peninsular War. Owain told me about it. Napoleon became quite distracted, and had not the faintest idea how to deal with the brigands. By the time he worked out where they were coming from, they were gone. The Welsh princes did the same in the battles against the Normans. Here today, and tomorrow twenty miles away. Brilliant! You can only defeat the dragoons and the fusiliers, Bessie, if they cannot deploy their usual military tactics. Also, if you are to keep public sympathy, the cry should be "bricks and mortar, not flesh and blood!" Respect for human life at all times, that is what must be insisted upon. If you harm people, and allow brutality and ill-discipline to infect your activities, people will turn against you, and then you are lost."

During this exposition of my military theories Bessie had been looking at me with wide eyes, with her hands buried in a great mound of bread dough. She could not contain herself, and burst into laughter. "Mistress Martha!" she gurgled, with tears rolling down her cheeks. "You sound like King Henry Tudor on the battle field at Bosworth. Never have I heard such a thing in all my life! And God help the cream of the British Army if they should ever find you on the side of the enemy!"

I had to laugh too at the intensity of my own feelings and at my foray into men's business. I let the matter drop, and we talked about bread instead. But now that I am alone in my room, mulling over the story told by Master Williams, I have a feeling that his visit was not a matter of chance. There is still a glowing anger in my breast, and a feeling that men who worship force and who act upon impulse are their own worst enemies, even when they are driven by reforming zeal. The sword of justice and the shield of righteousness may both shine like the sun, but David defeated Goliath with a short strip of leather and a little pebble.

ΩΩΩΩΩΩΩΩΩΩΩ

23rd January 1833

Today I have been for a long walk, in grey and miserable weather, to Ty Canol Wood and up to the high and windy crags of Carnedd Meibion Owen. Those are the skyline rocks which I see every day when I look across the *cwm* from my bedroom window. There are four rough and tumbled crags jutting out of the common, and they are said to be the petrified remains of the four last giants -- three sons and a father -- who lived in this territory in ancient times. I climbed each crag in turn, and as I did so I was reminded that according to the legend the three brothers killed each other in a mighty battle, because the stupid father could not decide on how to settle his inheritance. Then, when the sons were dead, the old father died of a broken heart. As I sat on the top of the highest crag, I thought about brute force, and blundering giants, and the means by which they had precipitated the end of their world.

That led me to give a good deal of thought to the story told to me by Master Williams, and to the debate which is currently raging in my newspapers about Moral Force and Physical Force as the means of righting the wrongs which plague our country. "Moral Force!" say the Nonconformists and the more thoughtful leaders of the Reform movement, citing the Bible and the Law of the Land as their justifications. "Physical Force!" thunder the radicals and the tub-thumpers, citing the fact that the Government, the captains of industry and the gentry are apparently impervious to reasoned debate.

And then something else came into my mind. That strange premonition which disturbed my peace of mind less than two months ago, with mighty waves sweeping in from the sea and smashing to pieces the gentry houses while leaving the hovels and cottages of the poor quite unharmed. Plas Ingli, I recalled, came out of the cataclysm virtually unharmed. I began to realise what that premonition meant, and perceived that I was destined to play some role in turbulent events. Had not Joseph, on his death-bed, told me that it was my destiny to change the world for the better? Had not Shemi, Joseph's natural successor, told me that I had work to do? I knew it myself, but I could not predict where or when I might be called upon, or the nature of the great cause in which I would become embroiled.

ΩΩΩΩΩΩΩΩΩΩΩ

PART TWO: 1837-39

4. Awakening

6th June 1837

It is more than four years since I last communicated with my diary, and for the most part they have been good years. There is a new little Queen called Victoria on the English throne. The estate has not exactly prospered, but it has survived intact, and on that I congratulate myself. And my family members, scattered as they are across North Pembrokeshire, have enjoyed good relations one with another. Brynach and Ioan have become firm friends, as have Betsi and Anne. There have been certain changes in my domestic arrangements, and I shall describe these in due course.

But my reason for picking up my pen again is that I sense the early rumblings of what might become a mighty earthquake. These rumblings are not far away in the great centres of coal mining or iron manufacture in South Wales, but much closer to home. Ostensibly, the cause of the trouble is the high price of corn, but other food prices are higher than they have ever been before, which is good for the big gentry of the lowlands but a tragedy for the hill farmers and others who live in this area. They have only a little barley and oats to sell, and hardly any wheat; and for their livelihoods they depend upon sales of animal products like beef, mutton, butter and cheese, at depressed prices. Then I know from my discussions with my tenants and my labourers that they are assailed by a whole host of other problems. There are still far too many people on the land, and there are too many men and boys seeking labouring work. Local people are having to compete with those fleeing into the West Wales countryside from hunger in Ireland and from a sudden decline in the fortunes of the mines and the iron-works. That causes great trouble, especially in the ale-houses of Newport late at night. Havard Medical complains that he is having to deal with broken limbs and bloodied heads almost every night, and the lock-up on Long Street is in constant use.

Enclosures are another problem. I recall that many years ago Owain was in dispute with Squire George Price when the latter sought to enclose parts of the common previously used for grazing by his tenants and by the landless poor. But in recent years it has been happening again, and Parliament has been passing Enclosure Acts for all the gentlemen who ask for them, without having any regard for the consequences. So the Squires say that their enclosures of the best grazing areas are legal, even though the process has forced more and more animals onto the moorlands covered by rocks and bracken, and more and more small farmers into destitution. In the last six months, four well-established *ty unnos* hovels have been smashed down by the local squires, who have been perfectly impervious to the cries of those who have been made homeless and to the pleas which I have entered on their behalf. I will have nothing to do with these enclosures, since my animals need the common too, but the common grazing area on Carningli and Dinas mountain has been reduced by about thirty per cent since I first came to the Plas.

Another process which is gathering momentum is the combining of farms into larger and larger units which are now directly administered by the big squires and their stewards. On the Bayvil estate, four tenant farming families have had their tenancy agreements revoked, and they are now reduced to the status of labourers. The same thing has happened on the Gelli Fawr estate, and even Walter Phillips of Ambleston has gone against the wishes of his wife Ellie (my dear friend) by combining three tenant farms into one.

All of this appears to have been carefully calculated to cause trouble, and it has. This very afternoon, as I was walking down the Cilgwyn Road towards town, minding my business and enjoying one of the few decent days of the last month, I suddenly came across an assembly of about a hundred men outside the Rising Sun Inn. They recognized me, as I recognized many of them. "Good afternoon, Mistress Martha!" they shouted. Their leader, one Dafydd Ifan from Gamallt, explained to me that they had work to do, and that it might be best for me to follow them down Greystones Hill at a safe distance, if I was really intent on going into town. I nodded and said that I was perfectly happy to keep out of their way. "*Ceffyl Pren*?" I asked. "Yes, Mistress. And not before time. There are two gentlemen who deserve our loving attention, and they will get it."

I was flattered that the men were prepared to trust me. As I watched, they blackened their faces with soot from a bucket, unpacked some bundles of old clothes, and dressed up in an assortment of women's skirts and aprons, petticoats, jackets and bonnets. One of the men had a bugle, and two of them carried drums. Two others carried a wooden ladder. When all was ready, Master Ifan gave a signal, and off they marched down the hill, making a fearful noise with their "musical" instruments, and shouting "Master Lord and Master Eynon, your time has come!" over and again. I followed fifty yards behind, as did assorted labourers and their wives and small children, all out for an afternoon's entertainment. I knew, as did everybody else, that the men who were about to be brought to justice were Richard Lord, the steward of the Bayvil estate, and Henry Eynon, the most senior and most despised of the local bailiffs. The former had recently been instrumental in revoking the tenancy agreements of families who had worked the Bayvil land for three generations, and the latter had spent the greater part of the last three weeks taking furniture and other possessions from local families who had defaulted on their rents or on tithe payments.

We all knew what would happen. When the procession reached town, it made its noisy way to the Black Lion, where the two accused had already been apprehended by an advance guard of the judicial party. They looked very frightened indeed, and with good reason. They were stripped down to their undergarments, and then strapped onto the ladder. They both had notices hung round their necks, which read "This man steals from the poor and gives to the rich". The ladder with its double burden was then raised shoulder-high and paraded round town, during which perambulation the two guilty men were jeered and pelted with food scraps and other rubbish. At the crossroads in the centre of town an impromptu court was held. The "foreman" read out the charges against the two prisoners, who were given no opportunity to defend themselves. "What says the jury?" demanded the foreman. "Guilty! Guilty!" shouted the mob of black-faced men and the crowd of onlookers.

"What shall be the penalty?" asked the foreman.

"New tenancies in place of the old! And return of all confiscated property!" yelled the mob.

"And if they disobey?"

"String them from the gallows tree!"

"And as a token of intent?"

"A short swim in the salty sea!"

This ended the formal proceedings of the court, and with a cheer from the crowd, the procession set off down Long Street, passing the town Lock-up on the way. There was a special cheer for the three constables, who had locked themselves inside so as to avoid contact with anything unlawful. The bugle blared, and the drums were banged, and at last the procession reached the shore of the estuary. It was, by design rather than accident, high tide. Then Master Lord and Master Eynon were untied from the ladder. Their underclothes were removed, and as they screamed with terror, they were forced to stand naked and watch while all of their clothes were placed in a little pile and burned to ashes. Then they were both flung without further ado into the water. They did not come to any harm, for the water was only two feet deep close to the shore, but they emerged very wet and covered in black mud.

Then the mob, and the watching crowd, melted away, leaving the two wretched fellows to cover their shame and their indignity, and to find their way home as best they could. At least they still had their boots. Later on, as I went about my business in town, the talk was of nothing other than the punishment of the *Ceffyl Pren* which had been meted out to the two cronies of Squire Huws of Bayvil, and I must say that I found not a word of sympathy for either of them. Rough justice maybe, but if the law will not protect the poor, then the mob has to dispense justice itself, and provide a little innocent entertainment into the bargain.

ΩΩΩΩΩΩΩΩΩΩΩ

7th June 1837

This morning I had a visit from Squire Madoc Huws of Bayvil. He is not a very nice fellow, and he was not in a happy mood. He was accompanied by Squire John Owen of Gelli Fawr, who can always be depended upon to uphold virtue and privilege and to come down heavily on those who presume to object to anything whatsoever.

"Why, gentlemen!" said I, giving an exaggerated and obviously insincere curtsy. "What a pleasure it is to welcome you to the Plas! And what can I do for you on this fine summer's day?"

"I think you know, Mistress Morgan," growled Master Huws.

"Indeed. sir, I do not. I have a modest number of skills, but reading minds is not one of them. Pray enlighten me."

"In private, if you please, Mistress. This is a delicate matter."

I nodded and led the two gentlemen along the passage to the parlour. I sat them down, and asked Gwenno if she would be so kind as to fetch some apple cordial and three glasses. Then I shut the door and lifted my eyebrows as an indication that I was all ears.

"There was an outrage in town yesterday, Mistress," said Squire Owen. "An unruly mob of vicious criminals committed a whole string of despicable offences against two innocent gentlemen of my acquaintance. Assault, unlawful arrest, and theft, to name but three. The ringleaders must be brought to justice immediately, and we are minded to hold a Petty Sessions this very day in order to commit them for trial at the Quarter Sessions. Transportation for the guilty is the least we will expect."

"It has come to our notice, Mistress Morgan," added Squire Huws, "that you were present as a witness, and we assume therefore that you will do your public duty by identifying the fellows in charge of the mob."

"And what makes you think that I was present, sir?"

"The aggrieved parties, Master Lord and Master Eynon, swear that you were one of the bystanders, and that they saw you during their most unfortunate ordeal no less than three times, at the Black Lion, on the town crossroads, and near the water's edge on the estuary."

"I cannot deny, sir, that I was caught up in the affair as an onlooker, although in truth I was in town simply to do some shopping."

"Well, there we are then," smiled Squire Owen, spreading his fat hands across his expansive stomach. "So the names of the leaders, Mistress, if you please."

"Quite impossible, sir," I replied. "The fellows involved were all dressed in a most peculiar fashion, and they had black faces. They might have been tribesmen from some African jungle, for all I know."

"Come come, Mistress Morgan. You are not so stupid nor so naive as you pretend. Now then, the names, so that we can issue arrest warrants as appropriate."

"Even if I knew them, sir, I would not give them to you. What I saw yesterday was a harmless bit of tomfoolery involving the *Ceffyl Pren*. But it was also a citizen's court, properly convened and conducted, with public acclamation, according to the Ancient Laws of Hywel Dda. Do you yourselves, as good Welshmen and magistrates, not accept the primacy of these laws over those made in England? The fellows who were captured were certainly guilty of the crimes with which they were charged under Welsh law, and their punishments were undignified but very modest in the circumstances. So far as I could see, the only thing hurt was their pride."

The two of them were about to explode with fury, but at that moment Gwenno knocked on the door and came sailing in, looking as soft and sweet as a summer peach, with a tray of liquid refreshments. As I served drinks to my guests I changed the subject and talked of the prospects for the hay harvest instead. No matter how much they tried to return to the business of the trial and punishment of their cronies, I refused to cooperate, and in the end they had to go on their way empty-handed.

Nobody, and not even the town constables, will testify as to the identities of the leaders of the mob, and no further action will be taken. Master Lord and Master Eynon will not take out indictments or give evidence before a Petty Sessions either, for they know that that would result in further summary justice from the community. Next time it might be a severe beating, or worse.

Tomorrow the town will be back to normal. But I now have two new enemies in Squire Owen and Squire Huws, with whom I had previously been on moderately good terms. In their eyes, I am now certainly seen as an agitator and as someone who condones unruly and unlawful behaviour. I will be carefully watched. I find that I am not at all worried by the prospect, since I can do some watching too.

ΩΩΩΩΩΩΩΩΩΩΩ

15th June 1837

There have been developments. This morning, upon delivery of my weekly *Welshman*, I was amazed to see that the recent outing of the *Ceffyl Pren* was reported in some detail, under the heading "Rough Justice in

Pembrokeshire."   One might have expected the event to have been reported as an "outrage" or some such thing, but no -- the action of the mob was reported with some sympathy, and in considerable detail. Somebody who was present at the event, either as a black-faced "jury member" or as an onlooker, must have made detailed notes and sent them off to the newspaper. Now who could that have been? I saw no strangers in the crowd, and no other members of the gentry, so one of the locals who is good with words must have been responsible. I think I have a natural ally in town, and in due course I will discover who he -- or she -- might be.

Three days after the "trial" of Master Lord and Master Eynon, a notice was pinned to the door of the parish church in the centre of town. Its contents were soon common knowledge. It read: *"To Master Richard Lord and Master Henry Eynon and whomsoever it may concern. It has come to our notice, and disagreeable it is indeed, that the poor people who have suffered at your hands have not received recompense. Neither have you acted as required by the Court. You have eight days to do as you were bidden. If you do not, it will go ill with you. Signed the Foreman of the Jury of the Court of Ceffyl Pren."*

And yesterday, with the two guilty men still hiding away somewhere on the Bayvil estate, it did go ill with them. I understand from my sources that at two o'clock in the morning the members of a black-faced mob, again dressed in women's clothing, descended on Richard Lord's well-appointed house in Bayvil, carrying torches and beating on a drum. They made as much noise as possible, and they were clearly confident that the forces of law and order would be nowhere to be seen. They ejected the steward and his family into the yard. They then took every single piece of furniture from the house, and assorted other possessions as well, and piled them high onto horse-drawn gambos and carts. Then off they went back towards Newport, marching to a drum-beat. At the same time another mob did exactly the same thing at the modest cottage of Henry Eynon. And a third mob, operating this time without the drum and without drawing attention to themselves in any way, entered Squire Huws's rick yard adjacent to the big house and set fire to all four of the remaining ricks built last year. The Squire was not in residence at the time. The ricks were utterly destroyed, and it is rumoured that the Bayvil farm servants did not try terribly hard to save them. At all three locations, brief notes were left demanding new tenancies for Zeke Tomos, Nathaniel Evans, George

Billings and Hywel Lewis, the four men who had had their old tenancies revoked by the Squire. By six o'clock in the morning, with the sun already well up, all of the confiscated furniture and other things had been distributed to the poor people of the neighbourhood, with the largest items going to those who had suffered as a result of the recent flood of distraint orders.

When I came down to breakfast Bryn and Gomer were already at the kitchen table, tucking in to their toasted barley bread and cheese. They both looked more than a little the worse for wear. "Good morning, gentlemen!" said I. "You look as if you could do with more sleep, the pair of you. And try to be more presentable at the breakfast table, if you please. You both have filthy black marks all over your collars, and I think it might be best for those shirts of yours to go straight into the washtub."

They grinned and pulled off their shirts. Bessie found some clean replacements which used to belong to Billy, and they put those on instead. "Very sorry we are, Mistress," said Bryn. "We will try to be tidier in future, for the sake of this house's good reputation."

ΩΩΩΩΩΩΩΩΩΩ

16th June 1837

It will be perceived from the foregoing that Bryn Williams is now in residence in one of the servants' rooms at the Plas, and that he is established as a member of my strange extended family. I must explain how it is that I came to need an extra pair of hands on the estate.

Not long after my first meeting with Master Bryn, in the early spring of 1833, we had a visit from Herbert Herbal, the itinerant Green Man. He travels all over the kingdom, selling plant extracts, roots, leaves and powders to wizards and apothecaries, and he calls in at the Plas at highly irregular intervals which might range from a year to a decade. I am a good customer, and as a result of all my lessons with Joseph over the years I can claim quite a comprehensive knowledge of natural remedies for most of the common ailments which afflict human beings in this region. I keep a collection of maybe one hundred essences, oils, tinctures and dried leaves and roots native to my home area, but I depend upon Herbert for my supplies of exotic things like peppers, Oriental spices, cloves and opium poppy latex. When he called, he had just discovered that Joseph was dead, and he was distraught. I had to tell him about the accident and its aftermath, and that was not easy for either of us.

I spent £3 on essential items for my pharmacy cupboard, and then we sat down and had a cup of tea and a slice of rich currant cake. Herbert thought for a while, and then said; "You know, Mistress Martha, that Joseph wanted that young fellow of yours to take over when he came to the end of his days? He said so to me once. I think that he had a premonition."

"Do you mean Shemi Jenkins, my head man?"

"That would be the fellow. The one who knows the weather, and talks to animals."

"But he is the one who keeps this estate going," I blurted out. "I need him here at the Plas!"

"You probably need him less than you think, Mistress Martha. And what does he need, for his own happiness? Did Joseph never mention anything to you?"

"Well, now that you come to mention it, he did say to me, with almost his last breath, that Shemi would one day be a great wizard, and that I should pass on to him his big book, and his library, and all his other possessions when the time was right."

"And when might the time be right, Mistress?" asked the Green Man, with an enigmatic smile on his face.

When he had gone on his way, I sat down in my bedroom and gazed out over the *cwm*, deep in thought. Master Herbert was quite correct. Shemi had shown a natural aptitude for reading and study from a very young age, when he first attended the sessions of the Circulating School at the Plas. His ability to speak to animals, and to control them when they were disturbed or unruly, was legendary in the community. He could see changes in the weather a month ahead of any other weather man. He certainly had special powers, and I know that he shared my visions and experienced many of his own. He had acute powers of observation and deduction, and a natural empathy with those less fortunate than himself. When I came to think of it, he was already a *dyn hysbys*. It was perfectly obvious that he was a natural successor to Joseph, and that his talents were wasted in the cowshed and the potato field. Perhaps I had been misled by his appearance. He was a big man, over six feet tall and as broad as a front door, with blue eyes and fair hair and a chin which was sometimes smooth but more often stubbly. So different from Joseph, who had been lightly built, with piercing eyes, sharp features, a high forehead and wispy hair. There was no reason at all, I concluded, why any of the wizards of the future should look anything at all like my dear departed friend.

So it was that when Shemi came in for dinner I asked him to step in to the parlour with me. He sat down and looked awkward, like a small child expecting some admonishment. I smiled, and he relaxed. "Now then, Shemi," said I, "how old are you?"

"Fifty, Mistress. Been here at the Plas for over thirty-five years. Old enough to be a grandfather, I am, as Sian reminded me the other day."

"I want to ask you a serious question, and I want a serious answer." I looked him straight in the eye, and he nodded. So I continued. "Shemi, what is your true calling?"

"Why, Mistress, what a strange thing to ask me!"

"Think hard, and give me a truthful answer, if you please."

He thought for several minutes, looking alternately at me and at the floor. Then he swallowed hard and said: "If it does not sound presumptuous, Mistress, I think that I am called to be a wizard like Master Harries, but I fear that I am too stupid, and that it is already far too late for me to learn."

I got up and crossed the floor, and gave him a kiss on the cheek. Then I sat beside him. "You shall be a wizard, Shemi. You are neither too stupid nor too old, and I have it on good authority from the Green Man that you are exactly the right age. Old enough to be wise in the ways of the world. Are you prepared to study?"

"Of course, Mistress. Studying has always been a great joy to me."

"Very well. In due course you will have Joseph's big book and his library and other things which are in my possession. But the time is not yet right. First, I want you to go to Cwrt-y-Cadno to study with Doctor John Harries. No relation of Joseph, but a great wizard and a wise and kind man. He lives forty miles away, on the other side of Carmarthen. That will mean long separations from Sian and the family. Are you prepared for that?"

Awakening

"Yes, Mistress, if they will all agree to it."

Our interview was at an end. Shemi spoke to Sian and the three children, who are all now old enough to have minds of their own, and they all realized that it was his destiny to continue Joseph's work. A few days later I travelled with him to Cwrt-y-Cadno for an interview with Doctor Harries. The old wizard picked up immediately on Shemi's talents and agreed to take him on for three years as an apprentice. I agreed to pay the fees, and for his keep. Shemi started there in June of that year, and finished his apprenticeship in the summer of 1836. While he was away I renovated Werndew, which I had inherited in 1832 under the terms of Joseph's will. I was lucky that it was still intact, for wizards' houses are traditionally burnt down by silly people who believe that that is the only way to get rid of evil spirits. But I had called in to see all those who lived near Werndew within a few days of Joseph's funeral, and had told them that the devil whom they had presumed to be in residence many years before had in fact been Master Iestyn Price of Plas Llanychaer, undergoing treatment for truly terrible wartime injuries. The house is quite safe, I said, and as a sign of goodwill I let it at a peppercorn rent to a homeless old gentleman named Jac Blossom who agreed to look after the garden. I knew that Joseph's medical herb collection was a good deal more valuable than his cottage, for it contained hundreds of herbs, flowers and other medicinal plants which he had collected and nurtured throughout his life. It was, I thought, his true memorial.

Early in 1836, I paid for the cottage to be enlarged from a simple two-room structure to a pleasant house with six rooms, including a pharmacy and consulting room in which Shemi could meet his patients. Clom and thatch were replaced with stone and slate. Dear old Jac helped with the building work, and was delighted to do so. Then when Shemi returned, he and Sian moved to Werndew, and Jac moved into their small cottage on the edge of the Plas Ingli estate. I gave him part-time work in my own garden. All three of them were very happy indeed.

As for Master Bryn Williams, he simply happened to be in the right place at the right time. I gave him labouring work in the spring following our original meeting, and found him to be a perfectly competent and trustworthy fellow. The ironworks had affected his lungs, but he was otherwise strong and willing, and intelligent to boot. And he had wondrous tales to tell of his wild days and nights in the iron town of

Merthyr Tydfil. When Shemi went off to be a sorcerer's apprentice I promoted Will to be head man and gave Bryn the cattle to look after. I gave him the room next to Gomer, who was delighted to have another man as company beneath our roof, as a counterbalance to a considerable weight of emotional females.

So it was that the visit of the Green Man led Shemi to his true vocation and made at least a dozen people more contented than they were before. Such, perhaps, is the function of Green Men.

ΩΩΩΩΩΩΩΩΩΩ

17th June 1837

Thus morning, a year after Shemi and Sian moved in to Werndew, I decided that my erstwhile head man had proved himself as a worthy successor to Joseph. The reports from the old and the infirm who have sought treatment from him are universally good, and I know that he has treated broken limbs and other injuries with great skill and tenderness. He has the true calling of a wizard, the true instincts of a doctor, and the hands of a healer. He has also shown that he has the ability to solve great mysteries and to deal with petty crimes in a way that allows justice to be done without resort to the constables or the magistrates. He is also as lovely and as humble as ever, and said to me the other day that he really needed another twenty years of study in order to master a fraction of what Joseph had stored inside that masterful brain of his.

The time had come to pass over to our new wizard Joseph's big book and his library, and his other things. Shemi and Sian came over with their pony and trap, and while Sian went to help in the dairy I took her husband upstairs to the room which at one time had been the nursery for my small children. I told him that I now wanted to give him all of Joseph's possessions, as the dear man had requested shortly before his death. "Shemi," I said, "these items have always been destined for you. Now it is my great pleasure to hand them over into your safe keeping. Following your studies, you know far better than I what to do with them."

Awakening

"Why, thank you, Mistress! I hardly know what to say....."

"There is a price to be paid, Shemi. Two prices, in fact. The first is that you must embrace me, since I always embrace my wizards and derive great strength from it. And the second is that you will finish with subservience, and never call me "Mistress" again. From now on I will be "Martha" to you, as you are "Shemi" to me. Are we agreed?"

"Quite agreed, Martha," said Shemi. "It is more than my life's worth to disagree with the Mistress of Plas Ingli." And he gave me a great bear-hug and a kiss on the cheek, which I found very pleasurable.

Then I handed over to Shemi the Werndew library of books, some of which were printed more than two hundred years ago. There were herbals from France, Germany and England, and three editions of Culpeper. Then there was a large Bible, and for good measure the ancient works of the Kabbalah. Then there was the old German book called *Hammer of Witches* and the infamous *Discovery of Witches* written around 1650 by that insane Witchfinder General, Matthew Hopkins. And so it went on -- worthy tomes by Adam Smith, John Howard, Mary Wollstonecraft and Tom Paine; novels by Tobias Smollett, Jonathan Swift, Samuel Richardson, Henry Fielding and even Mistress Jane Austen; volumes on science and natural history, gardens and cooking; grand tours and agriculture; history, dictionaries and chronicles; poetry and the ancient myths of the Greeks. Joseph's choice of reading matter had been nothing if not catholic, and I was reminded, on handing over all his volumes, that he had been able to read in Welsh, English, French, German and Latin.

Joseph's big book, about which there had been endless speculation since his death, was a great prize for Shemi. It was reputed to be protected by demons, but I had looked through it before without being struck dead, and I assumed that Shemi might also survive. I knew that it contained an extraordinary compendium of information, written in at least five different hands. There were some dates at the beginning of the book which showed that its first owner had lived around 1680. There were no names or signatures, but it was indisputable that the first wizard had handed the book on to his apprentice or successor, and so on in an unbroken line until it reached Joseph. Now it was going to Shemi, and I noted with pleasure that there were at least twenty blank pages at the end of the mighty tome which were available for him to write on. And the contents? The laws of Hywel Dda relating to the office and privileges of true physicians; a translation of the manuscript of the Physicians of Myddfai including a list of medicinal plants, descriptions of medical practice, and a list of the essential virtues of a physician; hundreds of recipes for the making up of herbal remedies; lists of the symptoms of common and uncommon ailments; notes relating to the anatomy of human beings and of many animals and birds; descriptions of systems of medicine from foreign lands including China and India; recipes for jams and chutneys; the Ten Commandments and the Beatitudes; tips on the making of good wine, ale and cider; notes on hypnosis and on the workings of the human mind; astrological tables; scales of charges for services rendered; spells and invocations; rituals, charms and symbols; detailed notes on the weather and seasonal patterns of flowering, leaf fall and so forth; and some sections which were written in a script which I did not understand and which I thought might be Arabic. "There is enough in here to keep you occupied as a student for the rest of your life," I said to Shemi. "I have studied much of it myself, in my lessons with Joseph. But there are some mysteries here that I have not even tried to understand, relating to good and bad spirits and to *Yr Hen Fachgen* or the Devil. Now that Harries Cwrt-y-Cadno has given you the key to at least some of this esoteric knowledge, it is your privilege as Joseph's successor to hide it or reveal it as you see fit."

Finally I handed over Joseph's black cloak embroidered with zodiac and cabalistic signs, and other garments made from cloths of various colours -- white, gold, purple, silver and green. I had never seen him wearing any of these, but I assume that he must have done so during his own private rituals. There was no hat apart from the battered stovepipe hat which Joseph used to wear when it rained. I passed over five wands, three made from hazel and bound with rings of copper and zinc, and two made from mountain ash. There was a long staff which was almost as thick as my wrist. Much to my surprise, there was a Christian crucifix fashioned out of silver. One small box contained wax candles, and a silk pouch contained three beautiful crystals. Another box contained his glass ball, which was about six inches in diameter. There were some small animal skulls, and a few leather thongs, one of which looked like an eel skin. There were various feathers, semi-precious stones, chains and chalices. There were about fifteen glass vessels containing sacred oils and smelling of cinnamon, myrrh, olive and other scents I did not recognize. There were glass bottles, tubes and jars used for distillation and various chemical processes, and pestles and mortars, knives and spoons, and carved pieces of wood. And finally there was his pharmacy, containing hundreds of small bottles and jars, carefully labelled, containing roots and herbs, powders and dried flowers, fruits and leaves.

I had never felt bothered by having all these items stored at the Plas, but it was good that they were now all going back to Werndew where they belonged. When everything was packed safely onto the chaise, and when Shemi and Sian were ready to go, our new wizard gave me another hug. "Thank you from the bottom of my heart, Martha," he said. "You have given me the means, through your support and your money, to serve this beloved neighbourhood just as Joseph did. I will never forget your kindness. As I leave, I will do you one small service. Last night, as I sat in silence, it came to me that you have five days of hot weather to get all the hay cut and carted. After that, the rain will come, and it will not stop until mid-September, by which time the corn harvest will be ruined. Those who do not cut the hay tomorrow are lost. I urge you to organize the harvesters for an early start. I will be here myself to help you at seven o'clock in the morning."

Shemi is never wrong, and after waving him farewell I sent messages to all of my tenants and labourers, and to five of the Irish itinerants who are currently in town, asking them to drop everything, and to turn up before seven with their scythes ready-sharpened.

ΩΩΩΩΩΩΩΩΩΩΩ

25th June 1837

The rain is sluicing down out of a black sky, but the hay harvest is in. Shemi came, and I had ten men scything and twenty women and children raking and turning. The grass was not as high as I would have liked, because of the coldness of the early summer, but at least I now have full hay lofts in the stable and the cowshed, and two new hayricks in the yard. I tried to warn all of my neighbours that the weather would break soon, and I said that Shemi had predicted rain for weeks to come, but with the exception of two of my tenants they all said that they would take a chance and wait for a little more growth. Now they will have to pay a price for their greed. They will have nothing but flattened grass and muddy puddles in their hayfields, and starvation will be staring them in the face before the summer is out.

That knowledge of misery to come has quite destroyed the joy of the hay harvest and the pleasure that I normally feel once the crop is in. The laughter, the camaraderie that comes from shared and sweated labour, the smell of new-mown hay beneath the high sun, the creaking wagons heading for the rick yard, and the meals taken together in the blessed shade of tall trees -- all of this brought euphoria then but apprehension now, as I realise that I will not be able to escape from the consequences of other people's failed harvests. There will be no hay to be had once autumn turns to winter, and prices will spiral upwards. I will be pressed to sell hay that I want to keep, just to keep other animals alive and other farmers from destitution. I truly hate the process of making decisions in such circumstances, and sometimes think that it would be better to share the misery of those who do not have the wisdom of a wizard to call upon.

While my mind is settled onto miserable things, I recall that in the pages of this diary I have already given expression to my concerns about high rents, about the religious and political awakening of the common man, and about food prices, and too many people on the land, and enclosures and evictions, and farm amalgamations. A miserable catalogue indeed, and one might have thought that that would be enough to be going on with, but now we have a new misery dumped upon the heads of ordinary people by our infinitely wise political masters. Since the passing of the Reform Act five years ago, and the addition of new Members of Parliament elected by people other than their cronies, we have assumed that fresh air would sweep through the House of Commons and blow away the cobwebs. I for one thought that sensible laws would be brought in to deal with poverty and distress. But no -- our new leaders appear to be more remote and even more idiotic than their predecessors.

If anything could have been designed to create more revolutionary fervour than the Poor Law Amendment Act, I should be very interested to hear about it. This Act, which is now about three years old, requires that the poor rate which we all pay to the parish should no longer be used to alleviate poverty where we find it, at the discretion of the Overseers of the Poor. Instead, the money that is collected goes to a Union of parishes, governed by an elected body of men called the Guardians of the Poor, who meet in Cardigan. The members of that body, who are supposed to work without recompense, are generally illiterate and ill-qualified for responsibility of any sort, and yet they are supposed to oversee the building of a Workhouse in Cardigan. Thank God that it is not yet built, but once it is in commission poverty will in effect become a crime, and those who are unable to earn a living through old age, infirmity or other misfortune will be shut away there under a regime that will be worse than that of Cardigan Gaol. I know this because I have read about the workhouses already in use in the big cities in other parts of the country. Some of them are likened to the Bastille. Husbands are separated from their wives, and children from their mothers. Rations are deliberately kept small so as to deter people from falling into poverty! Women spend their time washing clothes or sewing and knitting, but the "honest toil" for men apparently consists of breaking up one and a half tons of stones per day, to be used for the building of roads. If any man refuses to cooperate in this, he is brought before the magistrates and generally sentenced to spend a month or two on the treadmill. In a world which is supposedly enlightened, the shadows that afflict the poor are dark and grim indeed.

ΩΩΩΩΩΩΩΩΩΩ

26th June 1837

On another windy and rainy day, with nothing to be done at home other than moaning about the weather, I was happy to accept an invitation to dinner from Betsi and Ioan at Brithdir. I walked down from the Plas in the rain, and found that Brynach and Anne and their children had also been invited, and were there already. An unexpected pleasure indeed, with all the members of my family gathered together in one place for a convivial meal. But for me the greatest pleasure was to spend a little time with my five grandchildren, who are growing up too quickly for my liking. The Brithdir boys are Benjamin who is now sixteen, Abel who is thirteen, and

Awakening

Owain who is eight. And Brynach and Anne have two delightful little ones, Rose who is six and David who is now three. Betsi says she is finished with child-bearing, and I hope that she is right since she has miscarried twice since Owain was born. But Anne is with child again, and is round and beautiful with seven months gone. It would be good to have another girl in the family, and she says she will do her best to oblige.

After a splendid meal we five adults settled into the parlour with a cup of tea while the two older boys played chess in the kitchen and the three little ones played in the nursery. We talked of this and that, and occasionally I allowed myself the privilege of drifting out of the conversation and into a reverie on the good relationships which now exist between us. We have had our difficult times, especially during the period when Betsi's family was stranded at the Plas with nowhere else to go, but now that both families have their own homes and their own farms to run, I sense much greater contentment. Ioan struggles to make ends meet on the sixty acres he has at Brithdir, but he is a good farmer and brings in enough to keep the family in reasonable comfort. Brynach has a large estate to run, and while he is guaranteed a reasonable income from his tenancies, he has to employ a much wider range of skills than his brother-in-law, and has to cope with greater pressures. But I am very proud of him. He manages remarkably well, even with two small and very lively children constantly demanding his attention.

"Mother, a penny for your thoughts, if you please," said Brynach suddenly. "You were a million miles away, if I am not mistaken, and we asked you for your assessment of the contribution of Master Cobbett in the matter of good husbandry."

"Is that so? I fear that I was not concentrating. That is one of the privileges of being a grandmother."

Brynach grinned. "Come now, Mother. You are not as old as you pretend, and you are still perfectly capable of turning gentlemen's heads in the streets of Newport. Be that as it may, I asked you about the irritating Master Cobbett."

"Well, he was certainly, before his untimely death, a thorn in the flesh of the political establishment. I suspect that he did more in the cause of free speech than he did in the cause of agriculture."

"Quite so," said Ioan. "I thought of him as a great man, driven by the desire to see justice done. We could do with such a man in Wales. He would pretty soon, with his sharp pen, cut down to size the Campbells of Stackpole, or the Owens of Orielton, or the Philippses of Picton."

"To Hell with the lot of them!" stormed Brynach. "Self-serving, arrogant and corrupt from the top of the gentry tree to the bottom! They should all be swept away and replaced with good men and true, with real contributions to make, who are elected by the secret votes of free men!"

"Come now, husband," said Anne, with a flush upon her cheeks. "You yourself have gentry blood in you, as do all of us in this room. Does our blood infect us with vices and prevent virtue from flowing in our veins?"

"And even the big gentry have their moments," I added. "You young people may not know it, but the old Lord Cawdor once saved Pembrokeshire from the French invader and saved me from the gallows. And the Bowens of Llwyngwair are good God-fearing people with a code of honour to which the rest of us should aspire. If it had not been for the steadfastness and skill of John Bowen, the old squire, the Plas Ingli estate might have been lost to charlatans before the turn of the century. And do not forget............"

"Yes, Mother," interrupted Betsi. "We know all of that. Some of them are good and benevolent people who know about duty, and who are paternalistic in the best sense of the word. But surely those who sit in Parliament on our behalf, making laws and raising taxes, would be empowered rather than threatened if only the demands of the Chartists could be met?"

"The Chartists? Who are they?"

"You will hear more of them, Mother, that is for sure," said Brynach. "You will even read of them in the *Welshman* before the year is out. My informants tell me that there are six demands: votes for all men, regardless of wealth or status, electoral districts of equal size, secret ballots, payment for Members of Parliament, removal of the qualification based upon property value, and some other thing which I forget......."

"Annual elections," volunteered Ioan, sipping his China tea. "That one I do not agree with, since we would spend all our time in years to come either campaigning for elections or recovering from them. But the other demands are based upon natural justice, and cannot be denied."

"But they will be disputed, you may be sure," said Anne. "For those in power, to give in to Chartism would be unthinkable. Votes for the ignorant rabble? Never!" And she slammed her fist down onto the table in a passable imitation of old Squire Price in his heyday. She laughed, and so did the rest of us. Then our interesting conversation was brought to a premature end by a wail from upstairs, which turned out to have come from Rose who had been pushed over by her nasty little brother. So there was consoling and remonstrating to be done, and peace was eventually restored. We adults devoted the rest of the afternoon to the children, and that was as it should be.

As I walked home through the rain I could not get over the fact that my son and my daughter, and their spouses, were a good deal more aware of political matters than I had previously realized. Maybe I should not have been surprised. They were, after all, not children any longer, and I have always encouraged them to think, and not to accept injustice in any form. So who am I now to complain if I have two male firebrands in the family, and two wives who seem to have an equal lack of respect for authority? I am excited by the thought that they are all clearly willing to fight for virtue. But there is also a flutter of apprehension in my breast, for those who fight also run the risk of getting hurt.

ΩΩΩΩΩΩΩΩΩΩΩ

15th July 1837

It started to rain on the 23rd day of June, and it has still not stopped. The streaming water and the leaden skies have had a debilitating effect upon the whole community. Sheep and cattle are wallowing in mud, and those who lost their hay harvest are now resigned to the loss of the corn harvest as well. Some of the labourers have blight on their potato crops, and those who plant on sloping ground have had the soil washed out from beneath the flattened potato leaves. Will tells me that the quantity of potatoes harvested from our own potato field will be hardly any greater than the weight of potatoes planted in March. Jac Blossom cannot do anything in the garden. Our milk supply, which should now be at its peak, is down by one third. That means less butter and cheese to sell and to put away in the pantry.

Awakening

As for the poor people, they already know that crabapple, blackberry, wild plum and bilberry will be in short supply, and I suspect that by the end of the year people will be doing as our ancient ancestors did -- eating seaweed and mussels from the seashore, badgers, starlings and brown rats where they can find them, and nettle and sorrell from the hedgerows. Then they will take trout and sewin from under the noses of the bailiffs, and steal turnips and cabbages from the fields and gardens of the gentry. What else can they do, when they have small children at home, wasting away before their eyes? Those who are caught, either by mantraps or by vigilant bailiffs, will go to the Quarter Sessions and will end up being transported to the colonies.

The same thing happened last year, when we had weeks of unbroken rain. Many local families left in search of a better life elsewhere. Some went to Paterchurch, in the hope of finding work in the Royal Naval Dockyard. Others went further afield, to the coal mines of Carmarthenshire or the ironworks of Glamorgan, only to pass hordes of refugees from those great industries who were fleeing in the opposite direction, intent upon making better lives for themselves in the farming counties of West Wales! We have had squatters on the common, and on Carningli and Carnffoi. The Irish have come into South Wales in their thousands. Some of them have built *ty unnos* hovels, but most of them have made crude shelters out of branches and leaves in feeble attempts to keep out the rain. Last week a small child died from cold and hunger on the mountain. A group of about twenty Irish moved into Pengelli Wood in the hope of finding shelter beneath the trees, but they were evicted in short order by Squire Rees Laugharne.

I am beginning to despair with regard to my own finances. Since I sold Llystyn and Fachongle, and gave Brithdir to Ioan and Betsi, I only have four tenanted farms on the estate -- Gelli, Penrhiw, and the upper and lower Dolrannogs. I need the rents, but last year I only got half of what I was owed, and this year I am no more optimistic. I should really evict my tenants as some of my neighbouring landowners have done, but I will not do that. I can receive payment in labour, or cattle, or turnips; but I need cash, and my reserves are now running desperately low. I hope to God that I do not have to dig up my treasure, but I am beginning to think that it may become inevitable.

With many people coming in from Wexford and Cork, it is ironic that the ports of Cardigan, Newport and Fishguard are seeing an increasing movement of emigrants who have had enough and who are now intent upon making new lives for themselves in America. The *Enterprise*, a vessel in which I hold a one-eighth share, has made five voyages to the New World already in the last two years, taking thirty passengers from Newport each time. There have been other ships too, heading west from Cardigan across the mighty Atlantic Ocean. I estimate that about a thousand people have gone already from North Pembrokeshire. In steerage the travellers have to find four pounds a head, which is more than the annual salary of a labourer; but by hook and by crook, some poor people have saved and saved, and have received gifts from relatives, and have sold all their possessions, in order to buy their passages. The Guardians of the Poor even found £20 to fund the passages of a pauper and his wife and children to Newfoundland, on the basis that this would be cheaper than keeping them in the Workhouse in years to come. But the quayside scenes are terrible indeed, for the travellers know that they will never again see the loved ones whom they leave behind, will never again see the sun setting behind Carningli, and never again hear their mother tongue spoken on busy streets.

A curse upon this weather! And a curse upon a world which drives people to flee, and leave their souls behind, just because of a few weeks of summer rain!

ΩΩΩΩΩΩΩΩΩΩΩ

22nd July 1837

The *Ceffyl Pren* has struck again. This time the target was Llewelyn Thomas, the Rector of Newport. He is not a bad fellow, but neither has he made himself very popular through his insistence upon the prompt payment of church rates and tithes.

The payment of church rates is bad enough at a level of two shillings or thereabouts in the pound, but in such matters we have the right to attend parish meetings and to postpone or change the rate. In the past, the rate has sometimes not been set, and in other years it has not been collected. Master John Devonald, our old rector, was content if just some of his parishioners paid up, and indeed those of us who used the parish church for weddings, funerals and so forth were happy enough to do so, in order to defray parochial expenses and to keep the church standing. The system almost became one of voluntary contributions. But the new man, since he was given the living in 1824, has become strict and implacable. Last year not only did he pack the vestry meeting with his cronies in order to get a rate set, but he then collected it with such vigour that some farmers who could not pay threatened him with physical violence. Undeterred, he then obtained distraint orders, and non-payers had items of their furniture taken away by the bailiffs and sold.

Outrage enough, one might have thought, but disputes over church rates pale into insignificance when set alongside the tithe problem. I have to pay a "great tithe" of ten percent of my crops of corn and hay, and so do my tenants. If the crops are poor, then according to the theory the tithe goes down. In the old days Rector Devonald used to come with his own cart, immediately after the harvest, to collect his due proportion, and he was always open to negotiation as to how many cartloads he should take away. But now the tithe does not go to the Rector at all, but to Squire Owen of Gelli Fawr, who purchased the right of tithe collection from the Lord Marcher last year. As the new impropriator, he also bought the right to collect pew rents in the nave of the church, and to collect burial fees. His steward, who is a thoroughly obnoxious young fellow, has visited all of the landowners and tenants in the parish of Newport and has insisted on accurate annual valuations of the size of the harvest from now on until the end of time, so that he can calculate the quantity of tithe due. Everybody knows that his valuations will always err on the high side. The squire has also claimed the right to a tithe on potatoes, on timber cut in the woods, on garden produce, and even on the milk produced by our cows. This is an outrage, but it appears that he is prepared to go to litigation in order to prove that he has an ancient right to a tithe on all of these products which has simply not been collected due to the negligence and inefficiency of several past rectors. There has been speculation that wool will come next, followed by a tithe on blackberries and mushrooms. The rector is not guiltless in all of this, and he has retained the right to collect the "little tithes" of calves, eggs, butter and cheese. In theory these products are collected for his own use, but of course the bulk of what he receives is sold at Newport market. Some of the produce goes back to the very households from which it was taken in the first place. And to add insult to injury, the new Tithe Commutation Act, passed last year by our wise political leaders, allows all tithes to be commuted to cash payments. I have calculated that roughly £600 per year from our little parish alone will go straight into the deep pocket of Squire Owen, in effect representing a private tax on the efforts of his neighbours. And it will all be legal. Those who do not pay will be taken to court, and distraint orders will be issued with gay abandon by the magistrates who connive with the Owens of Grili Fawr to maintain their control over the community.

It will not be tolerated, of course, and the deep rumblings which presage a mighty earthquake are getting closer and louder. Squire Owen's time will come, but for the present Rector Thomas is an adequate target. He and Squire Owen are seen as two of a kind, and the Nonconformists see no reason whatsoever why they should pay over any part of their produce, or any of their hard-earned sovereigns, to support either the Church or the gentry. They are both seen as belonging to an upper class which victimizes and oppresses them, and as part of an old order which must be swept away.

So it was that last night a mob assembled outside the Black Lion and held a public meeting. I was not there, but I heard about it this morning from Liza, who heard about it from her sister. Apparently there were about fifty men involved, all dressed in female garb and disguised by having blackened faces and straw "hair". This time they actually had a hobby horse, and somebody rode it round and round as the meeting was being held. There were bugles and drums again, and somebody had a musket which was fired off into the air on several occasions. No doubt that was simply an act of high spirits or bravado, but it was a development that caused my heart to sink. While I support the right of free men to protest as they will, I fear that firearms and inflamed passions do not go well together. The insurrection at Merthyr Tydfil some years ago showed that perfectly, and in a recent riot in Cardigan fifteen protestors sustained gunshot wounds. Where such weapons find their way into the hands of both the rioters and the constables, there will be times when they will be used with lethal consequences.

The point of the torchlight assembly in Newport was not difficult to discern, for a stuffed effigy of the Rector was prominently on display. The effigy had a rough sign attached to it, which read *"Blessed are the poor, for they keep me fed and clothed."* The straw man was placed in the middle of the road, and then it was "tried" by the foreman and jury. Various accusations were hurled at it, mostly to do with the injustice associated with tithes and church rates. One of the accusers shouted that Rector Thomas was a "lackey and a lickspittle" of the Squire of Gelli Fawr and of the Lord Marcher, and that that was a crime punishable by death. The crowd cheered and booed, and at last the black-faced and bonneted foreman held his hand up and shouted: "My sisters, you have heard the evidence and the charges. How find you this man?"

"Guilty! Guilty!"

"And how shall he be punished?"

"Send him off to Heaven, and the sooner the better!"

And with that, they hung up the effigy by the neck, using a rope and a long pole. When it was dead, they took it down and set fire to it, with a good deal of cheering and dancing round the flames. Then they shouted "To the Rectory!" and marched off along East Street towards the location of the Rector's substantial residence. Bugles were blared, and drums were banged, and I daresay that the whole town was woken up. When they got to the Rectory, still shouting and waving their torches in the air, they found that Master Thomas and his family were in residence, peeping out from behind their shutters like timid hedgehogs. But the mob left them alone, probably thinking that to direct personal violence against a man of God would be taking things too far. So they satisfied themselves with burning down one hayrick and one cornrick in his yard before returning into town. Then they all disappeared, leaving no trace of their activities other than a small pile of ashes in the middle of the road.

ΩΩΩΩΩΩΩΩΩΩΩ

25th July 1837

Just four days after the latest riot in Newport, another report has appeared in the *Welshman*. As on the previous occasion it matched in almost every detail the account which I received third-hand, and while it did not condone the actions of the rioters it did not condemn them either. Indeed, the editor of the newspaper devoted some space to an analysis of the causes of the riot in a decidedly sympathetic manner. He appeared to know more about the grievances of the rioters than some of the onlookers in town. Then there were little details in the description of the riot which led me to believe that the mysterious writer, referred to as "our special correspondent in North Pembrokeshire", had actually been involved in the riot himself. So my soul-mate is a man and a rioter, rather than a female bystander. I am increasingly intrigued.

The other notable development is that Squire Owen and the Rector have jointly made a complaint to the Mayor about intimidation and criminal damage, and they have formally complained that the town constables have now, on two separate occasions, hidden away from the rioters and have made no attempt to prevent unlawful activity. There has been a meeting of the magistrates and the Court Leet, as a consequence of which ten special constables have been sworn in. The townspeople are all highly amused, since they are all elderly fellows who are quite untrained and who will disappear at the first sound of a beating drum. Additionally, two letters have gone off from the Mayor, one to the Home Secretary requesting a detachment of Metropolitan Police officers to be billeted in the town, and the other to the Commanding Officer of the troops in Brecon, asking for dragoons or fusiliers to quell the violent countryside. Neither request will be acted upon, since the Newport riots have been small beer indeed. Nobody has been hurt, and the numbers of people involved have been relatively small. But all of this is a sign that those who govern this little community, and who traditionally expect people to jump when they are instructed to do so, are sleeping a little less well in their beds than they did a year ago.

ΩΩΩΩΩΩΩΩΩΩ

Awakening

3rd August 1837

Tragedy has struck my beloved family again, and my belief in a benign and protective God has been sorely tested. Brynach's lovely wife Anne, and her new baby daughter, are both dead.

It happened yesterday, in the middle of the night. Anne knew that her time for delivery was very close, because she had been experiencing birthing pains throughout the previous day. But she felt well, and there was no cause for apprehension since this was her third baby. And she was in good hands, with her mother Bronwen and her housekeeper Mags in attendance. Between them, they have supervised at least twenty births, and would surely know what to do in all circumstances. I stayed away, since Anne was not my daughter and this time it was not my privilege or my duty to be there.

I heard about it yesterday morning, from a hysterical servant who arrived on horseback from Plas Llanychaer, and then later, on my arrival, from all of them in that poor blighted household. What follows is all based upon hearsay, and I thank God that I was not there myself. If I had been I would certainly have made matters worse. After the breaking of her waters all seemed to be going on as normal with Anne, but then the poor girl started to become frightened because she sensed that not all was well. She worked hard, in the manner of all mothers. She struggled, and cried, but after two hours the baby still would not come, and upon close observance Bronwen realized that the umbilical cord was tangled up and that the little one was the wrong way round. She put her hand inside and tried to correct the matter, but Anne was in such pain, and was screaming so loudly, that she could not complete the task. Bronwen became so distressed herself that Mags had to take over.

Then Anne, who was quite a frail woman and not really built for child-rearing, became more and more exhausted and less and less able to help in the delivery. Three hours had passed. Mags made frantic attempts to complete the birth, and had to make a cut in order to ease the delivery. But she realized at last that the baby -- a little girl -- was dead. She held her in her arms, covered in blood and strangled by the very cord that had given her nine months of life in warm darkness. Suddenly Bronwen, who had been talking and shouting to Anne and urging her on, became hysterical, because her beloved daughter had given up the fight and had stopped breathing.

According to the servants, that was the point at which Shemi arrived. He had galloped on his white pony through the pitch black night and the pouring rain, without a glimmer of light to guide him, not because he had been called, but because he knew that something was wrong at Plas Llanychaer. He did not knock, but splashed in through the kitchen door, past Brynach and the children who were sitting at the fireside with terror writ large across their faces, and rushed up the stairs to the bedroom. He did not even stop to take off his hat or his oilskins. He immediately poured some reviving potion down Anne's throat and fought like a mad thing to bring her back, but it was too late.

He sat for some minutes while he composed himself. Then he ordered Bronwen from the room, and told her to go to Brynach and the children. She was exhausted herself, and as white as a sheet, and one of the servants had to help her down the stairs. She broke the news to Brynach and little Rose and David, who were mercifully too young to appreciate the full import of what had happened. God knows how I would have reacted had I been in that kitchen, but I am assured that Brynach took the news with a stoicism which the servants marvelled at. He sat on the settle by the kitchen fire for a long time, with one child on each knee, rocking gently back and forth, and gazing into the flames.

Shemi and Mags cut the umbilical cord and cleaned the little girl. She would, said Mags, have been called Martha. That was difficult for me to hear, and it is difficult for me to write now, after the passage of many hours. Then they tidied up the bed and put away all the bloodstained garments and bedclothes, and the birthing implements and containers of hot water. They laid Anne out so that she looked utterly beautiful in her final sleep. They dressed her in a clean white cotton nightdress. And finally they placed the little girl on her breast, enfolded by her delicate white arms. Mags says that Shemi and she then stood by the bed for some minutes, with their arms about each other's shoulders, until she felt that he was about to be overcome by emotion.

"Master Jenkins," she said to him, "I must now call my Master."

He nodded, and so the two of them went downstairs and into the kitchen. Mags, who is a wonderfully strong woman, took the two children from Brynach's knee, and said to them: "Come now, children, it is time for you to sleep. I will come with you, and we will sleep together, with our arms about each other." They looked at her, and obeyed. As they went off up the back staircase to the nursery, Shemi looked at Brynach. No words passed between them, but my beloved son got up and walked slowly across the kitchen, and up the stairs, and into the bedroom in which he and Anne had laughed and loved since their move to Llanychaer.

He stayed there until dawn, with his dead wife and his dead child. I know something of the emotions that he must have experienced at the end of that particular dark tunnel of the mind in the darkest hour before dawn, for I have been there myself. And because I have been there before, I am there again now in the darkness, and I am weeping for Anne and her little one, and for Brynach, and Rose, and David, and for myself.

ΩΩΩΩΩΩΩΩΩΩΩ

8th August 1837

Anne and her baby are at rest in hallowed ground, in that part of the Llanllawer churchyard set aside for the Squires of Plas Llanychaer and their families. Yesterday's double funeral was a very large one, conducted by the Vicar of the little church of St David and attended by a great throng of people from all over the north of the county. Without exception, people were touched and even moved to tears by the tragedy that had occurred, and by the bleak prospect that now faces Brynach and his two young children.

On the day of that tragedy, I rushed over to Llanychaer as soon as I received the news from Brynach's servant, and I found a household that was in shock. I insisted that Bronwen should go home to Trefach to rest for several days, and she agreed that there was little more that she could do in the house of her dead daughter. I stayed for five days, helping Brynach and the servants and knowing that the greatest trauma would come for all of them when they had recovered from the initial shock. That is how it transpired, and during my stay many tears were shed. Betsi came early on and took the children away to Brithdir to see their big cousins, while arrangements were made for the *Gwylnos* and the funeral.

Awakening

I became very concerned about Brynach, for he shed no tears at all, and became very closed in upon himself. I tried to reach out to him, and to give him all the affection and support that is there for a mother to give, but while he accepted my embraces and my words of consolation there was some barrier that I could not break down. I knew that I should not force him to express his grief, and I knew that it would come in time -- perhaps after a week, or a month, or a year. So I tried to work systematically at all that had to be done, and in the process I became very fond indeed of Mags, a lady who is seventy-five years old if she is a day, and who was a veritable rock in a turbulent sea of emotions.

On the day before the funeral Shemi came to Llanychaer to talk to Brynach, and the two men spent a long time walking together in the walled garden, apparently impervious to the drenching which they received from this accursed rain. I had almost forgotten what good friends they were, having shared mealtimes, good times and bad times at the Plas for about twenty-five years. I recalled the occasions when Shemi had given little Brynach piggybacks, and made kites for him, and picked him up out of the mud after childhood accidents, and made secret dens for him out of branches and leaves and grasses. Now they talked man to man.

When they were finished, Shemi came to see me in the room which I had temporarily occupied. The poor fellow was close to tears. "Martha, I fear that I am afflicted by guilt," he said. "I had a feeling that something was wrong at Plas Llanychaer, but instead of instantly accepting my intuition, as Joseph and Master Harries Cwrt-y-Cadno taught me, I delayed. At last I did obey my instinct, and came flying to the scene of the tragedy, but it was already too late. Had I been two minutes earlier........."

"You must never talk like that, Shemi. Hindsight is a curse which turns good intentions and noble ideals into a lethal poison. It can eat away at your insides and destroy you. What you did was far beyond the call of duty, and from what I hear your calming influence upon the household in the remaining hours of darkness on that terrible night brought succour to all and will long be remembered. You fulfilled your duty admirably, and you must never think otherwise."

"Do you really think so?"

"I have never lied to you, Shemi, and I will not start now. You are a worthy successor to Joseph, and you must have confidence in your own powers." I went over to him as he sat on the edge of the bed with hunched shoulders and a hanging head. I put my hand upon his arm, and when he looked up I said: "I am not sure that I am supposed to tell you this, but when Joseph was on his deathbed he told me that you would be a great wizard."

The tension drained out of him, and he even managed a smile. "He said that?"

"I swear it. And remember, my dear friend, that Joseph was never shown to be wrong in anything."

Shemi went on his way a good deal happier after our little talk, and I was greatly relieved that after his long conversation with Brynach, my dear son became more communicative and more involved in the arrangements for the funeral.

Now I am back at home, and need to recover myself from our ordeal. Betsi has gone to Llanychaer for a few days, since her own children are now old enough to manage without her. Ioan encouraged her to go, and during the crisis of the past week or so he has impressed me with his quiet support, his obvious affection and respect for his brother-in-law, and his capacity for clear thinking. I am lucky indeed to have Betsi, Ioan and Brynach as my nearest and dearest, and lucky that we have been able to support one another through this crisis. One day my beloved son will wish to talk with me, and when he does I will listen and give him sympathy. If he wishes it, I will give him advice founded on my own experience. God bless Anne and the little mite who would have been another Martha Morgan, had it not been for the intervention of Cruel Fate. I saw her, and she had brown eyes and black hair, and she was beautiful.

Now I am exhausted, and I need to sleep for a very long time.

ΩΩΩΩΩΩΩΩΩΩ

20th August 1837

Almost three weeks have passed since the death of Anne and the little one, and Brynach and his two children have gradually begun to adjust to life without a wife and a mother. I have been back and forth between Plas

Awakening

Ingli and Plas Llanychaer, staying for a few nights at a time, as have Betsi and Ioan. Now Brynach says that he must learn to cope on his own, and so we have withdrawn into the background. With old Mags at the helm, and with four other excellent servants in the house, including a young nursemaid, I am sure that things will settle down.

Last week I managed to find time with Brynach alone, and we seized the chance of a break in the rain to take a walk on the mountain above Llanychaer, leading up to the rocks of Garn Fawr and Garn Enoch. The sun even managed to peep out for a few minutes from behind the heavy ponderous clouds. At last he talked and at last he wept. I will not divulge what we talked about, but we opened our hearts to each other, as mother and son, and embraced each other beneath the wide sky. As we walked back downhill, soaked by the next spell of rain, he even laughed, and I knew that the process of healing was finally under way.

As I seek to adjust to the new circumstances at Llanychaer, I have to free myself from my recent obsession with family matters and lift my eyes to more distant horizons. Something has happened which confirms me in my belief that there is trouble ahead, but which has at the same time given me the confidence to believe that I will cope. It has also given all of us at the Plas something to smile about.

I decided two weeks ago that I would refuse to pay my tithe to Squire Owen of Gelli Fawr, on the grounds that it was now nothing more than a private tax which lined his pockets and brought no benefit to the Church. It was probably a foolish thing to do, but I was in a strange mood at the time and wanted a confrontation of some sort to divert my mind from family miseries. I said to his steward that there was no negotiating to do, and that I was perfectly able to pay, but chose not to. Because of last year's terrible harvest, the amount due to the Squire was quite modest, assessed at only five pounds and six shillings. It was simply that I refused to pay on principle. He said that my action was illegal and that he would bring down the full weight of the law upon me. Very well, said I, go ahead if you dare. I refused to attend the magistrates hearing last week, saying that I did not accept the jurisdiction of the Petty Sessions in such matters. I am not sure that I was expecting a distraint order to come my way, but five days ago one duly arrived, waved in the fist of none other than Master Henry Eynon the bailiff. I asked him politely if he had recovered from his recent ordeal at the hands of the *Ceffyl Pren*, and he scowled at me.

Awakening

"May I please see the order which you have in your hand?" I asked. "I am always very careful with documents."

Master Eynon handed it to me, and it gave authorization for the seizure of goods to the value of five pounds and ten shillings, being made up of the tithe due to Squire Owen and a few shillings added to cover the bailiff's costs. It was signed by Squire Owen and Squire Jobbins of Holmws. "Not good enough, Master Eynon," said I. "Squire Owen is not allowed by law to sign a distraint order when he himself is the beneficiary. I will keep this piece of paper in a safe place, in case the Lord Lieutenant wishes to see it at some future date. Now kindly go away and get another piece of paper with two impartial signatures on it as required by the law."

I really had no idea whether my complaint was justified or not, but Grandpa Isaac had tried this trick many years ago in my presence, and if it worked then, I saw no reason why it should not work again now. Master Eynon spluttered and growled, and grumbled that he was only doing his job. He said it was difficult and unpopular enough as it was, without awkward Mistresses quoting the law at him and making life even more miserable. So I sailed back indoors, leaving him and his henchmen to get back onto their cart and rumble off down the track to Newport, with countenances as black as thunder. When they were almost out of earshot I ran out and shouted after them: "Master Eynon, I will appreciate it if you do not call tomorrow as I have other pressing matters to attend to. Ten o'clock on Thursday would be convenient."

On Wednesday Will, Gomer and Bryn went to the barn and fetched a very heavy oak chest which had been buried under a pile of old horse harnesses for the past three years. It had come from Plas Cenarth when Betsi and Ioan had moved in with me some years back, but it had been too big and ugly to have in any of my rooms. We washed it and polished it, and put it in a prominent position in the parlour. Then we filled it with fine fabrics and other items designed to enhance its value. There was a good deal of giggling, which made me feel considerably better after the traumas of the recent past.

When Master Eynon arrived with his cart and his trusty assistants at ten of the clock yesterday morning, there was a crowd of about thirty people in the yard waiting to greet them with hissing and booing. I did not exactly rent them, but neither did I discourage their attendance. Purely by chance, they had all got to know that Martha Morgan, that troublesome

Awakening

Mistress of Plas Ingli, was due to have a distraint order served upon her by the bailiffs. This time Master Eynon had a piece of paper properly signed and sealed, and I let him into the house on condition that I would determine which furniture he should take into his possession. I said that the only thing I could part with was the valuable old chest in the parlour, which had been made by the Italian master craftsman Orlando Ernesto around the year 1650. I showed him the initials "OE" inscribed on the underside of the lid, and explained that it had been in my family for seven generations. "Unfortunately it is too big for this house," I explained, "and I am minded to put something lighter and smaller in its stead. Last time I had it valued I was offered twenty pounds for it. But you seem to be a reasonable and discerning fellow, and I know that times are not easy for bailiffs and their helpers, especially for those whose houses are lacking in furniture. Once I have emptied the chest of my personal possessions, you may carry it out of the Plas and dispose of it as you will. You may have it for fifteen pounds. Sell it at your next distraint sale. You will certainly get twenty pounds for it from a sophisticated buyer who knows good furniture when he sees it. Pay the Squire his five pounds and six shillings, take out your fee, and you are left with a very tidy profit."

"But Mistress, I have only come to collect goods to the value of five pounds and ten shillings. I do not want or need a big oak chest, even if it is made by Master Orlando Ernesto."

"Take it or leave it, Master Eynon. I assure you that nothing else is going to leave this house, and you are required by the rules of your employment to agree things amicably if at all possible. I am being as amicable as I can be."

Master Eynon and his fellows had a whispered consultation in the corner. "Ten pounds, Mistress. Not a penny more."

"Come now, Master Eynon. Thirteen pounds, and not a penny less."

So we settled on twelve pounds, counted out from his leather bag in clinking coinage. I gave him a written receipt, just to make matters official, and he gave me his official receipt for goods to the value of five pounds and ten shillings. There were plenty of witnesses. Then I took out all the linens and other fabrics and handed the chest over to its new owner. He and his fellows had quite a struggle to get it out of the house, and before bidding him farewell I warned him that the crowd outside might show some hostility towards him. "Oh, don't you worry, Mistress," said he. "We are used to that. It is a small enough price to pay for making an honest living."

So as the bailiffs loaded the crude chest made twenty years ago by fifteen-year-old Oliver Evans, apprentice carpenter at Plas Cenarth, they were jeered and shouted at by a goodly crowd of labourers and vagrants, and pelted with rotten eggs and vegetable scraps. "Shame on you, Henry Eynon!" they yelled. "Robbing a good lady just to feed that bastard squire! May you rot in Hell!"

When they had disappeared round the corner en route to the Cilgwyn road, we collapsed in hysterics, and invited the crowd in for a few jars of ale. I felt so benevolent that I paid them sixpence each for their contributions to the morning's entertainment.

ΩΩΩΩΩΩΩΩΩΩ

25th August 1837

News has reached me that Master Henry Eynon never did put that horrid chest into the distraint sale, and it may therefore be concluded that he has kept it himself as a long-term investment. He probably needed it anyway, since his household furnishings may be too sparse for his liking just now, following the furniture removals by the gentlemen of the *Ceffyl Pren*.

It is still less than a month since the tragedy at Llanychaer, but I have two very serious matters to deal with. The first, which comes as no surprise to me, is the inevitable failure of the corn harvest, for the second year running. Just as Shemi predicted, we have had rain every day for the last two months, and even if it stops tomorrow all of the barley, oats and wheat planted in this area is flattened and useless. For the most part the ears are not formed, but even where they are formed they are on the ground and germinating. Once the rain stops, which will be in mid-September according to Shemi, I will have to put the animals into the cornfields in the hope that they will eat something, and when they are done I will have to plough in everything that is left. This is confirmation, if any was needed, that hard times lie ahead. At least I have some hay in storage, which is more than can be said of my neighbours.

The other serious matter causes me to feel a tightness in the pit of my stomach, and I am still uncertain what to do about it. Today I managed to find a little time to myself, and I settled down to read three copies of the *Welshman* which have lain unopened on my bedside table. The first one was dated 8th August 1837, which was six days after Anne's death. There was nothing very exciting in it, but then when I was idly glancing through the small announcements I spotted this: *"The Editor and staff of this newspaper send our sincere condolences to our special correspondent in North Pembrokeshire, who has recently suffered a sad family bereavement where there should have been joy. We trust that he and his dear family will draw strength and consolation from the support of well-wishers near and far, and from the knowledge that they are held in the highest esteem and affection by the community."* There were no names, no dates, no addresses, but there was enough information contained in those words to set my heart beating wildly.

Then I remembered two other things. First, I recalled being considerably impressed by the vehemence of Brynach's expressions of opinion when we talked as a family many weeks ago on Chartism and such matters. He did seem to know a good deal about trade unionism and even about the editorial policy of the *Welshman* on matters which were not yet fully in the public domain. I was proud to discover the depth of his knowledge, but thought nothing further about it at the time. And second, I remembered that during the days spent at Plas Llanychaer between the tragedy and the funeral, at the beginning of the month, I had been helping Mags with domestic chores and had been gathering up garments for the washtub. Under a bench in the scullery I had found a canvas bag stuffed full of very old and dirty women's clothes -- a high-collared and long-sleeved cotton dress, a petticoat, a battered old straw bonnet, and a woollen shawl. I thought at the time that they must have belonged to one of the larger female servants, who had forgotten to put them into the wash. But now it came to me in a flash that there had been bits of straw stuck onto the shawl, and that there was so much black dirt around the collar of the dress and on the rim of the bonnet that it must have come from a face and neck covered in soot.

I may not have the wit or the intellect of my dear departed friend Joseph Harries, but at least I can add two and two together and make five.

5. A Growing Fury

8th October 1837

Since the rain stopped in mid-September we have had warm dry weather which has reduced hardship to some degree and also brought smiles to faces that were previously distorted by furrowed brows and hard lips.

I have been giving a good deal of thought to the matter of Brynach's involvement in the activities of the *Ceffyl Pren*. I have still not confronted him or asked him a direct question about his activities, because there is a part of me that thinks it is none of my business. But there is another part of me -- the maternal part -- which is seriously worried that he might get into trouble and then harm his two beloved children as a consequence. I admit to my own diary that I have been somewhat indecisive, not least because of my poor son's state of mind. I thought, after the passage of some weeks following the tragedy, that he had dealt with grief and had reached some accommodation with his changed circumstances. But no. His initial feelings of numbness and desolation, natural enough after losing the one and only great love of his life, have now given way to a bitterness and a cold anger that frightens me when I see it. On several occasions in the last fortnight he has vented his fury on the children when they have misbehaved, and has brought the poor mites running to me in tears. I have urged him to control his temper and to think of the needs of the children, and indeed he is filled with remorse immediately after every explosion of wrath, but he is having a very difficult time of it. Thank God for Betsi. She is proving to be an exemplary big sister, and having sensed the turmoil in his heart and soul, she has spent a good deal of time at Llanychaer of late, providing him and the children with the love and support which they need.

So I will bide my time before broaching this matter with Brynach, and will come to it when his anger has subsided. I have also been giving a good deal of thought to that premonition of five years ago, which I described at the beginning of this diary. I saw great waves coming in from the sea, overwhelming the community, and -- employing a strange sort of natural selection -- destroying only the houses of the rich and powerful. As

A Growing Fury

I have mulled over the many and varied causes of discontent among the poorer people, I am moving towards the idea that food prices, enclosures, lack of farm tenancies, rents and tithes are all contributing towards a growing fury, but that the thing which will finally tip this community from dumb acceptance into noisy conflict is the scandalous behaviour of the Turnpike Trusts. That may appear to be a strange conclusion for me to draw, but the evidence is incontrovertible.

When there is hardship or starvation in the countryside, and when costs are high and incomes low, it may be that one quite small thing may transform bearable suffering into something that is unbearable. Road tolls are quite small in themselves, and when they are low in comparison to a farmer's earnings he will accept them, especially if he sees that they are going to improve the highways that he needs for his daily and weekly journeys. But when the tolls are high, and rising, and his earnings are falling, and he sees corruption in the Turnpike Trusts, he immediately has a focus for his anger and frustration, and trouble will not be far away. I have had no startling vision to guide me in this matter, but my head tells me that there will be major confrontations on the highways in the coming months. I predict chaos, for I have inside knowledge.

For many years now I have been a trustee or a tally-holder of the Fishguard Turnpike Trust which was formed a long time ago, in 1791. Grandpa Isaac was a tally-holder, and so was my husband David, and so is Brynach. There are seventy-three of us altogether. The Trust, like all the others in West Wales, is supposed to levy road tolls at a standard rate as decreed by Parliament and to use the profits for the maintenance and improvement of the roads in its care. But sometimes there are no profits, since all of the income from the collection of tolls goes towards paying the clerk and the surveyor, defraying "expenses", and paying dividends to the tally-holders. So nothing is done to improve the roads, which are so full of pot-holes and ruts that it is sometimes safer for a coach and four to travel across adjacent fields than it is to follow the road. At meetings of the Trust, year after year, several of the tally-holders including Squires Byron Bailes, John Collyer, Mostyn Gittins and Dafydd Stokes have supported me in my complaints about bad management, but we have always found it difficult to prove corruption, and we are always outvoted by those who see the Trust as a tidy means of earning an income. There was an angry scene at last year's annual meeting of the Trust when I accused the trustees and the surveyor of siphoning off profits. Ten others supported me, but in the end we got nowhere. I thought of resigning there and then, but after talking to my young friend Nicholas Lloyd Cwmgloyn I decided in the end that it was easier to fight corruption from the inside than from the outside. Brynach advised me in similar terms. So for the time being there are three gates between Newport and Fishguard, and ten others to the south and west of Fishguard which are the focal points for more and more ugly confrontations between gatekeepers and local small farmers.

Following a new Act of Parliament, the Cemais Turnpike Trust has recently been formed, in order -- in theory -- to improve the roads to the east and south of Newport and to allow access from the outlying farms to the lime kilns at Parrog, Pwllgwaelod, Aberfforest and Ceibwr. I decided to take up my right to become a tally-holder, and for my sins I am now a part-owner of four Trusts, centred upon Fishguard, Cardigan, Cemais and Whitland. Most of the small farmers hate the Trusts, and they are uncertain of my motives in joining them, but I am determined to reform them if I can, and I will do it from within, by attending their somewhat irregular meetings and encouraging their trustees to keep good accounts, avoid abuses and spend their income wisely.

I predict that trouble is going to come from a recent trend which I have identified from my readings of the *Welshman* and the *Cambrian*. With many of the Trusts close to bankruptcy, there is a great move to increase the tolls. At the moment the tolls are three pence for a horse and rider, six pence for a horse drawing a carriage, six pence for a horse and cart, one shilling and sixpence for a score of cattle, and one shilling for a score of sheep. If lime is being carried, the toll is halved. There is no toll for mail coaches, or for carriages going to or coming from church, or attending funerals. Tally-holders and their animals and vehicles can pass through gates without charge. In this area, at the insistence of a number of tally-holders including myself, there is no toll for farmers who are carrying coal, manure, hay, corn or potatoes, or for farmers using a toll road for 300 yards or less for the purposes of husbandry. Return journeys are also toll free if within twenty-four hours of the outward journey. That all sounds good and reasonable, but it cannot be right for a farmer making a short journey to pay in tolls more than he pays a labourer for a day's work. I am gravely concerned that with gates surrounding towns like Newport and Whitland, farmers and other travellers making quite short journeys will have to pass through gates belonging to two or three different trusts who have different tolls and different rules as to exemptions. This is a recipe for disaster even if the tolls are not increased.

In the past each of the Trusts with which I have been identified has let its gates annually, usually to a local fellow who pays a fee for the privilege and then employs gatekeepers for a few shillings a week to collect the tolls. It is not a very profitable business in this area, since there is very little traffic, but inland, and towards the coalfields and industrial parts of Carmarthenshire, there is more business to be had. Recently we have seen the appearance of a new breed of toll-farmers who treat the gathering of tolls as big business. One such is Thomas Bullin, who lives somewhere towards Neath and who has bought his way into a powerful position in West Wales. He now holds all the gates of the Tavernspite, Milford and Cardigan Trusts, and I suspect that he has his beady eye on Fishguard, Whitland and Cemais as well. If Master Bullin and his cronies take control we will see a new harshness in toll collection, no allowance of credit, stronger use of the Petty Sessions to punish defaulters or those who evade or bypass the gates, and measures taken to block off small roads through the use of "side bars." I am in no doubt at all that Bullin will want new gates to be erected so as to increase his income. And I am sure we will also see unauthorized gates and chains going across roads which are actually maintained by the parishes and not by the trusts.

I will use whatever influence I have to keep Bullin out of this area and to hold down the tolls and the numbers of gates, but elsewhere there may be bigger battles to be fought.

ΩΩΩΩΩΩΩΩΩΩ

21st October 1837

Today Brynach and the little ones came to dinner, and we had a most convivial time together. After our meal we decided on a walk on the common. However, the children wanted to go and catch monster fish in the river, so they went off downhill in the company of Bessie with their nets and buckets, while Brynach and I walked arm in arm up the mountain.

We talked of Anne, and of that fateful day in August, and I was greatly relieved that he felt able to talk freely of his own feelings. I sensed that the anger which had burned in his breast had subsided somewhat, and told him so.

"Yes, I admit it, Mother," he said. "For some weeks I was consumed by a sort of hatred of the world, and I blamed it for my misery. I could see no joy or innocence, not even in the eyes of Rose and David. It was a sort of madness, I daresay. I convinced myself that I was responsible for the deaths of Anne and the baby. I thought that I was as strong as the next man, but I fear that I would have collapsed entirely under the weight of guilt had it not been for the support of you and Betsi and Ioan. I am truly blessed to have such a family around me."

"That, I daresay, is why families exist, my dear son, and why your father wanted you to be a part of one."

"I know, Mam, and I know why he wanted me to become one of the Morgans of Plas Ingli," said he, with a smile on his face. "I know, too, why he carefully arranged everything so that you would be my mother. I think he probably loved you, just like every other red-blooded man within a radius of twenty miles!"

I would not be drawn on that one. He kissed me gently on the cheek. Then he asked: "Has this whole time been as hard for you as it has been for me and the children?"

"Of course it has, *cariad*. I loved Anne as a daughter, you know that. And there has been another dagger in my heart arising from the knowledge that the little girl would have been baptized in the name of Martha. But what you may or may not understand is the manner in which a mother feels a son's pain. I have carried your pain with me from the day Anne died, not because you asked or expected it of me, but because that is something that goes with motherhood. Please do not ask me to explain it -- I do not understand it myself."

"Mother *bach*, I accept what you say, of course, and I love you all the more for it. You always did have a tendency to feel other people's pain. In the past I put it down to your special powers, but now you say that it is just a matter of maternity. Perhaps you feel maternal instincts towards all who suffer, or maybe you are just a natural martyr......."

I realized that he was grinning, and teasing me. So I boxed his ears, and we ended up, mother and son, laughing hysterically, lying on our backs on a patch of purple heather and looking up at the sky.

"How wonderful to hear you laughing again, Brynach," I said.

"Your fault entirely, Mother. Here you are, leading me astray again when I should be sitting at home feeling miserable."

"I have two missions in life, dearest son. The first is to lead people astray, and the second is to be a terrible mother."

He laughed again, and for several minutes we gazed up at the scudding clouds and enjoyed the warmth of the autumn sun on our faces. Strangely, I felt closer to Brynach then than I had done since he was a small baby.

"Brynach, can I ask you a straight question, and will you give me a straight answer?"

"I promise nothing, but try me."

"Have you been involved in the activities of the *Ceffyl Pren* in the neighbourhood in recent months?"

There was a long silence, and then he said: "Yes, Mother. I cannot tell a lie to you. But I will not apologize, for without the activities of the foreman and his jury there would be precious little justice for anybody in the country districts of West Wales."

"I can accept that. You have had a little harmless fun, and so have I, at the expense of a few arrogant and silly people. But do you realise that what you and your confederates have started will soon become less frivolous, and harder, and angrier, and will lead to people getting hurt?"

"I think we can control it, Mother."

"I doubt it, *cariad*. I have seen mass protests before, and I have seen men killed because of them. Your innocent escapades will spiral out of control, and soon you will have more than a few elderly gentlemen disguised as constables to deal with. You realise that if this escalates, we will have Metropolitan Policemen in town, and possibly even the Yeomanry and the Fusiliers marching along our lanes and across our green fields?"

"Why should anybody take little Newport seriously? Why, in the House of Commons they have probably not even heard of us!"

"Now there you are wrong. The Lord Marcher has friends in high places, and one of them is the Lord Lieutenant, who is charged with keeping the peace on behalf of the Queen. And pray do not forget,

A Growing Fury

Brynach, that this is not the only place where there are grievances, and where there will be riots and other disturbances in the months to come. The Home Secretary will not stand idly by while West Wales goes up in flames."

"You exaggerate, Mother."

"Indeed I do not. Shemi told me the other day that he had heard bugles, drums, galloping hooves, clashing sabres and cascades of muskets in the middle of a calm moonlit night. And then the shouts of a fleeing rabble, and the cries of wounded men and horses. That means fusiliers and dragoons in conflict with foolish fellows like you who have failed to predict the consequences of their actions."

"Mother, this country is rotten to the core, and I will not accept the suffering I see around me day after day. I am prepared to fight for what I believe in, and to take the consequences."

"Spoken like a hero and an idiot, Brynach. Do you realise that if you take part in an ill-considered riot, or are betrayed by somebody who wishes you ill, you could be arrested by the constables or taken by the army? And do you realise that you could end up rotting in the colonies, or rotting on the end of a rope?"

"Impossible, Mother. I am gentry, and they know it. They do not hang members of the gentry."

"That is where you are wrong, son. If you are involved in a riot in which a soldier or a magistrate is killed, they will look for exemplary justice. Look what happened to Dic Penderyn at Merthyr Tydfil. He was innocent, and the Home Secretary knew it, but they needed a scapegoat, so Dic was strung up on the gallows. A member of the minor gentry in this area would do very nicely, just to show that the justice system is impartial and that nobody is above the law. When I was young I was stripped to the waist and scourged behind the whipping cart from one end of town to the other, at a time when everybody thought that such a thing could not possibly happen to the Mistress of a fine estate."

Brynach looked thoughtful, so I continued, trying to keep my voice and my passions under control. "I admire your idealism and your foolhardy courage, Brynach. I admire the fact that you are prepared to risk everything -- including your life -- for the greater good. But since you started on this escapade, everything has changed. Your wife is dead, and you are now on your own with two very small children to bring up. They would be utterly destroyed, were they to lose a father, having already lost a mother. Do you not love them more than anything else on this earth?"

"Of course I do."

" So you would be insane to risk anything that might cause your bond with them to be broken."

"Life is dangerous, Mother. I could fall off a horse tomorrow and kill myself."

"That may be so. But not even the blackest villain would increase a thousand-fold the risk of leaving two beloved children alone in this world and blighted by misery." I turned over onto my front, and looked him straight in the eye. Then I said: "Your children love you, Brynach, and I will never, never forgive you if you betray them. I mean that."

He thought for a long time. "You may be right, Mother........"

"I know that I am right. Remember too, if you will, that you have other responsibilities. The servants, tenants and labourers of the Llanychaer estate depend upon you for their livelihoods. You are doing now what your father and your grandfather wanted you to do. You are also my beloved son and the rightful owner of this estate. At present I share your burden, but when I am gone you will have other farms and other people to look after. If you want to do something for the world, and something courageous, that is quite enough to be going on with."

Then he laughed. "Enough, Mother! You win, as ever."

"Will you promise me that you will never again take part in a riot or mass protest involving the *Ceffyl Pren*, or in any other riot for that matter?"

"Very well, if you insist upon it."

"And will you promise me that you will stay clear of any secret meetings or other gatherings of the rioters designed to plan actions against those they deem to be enemies, or against property, or against the forces of law and order?"

"You sound like an attorney, and drive a hard bargain, Mother. Yes, yes, I promise it."

"Thank God for that. Now, you may give me a kiss to show that you love me even though I may be a miserable old mother who is out to spoil your nocturnal boyish adventures."

So he kissed me, and stood up, and pulled me to my feet. "Mother *bach*, it is time to go home," he laughed. "Those children will probably be back by now, wanting to show us the giant fish which they have caught in the stream."

So we walked back down the slope to the Plas, arm in arm, and talking of this and that. Before we arrived, I said: "By the way, do not be too surprised, dearest son, if I show a little interest in the activities of the *Ceffyl Pren* myself. Unlike you, I have absolutely nothing to lose, and I enjoy a little excitement now and then."

His eyes opened wide in amazement, but before he could say anything, I added: "Good, good. No objections then. And since you do not object to that, I will not object if you continue with your interesting reports in that excellent newspaper called the *Welshman*. Your reports will be a little less detailed in the future, maybe, but I am sure that we will find ways and means of getting firsthand accounts of one thing or another over to your writing desk in Llanychaer. The public has a right to know."

And as he stood on the doorstep of my beloved house with his mouth open, I waltzed into the kitchen with a happy smile on my face.

ΩΩΩΩΩΩΩΩΩΩ

3rd March 1838

It has been a hard winter with widespread distress across the community, partly because of the harvest failures of last summer. I have tried to alleviate suffering where I have found it, but it has been difficult enough to keep my own tenants and labourers alive and fed. So severe was the food shortage that our Christmas celebrations were very curtailed, and I could not afford a Christmas Day feast at the Plas. Instead, our three households joined together and combined our resources of food and drink at Plas Llanychaer after the *Plygain* service in the parish church. That was no bad thing, and we all felt that for the sake of Brynach and the children the old house needed light and laughter to help in the recovery from the dark days following Anne's death. And it was a very happy time, in spite of the inevitable moments of poignancy and sadness. At *Hen Galan*, in January, having calculated with Bessie that there were modest resources left in our pantry, I invited all of our tenants and labourers and their families to the Plas for a jolly event. There was not much to eat, but we drank well, and there was some excellent singing. At the end of it, some people were incapable of finding their way home, and had to sleep on the kitchen floor. Even those with the sorest of heads insisted that they had had a good time, and I believed them.

To more serious matters. With such hardship across the community, one further shipload of emigrants has departed to America from the Parrog, and others have left to seek a better life in the industrial districts. Those who have stayed have been so pressed for cash that they have been defaulting on their payments of rent, tithes, and road tolls. Prosecutions have been frequent, and the magistrates have been issuing distraint orders by the score. Mean-spirited magistrates like John Owen and Thomas Watkins have apparently taken delight in applying the letter of the law, and have been quite impervious to the entreaties of the defaulters and the attorneys who have represented them. Brynach has been appointed a magistrate, and he has sat at many Petty Sessions himself, trying to exercise moderation and flexibility. But he says that he cannot for ever set aside the law and the penalties prescribed for defaulters, and that he often has to defer to the counsel of the older magistrates who sit on the bench beside him. Tolerant and kind magistrates like Dafydd Stokes and Byron Bayles have themselves had to make heartbreaking judgements against people who have no food in their larders and no pennies in their pockets. So Master Eynon and his fellow bailiffs have been hard at work, confiscating crude items of furniture and even precious personal possessions which are then sold at auction for a few shillings to defray debts and expenses.

Since the middle of January there have been five distraint sales in Newport, and they have each involved ugly confrontations between the bailiffs and the common people. The constables have tried to keep order, and there have been a number of arrests for violent behaviour and affray. At three of the sales no buyers would come forward for any of the items put up for auction. So the items were sold for pittances to various cronies of Squire Owen and to the thugs who assist Master Eynon in his work. These fellows have then gone to Fishguard and Cardigan and sold on these goods at a tidy profit, compounding the fury of the locals. And then, because the distraint sales have failed to make enough money to cover the debts of the defaulters, the bailiffs have gone back to their houses again and taken more goods to sell and make up the shortfall. The only consequence of this insanity is the reduction of more and more people to pauperism. They will throw themselves upon the mercy of the new Guardians of the Cardigan Union, who will, with the aid of contributions from me and the rest of the gentry, provide them with some poor relief for the time being. But soon, with the completion of the Cardigan Workhouse, these miserable people will be dragged out of their community and incarcerated there with virtually no prospect of returning to a normal life.

Inevitably there have been more riots, and the *Ceffyl Pren* has been out and about. Ricks have been burnt at Gelli Fawr, Pengelli Fawr, Trewern and Pentre Ifan, because those are places inhabited by men who are deemed to be enemies of the people. Effigies of Squire Owen, Thomas Watkins and the Rector have been burnt in broad daylight in the middle of town by crowds of up to a hundred men dressed in women's clothes and disguised with blackened faces. I saw one of these charades myself, and recognized many of the men who took part, and if I knew them, so did many others. But the constables are frightened, and no arrests are made because nobody will give evidence against the rioters. Thank God that Brynach is no longer involved, except in his capacity as a shadowy and furtive special correspondent for the *Welshman*. His reports have been good, though I say it myself, and when I read them I am reminded that he certainly has many friends within the *Ceffyl Pren* jury.

Very early this morning I was terrified when, about two hours before dawn, I awoke with a start and heard the bugles and the drums of the *Ceffyl Pren* mob in the distance. I opened the shutters, and saw the torches spluttering and sparking in the wind. There was no doubt that the mob was heading towards the Plas. I convinced myself immediately that the Plas was about the be attacked, and I also felt a deep sense of betrayal in the light of the fact that I have always supported the poor in their struggles against oppression. Not as blatantly as I might have done, perhaps, but evidently enough to have caused eyebrows to be raised and heads to be shaken in the fine gentry drawing rooms of North Pembrokeshire. Why should I now be singled out for the rough justice of the mob? Had I not made a stand against the injustice of the tithe system? Had I not argued to keep down the local toll rates when they were rising elsewhere? I was angry and close to tears. Were they now going to burn my precious ricks to the ground? Did these men not realise that without my gifts of hay over the last three months to the poor people of the neighbourhood, they would by now have no house cows to give them milk, and no porkers in their pig sties, and no sheep upon the common? Without me, starvation would have been rife, and more poor people would have died.........

In a panic I woke everybody in the house, and in our nightgowns and nightshirts we watched in horror as the mob came closer. They were shouting and waving their torches with gay abandon, and it appeared that many of them were drunk. As ever, the men all had blackened faces, and all wore old and battered women's clothes. I asked Bryn and Gomer to get dressed and to prepare to defend the ricks with their lives, and to their credit they threw some old clothes over their shoulders, lit candle lanterns, and ran out to the barn in order to assemble whatever weapons they could find. They then mounted guard in the rickyard, armed with sickles, pitchforks and billhooks. Then, much to my own surprise, I threw a cloak over my shoulders and ran out to the yard entrance, where I stood and awaited the arrival of the rioters. I thought that I would probably be somewhat less effective than King Canute when confronted by an incoming tide, but I thought that it was incumbent upon me to try and defend my little estate.

The mob approached to within five yards of me, with bugles still blaring and drums still thumping. The foreman of the jury, who had been riding on his hobbyhorse, dismounted very theatrically. Then he held up his hand for silence, and got it. I recognized him in spite of his black face and pretty dress as Dafydd Ifan from Gamallt, the man who had led the mob in town in the first of the riots. Then my heart sank when I noticed in the light of the torches that there was a horse and cart at the rear end of the procession. Oh no, I thought, they have come to confiscate possessions, as well as burning down my ricks. I felt my temperature rise, and I daresay that my eyes blazed. I took a step towards Master Ifan, and wagged my finger in his face. "Now then, Ifan Gamallt," I stormed. "This is just not good enough.........."

He held up his hand and shut me off in midstream. "My dear Mistress Morgan, you look very beautiful this morning, if I may make so bold. Hum hum. To the business in hand. It has come to the notice of certain gentlemen of this jury, to whom I refer as my beloved sisters, that you recently suffered a grave injustice when that evil bastard Eynon called upon you and took possession of valuable property that is rightfully yours. That was a gross violation of the home of a good lady. Correct, sisters?"

There was a low rumble of "Yes indeeds" and "Quite corrects" from the beautiful sisters.

"Well now, Mistress, it so happens that this very night we had certain business to conduct at the house of that snivelling bastard, if you will excuse the expression, with certain items of furniture and other possessions requiring repatriation. While we were in the process of emptying the house, which was indeed the least we could do in the circumstances, as I am sure you will agree, one of my sisters, who shall be nameless, said "Oh my goodness, is not that chest in the corner the very one that was taken away from Mistress Morgan some little time ago?" And another sister said "*Diawch*! I do believe it is." And so it was determined by a unanimous decision of the jury, Mistress........."

"Quite so, sister. By acclamation, indeed!" came a falsetto shout from the back of the mob.

".........that we should repatriate said chest to the place from whence it came. By damn it was heavy, Mistress, but that is the way with valuable furniture made by Italian master craftsmen. So we put it on the cart, and it is our privilege to return it to you here and now. Sisters, bring forth the chest, and place it where it rightfully belongs!"

So with due ceremony, four of the hairy black-faced sisters lifted the chest off the cart and carried it into the house. I was speechless and useless, but Bessie reacted with great presence of mind, and thanked them all profusely for their kindness. She showed the fellows into the parlour, and indicated exactly the "proper position" for the chest against the wall.

After that there was a good deal of cheering and laughing, and considerable relief on the part of the inhabitants of the Plas. The least we could do, in the circumstances, was to give the members of the mob a few jars of ale. Seldom has the kitchen of the Plas been graced by such a gathering of sophisticated and delicate sisters. At last they went on their way, heading off in various directions so as to change sex and be back in their beds before dawn.

After breakfast, when we had all recovered, we dragged that horrid ugly chest back to its proper position in the barn. And that is where it will stay, out of sight if not out of mind, covered once again by barley dust and old horse harnesses.

15th April 1838

On such a day as this, even the most resolute of atheists and the most pagan of witch-doctors could not doubt the existence of Heaven. It is here, all around me, and while I am immersed in it there is no place for dark thoughts and misery. Since I was woken up by a torrent of birdsong at dawn, celebration has been the order of the day, and I thought that there could be no better way to celebrate than to walk alone upon the mountain.

After breakfast I told Bessie and the others what I planned to do, and they were very encouraging. I daresay that they are always pleased when I am out of the way, for they occasionally need space around themselves just as I do. Gwenno made me up a little bundle of crusty bread and butter, cheese and ham, and one of the few apples we managed to harvest last autumn. She added a bottle of raspberry cordial, which is my favourite drink when I am in a mood for exercise and observation. By nine of the clock I was striding along the track towards the top edge of our enclosed land. Above me was a cloudless sky, and there was a warm sun upon my back. The air was perfectly still. In among the hedgerows and the old stone walls I counted the flowers in bloom -- primrose, violet, cowslip, white dead nettle, celandine, dandelion, and even the last of the daffodils and the first of the bluebells. On one shady bank, beneath a cluster of overhanging bushes, there was a sheet of delicate white wood anemones. And when I looked closely among the bursting greenery I found, hidden away, wild strawberry, toadflax, stitchwort, herb robin, ground ivy and forget-me-not. Self-effacing little flowers, all of them, unlike the brash and brave foxglove, cow parsley, red campion and sorrell which will take over their timid world within a fortnight. Although the big trees around the Plas were not yet in leaf, some of the bushes in sheltered places were well advanced, and I noticed with delight what exotic colourings there were on the first leaves of the spring. The colours of the bursting buds of honeysuckle and sycamore were so delicately tinted with pink and white and red that I thought them almost more beautiful than the flowers over which they would soon cast their protective canopy. As I climbed, the softer trees gave way to spiky furze and thorn bushes, and I was flanked by such masses of golden-yellow furze blossoms and snow-white mayflower as I have never seen before. Or maybe I had indeed seen them, but never noticed?

A Growing Fury

I followed the iron water pipe up towards Ffynnon Brynach, anointed my forehead with a few drops of the sacred water, and wandered off across the common. Underfoot were dry white grasses and the broken stalks of last year's bracken, and I was amazed to find little patches of violets in areas which will soon be devoid of light, shaded and overwhelmed by the new bracken which will spring up like a miniature forest. In the damp areas of the common there were trickling rivulets, little stony stream beds and patches of fresh green moss and cotton grass. Here and there I walked across areas burnt by Will and Gomer last month, or last year, or the year before that, all with the gaunt scorched branches of the furze bushes standing out in black relief above a carpet of fresh grass. Idly, as I walked, I wondered how many generations of burning there had been on this mountain, and how many generations of Morgans had walked across the scorched areas as they turned green, and thought "Ah yes, that's another three acres of good grazing for the sheep next summer."

Then I heard the cuckoo, singing that weird demented song of his in a little copse of small trees no more than twenty yards from where I stood. He flew off as I approached, and settled in a bush some way down the slope, and carried on giving his mad message to the world. I could not for the life of me work out how any small bird could possibly allow such a creature within a hundred yards of its precious nest. Up on the skyline a kestrel fluttered and swooped. A buzzard mewed somewhere, but I could not see it even though I narrowed my eyes and scanned the whole mighty sweep of the heavens. A pheasant called in alarm from some secret cover in Gelli Woods. And as I climbed onto the tumbled boulders which led eventually to the mountain summit, I was struck by the full force of the skylark choir and reminded that this was their natural and familiar territory, not mine or the Lord Marcher's.

I climbed up the steepest part of the slope, risking that I might fall or trip over my long skirts, but the rocks were dry and I was driven upwards by a sort of elation. So I leaped about from rock to rock like a mountain goat, and used my hands to help me in scrambling up the steepest slabs where cracks and crevices provided hand-holds and foot-holds. In truth it was not so much of an adventure, since I knew every inch of the way, having climbed across those rocks a hundred or a thousand times before. I laid a little wager with myself that when I reached the summit I would look down on where the coast should be and see nothing but sea mist. And so it was. The bay and the far cliffs and the little town that I loved and hated were quite invisible beneath a thick blanket of grey-white cloud which moved and heaved almost imperceptibly but on this occasion failed to make any progress inland. There it stayed, wrapped around the northern and eastern slopes of the mountain.

So I settled down on the grassy patch near the summit, feeling very smug and snug as I basked in warm sunshine and thought of the people of the town creeping about miserably in a damp cold drizzle. I ate my little picnic, and as I did so a green lizard scuttled towards me, spotted me, and hurried off again. Butterflies came and went at their leisure, settling onto the warm crusty rocks and spreading and closing their wings to some mysterious rhythm. The skylarks still sang. In the distance I could hear a flock of squabbling gulls following a harrow, but I thought that the stillness and the warmth of the day had made my sheep and those of my neighbours contented and even sleepy, for I could not hear a single lamb calling for its mother. What a contrast, I thought, to the month of March, when lambing had been in full swing and the sounds echoing around the *cwm* had been made by sheep and their lambs, and buffeting winds, and small boys in the newly-sown fields as they operated their assorted bird-scaring devices.

Silence, and skylarks, and tranquillity............

I woke with a start, and realized that the sun had come round a good ten degrees in the sky and that it was dropping westwards. The old raven was there on his crag, watching me. Perhaps he was even watching over me. So I thanked him for his kindness, and gathered up the remains of my picnic, and set off down the slope towards home. Master Raven preened his feathers nonchalantly, and watched me go.

As I scrambled down the slope I thought what a strange thing it was that on such a day I should feel so close to Heaven while knowing, in my heart of hearts, that in the little hovels and cottages of the *cwm* men, women and children were haunted by the twin spectres of starvation and poverty. While I had snoozed on the summit with my straw bonnet over my eyes they had probably been slaving away in one of my fields, or somebody else's, for a penny or two, or gathering sorrell leaves, or working out how best to catch a squirrel or a wood-pigeon for their supper. April and May, the two months painted in the brightest colours of a bountiful God, were the starvation months which all poor people anticipated with fear and struggled to survive. No bountiful God for them, at least not until June arrived and brought with it some relief in the form of edible things in the hedgerows, and money from the hay harvest, and food from my pantry for the haymakers.

When I arrived back at the house, Bessie was waiting for me on the doorstep. "Mistress Martha!" said she, looking and sounding very fierce. "I watched you as you climbed up there among those rocks, and thought that you had taken leave of your senses! Leaping about like a mad thing, you were. I was quite convinced that you would slip and disappear for ever down some mighty crevasse. If I may say so, it is not seemly for the Mistress of a grand estate to behave like a mountain goat, especially when she is being watched."

"Well, you have watched me before, Bessie, and you may watch me again. I may be a Mistress and a grandmother, but I am still in good working order, and I might as well leap about until rheumatism forces me into the settle by the fire."

Bessie grinned. "Quite so, Mistress. My concern arises largely from the fact that Squire Jobbins from Holmws was doing the watching with me. He was, I assure you, quite amazed by your antics."

I was immediately overtaken by a fit of the giggles, and the more I thought about Squire Jobbins and imagined the expression on his face as he looked up towards me and the mountain, the funnier it all became. I thought him to be the most serious and respectable gentleman within a radius of fifty miles of the Plas, who might be overcome with embarrassment by the most fleeting glimpse of a lady's ankle. Then Bessie burst out into laughter as well, and soon the pair of us were quite out of control, hooting and howling, and bursting our stays. We had to hold each other up, and at last staggered into the kitchen arm in arm, with tears of mirth rolling down our faces. There we encountered thoroughly disapproving looks from Gwenno and Liza, and for some inexplicable reason that compounded our amusement, and we took a very long time to return from hysterics to some sort of equilibrium.

At last Liza gave us a cup of tea each, and when she judged that I was once again capable of rational responses she handed me a letter. "Master Jobbins left this for you, Mistress," she said. "He jotted it down for you when he realized that you were heading up the mountain, and when we told him that you had a picnic with you and might be some time." I nodded, and opened the letter. Then I read it out loud, since I could not imagine that it contained anything that I would not wish to share with my handmaidens. This is what it said:

> *My dear Mistress Martha,*
>
> *My deepest apologies for arriving at the Plas unannounced. That was a most ungentlemanly thing to do, and I must further apologize for any embarrassment occasioned by my observance of your mountaineering activities, which I daresay you might have wished to keep to yourself. You may rest assured, Madam, that my lips are sealed.*

"My goodness," said Liza, "a very apologetic and discreet fellow he is, to be sure." Gwenno and Bessie giggled.

> *To more serious matters. Had we met today I might have communicated to you certain concerns. I bear you no ill will, and indeed I see much to admire in your good little estate and in the Llanychaer estate managed by your dear son Brynach. It would be a sad thing indeed should the good name of the Morgan family be adversely affected by ill-considered talk or by a loss of confidence among your neighbours.*

"He is threatening you, Mistress," said Bessie. "This is not the first time we have heard such language from those who purport to be your friends."

> *I will not elaborate further until we have an opportunity to meet. However, I will say just this -- there is some talk about the sympathy demonstrated by you and other members of your family for certain troublesome causes. There is further talk about some of the company you keep. If I may say so, your opinions on matters which are of no concern to a lady are a little too loudly voiced and a little too widely canvassed, and I urge you -- as a friend -- to be more discreet. Those of us who have been blessed with responsibility for the welfare of our fellow men, and who have been entrusted with the maintenance of law and order, are more than a little concerned that our united purpose is breaking down. I fear that should we be riven by dissension the consequence may be disaster for all civilized people.*
>
> *I am, Madam, yours faithfully,*
>
> *James Jobbins*
> *Squire, Holmws*

A Growing Fury

Twenty years ago I would have been greatly worried by such a letter, and even intimidated by its tone. But not any longer. Now I felt a sort of thrill, compounded perhaps by the sensuous delights of my day upon the mountain and by my recent very silly behaviour in the company of Bessie. "So Squire Jobbins is warning me, and watching me, on behalf of the forces of darkness," I said. "Neither his visit nor his scribbled words surprise me, and he has clearly come here as a one-man deputation. Maybe he has visited Ioan and Brynach as well, in an attempt to intimidate them....."

"Indeed he has, Mistress," said Gwenno. "He said as much while he was here watching you cavorting among the boulders on the mountain."

"I wager that he got short shrift from both of them. They may be young, but they are very modern young gentlemen. Their respect has to be earned, and I doubt that Master Jobbins has earned it."

"Quite right you are, Mistress," said Bessie. "He did seem to be somewhat displeased with the Morgan family in general. He did not say much, but I could read it in his demeanour. He was very agitated."

"Perhaps that was because, from a considerable distance, he had an exciting view of my petticoats?"

"I doubt that. I hope, for his sake, that he has seen waving petticoats before. But I urge you to be careful, Mistress. Master Jobbins has many cronies, and some of them are not very pleasant."

I nodded, and we left the matter there. I did not reply to the Squire's letter, since I thought that to do so would be a sign of weakness. But I did call Will in to the parlour for a little talk before he went home after his day's work. He knew about Master Jobbins' visit already, but I told him about the letter and about the suspicions of certain of the gentry that I was too close to some of the unlawful events that have occurred in the recent past. I also told him that I was probably being watched, and that great discretion was required of all of us.

"Don't you worry, Mistress *bach*," he said, giving me a wink. "All under control, it is. My mates have been watching the watchers for some little time, and one of them ended up in the river down at Trefelin the other day, just for his pains. Just a little wetting, mind -- nothing more serious. What with everything being so busy on the land now in the coming weeks and months, I doubt that much will happen, and you can be sure that if anything does occur it will not be here. My spies are older and more respectable than they were, Mistress, but there are none better in the business than Abby, Halfpint, Faggot and Daffy. When there is something that you need to know, Mistress, you may be sure that you will be the first to know it."

ΩΩΩΩΩΩΩΩΩΩ

22nd July 1838

The summer is set to be another disaster. After the mild spring we had a rapid spurt in the growth of the grass, and hopes were high that we would be blessed by a good hay harvest. But then in May, shortly after my 60th birthday, it started to rain, and since then we have hardly had three dry days in succession. For most of the farmers and labourers the hay harvest is lost, as it was last year. Luckily I had decided to cut hay off my sandiest field, Parc Haidd, this year, and in late June I managed to get it cut, turned, carted and ricked at high speed. It is too wet, and will probably ferment or ignite in the rick, but there is a chance that I will have something to feed to my animals during the coming winter.

Once again, the spectre of famine is sidling across the sodden landscape. Four people have died in Newport. Havard Medical puts the deaths down to cholera or some such thing, but the real cause of death in each case was poverty. Several more families have left in despair to seek work and a better life in the coal mining and iron-working districts to the east. And two weeks since, another thirty people joined the brigantine *Mary Louise* when it called at the Parrog en route for the United States. At this rate the inexorable rise and rise of the local population will be halted and even turned into a decline; and indeed there is something to be said for migration as an alternative to a slow and miserable death.

In recent weeks the hairy ladies of the *Ceffyl Pren* gang have been out and about three times, burning effigies and informing certain squires of their displeasure. There has been an attack on the Castle Mill, not aimed at the miller and his wife but at Thomas Lloyd the Lord Marcher, who lives far away in Carmarthenshire and who is seen by the locals as a parasite rather than as a benefactor and protector. But the most serious trouble has been down on the Parrog, where two of the warehouses have been burnt down, destroying all the imported corn and other goods stored in them. Skiff's warehouses were untouched, since he has a reputation for fair trading and for looking after those who still belong to the class from which he has extracted himself. I cannot see where all of this is going to end, since the gang is getting more and more daring and more contemptuous of the law. I am greatly afraid that somebody will be hurt or even killed if this unrest continues.

ΩΩΩΩΩΩΩΩΩΩ

30th July 1838

My fears have been confirmed, and the good-natured tomfoolery of the earliest *Ceffyl Pren* episodes has turned into something much more sinister. Now, not only do we have violence directed against property, and anger directed against those in authority, but also cruelty inflicted upon those who are themselves poor and vulnerable.

Three days ago my friend Patty paid a visit to the Plas, and she reported that an old widow woman called Mistress Jane Dafis, who lived three doors away from her on the Parrog, had been foolish enough to respond to a poster recently put up by the magistrates. That notice offered a reward of five pounds for any information leading to the arrest and conviction of the men who burned down the warehouses on the 15th day of July. The widow, probably driven by hunger rather than malice, reported to the constables that she recognized five of the men involved in the riot, and she proceeded to name them. All five were arrested and taken into custody, but they all insisted that they had been elsewhere at the time of the burnings, and since there was no other evidence to incriminate them they had to be released after two nights in the lock-up. On the very next night, at two o'clock in the morning, Mistress Dafis was visited by the *Ceffyl Pren* and evicted from her cottage. She was not handled roughly, but she was forced to watch while the "sisters" took all of her furniture and belongings from the cottage and piled them up on the trackway outside. Then they set her cottage on fire, and when it was reduced to a pile of smouldering rubble they advised the poor woman that she was no longer welcome in the neighbourhood, and disappeared into the night. Mistress Dafis was left there, dressed only in her nightgown, weeping and wailing as she stood surveying the smoking remnants of her home.

Patty took pity on her and took her in, but Mistress Dafis knew that she could not stay in Newport or the Parrog, and now she has gone with her meagre belongings to live with her daughter in Letterston. I hope that she will be safe there, but I fear that she is now known as a traitor and informer, and that this reputation will have travelled with her. Patty says she is not a malicious woman, but she is certainly a very foolish one, and we are all reminded that in the present circumstances small actions can have truly terrible repercussions.

Following Patty's visit, I thought long and hard about what to do next. I was sitting in my dressing-room, still thinking, when there was a knock on my door. "Come in!" I shouted, and in came a deputation consisting of all three of my menservants -- Will, Gomer and Bryn. "Please forgive us, Mistress," said Will, the natural leader. "We know that we have work to do, and should be out and about, but very concerned we are, and wish for a quiet word or two. Would that be acceptable?"

"By all means, Will," said I. "This visit is very opportune, since I wish for a quiet word with you too, and probably on the same matter. You first. Sit down and tell me what troubles you."

"Very delicate it is, Mistress." He swallowed hard, and looked like a small child who has stolen the last apple from the pantry. "Would you be surprised if I was to tell you that we three fellows have been out and about with the *Ceffyl Pren*?"

"Not in the least, Will. What you do in the middle of the night is up to you, but from your blackened collars and your red eyes I have long since drawn certain conclusions."

"Well, Mistress, times are hard, as you know only too well. Not for us, I hasten to add, for you are the best and kindest of Mistresses. But we have to support our brothers in distress, even if certain risks have to be taken. You take my point, Mistress?"

"Of course I do, Will. And I admire you, all three, for your courage and your loyalty to your comrades."

"Then there is the matter of Master Brynach........"

I felt my heart miss a beat. "Surely he is not still taking part in the administration of *Ceffyl Pren* justice?" I gasped. "He promised me that all that was behind him."

"Never fear, Mistress. Indeed it is behind him, and we have not seen him in action since last year. He met Bryn one day and explained that he had come to realise that what with his responsibilities to the children and the estate following the death of Mistress Anne, he had to retreat from public life for a while. We quite understand that, Mistress. He will support us in other ways, of that we have no doubt."

"You may count on it. But why do you mention him now?"

"Because, Mistress, since he left us there is nobody in the gang to speak with a voice of reason. As times get harder, the men are getting more and more angry, and there is a clamour for blood. Is that not right, boys *bach*?"

The two of them nodded, and I noticed a grim set to their jaws. There was a silence, and then Bryn said: "I have seen it all before, Mistress, before the Merthyr Insurrection six or seven years since. Once the wild men take control, there is no knowing what will happen. They act first, and think afterwards. And they love power just as much as the Squires do. But because they are not used to it, they get intoxicated by it when they should remain cold and sober. Somebody will get killed soon, Mistress, just you mark my words."

I moaned. "I hear you, Bryn," I said. "Nor am I surprised. I was appalled by what happened to that silly old woman on the Parrog. The punishment was a good deal more terrible than the crime."

"Thank God it was not worse, Mistress. Some of the fellows wanted her inside the cottage when it went up in flames."

"Surely that cannot be?" I whispered. But my enquiring eyes brought only nods of confirmation from Gomer and Will. There was no point in dwelling on the stupidity of men, or berating my menservants for the failings of others, but as inexorably as the clock ticked away another minute on the wall of my bedroom, I saw myself being sucked into a situation from which there might be no escape.

"So what do you want me to do?"

"Mistress, all of the men respect you," said Will, "and we think you are the only person in the neighbourhood who can talk some sense into them. Will you meet Dafydd Ifan and Zeke Tomos?"

"Very well. Tell them to come and see me after supper on Thursday next. I will see what I can do. I know Dafydd Ifan from Gamallt as an intelligent fellow and a tidy farmer. He was once a tenant of mine, and he caused me no trouble. But Zeke Tomos -- is he not one of the fellows evicted by Squire Huws of Bayvil?"

"Indeed he is, Mistress. Very bitter, he is, and although he has been given a new tenancy, it is less than half the size of his old one, and at twice the rent. The Squire blames him for the attentions of the *Ceffyl Pren*, and in that he would not be too wide of the mark. The old man wants to crush Zeke beneath his booted foot, if Zeke does not kill him first."

"That does not sound like a situation leading to peace and harmony, my dear Will."

"Afraid not, Mistress. If Zeke cannot revenge himself upon the Squire, he will let out his anger in some other direction. His youngest daughter died of starvation, so they say, some three weeks past, and he is near enough mad with grief. He and a few others are set upon a real insurrection, and I do believe, Mistress, that they are not concerned whether they live or die as a consequence of it. Zeke will probably end up a martyr, like Dic Penderyn."

"I will try to save him from himself," I said. "One last thing. When they walk here on Thursday, I do not want them walking together, and I want them to come from different directions. From this point on, brains are needed as well as brawn. Understood?"

The three of them nodded, and our interview was at an end. I got up, and they thanked me profusely for agreeing to help. They returned to their tasks in the farmyard and in the garden. I sat alone for a long time, lost in thought and with an increasing awareness that I, the feeble Mistress of Plas Ingli, was about to become embroiled in men's business. Not just the simple business of farms and estates, but the business of lives and livelihoods. And I know that blood will be spilt.

ΩΩΩΩΩΩΩΩΩΩ

A Growing Fury

4th August 1838

Suddenly I am in great demand, and I am quite enjoying myself. This morning I woke up, yet again in this infernal summer, to the sound of rain beating on my window and sluicing off the roof and into the gutters. It was so cold at six o'clock that Liza had to light the fire in my bedroom grate so that I could get up and get dressed in reasonable comfort. "Big day today, then, Mistress?" she asked as she knelt in the fireplace and nursed the kindling into flames.

"Yes and no, Liza," said I. "I have had bigger days in my time. I doubt that my expected visitation will be sufficiently hilarious for me to burst my stays, but I do indeed have a challenge on my hands. I hope that my diplomatic skills are up to it."

"No doubt about it, Mistress. Those gentlemen will be like clay in the hands of a potter."

"Very poetic, Liza," I replied. "I hope your confidence is not misplaced. Thank you for the fire. Now then, is my hot water ready? And my burgundy-coloured velvet dress today, I think, since that might help me to convert my enemies into friends."

At ten o'clock in the morning, at their prior request, Squire Huws of Bayvil, Squire Jobbins of Holmws and Squire Owen of Gelli Fawr arrived in a very elegant coach pulled by four white horses. Gomer helped each of them down in turn and sheltered them with my largest umbrella as they splashed across the yard to my front door. I gave each of them in turn a deep curtsy, as did Bessie, Liza and Gwenno when I introduced them. Seldom, I thought, can these three squires have come across three such pretty servants, and I was very proud of both their looks and their gracious manners. I could see that the gentlemen were impressed too, and that they were delighted to see that all four of us women were showing a little more *décolletage* than is strictly allowed these days in smart circles. I learned long since that there is nothing like a little display of femininity when one needs to cope with pompous and aggressive gentlemen.

When Gwenno had served the gentlemen and myself with crystal glasses of my best duty-free claret, and when we had finished with small talk, Squire John Owen cleared his throat and opened the attack. "My dear Mistress Morgan," he said. "Most excellent claret, if I may say so. Almost identical, indeed, to the claret which has been discovered in many

149

of the local houses following a recent illegal landing at Aberrhigian."

"Is that so?" said I, with my eyes wide and innocent. "What a very strange coincidence. It is good, though I say it myself. I pride myself on making sensible purchases. My cellar is small but well-stocked, and since you too, Master Owen, are a connoisseur, you will know that I can reveal neither my budget nor my sources."

"Quite so, quite so, Mistress Martha," he mumbled.

"Enough of wine, Master Owen," said Squire Jobbins. "There are other matters to be discussed. Now then, Mistress Martha, I trust that you recall a visit which I made to the Plas some six months back?"

"Indeed I do, sir. I think that your visit was unannounced, as a consequence of which I was not here to receive you. I am very sorry about that. I think that I was taking a quiet stroll on the mountain at the time........" I smiled sweetly at him, knowing full well that his mind was full of images of me frolicking about among the mountain boulders like a frisky kid goat.

"So you were, Mistress. Yes indeed. Indeed yes. But you received my hurriedly composed note?"

"Yes sir, I did. And if I may be perfectly honest with you, I did not judge that it required a reply."

"Oh? And why might that be?"

"Sir, six months have passed, and I no longer recall your exact words, but I seem to remember that in your letter you were threatening me. Very obliquely, of course, but your intention was nonetheless clear. And when I receive threatening letters, I always follow the advice which my father gave me when I was very young, and that was to throw them in the fire."

I saw the colour rising in Squire Jobbins' cheeks, and I thought that things might become interesting, but Squire Huws retrieved the situation with a loud guffaw, upon which we all burst out into laughter. The Squire of Bayvil was particularly entertained by the thought of me scattering letters onto the flames, and he spluttered: "God bless my soul, Master Jobbins, I always did tell you that letter writing was not your strong point! If there is something to be said to a lady, it should be said face to face. Would you not agree, Mistress Martha?"

"Indeed I would, sir. So shall we get to the point? We have generated more heat than light here this morning thus far, and I seek enlightenment."

A Growing Fury

Squire Owen intervened. "Mistress, you have been at the Plas for more than forty years," he said, "and you have suffered from hard times like the rest of us. We have had our disagreements over tithes and such matters, but I am sure that we can put such things down to misunderstandings and misjudgements, and that in future our relations will be perfectly amicable......"

I felt my temperature rise, but I kept my composure and said in a level voice: "Sir, let me assure you that when I withheld my tithe payments last year, that was the result of neither a misjudgement nor a misunderstanding on my part. I knew what I was doing, and in case there is any uncertainty in your mind as to my current intentions, I give you notice that I will withhold payment this year as well. Prosecute me if you will."

Squire John Owen is only a little older than me, but he looked for a moment like an old man of ninety, with a pale face and haunted eyes. He was rescued by Squire Jobbins, who chortled; "My goodness, gentlemen, we have found Mistress Martha on fine form today. I do believe that she is intent upon insulting each one of us in turn, and all within the space of fifteen minutes!"

"Master Jobbins," I replied, "let me assure you that it is not my intention to insult anybody. But I will not put up with hurtful remarks or insinuations even from respectable gentlemen such as yourselves. You should know me well enough, after all these years, to understand that I will defend myself. This is my house, and I make the rules. Now, for the last time, what is the purpose of your visit?"

The three of them exchanged sheepish glances, and Squire Huws spoke. "We apologize, Mistress, for our less than gentlemanly behaviour. Please forgive us." I nodded as graciously as our new Queen in her palace, and the Squire cleared his throat. "You are aware, Mistress, that we have all suffered grievously in recent weeks and months because of the vicious criminal activities of these fellows who carry the *Ceffyl Pren* around and who dress up in female disguises?"

"Yes, of course I am aware of it."

"Squire Owen here has seen his ricks going up in flames, as has my friend from Holmws, and I too have had to endure the depradations of the mob. My steward has been beaten and humiliated, and I have lost ricks as well. Furthermore, I have been forced, against my better judgement, to give back three tenancies to rough fellows who have given me nothing but

151

trouble since I took over the estate from my father."

"You may spare me the details, Master Huws. I think that the whole neighbourhood knows about the exciting nocturnal events which have taken place on your land."

"Exciting nocturnal events, indeed!" shouted the Squire. "The fellows responsible are thugs and criminals, and their leaders deserve nothing better than to be hung, drawn and quartered! We will catch them, never fear. The leaders will be strung up and the others will be transported. Letters have gone to the Home Secretary, and we expect troops within a fortnight."

I was very interested to hear that, but I made sure that my face remained quite expressionless. "Sir, I can but sympathize with your predicament, but I would remind all three of you gentlemen that you make your beds and you lie in them. Those who have been targetted by the mob are, in my estimation, those who have caused distress to common people and who have been, shall we say, less than sensitive to the needs of those who are penniless and starving."

"So you do not condemn the suffering which we gentlemen have all had to endure over the past months?"

"I condemn all suffering and cruelty, sir, but I reserve my harshest condemnation for the rich and the strong when they inflict misery on the poor and the weak. Call that a woman's passion, if you like, but that is what I experience, and I will not attempt to hide it from gentlemen such as yourselves. Now, gentlemen, to the point, if you please. What do you want of me? I take it that you did not simply call on me in order to check out the provenance of my claret?"

"Very well, Mistress Martha," grumbled Squire Owen. "We need your help."

"And how might I be of assistance?" I asked, as I got to my feet and served more claret from my finest decanter.

"Well, we have a good deal of lawlessness on our hands, and neither the Mayor, nor the constables, nor the magistrates can prevent it. When we seek information, people refuse to speak. And when somebody like Mistress Dafis does speak up, she is treated most abominably........"

"I would agree with you most heartily on that point, Master Owen."

"Good, good. Very pleased to hear it. But I fear that there is little chance of arrests and prosecutions in the present climate of fear and intimidation, and I consider that matters can only get worse."

"Yet again, Mistress, the harvest is lost," added Master Jobbins. "This accursed rain has once again flattened the hay, and there will be no corn harvest to speak of, even if the rain stops tomorrow. Once again, the potato harvest is rotting in the ground. More starvation, more unrest. More riots are inevitable."

"But I thought that you said there were troops on the way, and that they would maintain law and order?"

"A vain hope, Mistress Martha," said Master Huws. "Three times in the last year we have written to the Home Secretary, to ask for extra constables or infantry, and three times he has refused. He says that there are troubles all over the kingdom, and that the maintenance of law and order is entirely a matter for us as magistrates. He says we must swear in special constables. We have done that before, but they are always worse than the regular constables, and in future will probably cheer on the rioters rather than apprehending them."

"We need your help, Mistress. We have had a number of meetings of the magistrates of late, and we have become aware that if there is one landowner in the north of this county who has the ability to urge restraint upon the *Ceffyl Pren* gang, it is you. No matter how uncomfortable it may be for us to say so, you do have the respect and even the affection of the common people, and you appear to be immune to the poison which is afflicting the rest of us. Do you know who leads the gang, and who participates in the riots?"

"I will admit to nothing, Master Jobbins, and neither should you expect me to."

"So will you help us?"

I thought for a long time, or at least pretended to think, and in truth I quite enjoyed observing the growing tension and agitation in the three foolish fellows who were seated opposite me. Then at last I said: "Very well. I thank you, gentlemen, for your confidence. I know very little myself, but it is quite possible that I might have some role as an intermediary, and get messages to those who know more and who might even provide leadership. I hate conflict and violence, and it is my duty to seek to keep both of those monsters at bay. I will urge caution, and will seek to control the excesses of the wild men."

"Such a gesture would be much appreciated, Mistress Martha. I think that I speak for all of the squires who live within twenty miles of the Plas."

"And now, gentlemen, I come to my conditions."

"Conditions?" squeaked Master Owen.

"Yes, conditions. In matters of diplomacy, you take something from your adversaries, but you must also give in return. You want restraint and respect for the law from those who are starving. Very well. But in return I want you to promise, on behalf of yourselves and all the other gentlemen of this area, that while current conditions of hardship prevail, there will be no more evictions, no more prosecutions for petty poaching offences, no destruction of *ty unnos* cottages, no prosecutions for nonpayment of tithes or church rates, and no more distraint seizures and sales. Oh, and while we are about it, no more enclosures on the common. And more generosity in the matter of poor relief would not come amiss. Are we agreed?"

"But that is preposterous!" spluttered Squire Huws. "It is not in our power to deliver on any of these things!"

"Oh, I think it is, sir. I am not asking for public announcements. Actions will speak louder than words. Where the common people see compassion, you may be assured that they will respond in a generous fashion. Do you want to stop the predations of the *Ceffyl Pren* and his jury, or do you not?"

There was a long silence, and at last the three gentlemen exchanged glances, and all three of them nodded. "Very well, Mistress Martha. If you will use your good offices as you have indicated, we will use ours with our confederates. We pray to God that the result will be peace in our community, if not in others."

"I seek nothing in return for my good offices," said I, probably sounding like a saint, "but I will appreciate it if you, Squire Owen, will take away those silly fellows who have been spying on the Plas for the best part of eight months. It is very irritating, and my servants have had to throw three of them into the river already."

"Spying, Mistress Martha? I do not know what you mean..........."

"Come now, Master Owen. Everybody in the neighbourhood knows what is going on, and everybody knows that these fellows are paid by you. They have admitted it themselves. Do I have your word?" He looked rather shamefaced, and said nothing, but then he nodded slowly and reluctantly. "I thank you, sir. I take that assent to cover the withdrawal of spies and informers paid by other gentlemen as well. We will make no progress at all without trust and mutual respect, as I am sure we all agree."

We all got to our feet, and I said: "Well, gentlemen, after all that hard work, a little refreshment might be in order. Can I offer you a small selection of good things from my larder before you go on your way?"

"But Mistress Martha, that was not at all our expectation," said Master Jobbins. "We really must be on our way........."

"I will not hear of it, gentlemen, and I am sure that Bessie will be most disappointed if you do not take at least a little of the game pie which I can smell even as we speak. Please join me in the dining room."

And so the four of us migrated to the dining room, which is used all too seldom, to find it beautifully laid up for a feast of considerable proportions. Let us just say that the meal was a good investment, and that when the three squires went on their merry way at three in the afternoon we were all the best of friends.

ΩΩΩΩΩΩΩΩΩΩΩ

5th August 1838

A sunny day at last, but I have had little chance to enjoy it since I spent the morning recovering from the exertions of yesterday's meeting, and the afternoon preparing for my discussion with Master Ifan and Master Tomos. Now it is late at night. The house is dark and quiet, and as I sit at my writing desk, with the pages of my diary illuminated by two flickering candles, I can collect my thoughts and report on another job completed to my satisfaction.

After supper, more or less on time, Zeke Tomos came up the track from Dolrannog and Dafydd Ifan came down the moorland track on the western flank of the mountain. Both of them did their best to look invisible, but it did not greatly matter, since Will informs me that the spies have departed, just as Squire Owen promised they would. So far, so good, I thought, as I welcomed the two *Ceffyl Pren* conspirators into my drawing room.

They were a strange pair, and I was not entirely surprised that they might have difficulty in working together. Dafydd is a lean and upright fellow with fair hair and bright eyes. He has a smooth chin, and the creases around his mouth and eyes show that he is capable of laughter, even in these hard times. He has good manners too, and indeed in the days when he was a tenant of mine on land belonging to Llystyn I found him to be articulate and surprisingly aware of political and social issues. He is a good reader too, and I recall with pleasure the great progress which he made as a young man attending Madam Bevan's School in Newport. He is a natural leader for the small farmers of the area. Zeke is a man of modest build, with broad shoulders and big hands. He has a weatherbeaten face partly covered with a wispy beard, and dark deep-set eyes. He has hard lips which turn down at the edges, and a permanently furrowed brow. An angry man, I thought when I met him, and one who has suffered. He did not talk much, but listened with a rare intensity. I thought from the beginning that I might have problems with him, and that he might mistrust me as he mistrusted every other member of the gentry.

I should have offered them each a jar of ale, but I was moved by an impulse to treat them just as I had treated the three squires, and at the risk of appearing ostentatious I offered each of them a glass of claret instead. Much to my surprise, they accepted, and Gwenno served the ruby liquid to them in crystal glasses.

"I thank you, gentlemen, for coming to see me," I said. "This is not my idea, but it comes from some of your fellows. Let me say at the outset that you may trust me completely, and that I will never betray you. I know of your involvement with the *Ceffyl Pren*, and I know most of the men who have participated in your activities over the past months. I sympathize with your aims and approve of most of your actions. And I thank you once again for returning my valuable Italian chest."

"Not here any longer, Mistress?" said Dafydd, having cast his eyes across the room to where the chest should have been standing.

"I have put it somewhere safe, where the bailiffs cannot find it, should they pay me another visit."

Zeke remained expressionless, but Dafydd grinned. Then he said: "Will said that he and some other fellows have talked to you, Mistress, and that you might have certain information which might be of use to us."

"He said that, did he? Well, he may be right. But before we get onto the matter of intelligence gathering, I need to say one thing to you. I fear that you are in grave danger of destroying your cause if you start to harm the poor instead of the rich and if you allow your discipline to slip. Do you know what I am talking about, gentlemen?"

"Mistress Jane Dafis and her cottage?" asked Dafydd.

"Yes, and the corn warehouses on the Parrog. Burning them was stupid, not only because the buildings are now in ruins, but because the corn that was in them is also destroyed. Burning corn is not very clever at a time of starvation."

At last I got a word out of Zeke. His eyes blazed, and he growled: "But those bastards Harry and Shinkins were simply sitting in there, on hundreds of sacks of wheat and barley, and watching the price rise while we and our families were starving outside on the streets."

"I understand you, Master Tomos. But with a little less anger you might have "saved" the corn instead of burning it. Then at least some of you might have had bread in your bellies by now."

"Quite right you are, Mistress Martha," said Dafydd. "We never thought of that........"

Then Zeke turned on his colleague. "As brazen as a hussy you are, Dafydd, to change your tune now, when you were the first one in there with your flaming torch and your mad shouting and cheering!"

Having observed that there was a satisfactory degree of dissension in the ranks, I thought it best to restore good order. "Please, please, gentlemen," I pleaded. "I will appreciate it if you will keep your voices down. I simply wish to make this point. You have a chance of succeeding in your fight for justice if you remain united, and if you have just one enemy -- the group of gentlemen who control the land and who administer justice. But if you make enemies of the merchants as well, your task is suddenly a much greater one. And if you make enemies of some of the poor people -- the very ones whom you seek to represent -- everything will be lost."

"Huh!" said Zeke. "That Jane Dafis was a traitor, and good riddance to her!"

"She was also weak, and vulnerable, and starving, and in the eyes of many of the local people what you did to her was thuggish, brutal and cowardly. If you are not careful, Zeke, your support will slip away, and other traitors will sell names for hard cash."

Zeke's eyes blazed again, and although Dafydd tried to restrain him, he rose to his feet and confronted me, wagging his finger a few inches from the end of my nose. "It's all very well for you to talk, Mistress Morgan of Plas Ingli, sitting here in your fine mansion and serving up tax-free claret to your guests! You are one of them, the bastards who suck the blood out of us and break our backs and watch us starve. I have watched my baby girl starve to death. I have been evicted from my home and I have seen all my possessions disappear down the lane on the back of a bailiff's cart. That is what poverty is, Mistress Morgan! What do you know about starvation, and suffering, and grief? And you presume to preach to us?"

The poor man stood there in front of me, quaking with emotion and with a terrible tragic fury in his eyes. I thought that he was close to tears. Dafydd put his arm around him and guided him back to his seat. "Zeke! Zeke!" he pleaded. "I beg of you not to insult Mistress Martha. She is one of the few friends we have -- you know that."

Zeke slumped in the chair, and buried his face in his hands. He drew in great gulps of air as he tried to control himself. I was shaking with emotion too, and poured out some more claret for my guests while I composed my thoughts. Considerable diplomacy was required. At last Zeke raised his eyes to meet mine. "Do not worry about being honest with me, Master Tomos," I said. "I try to make a virtue of it myself. I am not offended by your words. Of course I will never understand starvation, although I will say in my defence that I try harder than many others to avoid it and to plan months and years ahead. And my servants will tell you that I share their fare, and at the same table. When the larder is empty, I go hungry as they do. If you doubt that, ask Will and Bryn."

"I can confirm that, Zeke," said Dafydd. "Those fellows have said as much to me, and that is one of the reasons behind the fierce loyalty which they feel towards their Mistress."

I continued. "I do not want to labour the point, Zeke, but I have felt grief as you have following the loss of a child. I have lost two young people, one son and one daughter, who were both greatly loved. My husband David was murdered by members of his own class, and I lost another dear man to whom I was betrothed, to a terrible wasting illness. And I think I know a little about suffering at the hands of so-called gentlemen. When I was young I was falsely accused of some petty theft and I was stripped to the waist and dragged behind the whipping cart and scourged through the streets of Newport like a common criminal. I still have the stripes upon my back to prove it. Then I was incarcerated in a dungeon in Haverfordwest Gaol, and believed for a while that I would be strung up on the gallows. Believe me, Zeke, I have no great respect for the gentry and no great faith in this thing we call justice. But I do want to make the world a better place, just as you do. And that is why we are sitting here this evening, facing each other and shaking with emotion."

Zeke nodded and even managed a little smile. "I apologize, Mistress," he said. "That outburst was uncalled for, and I have to admit to being only vaguely aware of your own troubles. What can we do?"

"First, take heed of this intelligence. Yesterday, I was visited by three squires. I can tell you that letters have gone to the Home Secretary requesting troops. Thus far, he has resisted the requests, but if there are any further incidents locally I fear that you will be apprehended by the Yeomanry, or by the Light Dragoons. Their methods are well known, and they are not pleasant."

"Good God! That is news to us, Mistress! We will pass that on to our confederates."

"Now then. I can promise nothing, but if you wish it, I will try to use my good offices with the gentlemen of this neighbourhood to relieve some of the burdens which you currently feel. With the failure of yet another harvest, starvation will be with us for at least another eight months, and people will die because of it. But I will ask for tolerance in the matter of debts, and I will ask for compassion in the administration of justice. I will ask for other things too, but those will be resolved between me and the squires."

"And tolls, Mistress?" asked Dafydd. "There are rumours that the Fishguard Trust wants another gate at the west end of town, and that the Cemais Trust wants three new gates, on the Cardigan, Moylgrove and Cilgwyn roads. If those gates go up, we will not be able to control the men."

"I understand that full well, Dafydd. But leave that matter with me, if you will."

"And what do you want in return, Mistress?"

"First, I want you to talk to Bryn. He knows better than any of us what happens when large crowds of angry men get out of control, and when they threaten life as well as property. In Merthyr Tydfil, some years ago, God only knows how many poor people died at the hands of the soldiers because men acted too quickly and thought too slowly. And I urge you to call a halt to your activities for the time being. Zeke, I think it is within my power to encourage even the most cruel of squires, such as your own Master Huws at Bayvil, to act with greater tolerance and understanding in the future."

"Do you really believe that, Mistress?"

"Never underestimate a woman's influence, Zeke. The women of this district may not have much power, but we do have more influence than you might imagine. Give me six months, and if after that time you and your friends do not see any improvement in your circumstances, then nobody will be surprised if the *Ceffyl Pren* resumes his activities. But if that should prove necessary, I beg of you to hold fast to two principles."

"Only two, mistress?" asked Dafydd. "The Chartists have six, and good ones they are, too."

"Hold fast to those if you will, gentlemen. I agree with all of them except the one about annual elections. But add mine onto the front of the list, if you will. First, think long and hard before you act. Second, use subtlety instead of brute force if at all possible. Never harm the interests of those upon whom you depend for your support. Change your tactics and your leaders frequently. And let your targets be stones and timbers rather than flesh and blood, for if you do not........."

Now both of the rough fellows in front of me burst out laughing. "My goodness, Mistress Martha!" chortled Zeke. "Enough, if you please! That seems like a lot more principles than two, if I am not greatly mistaken. I thought that I was a revolting enough sort of a fellow, but you are considerably more revolting still, and I see that you have planned the collapse of civilization in greater detail than Master Guy Fawkes ever did!"

I had to laugh with them, and soon the three of us were swept away in a gale of hilarity. At last I recovered my composure, and as I wiped the tears from my eyes I said: "Enough, enough. Quite right you are, Zeke. If I had been a man, I should have been a preacher. I will not say another word about putting the world to rights. Now then, you gentlemen have already eaten your suppers, I daresay, but after all this talking I assume that you could manage a little something before you set out for home?"

"But that would put your servants to some inconvenience, Mistress, would it not?"

"I insist on it. If we go through to the kitchen, I think that we might find that Bessie has already anticipated the imminent arrival of two hungry men and one hungry Mistress."

And so we enjoyed a most excellent late supper around the kitchen table, with Gwenno and Bessie in attendance and with Bryn and Gomer enjoying a very convivial hour or two in the company of their fellow conspirators.

When Zeke and Dafydd left, at eleven of the clock, I stood on the doorstep and bid them goodnight. I watched the dull glow of their candle lanterns disappearing down the track towards the Cilgwyn Road, and realized that I was now, more by accident than design, in a position of considerable power.

ΩΩΩΩΩΩΩΩΩΩ

6th December 1838

During the last four months there have been no further incidents involving the *Ceffyl Pren*, and I thank God that my allies on both sides of the law have respected our agreements. I have had various short meetings with the squires, and with Zeke and Dafydd, and for better or for worse it is now quite widely known that I am acting as a sort of intermediary. That may place me in danger in the future, but for the moment I feel safe enough, and I am well protected by the network of spies which is operated by Will and his disreputable friends.

There have been no new tithe or rent default prosecutions or distraint sales in the neighbourhood, and it is good to see that even Squire Huws and Squire Owen have acted with moderation and even compassion when circumstances have demanded it. Squire Jobbins, whom I have never looked upon as an evil fellow, has even allowed a temporary reduction in his rents in view of the failure of yet another harvest, and that has greatly enhanced his reputation in the community. And just the other day Brynach said to me that the local magistrates are well pleased with my diplomatic efforts, and have noticed a reduction in petty crimes as local antagonism towards the gentry has eased. Indictments and complaints have become rare. On the bench, the justices have themselves shown such remarkable tolerance of minor misdemeanours and human frailty that the constables are complaining that they have too little to do. I never thought that I would be able to write such a thing about this rough and lovely town. This outbreak of virtue cannot last, of course, but we must enjoy it while we can. And we have little enough to enjoy, with the signs of hunger and illness on all sides, and with deaths almost every day. The weather has improved, but we will all have to face another frugal Christmas.

In September I attended two crucial meetings in the company of Ioan and Brynach. They were the meetings of the Fishguard Turnpike Trust in the Castle Hotel, and the Cemais Turnpike Trust in the Black Lion Inn. Both meetings were attended by Master Thomas Bullin, a toll farmer whose ambitions seem to have no limits. He is also wealthy and persuasive. He spoke with a rough English accent, and he seemed to me to be a perfect example of that new breed of merchants and money-men who will no doubt eventually rule the world. At both meetings he offered to take over the collection of tolls at fees twice as high as those paid by the present license holders. But he also wanted to build more gates so as to cover his investments. This had already been widely expected of Master Bullin within the community, for he and his surveyor had already been spotted at work during the summer, making measurements on all of the roads leading out of town.

At the meeting of the Fishguard Trust on the tenth day of the month, many of the trustees and tally-holders wanted to go along with Master Bullin, for the Trust is in dire straits because of maladministration and corruption. But I had taken the precaution of encouraging all of my allies to be there, and I had also reminded Squire Jobbins and his cronies that new gates or higher tolls would certainly bring out the beautiful hairy ladies and the *Ceffyl Pren* again. Much against the instincts of the Chairman, who thinks that women have their place, so long as it is not in gentlemen's meetings, I managed to occupy the floor for a few minutes and to plead for moderation. Master Bullin, said I, was a businessman whose business was making money, but I said that we who were trustees had wider responsibilities, and one of those was to be mindful of the distress which currently afflicted both town and country. I warned that new gates and higher tolls would lead to civil disorder and would leave the Trust worse off than it was already. The Chairman got very red in the face, and asked me whether I was threatening the trustees. "Indeed not, sir," said I, as sweetly as I could. "But I do have my ear close to the ground, as do many of the gentlemen in this room, and we do not like what we hear. I urge you to reject this proposal and to leave things as they are." Luckily Master Byron Bailes and Master Nicholas Lloyd supported me, and so did several others, and the vote which we had feared in support of Master Bullin's plans did not materialize. He went away at the end of the meeting with a face as black as thunder.

The same thing happened at the meeting of the Cemais Trust on 20th September. Again Master Bullin was there to present a careful case for "modernization". Again I did my canvassing in advance and opposed him from the floor, and again my allies stood firm to reject his proposals. Thank God for common sense. At least for the time being, we will have no new gates around Newport and no increases in tolls. I communicated the results of these meetings immediately to Zeke and Dafydd, and received the thanks of all the beautiful sisters, together with an assurance that their party dresses would remain in their wardrobes for the time being.

Locally, there is a good deal to be thankful for, but further afield I fear that the storm clouds are gathering. Just three days ago, I received an invitation from Will to attend a meeting, under conditions of some secrecy, in Brynberian at a place called Trehaidd. We travelled there together in the chaise, on a cold and blustery winter's evening. When we got there it was too dark to see much of the house, but there was a warm welcome within from six or seven fellows gathered around the *simnai fawr*. The mistress of the house, Ellen Mathias, proved to be one of Will's multitude of cousins. She gave us mugs of hot tea to warm us up, and her husband George introduced us to the others, none of whom I had met before. There were bows and curtseys, and although they were all small farmers and labourers I thought all of them remarkably well mannered.

"You were not followed this evening, Will?" asked George. "You took precautions?"

"Yes indeed, George *bach*," replied my head man. "Nobody but the Mistress and me knew that this was our destination, and I stopped several times on the way and covered our candle lanterns. There were no lights behind us, and no sounds as we came up out of the *cwm*."

It turned out that two of the other fellows huddled around the fire were also Will's cousins. One was Master Lloyd Davies of Glynsaithmaen, on the south side of Mynydd Preseli, and the other was a huge fellow called Thomas Rees, whom they call Twm Carnabwth because he lives in a stone cottage on the edge of the moor. Twm told me that he built it himself as a *ty unnos* on the edge of Glynsaithmaen land some years since, and that he had been allowed to stay without molestation -- in the first place because the land he occupied was wet and useless, and in the second place because he was bigger and uglier than his cousin Lloyd and would not have taken kindly to being evicted. At this Lloyd roared with laughter and said: "Quite right he is, Mistress Martha. Only a fool interferes with my cousin Twm. He is a God-fearing Baptist and a chief reciter at the *Pwnc*, but only when it suits him. When it does not suit him, he can hold half the contents of a beer barrel, and he can beat any bare-knuckle fighter this side of Swansea even though he only has one eye. *Diawl*, is that not right, Twm *bach*?"

Twm chuckled, and such a chuckle would surely have shaken down the walls of Jericho in short order had he been employed by Master Joshua. "No ale tonight, boys, for we have a lady in our midst," he said. "Tea it is, and sober thought. We welcome you, Mistress, as one who knows our suffering and who does more than any other to bring comfort and peace."

"Amen to that!" said another man in the corner. "Now then. We know of Mistress Martha's credentials. Might we move on to the business of the day?"

"Of course, and high time it is," said Master Lloyd Davies, asserting his authority. He was clearly the leader of the group, and as I looked around me I could see that he was well liked and respected. He turned to me. "Mistress," he said, "there are meetings like this going on all over West Wales just now -- some on this very evening, some yesterday and some tomorrow. We are not very organized, and nor do we want to be, but we have terrible burdens to bear, and there is a limit to our suffering. You know what the problems are, Mistress. Change has to come, and it will not happen unless men and women of courage act together."

"And what can I do?" I asked. "I am flattered to have been asked to join you, but as a mere woman my influence is very limited. I do not spend a lot of my time moving in polite circles......."

"But you are a tally holder of the Whitland trust?"

"Indeed I am, but I have to admit that I very rarely attend its meetings, infrequent though they are."

164

A Growing Fury

"Do not worry about that, Mistress. You will see where this is heading. You appear to have achieved a certain harmony between the squires and the common people around Newport, and that is a cause for celebration. But we are not so lucky elsewhere. The squires and their cronies are getting ever more rapacious and cruel, and there is a major risk of insurrection and bloodshed to the east of here and into Carmarthenshire. I think we will need your advice, Mistress."

"I will give it if I can. But first I need to inform myself. Do you mind if I simply listen to what you all have to say? Then, once I know what the issues are, I will give you my thoughts. It will then be down to you to decide what to do with them."

The men all agreed to that. And so they talked, at length and with passion, about starvation and poverty, about tithes and church rates, about the administration of justice and the corruption of the magistrates, and about the workings of the Poor Law. It transpired that the new Workhouse at Narberth was almost completed and ready to receive its first paupers, and it became clear to me that the place would become a focus for future action. And it transpired that the burden of the road tolls was much more severe to the east than in the Newport area, since the Whitland Trust in particular was more efficiently run. Tolls were extracted with a good deal more enthusiasm than they were by the lazy gatekeepers of Newport, and it was rumoured that Master Thomas Bullin and his surveyor had been spotted on almost all of the toll roads under Whitland control. Will, Twm and the others were quite convinced that at the next meeting of the Whitland Trust, Bullin would come forward with a new offer for the tollgate contract, and that that offer would be accepted.

The discussion moved on to future action, either in response to any moves that the squires might make to grind the poor people into the mud, or of a preemptive kind. Two of the wilder fellows from south of the mountain argued that it was time to make an example of certain hated squires, and that it might be necessary to ambush the occasional coach or to burn down one or two of the grand houses. Somebody else argued that if a thousand men could be assembled to march on Whitland, on the day of the next Trust meeting, that might have the effect of frightening Bullin away. I moaned when I heard that, and that attracted the attention of all the men in the room. "You have concerns about that, Mistress Martha?" asked Twm. "In my humble opinion, unless we can show that thousands of people are with us, we will never influence the squires and the magistrates, and never catch the attention of the Government. Twenty or thirty men here and there can be swatted by the Yeomanry as if they are flies, and we will be no further forward in our demands for justice."

"That is where you are wrong, Twm," said I. "My man Bryn was at Merthyr Tydfil in 1831. He will tell you, if you ask him, what happens when you get a thousand angry men together in one place. Some of them will carry weapons, including firearms. The magistrates will get wind of it, and they will ask for the protection of the Yeomanry. They will get it. And if the crowd is then displeased by the findings of the meeting, the madmen will shout down the moderates, and there will be a great press forward. The Yeomanry will lose their discipline, shots will be fired, and lives will be lost. Is that really what you want, gentlemen?"

"I daresay that it is not, Mistress," said Master Lloyd Davies. "But what else can we do to further our cause?"

"In my view, Master Davies, you have the solution within the great traditions of the area. Let the *Ceffyl Pren* do your work for you."

"The *Ceffyl Pren*? That is all very well for meting out justice to the fathers of bastard children, or to over-zealous bailiffs or mean-spirited magistrates, but how can we use such silly charades to change the law, or even to bring down a Government? I do not see it, Mistress Martha......"

"The activities of a few intelligent men dressed in silly costumes in Newport have had an effect which none of us could have dreamt of, Master Davies. Please tell him, Will."

So Will described for the other men in the room how he and his confederates had brought together the *Ceffyl Pren* gang and how they had sought to win public sympathy and to target those who were most responsible for the sufferings of the poor. He was even honest enough to describe the disagreements that had occurred between the members of the group, and kind enough to give me some credit for bringing in discipline when there might have been a descent into mindless violence. When he had finished, there was a long silence.

Then Master Lloyd Davies said: "Mistress Martha, you and Will have given us cause for thought. Will you help us further, if action should be needed, for example, to deal with the Whitland Trust?"

"Of course I will. I will give this further consideration. But I will only help you by using my contacts and passing intelligence over to you if you will promise me that any violence that may be needed will be directed strictly against property and not against persons. Damage toll gates if you will, but do not harm the gatekeepers and their families. Once innocent people are hurt, that will be the beginning of the end, and justice will remain for ever beyond your reach. I say this to you as a feeble woman, but I think I know what I am talking about."

"I accept that, Mistress. I will agree to it, as I hope will the others here present."

Much to my relief, all of them agreed, including the pugilist Twm Carnabwth. It was time to go. I urged the men to take no action against authority for the time being, and I promised them that I would see them immediately after the next meeting of the Whitland Trust in January, to pass on news of the trustees' decisions.

As Will and I made our way homewards, with the candle lanterns faintly illuminating the way ahead, we were both as excited as small children at a birthday party. We chatted endlessly about strategies and targets and tactics, as if we were two great generals preparing for a campaign of conquest. We knew full well that what lay ahead of us would be a severe test of discipline for undisciplined people, but we knew that optimism and determination would be crucial. We also knew that once the action started, there would be no stopping it until either the poor or the rich could declare a great victory.

ΩΩΩΩΩΩΩΩΩΩΩ

Editor's Note:
For Mistress Martha's simplified map of turnpike trust roadways and key locations in West Wales, see Pages 274 and 275.

6. Set upon a Certain Course

6th January 1839

We have had a white Christmas, blessed by a mighty snowfall. That is unusual in these parts, since winter does not normally start until the turn of the year.

As it happened, the snow did not cause too much disruption to our plans for the celebration of the season, since I had already made the miserable decision to hold a small Christmas rather than a large one. That meant that for the second Christmas in succession my tenants and labourers and their families were not invited to the Plas. I hated the situation in which I found myself, but I really had no options in the matter, for another harvest failure meant that my larder was far too bare even for the feeding of fifty people. I knew that Christmas dinner in the cottages and hovels of the *cwm* would consist of barley bread, buttermilk and salted herrings, but mine at the Plas would not be much better. We would have ham, beef and wheat bread, but there would be no potatoes on our table, and no apples, and I had long since relieved my tenants of their seasonal obligations to provide me with eggs, chickens, geese and other provisions. I will have to make do with labour instead, when the weather permits me to think of such things as stone clearance, hedging and ditching.

But back to the snow. And what a delicate and wonderful deluge it was! The prelude occurred four days before Christmas, when the wind shifted round to the east and stayed there. Within a day everything was frozen, and Will and the other men warmed the bitter air with their cursing as they tried to keep the animals watered and fed. The sheep and cattle were for the most part close to the Plas, or under cover, and the only beasts left on the mountain were a few old ewes and some of the mountain ponies. They were all tough enough to survive the end of the world, we thought, so we were not too worried about fetching them in. Two days before Christmas the air felt less cold, and the clear sky was obliterated by a mass of dark cloud that rolled in from the east. At midday it was as black as midnight, and then the snow started to fall, with small hard grains at first, and then with big and beautiful flakes that tumbled and swirled in the gentlest of breezes and settled on every accessible surface. I listened to the complaints of the servants, of course, since they hate heavy snowfalls, but secretly I exulted, for I have never lost my childish fascination with the short-lived beauty of snowflakes, and the way in which a snowfall shuts off the landscape for hours or days and then reveals it again, transformed and cleansed.

It snowed without a break for two days, with hardly any wind to cause drifting, and then, acting on instructions from Heaven, the snow stopped on Christmas morning. The cloud disappeared and in an instant the silver landscape was flooded with golden sunshine. I stood in the window of my bedroom, looking out over the *cwm*. I had to narrow my eyes because of the intensity of the light, and although I pricked my ears I could not hear a single sound. For a few blessed moments every bird, every animal, every human being in the *cwm* was transfixed by the beauty of our little world. I entered a sort of reverie, and in my mind's eye I looked back thirty years and saw my own small children out in the snowy field beneath my window. They shouted and screamed and laughed, and rolled in the snow, and threw snowballs at each other, and lay down and made the shapes of angels. Betsi chased little Dewi, and he ran away giggling. Daisy made a snow house, and Sara had a tantrum. Strange creature that I am, I wept -- not out of sadness or out of joy, but out of a strange sort of love and reverence which I am even now incapable of describing. The moods and mysteries of motherhood are still, after all these years, beyond my understanding.

"Tears for the beauty of the world, Mistress?" asked Bessie, coming up behind me and placing her hand upon my shoulder.

"Why yes, Bessie. And remembrances of the past. Forgive me, if you please. Put it down to the sentimentality that goes with old age."

"I understand you well enough, Mistress," said she. "Thank God for sentimentality, and for the fact that you have no other cause to weep. The snowfall has disrupted Christmas with a vengeance, but now that it has stopped, I need to trouble you for instructions. This morning, with the snow still falling and nothing moving, I assumed that Christmas dinner would be enjoyed by you and me, Gwenno, Gomer and Bryn. But now that it has stopped, should I assume that Betsi and Brynach and their families will fight their way through the snow to join us?"

"Your guess is as good as mine, Bessie. They are certainly invited and want to come. But the snow is three feet deep, and it looks soft, so horses and sledges are out of the question. I am sure that Betsi and Ioan and the boys will come, since they have but a short plod up the hill from Brithdir. But Brynach, Rose and little David have more of a challenge, if they are to walk all the way from Llanychaer. They will come if they can, probably over the common rather than along the valley. They have snowshoes, and they know how to use them. But five miles in deep snow is almost too much for little children with short legs."

So we hoped that the Llanychaer family would come, although in truth I was worried since there were only four hours of daylight left for them to make the journey. We ate a light mid-day meal, and at two of the clock Betsi and Ioan and the three boys arrived and filled the kitchen with laughter and lumps of snow as they shook their outer garments and stamped their feet. By four of the clock it was almost dark, and there was still no sign of Brynach and his two children. Betsi saw the concern writ large across my brow, and said; "Don't worry, Mother. They have probably taken one look at the snow and decided to stay put. Let us assume that they are enjoying their Christmas at home. Now then, we must concentrate on enjoying ours."

I nodded, but there was a nagging doubt in my breast, and so I went to my room and sat there in something approximating to silence, while the sounds of clanking pots and pans, and conversation and laughter, echoed up the stairs. I managed at last to empty my head and listen to my heart, and suddenly I knew that Brynach and the two children were at Carn Edward. And they were in trouble.

I rushed down the stairs, no doubt looking as pale as a ghost and as wild-eyed as a cornered rabbit. I met Betsi as she carried a tray of plates and cutlery from the kitchen to the dining room. "Mother!" she said. "You have seen something. What is it?"

"Brynach, Rose and David are at Carn Edward, and if we do not get to them soon they will freeze to death!"

I rushed into the kitchen, and all of the Christmas activity stopped. I kept as calm as I could, with all eyes fixed upon me. "We do not have a moment to lose," I said. "I know where they are. Bryn, how many pairs of snowshoes do we have?"

"Four, Mistress."

"Very well. Enough for Gomer, Bryn, Ioan and me. And the light sledge? Can we pull it between us?"

"It is not that light, Mistress. But we three men can drag it if we work together.........."

"Good. Let us go then. Bessie, when we return we will need lots of hot water and a house as warm as toast. Will you see to that?"

And as Bessie nodded, we four mountaineers rushed about, gathering our warmest coats and cloaks, and scarves and mittens, and pulling on our thickest boots. We wore whatever hats came to hand, and muffled our faces so that only our eyes were visible. I daresay that we looked like a group of intrepid Arctic explorers. Ioan fetched two of our biggest shovels from the cowshed. Bryn and Gomer ran out into the stable and collected ropes which they tied onto the sledge. Then they made three crude harnesses for man-hauling, while Ioan and I made ready our candle lanterns and collected the extra blankets which we assumed would be needed for the stranded and frozen travellers. Ioan was a good deal more frantic and worried than I, for he is a man of emotional extremes. Somehow I managed to keep calm, and surprised myself in the process. Within five minutes we were away, with our heavy snowshoes strapped to our feet just as that blessed man Iestyn, Brynach's father, had taught us many years ago. He had learnt the Red Indian method of walking over thick snow from an old soldier who had been in the American War of Independence; how fitting, I thought, that these simple flat things, made out of wickerwork and leather, should now give us the opportunity of saving Iestyn's son and grandchildren when otherwise they might perish.

I led the way with a lantern on a long pole, trying to find the easiest route up the lane towards the common. We had to struggle over three gates, since the snow was too deep for us to open them, and in a few places we had to scramble up and over hedges and stone banks with a good deal of slipping and falling and cursing. But the night was calm, and once our eyes had adjusted to the darkness we found that the starlight and the whiteness of the snow-covered landscape enabled us to see all but the smallest details of the terrain. There was a thin moon down near the horizon. Above us and to our right towered the bulk of Carningli, clean and white against a star-studded sky, and when I looked back I could see the wide expanse of the *cwm*, with pinpricks of light and columns of smoke showing the locations of Gelli, Fachongle, Cilwen, and other houses. In all of them, I thought, there are Christmas dinners in the oven or on the table, and yule logs and roaring fires and ruddy faces, while we spend our Christmas Day struggling up the rocky slope towards the common, fighting for breath and mocked by a snow blanket so powdery that we sink into it up to our knees in spite of our excellent snowshoes.

We had to travel no more than half a mile, but with snow as difficult as this I quickly came to realise why Brynach and the children had failed to complete their journey. We had a truly terrible time of it, and our passage brought us to the very edge of exhaustion. We had to struggle with every step of the way, and as I encouraged the three men onwards and tried to find the best route for them and their loaded sledge I marvelled at the fact that they had not for a moment doubted my strange prophesy that Brynach and the children would be at Carn Edward. That said something for their faith in my special powers, but as we battled onwards, not daring to stop for a moment in order to catch our breath, doubts began to enter my own mind. What if they were not there? What if they were somewhere else, lost in the snowy wilderness with nothing to guide us towards them? What if they were dead already, frozen in a last embrace in some icy tomb? Oh God, let that not be true. Please God, do not take Brynach and the children from me! Have you not had your fill of sacrifices from this beloved family? Do you not realise, in your fatherly wisdom, that I have been tested to the limit, and cannot cope with yet more tragedy? Let it not be true. Let it not be true........

"Mistress!" shouted Gomer. "I think there is a light at Carn Edward!"

Thus jolted back into the real world, I stopped in my tracks. The men stopped too, and we all strained our eyes to see what lay ahead of us. There, no more than two hundred yards away, was the outline of Carn Edward, softened and changed somewhat by the blanket of snow, but unmistakable nonetheless. And on the highest part of the rock a dim light was flickering. Somebody -- probably Brynach -- had placed a candle lantern there, in the hope or the expectation that it would be spotted by somebody out searching on the common.

Like mad things we resumed our struggle through the unforgiving snow, with poor Bryn so exhausted that he kept on stumbling and falling. I also realized, from my acheing limbs and burning lungs and pounding heart, that age was beginning to take its toll. But after five minutes we reached the rock. My heart leapt when in the dim light of my own lantern I saw the tracks of snowshoes and sledge runners, and then we spotted the sledge itself standing out starkly against a mound of disturbed snow. "Brynach, are you there? Can you hear me?" I shouted. The four of us stood perfectly still and waited for a reply. There was none. Although I was sweating profusely as a result of my exertions in the snow, ice began to enter my heart, and I stood frozen to the spot. So the men shouted together, and waited for a few seconds for a reply. Still there was none. I was quite petrified, and knew not what to do. Then Ioan took charge. He and Gomer and Bryn threw off their sledge harnesses and called upon some hidden reserves of energy to search among the snow-covered rocks. Bryn examined the abandoned sledge, and said that it was loaded with a bundle of blankets and ropes. More to the point, it had a broken runner. Gomer looked at the lantern on the topmost rock. "Mistress, I am quite sure that this candle has not been burning for more than an hour," he shouted. "There has to be hope for them, indeed, if they are tucked away somewhere nice and cosy."

There was a large area of disturbed snow, and the men followed every track and trail between the icy crags, intermittently shouting and listening. Having overcome my initial sense of horror, I started to search too, and once I had composed myself I realized that Brynach and the children would be at the western end of the *carn*, in a narrow crevice in which he had often hidden as a small child during our birthday picnic visits. His favourite place, I thought, and maybe the perfect place to die? I refused to give in to such thoughts, and I shouted to the men to follow me. "I think I know where to look!" I said, and led them off the summit of the *carn* and down onto the lower area at the base of the rocks. We skirted round the southern outcrops, and suddenly we were into a new area of disturbed snow. It was piled up high at the entrance of the hidden crevice, and it was clear that Brynach had worked like a madman to create a sort of cave between the rock faces. They were bound to be somewhere behind that pile of snow.

"Excuse us, Martha *bach*," said Ioan, and the three men pushed me aside and started burrowing with their mittened hands like excited terriers digging out a badger sett. I hardly dared to look. Then Gomer found an opening, and after more frenzied excavation managed to squeeze himself into the snow cave. "They are here! They are here!" he shouted.

"Are they all right?"

173

Then I heard him shouting: "Master Brynach! Master Brynach! Wake up! You must wake up! Come along now! Children, wake up!" And I could hear that he was shaking them and slapping faces in an attempt to bring them back from the cold clutches of death.

"Mistress! They are breathing! They are all alive! But we must get them out of here and home as quickly as may be!"

So Bryn and Ioan and I resumed the digging, and soon we had cleared most of the snow from the cave entrance. Then I saw Brynach and the children, crammed into a little space no more than four feet wide and four feet high, dimly illuminated by another candle lantern which was propped against the rock face. Brynach had his arms around the children, and all three of them were enveloped in a large black cloak. I recognized it at once as the Nightwalker's cloak, used by Iestyn Price on his mysterious expeditions onto the mountain when Brynach had been a small baby and a growing child. Then it had terrified me and terrorized the neighbourhood, but now, in another strange twist of fate, it had kept three beloved members of my family alive when they would otherwise surely have died from cold and exhaustion. Iestyn, I thought, might well be looking down from Heaven at this precise moment, with a self-satisfied smile upon his face.

At last the entombed travellers opened their eyes. "Hello boys. Hello Mother," said Brynach. "Wherever have you been until now?"

"*Mam-gu*, is Christmas dinner ready yet?" said Rose.

"Have I got any nice presents?" said David.

Then I stood outside the snow cave and wept while Ioan and Bryn dived inside and laughed and shouted, and hugged Brynach and the children, and Gomer, and each other. How they all fitted into such a small space I will never know. But at last they extricated themselves, and I realized that Brynach and the children had done everything that was needed for survival in such conditions. They had left a signal to guide us. They were well dressed for the freezing weather, and they were as warm as kittens in their little cave. They had shut themselves into a place where, if the wind had sprung up, they would have been protected. They had a lantern and spare candles. They had three sheepskins to keep them warm. I concluded that their deep sleep had been induced by exhaustion rather than frostbite, and I could see from the debris littered about that they had been nibbling dried fruits and sweetmeats before sleep had overtaken them. They even had with them a little bundle of food, and when I embraced them and kissed them I realized that they had smeared their faces with goose grease. I was inordinately proud of them all, as any old mother and grandmother would be.

Soon the three of them were out in the open, and Brynach explained to us what had happened on their journey. "We knew that it would be difficult," he said, "but the children were determined to come to the Plas. So while it was still snowing we planned everything in detail. When the snow stopped we set out straight away, with Rose and I walking and little David on the sledge. His four-year-old legs are still too short for plodding about in snowshoes. But the snow was more difficult than we had anticipated, and when we got up onto the open common it was so soft and powdery that the sledge would not slide on the surface. It kept on sinking down, and even with Rose's help it became more and more difficult to pull it along. Then, as we passed Bedd Morris, two things happened. One of the sledge runners broke, and even though it was still light enough for me to see what I was doing, my fingers were so frozen that I could not repair it properly. And then Rose fell and twisted her ankle. Suddenly she could not walk properly, let alone help me with the sledge. So I fitted her snowshoes onto David's little feet, and he struggled along like a hero. I had to take Rose on my shoulders, and without David's weight on the broken sledge I managed to pull it along, ten yards at a time. I was determined not to abandon our blankets and sheepskins in case we should need them..............."

"My dad is so strong, *Mam-gu*, that he could pull along a whole ox wagon all by himself!" shouted David.

"Thank you, *cariad*," smiled Brynach. "You are very kind. I knew that there is nowhere on this open part of the common where we could find shelter -- not a rock, not a tree, not a single stone wall. But I knew that if we could reach Carn Edward we would have a chance of survival. We had about a mile to cover, as the light faded. God knows how we did it. We fell over time and again, and we had to stop frequently as we were, all three, overcome by exhaustion. At last we reached the snow-covered *carn*. We hunted about, looking for a good place to dig a snow hole. Then I remembered my childhood den, and so I left one lantern on the top of the rock, and down we went with the other to find the entrance of the crevice. It was obliterated by the snow, but we dug and dug, and at last we found

175

the way in. Then we dug and dug again, did we not, children?"

"Oh yes, since it was a matter of life and death," said Rose, sounding like an old matron rather than a seven-year-old. "Dad said we must dig until we had a cosy cave, but we were very tired indeed..........."

"Then it was ready," added David. "And we ate some food, and brought the lantern and sheepskins in with us, and wrapped ourselves up in the old cloak that used to belong to my grandpa, and cuddled up nice and warm, and went to sleep."

"Just like that?"

"Oh yes. Just like that. It was very exciting."

"Too exciting for my taste," said Ioan with a grin. "Will you children please promise to do something a little less exciting next Christmas?" And without waiting for an answer, he picked up Rose and started to plod round the flank of the *carn* back towards the place where we had left the sledge. Gomer picked up little David and followed, and ten minutes later we were all on our way home.

We abandoned Brynach's broken sledge, and placed his possessions onto ours. Then we put the two children on the sheepskins, wrapped them up in piles of blankets, and set off down the slope back to the Plas. Brynach looked so weak that he could well have taken a ride on the sledge as well, but he insisted on walking, so he and I went ahead of the sledge, swinging our lanterns and lighting the way. Bryn, Gomer and Ioan had to do the hard work of pulling the sledge, but now it was easier, for the route led downhill all the way, and we had our old tracks to travel in. There was a good deal of slipping and sliding, and on four occasions the sledge tipped over, spilling its load of laughing children into the powdery snow. They thought it was all a hilarious adventure, and I thanked God that they appeared oblivious to the fact that they had come very close to death and had survived only because of a wondrous and blessed combination of circumstances.

Soon we were all singing lustily as we made for the warmth of the Plas kitchen and as we all thought of our Christmas dinner. They must have been watching and listening from the upstairs windows of the house, for as we dropped down into the snow-filled lane leading to the farmyard, I saw the rest of the household come out to greet us. There was pandemonium, of course, with tears and laughter and embraces and admonishments, and with everybody talking at once.

It may have been a small Christmas this year, but it was certainly one that I will never forget. Rose has a badly swollen ankle, but otherwise the three intrepid explorers are none the worse for wear, and after a couple of nights at the Plas they moved down to Brithdir for a short stay with Betsi and her family. Once again, through following my intuition, I have managed to keep my family together and have managed to avoid a terrible tragedy. And again I have been blessed by my angels.

The snow has now melted away, and we are getting back to normal. Brynach and the children have returned to Plas Llanychaer, travelling, at my insistence, in my light chaise. There is just one little footnote to this episode. On the day that the thaw set in, Brynach and I walked once again up to Carn Edward in bright sunshine, to recover a tall black hat. He had left it behind in the little snow cave on Christmas Day, in the euphoria of the moment. He said that both he and the children were very fond of it, and referred to it as "the Grandpa Hat." He knew, and I knew, that it was the very same hat which had been worn up until the time of his death in 1822 by his father whom we called the Nightwalker.

ΩΩΩΩΩΩΩΩΩΩ

18th January 1839

Hen Galan has come and gone, and the days are beginning to lengthen. The weather is now coming in from the west, with one spell of wind and rain following another. The sun shines occasionally, but never with any strength, and never for long enough to dry out the yard or the fields. Working outside is miserable indeed, and I have tried to set the men tasks inside the barn and the other buildings, repairing harnesses and harrows and ploughs, shaping new handles for forks and rakes, greasing cartwheels and tending the animals. Shemi and Sian came and stayed for three days and entertained us hugely with their tales of strange events, and silly people, and the little dramas that come to the attention of a wizard and his wife. I rode down to the Parrog to visit my beloved friends Patty and Jake. I stayed there for a night, and observed a remarkably high tide which washed right across meadows and gardens and left the warehouses standing up like islands in a muddy sea. Small news indeed. But there is bigger news from further afield, and it has been delivered to me by Brynach.

On the ninth day of the month he left the children with me at the Plas and travelled up to Carmarthen on mysterious business. He was not very forthcoming, and would say only that he was going to report on certain matters concerning the Chartists. I was intrigued, but not greatly worried, and I trusted him to keep his promise that he would not get involved in any violent disorder. So for two days I had a very jolly time with Rose and David. We played games, went for walks, told each other stories, and painted messy pictures. I daresay that I had even more fun than the children, and Bessie had to tell me off for getting paint all over my dress and for carrying mud into the house on my boots.

Brynach came back very late at night, and over a belated supper in the dining room he told me about the Carmarthen meeting. It should have been held in the Guildhall, but the town council withdrew its consent at the last minute, and so thousands of men carrying torches and lanterns were left milling around in the streets, chanting and shouting. Because of that, said Brynach, many more men came out from their houses and cottages to join the marchers, and he estimated that the crowd eventually numbered about four thousand. It was all very good-humoured, and at last the organizers of the meeting encouraged the demonstrators to march to the Picton Monument, where they listened to speeches. The most impassioned speech, said Brynach, came from a Carmarthen solicitor named Hugh Williams, who was clearly in close touch with the leaders of the Chartist movement in London. He appeared on personal good terms with men like William Lovett and Francis Place. He knew the contents of the People's Charter and its aspirations, and he clearly had great sympathy for the plight of the working man. Indeed, said Brynach, so blunt and brash were his comments about the Prime Minister and the nobility that some thought his speech to be treasonable. Treasonable or not, Master Williams was elected by acclamation as the delegate to attend a great Convention of Chartists in London in the month of March.

"This Master Williams sounds like a fellow with whom one could do business," said I.

Brynach looked surprised. "Indeed, Mother?" he said. "He will end up in prison like Master Lovett and the rest of the leaders from London and Birmingham."

"Well, I am used to spending time in the company of felons and revolutionaries. I find them a good deal more interesting than the petty gentry of West Wales. Remember, if you will be so kind, that I am an ex-convict myself."

"Yes, yes, Mother," he laughed, "as you frequently remind me. But Master Williams might be a danger in more ways than one. His private life is, shall we say, just a little unsavoury."

"Even more interesting. And how do you know what he gets up to behind closed doors?"

"People talk, Mother. After the rally at the Picton Monument, the crowds dispersed in a perfectly orderly fashion, and a number of us found our way to the Red Lion Hotel, where we enjoyed a convivial hot supper. Dafydd Stokes Trecwn was there, as was Squire William Bowen from Llwyngwair and Nicholas Lloyd Cwmgloyn............"

"Really? And other gentry too, risking the displeasure and condemnation of their fellows?"

"A few from Carmarthenshire whom I did not recognize. Some of them were there in their capacity as magistrates, keeping an eye on things. Others might have been acting as spies for the Home Secretary -- I cannot be sure. But I have no doubt, Mother, about the integrity of my colleagues from this area; they spoke with great conviction about the justice of the Chartist cause, and appeared not to be at all concerned about whom their listeners might be."

"That's useful to know, Brynach. Now, can we return to Master Williams? Was he at the jolly supper, and did you meet him?"

"Yes and yes again. I should say that he is somewhat over forty. He has bright blue eyes, high cheekbones and a hook nose. He has a high forehead and unkempt side whiskers, and a rather hard mouth. He dresses soberly, with a heavy black woollen jacket and a black waistcoat. I should imagine that frivolity does not come easily to him. On the contrary, he appears to me to be a very serious fellow, with a strong personality and a ferocious intellect. He is very eloquent, and expresses his views in a most forthright manner. I imagine that he likes nothing better than a good argument in a London coffee house."

"More and more interesting.........."

"Come now, Mother. I should have thought that the gentle sex would not take to him at all, for he is far too domineering and intimidating. I think he might even be cynical and cruel. In my estimation he is also very arrogant."

"Even more interesting, my dear son. You might be surprised about those features in a gentleman which prove attractive to a woman. And on the matter of his unsavoury private life? What do you know about that?

"Not a great deal. But Dafydd Stokes, as you know, has his ear very close to the ground, and he told me that Master Williams is married to a lady from St Clears who is even older then you............"

"Be careful, son, or I will box your ears."

"Yes, Mother," he laughed. "I promise to be careful, and to move away swiftly if attacked. At any rate, it is said that Mistress Williams of Gardde is a good twenty-five years older than him, and that he married her simply as a means of acquiring her property and her fortune. He spends hardly any time with her at the marital home, and lives mostly in Ferryside. More to the point, according to Dafydd he is a thoroughly disreputable fellow who has scattered his wild oats across much of the Carmarthenshire countryside. It is said that he has more than fifty bastard children, and that if you look through the magistrates' records you will find his name in paternity suits galore. It is also said that much of his income as an attorney, and a good deal of his wife's fortune, goes out for the support of his bastard flock."

"Oh dear, I fear that he will never make a good Methodist."

"This is not a frivolous matter, Mother. If I were you, I would steer well away from the fellow." He got up and yawned, and then came and kissed me on the cheek. "Thank you for the supper. Now I must wish you goodnight. I am very tired, and could do with a good night's sleep. First thing in the morning, I must get back to Llanychaer with the children and prepare my report of the Chartist gathering for the *Welshman*. Anonymously, of course, as ever."

So I wished him goodnight, and off he went to bed. I sat up for a while in the quiet dining room, gazing into the embers of the fire, thinking and making plans. One of my plans is to meet that revolutionary gentleman Master Hugh Williams, and preferably quite soon.

19th January 1839

Today Dai Darjeeling called to see Bessie and to declare -- no doubt for the thousandth time -- his undying love. Such devotion over so many years! I have told her over and again that she should marry him and enjoy happiness and good tea for what remains of her life, but she insists that happiness resides within the Plas. She says that she does indeed love Dai, and has told him as much, but that he is too set in his bachelor ways to change now, and that a wedding and a new house would be burdensome to her. I suspect that he quite enjoys his freedom too, and would feel greatly restricted within a marriage. He may even feel that something would go out of his life if the chase were to end in success. His poems and his romantic gestures require a good deal of planning, and Bessie loves them as much as she loves the dear fellow himself. And I am sure that he has enjoyed a measure of success, for following several of my absences from the Plas I have returned to find fresh tea in the larder, a rosy glow upon Bessie's face and innocence writ large across the faces of her fellow servants. I have asked no questions and have been told no lies.

Dai was in Narberth two days since, and as we sat around the kitchen table drinking Chinese tea he relayed the news that an attempt has been made to burn down the Narberth Workhouse, which stands on a hill just outside the town. He said that the building was almost complete and ready to take its first paupers. But it was universally hated in all of the 48 parishes of the Narberth Union, and the poor people who occupy the two current poor-houses in the town do not want to move. Dai does not know who was behind the riot, but news of it must have reached the magistrates before it happened, for they swore in a crowd of special constables, and they were all on duty when the mob arrived with their flaming torches. Some damage was done, but the mob was sent packing, much to the surprise of the magistrates and the constables, who have never had such a victory in West Wales before.

When I had finished my tea I left Dai and Bessie to their chatting and flirting in the kitchen, and went upstairs to my room. I thought long and hard about this business of mobs trying to correct the evils that afflict the common people, and became even more convinced that great crowds are their own worst enemies. They advertise their presence far too widely and noisily, and secrecy is impossible. If a few elderly and rheumatic special constables can send a mob packing in Narberth, what will happen when the Yeomanry or the Light Dragoons are pressed into service? Slaughter, and even more discontent and riotous behaviour, and then even more suppression. Our feeble Prime Minister Lord Melbourne will do nothing, since he is reported in the *Cambrian* as neither wishing to see the poor nor to think about them. Stupid man -- does he assume, while he fawns before our new little Queen and ponders on the glories of the Empire, that the discontent that disfigures our countryside will simply go away? I, for one, will ensure that he is forced to notice it and to deal with it, for my single ambition from this point on is to bring back a smile to the face of this miserable land.

ΩΩΩΩΩΩΩΩΩΩΩ

26th January 1839

Two days since I attended a meeting of the Whitland Trust, called at the Red Dragon Inn to consider the letting of the gates for the coming year. I travelled to Whitland with Brynach and Ioan in the small carriage, and we were lucky to complete the journey in icy conditions without the loss of a horse or a wheel. The roads get worse each year where they should be getting better, and I daresay that when the railways get to Pembrokeshire we will all rush about by train and forget about the miseries of pot-holes and frozen mud. I cannot wait, and at my time of life I deserve a little speed and comfort.

Between Newport and Whitland we passed through eight tollgates, and if I had not been a tally-holder in each of the trusts responsible I would have ended up four shillings worse off than when I set out in the morning. Iniquity indeed, and I was seething with indignation even before the meeting started. It was a very silly meeting, with about forty people present. Master Thomas Bullin and his surveyor were there, and when he entered the room I caught his eye. I hoped that I might defeat him again, as I had done twice back in the autumn. But this time everything had been fixed in advance. The chairman, Squire Lewis of Henllan, was in a great hurry, and was clearly intent upon getting away for an early supper. He asked for a financial report, and when the figures were presented it was apparent that the Trust was still far from meeting the costs of the renewal of the Whitland Trust Act in 1832. From my limited understanding of such matters, it appeared to me that the Trust was bankrupt, and I could not see how it could continue to operate so long as its costs outstripped its income. This is where Master Bullin came in. Quicker than a wink of the eye, he was on his feet giving a presentation on the effective running of turnpike trusts. He explained that he was the very man to turn the Trust's loss into profit. All that was needed, said he, was that the trustees should accept his generous offer of £800 for the toll contract. A full £300 more than was offered by the old contract holder, and cash on the nail. Within a few months, said he, the trustees could reduce their debts by a considerable amount, pay interest to the tally-holders, and be left with at least £200 for the completion of major improvements to the roads and bridges which were under the care of the Trust. Better roads and fewer pot-holes would lead to greater satisfaction on the part of travellers, and thence to greater quantities of traffic. That would mean more revenues from the tollgates, as a result of which he hoped to return to the trustees in twelve months time with an enhanced offer for the letting of the gates for another year. A thousand pounds a year was not at all an unreasonable expectation, said he, with gold in his eyes and silver slipping off his tongue.

"Master Chairman," said I, "through your good office, might I direct a question towards Master Bullin?"

"Very well, Mistress Morgan, if you make it short."

"Thank you indeed. Master Bullin, this is clearly not the first presentation which you have made to a beleaguered Trust. If you now invest £800 in the tollgate contract, and place your cash immediately at the disposal of the trustees, you will clearly wish to recoup your investment as rapidly as possible, and long before the improvements of which you speak are affected. You must raise more tolls, and soon. How many more tollgates do you want, Master Bullin?"

"Well now," said he, getting red in the face, "I was coming to that in due course."

"You and your surveyors have been seen here, there and everywhere, sir!" shouted somebody from the back of the room. "There are rumours abroad that you want a dozen new gates!"

"Order, gentlemen, if you please!" pleaded the Chairman. "Master Bullin, perhaps you will explain?"

"Gentlemen, and Mistress Morgan, I am happy to oblige. I need only four new gates in order to recoup my investment. If I cannot obtain your consent for those, I withdraw my offer." He paused for effect, and then continued. "You may have it on oath from me that this is the most generous offer I have ever made in an area with such a small population. I am taking a very considerable gamble, but I do it out of a warm regard for those present in this room, and out of a sincere desire to see prosperity in these beloved counties of West Wales."

"Hear, hear!" said one of Squire Lewis's cronies. "A noble sentiment indeed, sir."

"And one last thing, Master Chairman," said Master Bullin, with all the sincerity of Shylock. "My offer is to take the contract for a minimum of three years at a minimum of £800 per year. I dare to suggest that you will not obtain a better offer."

He sat down heavily, with the look of a small child who has just enjoyed the consumption of an illicit plum pudding. Instantly another of the chairman's cronies leaped to his feet. "I venture to suggest, Master Chairman," said he, "that we have heard all we wish to hear. It is self-evident that we must accept Master Bullin's proposals in their entirety. I therefore thank him for his generosity and move acceptance."

"Seconded!" shouted another crony.

Those of us who had travelled from the far west were not used to this method of fixing decisions, and we saw that things were spiralling out of control. Before I could react, Ioan leapt to his feet and shouted: "Master Chairman, I object! We are not ready to move to a vote on this matter, since we have had no discussion. I have very grave reservations about Master Bullin's plan, and I wish to canvass the views of others present in this room."

"Out of order, Master Rhys," said the Chairman. "We have a seconded proposal. We must move on. You may, if you wish, propose an amendment."

At this, I could remain silent no longer. I sprang to my feet, while Master Lewis spluttered and flapped his hands at me. "Sir, this is an outrage! Master Rhys makes a sound point, and I support him. You must allow discussion. Master Bullin's presentation is based upon fantasy, not fact. With all due respect to him, he is an Englishman who speaks no Welsh. He does not know the circumstances of the small farmers of this neighbourhood. If he is allowed to put up these four new gates discontent could well be transformed overnight into open rebellion. The burden to be carried by the farmers during the spring and summer will be unbearable. And what will be the consequences of that? For a start, riot and disorder, and probably death and destruction. Then fewer travellers. And then less revenue rather than more. Less revenue means less money for road repairs and improvements. And that means more anger burning in the breasts of travellers, and fury directed at trustees and tally-holders. Master Bullin will be vilified to such a degree that he would be well advised to get out of Wales altogether..........."

"Mistress Morgan, I must rule you out of order! In any case I do not, as Chairman of this meeting, accept your wild pronouncements on the likely course of events. Our people are for the most part God-fearing folk with the greatest of respect for the rule of law."

"Sir, that may be so," said Brynach, leaping to my defence. "But they are also proud people who have suffered two successive harvest failures. They will be pushed only so far before they take action on behalf of their starving children."

I could sense that we three had little support in the room, but I decided that we might as well go down fighting. I stood up again, before Squire Lewis could stop me. "Sir, I propose an amendment. I propose that Master Bullin be awarded the contract for the gates in exchange for a sum of £700 for one year only, renewable for a second year on receipt of reports of satisfactory management on his part, and conditional upon an assurance that he will erect no further gates or side-bars within the area of interest of this Trust."

I knew that this would not be accepted, but I had to try. Master Bullin, with a face like thunder, stood up and addressed the Chairman. "Sir," he said, "I give notice that I will not accept the terms and conditions outlined in Mistress Morgan's amendment. You know my proposal. Take it or leave it."

So the proposal was voted through, with only three votes against. The chairman was instructed to complete the contract with Master Bullin, and to make an order for the four new gates. We three revolutionaries had to accept the decisions of the meeting with good grace, and indeed we stayed behind afterwards and enjoyed an ample supper with our fellow trustees. We even spent a jovial half hour in the presence of Master Bullin, who is not a bad fellow. He is insensitive and lacking in sophistication, but I think that he is honest, and he makes no bones about the fact that he is involved in the business of tollgates and turnpike trusts simply in order to make a tidy fortune. He knows what the risks are, and one has to admire him for risking his own money in a way that I could never contemplate.

After the meeting we three stayed for the night at the Red Dragon, for it would have been suicidal to travel home in the pitch darkness with the temperatures well below freezing. Twenty years ago, after such a frustrating and infuriating encounter with incompetent squires, I would have spent the night wallowing in the depths of despair. Not any more. Thank God that I have grown a little wiser as I have grown older. I am certain that before long there will be big trouble in the countryside, by comparison with which our little adventures with the *Ceffyl Pren* in Newport will pale into insignificance. But I face the prospect of social unrest with a degree of equanimity. Indeed, if I am honest with myself, I will admit to a feeling of anticipation and even excitement. Now that I am almost too old for lust, the thrill of insurrection will keep me going for the time being.

ΩΩΩΩΩΩΩΩΩΩΩ

17th March 1839

Shortly after the meeting of the Whitland Trust I sent Will over the mountain with a verbal message for Master Mathias Trehaidd, Master Lloyd Davies Glynsaithmaen and Master Twm Carnabwth. It was necessary for me to keep my promise to the plotters whom I had met before Christmas. I put nothing in writing, and will hold fast to that principle so long as there are vindictive magistrates and smart attorneys in this wicked world. Will passed on the intelligence that Bullin now had in his possession an order for four new gates, and that two of them, at Efailwen and Maes-gwyn, were in remote places which had previously been free of gates. Will also advised the men on the south side of the mountain that I would be prepared to travel to another meeting in due course, if they thought that further information from me might be of use.

News has now reached me that work is under way on the new gates and on the construction of gatekeepers' houses adjacent to them. There is growing resentment against Master Bullin and against the Whitland trustees, and some of them have been abused and even threatened with violence. At the Trust's existing gates there have been heated arguments, mostly arising out of Master Bullin's recent instruction to his gatekeepers that they should never allow credit. In the past, it was the custom to allow farmers to pass through the gates when they were on their way to market with animals or produce for sale, and to accept payment from them on their return journeys, when they had a few coppers in their pockets. Not any more. I have to say that the fellow appears to have an instinct for causing trouble where it could easily be avoided, and Brynach is of the view that he is actually seeking to provoke confrontation so that he can call down the forces of law and order for his protection.

I have met this fellow Hugh Williams, and I am intrigued by him. It happened like this. Four days since Master Williams and a colleague called William Jenkins called in at Newport during their tour of West Wales. They were preaching the Chartist cause and seeking to win recruits from among the local population. Posters were put up in advance in the town, announcing an evening meeting in the upstairs room of the Black Lion Inn. The magistrates wanted to stop them, but there was nothing illegal about their gathering, and so it went ahead.

I travelled down to town in the light carriage, and entered the meeting in the company of Brynach and Ioan, just to see what it was all about. There were maybe forty people in the room, including some whom I would not have expected to be there. Squire Jobbins was there, and so was Mayor Edward Rees, and so was George Havard Medical. Three of my own tenants were there -- Waldo Tucker Penrhiw, Gwyn Williams Gelli and Owen Pritchard Dolrannog Uchaf. I raised an eyebrow at that, since I had not previously been aware of their interest in political matters. Zeke Tomos and Dafydd Ifan were sitting at the back of the room in the shadows, and that did not surprise me. Then, among the younger generation, I spotted Jack and Hubert Nicholas, the two sons of my friends

Patty and Jake, and also young Bobby Morris, taking an evening off from courting Gwenno in my kitchen. Sitting with them were Shemi's son John and Will's son Gerallt. Then I saw my own nephew Mark, the youngest son of my sister Catrin, sitting with Samuel Stokes, the youngest son of my dear friend Mary Jane. My old friend Skiff Abraham was there, looking prosperous and surrounded by three or four of his confederates. Some of Skiff's spies were there, as were some of mine. And there were maybe twenty faces which I did not recognize. Friends or foes? I could not be sure, and concluded that it was probably wise to assume that they were foes, who would quietly be making lists of names and then reporting back to the powers of darkness.

In truth it was rather a boring meeting. Master Jenkins spoke first, and became tangled up in a complicated discourse about the Charter and about representation and conventions and petitions and so forth. Master Williams spoke with much more passion about injustices and rights, and fixed the members of his audience with his cold green eyes as he confronted them with the need for reform by the people and for the people. He developed his arguments well, as one might expect of an attorney, and at times he quivered with emotion. He gesticulated a good deal. He modulated his voice like a Nonconformist minister, sometimes speaking in a barely audible whisper, sometimes pleading and cajoling, sometimes declaiming, sometimes explaining as a father might speak to a child, and sometimes thundering out his challenges to his audience to take action within the law. He talked for maybe thirty minutes, and I was so taken with his delivery and his speaking technique that I have to admit, with a degree of shame, that I cannot recall much of what he actually said. I could not work out whether he was acting, or whether he genuinely believed, with great passion, every word that passed his lips. His eyes caught mine on more than one occasion, and indeed I thought he looked at me a good deal more frequently during his discourse than was appropriate in a public gathering. That caused my cheeks to burn, and I hope that in that dimly lit room nobody noticed.

I do remember his conclusion. "Brothers and sisters," he roared, "this is a moment of destiny in the history of our nation. We will, if we are not careful, subside into apathy and allow a government of arrogant and self-appointed gentlemen to control every aspect of our lives -- what we eat and drink, what we pay in taxes, what we say and what we do, and even what we think. Regulation and control on all sides! And what does that mean for you and for me? Suppression and misery, brothers and sisters -- nothing more and nothing less! Is that what men want? Is that what women want? Infamy, brothers and sisters! This Government cannot and will not change of its own accord, but Lord Melbourne and his cronies wish only to deny the aspirations of good men and women and to extinguish the flame of freedom which burns within their breasts. They must not succeed in this wicked enterprise, for if they do, we will deserve the ire -- nay, the condemnation -- of our children and our grand-children! Join us, brothers and sisters, and swell the great choir of voices across the land in demanding a new representation and a new beginning! You know our six demands. Sign the Charter. March with us if you will! God bless Wales!"

Master Williams sat down to polite applause, having been heard with a fair degree of respect by his somewhat naive audience. Most of those present in the room, including myself, signed his petition and agreed to support the aspirations of the Chartist Movement, but it occurred to me that the real issues that concerned the audience were not the great matters of state such as voting rights but the small things that affected them on a daily basis. Master Jenkins and Master Williams may be revolutionaries at heart, but I am not sure that they have found a hotbed of revolutionary fervour in our little town. We may yet see insurrection and revolution in West Wales, but its causes, and its solutions, will be so complex and so localized that our young Queen and our old Prime Minister will in my estimation be quite incapable of understanding them. Therein lies a very great danger.

After the meeting most of the audience departed, and George Havard Medical introduced me to Master Williams and his friend Jenkins. They both bowed deeply, and I lowered my eyes and curtseyed. "Mistress Morgan of Plas Ingli!" said Master Williams, with his green eyes sparkling. "Why, what a pleasure it is to meet you! I spotted you in our small but excellent audience, and wondered who you were. I should have known, having heard so much about your elegant beauty and about your interest in the affairs of gentlemen......."

"Sir, gentlemen should not have affairs in isolation. I daresay that most of them are improved by a certain amount of female participation."

He looked shocked, just for a moment, and then roared with laughter. "Checkmate, madam!" he chortled. "As an attorney, I should be more careful with my choice of words. I should of course have said the **political** affairs of gentlemen."

"Quite so, Master Williams. That was exactly what I understood you to mean. Indeed, I have no idea how else your words might have been interpreted by other gentlemen in the circumstances. Now then, I need to know more about your Chartist Convention. And I need to know what is going on in Birmingham just now. Would you oblige?"

Then Skiff intervened, and it became clear to me that he had had much to do with the organization of the meeting. He invited the speakers, and Havard Medical, and Brynach, Ioan and me, to a light supper at his substantial house just a few doors away from the Black Lion. We were all delighted to accept, and before Brynach could offer me his arm Master Williams offered his. I thanked him for his courtesy, and so he assisted me down the stairs. I let go before we went out onto the street, much to Brynach's relief, since the sight of Mistress Morgan on the arm of a dangerous stranger would certainly have set tongues wagging.

We enjoyed a good supper, and Skiff proved to be a generous host. Then we retired to the drawing room. Master Williams and I exchanged glances, and sat opposite each other more by design than accident. As the evening progressed we exchanged further glances, and I derived some pleasure from the realization that he looked at me a good deal more than he looked at Mistress Abraham or any other of those present. Skiff proved to be remarkably well informed on those matters which are of greatest concern to the Chartists, and I was reminded while I listened to him that Chartism provided a perfect route by which he and his merchant fellows might follow their aspirations. We talked and drank good wine far into the night, and while there was no mention of subversion, disorder or violence these things were never far beneath the surface, and that helped to put a frisson of excitement into the air. We made no firm plans for action, and spoke only in generalities. But while the meeting was genteel and orderly, there was no doubt that we all shared one agenda -- namely the changing of the old order.

At last it was time to go. Brynach called his man from the kitchen, and when his chaise was ready the two of them set off for Llanychaer along the valley road. Then I asked Gomer to get my light carriage ready, and soon he and the conveyance were outside the door of the Abraham residence. Ioan and I gave our thanks to Skiff and his sweet wife and said our farewells to the others, and I was pleased to receive a lavish bow and a kiss on the hand from Master Williams before we clattered off up the Cilgwyn road.

As we went slowly up Greystones Hill in a pool of dim light from our candle lanterns, I discussed the evening with Ioan, and declared myself well satisfied. He looked agitated, and at last he plucked up his courage and said: "Martha, I too found it a very satisfactory and interesting evening. But if I may say so, your behaviour towards Master Hugh Williams was a little less discreet than it might have been."

"Indeed, Ioan? I thought that I behaved myself very well. I did not exactly flirt with him, did I?"

"Well, no. But I could not help noticing the little shared glances, and the pleasure which you derived from his attention. I urge you, Martha, to remember your station. You are a gentlewoman and he is simply an attorney. You are also a grandmother, and twenty years older than him. He is also a dangerous fellow with an unsavoury reputation. Please be careful. I say this as a loving son-in-law who is concerned for your happiness. You have had enough pain in your life already........."

"Dear Ioan!" said I, holding his hand and giving him a kiss on the cheek. "I love you dearly, and I thank you for your concern. But do not worry about me. I am more than a little flattered by his attention. I am also old enough to look after myself, and I know exactly what I am doing."

We dropped Ioan off at the front gate of Brithdir, and continued on our bumpy way back to the Plas. I wrapped myself up in my travelling blanket, and could not resist smiling to myself. Not a bad evening, I thought, and a job well done.

ΩΩΩΩΩΩΩΩΩΩ

24th March 1839

I have had reports from Jacob Jones, who is one of my elderly spies. He does not look like a spy, for he has snow-white hair, a weatherbeaten face and a body racked by rheumatism. He spies for me because I help him with potions and ointments which ease his pain, and because he gets a square meal every time he calls on me at the Plas. He has the eyes and ears of a tawny owl, and he was at the Chartist meeting in the Black Lion and at the bar afterwards. He called on me yesterday, and as he gobbled down his smoked ham and wheat bread he told me that the Mayor has been given instructions by the Lord Marcher to keep all those present at the meeting under close observation. He also reported that the Mayor has sent a list of suspected Chartist sympathizers -- including Ioan, Brynach and myself -- to the Lord Lieutenant and to the county Sheriff. By now, he thought, it was probably on the desk of the Home Secretary.

When I heard this, I was outraged, and said that I was minded to go straight to the Mayor in order to give him a piece of my mind, on the basis that I had broken no law and that I would not put up with being placed under surveillance or branded as a radical or a subversive.

"If I was you, Mistress," said Jacob, "I would not bother. That would alert the Mayor and the Court Leet. Master Rees is as thick as an apprentice's plank, he is, and he is well watched. Dammo, he does not have the resources to watch you or any of the others who were in the room, and indeed he does not enjoy good relations with Squire Owen and the other magistrates. Very resentful he is, that they exclude him from their little plots and plans."

"Are you sure of that, Jacob?"

"Absolutely, Mistress. He is not only stupid, but he talks too much. Keep him in the dark, if you please. Me and my boys have the measure of him, and we will let you know if there is any danger."

So I agreed with that, but as Jacob went off down the drive with a full belly and a pocket full of potions I thought that great care would be needed in the weeks to come. In my own mind, and without mentioning it to anybody else, I began to formulate certain rules of behaviour so as to safeguard my future security.

As fully expected, I have received a letter from Master Hugh Williams. It was delivered by hand this morning, shortly after breakfast. At the time I was alone with Bessie in the kitchen, while Gwenno was churning in the dairy and Liza was cleaning upstairs. The messenger came inside and waited to see if there might be a reply. I sat down at the table and read the letter quietly while Bessie gave him some bread and cheese and a mug of ale. This is what the letter said:

Set Upon a Certain Course

Kidwelly, on the 22nd day of March 1839

My dear Mistress Martha,

I write to place on record my very great pleasure at meeting you some days since. Having heard a good deal about you in advance of my first visit to Newport, I had dared to hope that you might be present at our Chartist presentation in the Black Lion. And when I saw you in the audience, flanked by your son and your son-in-law, I was instantly swept away by your beauty and your elegance. I had heard that the most beautiful woman in Wales lived in Newport, and had dismissed the idea as fanciful in the extreme; but now I know it to be true.

And having now heard you speak I find myself utterly captivated by your wit and your erudition. I declare that I have never before met a woman with such a firm grasp of political and economic affairs, and I think I now understand those who have warned me that it is better to have Mistress Martha Morgan as an ally than as an adversary.

I believe that we share common ideals, and that it would be to our common advantage to work together. Indeed, it is my firm belief that the destiny of our beloved country may rest in our hands. If we cooperate and exchange information and plans for action, I believe that we will achieve our objectives.

May I call and see you at the Plas on my next visit to Pembrokeshire? I should like nothing more, and will await your reply with keen anticipation.

Your admiring friend
Hugh Williams

I took a few minutes to recover from the initial impact of this strange epistle, and then I decided that I would not transmit an immediate reply. So I asked the messenger to thank Master Williams for his communication and said that a reply would be sent very shortly. Then I sent the fellow on his way.

I have nothing to hide from Bessie, and so I showed her the letter. She read it quietly, and then burst out into laughter. "What an extraordinary letter, Mistress!" she said. "It is almost a declaration of undying love. And considering that the fellow has only met you once, in the company of a large crowd of other gentlemen, he is certainly not backward in coming forward."

"My thoughts exactly, Bessie. He is a gentleman who does not let the grass grow beneath his polished boots."

"Are you flattered by his attentions, Mistress?"

"Of course I am, Bessie. It is not often, I daresay, that a grandmother in her sixty-first year receives such an epistle from a man who is young enough to be her son."

"And do you feel just a little flutter in your breast when you think of this sallow youth?"

At this, I thought long and hard, and decided to be honest with both Bessie and myself. "I do not think so," I said. "Besides, he already has a wife who is older than me, and a reputation which makes Don Juan look like a shrinking violet. He is a thoroughly disreputable fellow, and much too full of himself for my liking. Besides, he has green eyes. Green eyes are perfectly acceptable in an Irishman, but not in a Welshman."

Bessie slapped her knees and giggled. "My goodness, Mistress!" she chortled. "It appears that Master Williams has a challenge on his hands, unless he gets himself some tinted spectacles. So what was his purpose in writing the letter?"

"Conquest, Bessie. Nothing more and nothing less."

"You are probably right. For a gentleman such as he, virgins and dairymaids present one sort of challenge, and mature and elegant ladies such as you present quite another. So what will you do?"

"The image comes into my mind of a large fish on the end of a fragile line. In the circumstances, my father taught me that you should always play out the line, and then reel it in a little, and then repeat the process.............."

"Do you mean that you set out the other evening to get him onto your barbed hook?"

"I may be old, Bessie, but I still have a good figure, and a firm bosom, and only a few wrinkles and grey hairs. And I have not forgotten how to use my eyes."

"Mistress, you are quite indefatigable! I always said that you would have made a wonderful courtesan. So what comes next?"

"When a fish is landed, Bessie, you should always examine it carefully, and if it is not the right sort of fish for a good supper, you should throw it back into the sea."

194

"You sound very callous, Mistress."

"Not at all, Bessie. Master Williams knows full well that he has very little chance of ever getting me between the sheets. But the chase is all that matters to a fellow such as he. If I make it my objective to firm up his resolve, and to harden the contents of his breeches every now and then, both he and I may obtain some innocent pleasure from the exercise."

At this, Bessie could contain herself no longer. Her giggles turned into hysterics, and that set me off as well, and soon the pair of us were wandering around the kitchen with our arms around each other, laughing so much that we would certainly have fallen over had it not been for the mutual support provided. In the middle of this performance Liza appeared with a bundle of sheets destined for the scullery. She looked very fierce and disapproving, and for some strange reason that made us even more amused. At last she had to sit us down and give each of us a glass of water.

"Oh, Liza!" moaned Bessie. "Our mistress becomes more and more disreputable with every year that passes. I think we will have to take her in hand and teach her something about refinement."

"I have had my fill of refinement, Bessie. What I need is excitement, and more time spent in the company of rogues and vagabonds."

Poor Lizzie was mystified by all of this, and with a pained look on her face, she said: "May I ask, Mistress, what this is all about? Or is it a secret between the pair of you?"

"No secret, Liza. I have had a very silly letter from a certain gentleman, and Bessie and I are considerably amused."

"That much is obvious, Mistress."

There was nothing for it but to take Liza into my confidence as well. So the three of us talked further, not only about Master Williams' amorous intentions, but also about his clear desire to work with me in the pursuit of justice. Bessie and Liza know all about my concerns regarding tolls and tithes and matters relating to the Poor Law, and they agreed with me that if Master Williams' political objectives are close to mine, there would be no great harm in working together if discretion and secrecy could be maintained. "I urge you to have caution as your watchword, Mistress," said Liza. "My good man Tomos has been out and about in town, and has already picked up some gossip about that Chartist meeting. People are entirely uninterested in the meeting itself, but they are very interested in the fact that Master Williams was quite bowled over by the Mistress of Plas Ingli."

"You cannot mean that, Liza?"

"Indeed I do, Mistress. He stayed at the Black Lion overnight, and the landlord says that when he stood at the bar with a mug of ale in his hand he spent all his time asking questions about you and extolling your virtues."

"Now that is very interesting, Liza. Thank you so much. I will reply to Master Williams in due course, having made him wait a little and sweat a little. Now then, can I count on total secrecy concerning everything that we have talked about this morning?"

They nodded, and I know that I can count upon both Bessie and Liza to say not a word to anybody. We all got on with the business of the day. It is now evening, and I have been pondering on how best I might reply to Master Williams. From this point on, I will follow Liza's advice and make caution my watchword.

ΩΩΩΩΩΩΩΩΩΩ

25th March 1839

Today I have done two notable things. I have forged another valuable alliance, and written a letter.

On a cheerful spring morning I was up early, and took a walk upon the common immediately after breakfast. I needed to think. I chatted for a while to Will and Gomer, who were in Parc Mawr with the mature ewes, supervising the arrival of the spring lambs. They said that they were well content with progress thus far, with more than half already delivered and with perfect dry and cool weather. The little birds were hard at work on their nest-building operations, but I fear that I could not concentrate upon the beauties and the joys of nature since I had other things on my mind. For most of my walk I was lost in my thoughts, and I daresay that even if the old blue mountain had collapsed before my very eyes, I might not have noticed it.

Set Upon a Certain Course

On my return to the Plas I asked Bryn to make ready my bay pony, and after changing into my riding habit I set off for town. At nine of the clock I knocked on the door of Master George Havard Medical, having made a great show of blowing my nose on his doorstep and convincing the neighbours that I was suffering from a spring chill.

"Why, Mistress Martha!" said Master Havard, when he opened the door. "A very good morning to you. Come inside, if you please. I trust that I can be of some assistance?"

"Good morning, sir. A brief consultation, if you would be so kind."

And so I stepped inside to his consulting room, and told him that I wished to discuss a matter of some delicacy. I added: "I trust, sir, that we will not be disturbed?"

"Complete privacy guaranteed, Mistress Martha," said he, placing a little notice which said *CONSULTATION IN PROGRESS* on the outside of his consulting room door.

Master Havard owed me something, for I have provided him on many occasions with the recipes for herbal remedies when he has had difficulties in treating his patients. I did not know him particularly well, but took some comfort from the fact that he drinks less than his old father and is a good deal more reliable. I did not beat about the bush. "George," I said, "I have a great deal of respect for your professionalism and your devotion to the people of this neighbourhood. But I have not called on a medical matter. I saw you at the Chartist meeting in town the other day. May I assume from that a degree of sympathy for the Chartist cause?"

"Why yes, Martha. You were there yourself. Through the very fact of attendance you risked the disapprobation and emnity of the Mayor and his cronies, just as I did. I have already been reprimanded."

I laughed. "I daresay you can cope with that, George. But we have more than petty local politics to deal with. You know that trouble is coming?"

"That is clear to all of us who talk to the common people, Martha. I talk and listen. I know that you have made valiant efforts to prevent trouble in and around Newport, and I applaud you for it."

"I am committed to do what I can, as a powerless woman, to prevent violence. I ask you, George, to take that on trust. But I am also committed to greater representation for the people, and to the removal of injustices where I see them. Do I have your support in those two enterprises?"

"You do, Martha. And you have come here this morning because you want my help?"

"I have. You are a man who knows all about discretion, and you are greatly respected. By comparison, I am a wild and troublesome creature............"

"Come come, Martha. Certainly, it is my impression that there are some squires who mistrust you for your public pronouncements, but you are a member of the gentry yourself. And I know from talking to them that they give you credit for delivering a degree of stability to Newport and for encouraging the gentlemen of the *Ceffyl Pren* jury to keep their silly costumes in their cupboards."

I grinned. "Thank you, George. Now, on the matter of cooperation. As I see it, one of the greatest assets enjoyed by a medical man such as yourself is that people call at your house at all hours of the day and night without attracting the slightest bit of attention apart from idle speculation about the origins and severity of the ailments from which your patients are suffering. You come and go all the time, spend long hours away from home, and receive and send messages with alarming frequency during the course of every single day. You even receive and send bulky parcels of medicaments, and welcome many strangers to your house. Most of them, I daresay, are travelling salesmen seeking to sell you their latest wonder cures, but that does not matter."

"Agreed, Martha. But how does that help the cause of justice?"

"In two ways, George. First, you are the last person likely to be watched by the Mayor and his spies, or by any spies working for others. They could not possibly keep a track of either your movements or your correspondence. And second, you are perfectly placed for the posting and receiving of messages."

Master Havard's eyes lit up. "You mean that you want me to be a sort of spy myself, or a sort of postmaster?"

"If you would agree to it. If I am to mediate between the forces of reason and the forces of prejudice, there may be occasions when I need to meet others away from the Plas, or when I need to communicate with people who are themselves in danger. Your assistance would be invaluable in that regard. It is important that nothing should happen at the Plas which might implicate either me or my family, and that no messengers from outside the neighbourhood should be seen either coming or going.

Will you do it, George?"

"Of course, Martha! I have been wondering how I might best help to effect change in high places, and this might be a perfect opportunity for me to do something useful."

"Wonderful! You are very kind!" And I got to my feet and gave him a kiss on the cheek. He was greatly surprised, for in truth I do not normally kiss my doctors, but I have found that little gestures are often greatly appreciated. Before I took my leave, I made one further commitment to Master Havard. "George, if you help in the manner indicated, I promise you that I will never betray you, and I further promise that I will never ask you to do anything illegal or to involve you in violence. Your reputation is as important to me as it is to you, and I am aware that if you get into trouble you might lose your livelihood. That is a risk which I do not run. Thank you again. I might have a message for you to forward tomorrow, if that is acceptable........."

"Only too pleased to oblige, Martha."

So I took my leave, and gave him a curtsy on the front doorstep although that was not strictly necessary. I blew my nose and gave a delicate cough, for the observance of interested passers-by, and returned to the Plas on my pony.

This afternoon I shut myself into my dressing room and penned the following epistle:

Plas Ingli, 26th day of March 1839

My Dear Master Williams,
I thank you for your communication, which I found most interesting. Your kind words are greatly appreciated, and have indeed given me much pleasure.

It is clear that we have a good deal in common, and it would give me great satisfaction to explore with you one or two matters of mutual concern. We share a common purpose, and it may well be that we can bring things to a happy conclusion more effectively together than in isolation.

You may not be aware that I am being watched. That is the reason for the delivery of this letter via an intermediary. May I suggest that if we are to develop our working relationship we should adhere to certain very strict rules?

199

Set Upon a Certain Course

1.   *We should never meet either at my house or yours, for fear that we might be linked together in some way in the minds of others who may seek to harm us.*

2.   *We should never communicate directly, and we should destroy all correspondence and thus remove any chance of incrimination on either side. I have already burnt your letter, and I ask you to do the same as soon as you have read this.*

3.   *We should beware of idle talk.   I was more than a little distressed to hear that your interest in me was advertised too loudly for comfort at the bar of the Black Lion on the night following the Chartist meeting in Newport.   That found its way back to me more quickly than I would have liked.   Would you please, therefore, ensure absolute discretion on your part at all times, if I give you a guarantee that I will do the same?*

I suggest that we should not meet in the near future, since there are too many people showing an interest in your affairs and mine.   When things are quieter, I will contact you again.

In the meantime, I send you my warmest greetings and an assurance of my admiration for the great objective which you have set yourself.

Martha Morgan
Mistress

When I had finished this, I was well pleased with it.   It had enough in it to appeal to Master Williams' vanity, and it contained quite enough *doubles entendres* to fill a pig swill bucket.   If he is not titillated and tempted by my words, then he is a heartless fellow indeed, and not worth a lady's attention. But he will shortly be in possession of my ground rules, and I can only hope that he will agree with them and adopt them himself.

Tomorrow I will send the letter via Master Havard, and on the next day Master Williams will receive it in Kidwelly.   By then, five days will have elapsed since he wrote his letter to me, and he will be in a merry stew since he will be on the verge of believing that I have spurned his advances.

Tonight I will go to sleep at peace with the world, and with a happy smile upon my lips.

10th May 1839

In two days' time I will celebrate my 61st birthday, but just now I do not have birthday planning in mind, for I have read something of considerable import in the latest edition of the *Welshman*.

There has been a serious disturbance in Llanidloes, a woollen industry town which is a long way from here, in mid Wales. The town has been suffering great hardship because of changes in the weaving and flannel-making factories. There has also been great poverty and distress in the farming districts, so that townspeople and country people have together risen to a state of great militancy. Fertile ground indeed for the activities of certain Chartist orators. One of them, Master Thomas Powell, has been accused by the newspapers of making inflammatory and seditious speeches in various parts of mid-Wales.

It all started last year, with minor disturbances instigated by the local Chartist branch. Then there was a peaceful meeting in early April addressed by Master Heatherington from London, after which a group of violent men from the ironworks and coal mines of Merthyr Tydfil arrived in the town. The magistrates convinced themselves that an armed uprising was imminent, and swore in more than 300 special constables who were then armed with staves. They also called in some constables from London. Three of the Chartist leaders were arrested and taken away, although it is not clear that they had done anything illegal. That was bound to cause trouble, and it did.

On the morning of 30th April a big open-air meeting was organized by the Chartists in the town. Master William Jenkins was there, and he must have travelled to that district shortly after his visit to Newport. If he was acting true to form, he would not have set the world alight with his oratory. But during the meeting somebody arrived with news of the arrests. Immediately there was uproar, and the local men, and the fellows from Merthyr Tydfil, all became so furious that they went out hunting for the constables and the magistrates with the intention of releasing the prisoners.

They found them in the Trewythen Arms Hotel, upon which they battered their way inside and rescued their colleagues. Then they sacked and looted the place, and dragged out the law men. They beat them mercilessly and sent them packing from the town. Greatly encouraged by this success, they organized themselves on military lines, armed with an assortment of weapons including firearms, and declared the place to be a Chartist stronghold. There must have been many ex-soldiers among them, for their discipline was good.

They occupied and patrolled the town for a week, flaunting their weapons, taunting the authorities, and holding grand military parades. Stupid fellows. It could not last, of course. According to the *Welshman* the Lord Lieutenant, Lord Clive, gathered up all the troops he could find, and then re-took the town when two hundred Yeoman Cavalrymen galloped through the streets with sabres drawn. Forty of the insurrectionists, including three women, were captured and thrown into goal. There is now a military garrison in the town, and I daresay it will stay there until all resistance is subdued.

It is certain that the authorities will want to make an example of the Chartist rioters, and the newspaper reports that Master Hugh Williams of Carmarthen has been assigned to organize their defence when they are tried at the Welshpool Assizes. That, I daresay, will keep him occupied for a little while, and I look forward to meeting him on his return in order to find out more about the events and objectives of this idiotic insurrection. I suspect that it had no clear objectives, and I further suspect that the only skills of its leaders were those learnt on parade grounds and in ale-houses. God help the Chartists if they are led in the future by such men! If they cannot show me that they have brains inside their skulls, and that they are prepared to use them, I for one will turn my back on them and leave them to march down the rocky slope to Hell.

ΩΩΩΩΩΩΩΩΩΩ

7. Collision

11th May 1839

I am now convinced that I cannot prevent trouble, for the four new gates sanctioned by the Whitland Trust have been completed, and are being used by Master Bullin for the collection of tolls. This has come right at the start of the lime-carting season, when almost all of the farmers of West Wales have to make frequent journeys to the kilns for the collection of the lump lime which they need to keep up the fertility of their fields. Some poor fellows have to make twenty journeys or more in the month of May, and if they have to go through a toll gate every time, even the special lime carting toll is an insufferable burden to them. At the Efailwen and Maes-gwyn gates there have already been ugly confrontations, and special constables have been sworn in for guard duty.

Yesterday Will brought me a message to say that my attendance was desired at a meeting at Glynsaithmaen, the residence of Master Lloyd Davies. I agreed to go, and we travelled together in the light chaise over the mountain. Since I had no wish to be ostentatious in a meeting of angry men, I wore a dark woollen dress and a grey shawl, with a black felt bonnet on my head. The house was beautifully situated in a wooded hollow tight up against the flank of the mountain, with the common to the north and good-looking fields to the south. The gathering proved to be taking place in the barn, and as we drove into the yard we saw a multitude of small farmers and labourers arriving, some on foot, some on horseback, and others travelling in groups and sitting on horse-drawn gambos. Most of them were coming from the east. There were hearty greetings, but there were also scowls, and I picked up a feeling of stern resolve in the air.

I was apprehensive even before I entered the barn, which was crowded with maybe two hundred men standing, sitting on the threshing floor and perched on carts and sacks of barley. When the men saw that there was a woman in their midst I heard a rumble of discontent. I thought it best for me to leave, and to wait outside until things were over and done with, but then Twm Carnabwth saw me, and realized what was happening. He jumped up onto a *gambo* which was obviously intended to

Collision

serve as a speaker's platform. "Now then, boys *bach*," he roared. "I hear some mumbles that there is a woman in our midst. Dammo, that's not just a woman. That's Mistress Martha from the Plas!" At that, laughter melted away the ice, and it transpired that my reputation had preceded me. Many fellows whom I had not met before came up and introduced themselves, and insisted on shaking my hand and thanking me for my past and present assistance to the poor and the hungry. I was very touched and humbled by these expressions of gratitude and solidarity.

As the meeting proceeded the anger returned, and Masters Lloyd Davies, George Mathias and Twm Carnabwth, who were all perched on the *gambo* at the far end of the barn, found it difficult to keep order. Nobody was in charge, and sometimes ten people were talking at once. But the theme was simple enough -- the iniquity of the new gate and the additional tolls at Efailwen. And the abuse was all directed at one man -- Thomas Bullin.

Master Davies explained that I had done my best, through negotiation and discussion, to prevent the construction of the gate and to send Master Bullin off to greener pastures. I had failed in that enterprise, he said, because of the greed and the incompetence of the majority of Whitland Trust tally-holders. So the unanimous decision was taken that the gate would have to be removed by force. Next came the discussion of how and when. Some hotheads called for blood and demanded that Bullin should be hunted down, but the majority were against that, and passions were brought under control, to some degree, when a young fellow from the front of the crowd spoke up and argued passionately but clearly for the use of the minimum amount of force required to achieve set objectives. I recognized the voice but could not see the face. There were murmurs of agreement from many of the older men present who had seen military service. "Brothers," said the young man. "I urge you to be very careful. Our objective is simply the destruction of a gate protected by a gatekeeper and a couple of old special constables who would rather be somewhere else. We do not need an army to do that. Twenty or thirty men who strike quickly, without warning, will suffice..........."

"Well spoken, young fellow!" said Master Davies. "That seems like good sense to me. What say you, brothers?"

Then there was uproar in the barn, with everybody talking at once. Some wanted overwhelming force, just to show the authorities that there was massive popular support for the destruction of the gate. Some wanted advance warnings and no violence at all. And some still wanted blood. With all of this arguing, things were going nowhere at all, and at last Twm Carnabwth held up both hands and thundered: "Brothers! Brothers! I urge you to be calm! This will get us nowhere, and we must have unanimity! Can I call upon Mistress Martha, in the hope that she might give us wise counsel?"

"Agreed! Agreed!" shouted the men, and at last the barn grew quiet. I had been sitting on an old butter churn at the back of the barn, but now I stood up and all the men turned to face me and to hear what I had to say. I was very nervous indeed, but tried not to show it.

"Gentlemen," said I, "I have no right to be here, for I am a tally-holder and I do not suffer as you do. I thank you from the bottom of my heart for welcoming me into your midst, and for trusting in my discretion. I will be brief. First, I agree that the Efailwen gate has to be removed. Second, I agree with the young gentleman from the front of the gathering that minimal force should be used. I have given this matter great thought, and I have been dismayed to learn of the events at Merthyr Tydfil some years since, when an insurrection was led by a great crowd which ran out of control and which then led to more than fifty people losing their lives. It also led to fierce retribution from the authorities, with the dragoons and the fusiliers brought in to do their worst. Something similar happened less than a fortnight since at Llanidloes, where a mob did wanton destruction and took over the town. As a result the cavalry was summoned, and mounted soldiers came galloping along the main street with sabres drawn. It is a miracle that nobody was killed. Forty of the insurrectionists are incarcerated in gaol as a result of their foolhardy actions. Gentlemen, I urge you to remember that excessive force will always be met with overwhelming force. The Government has limitless resources, and it is always easy for the generals and the colonels to take on and defeat a disorganized rabble, even if those involved have firearms."

"I agree with that, Mistress Martha," said Master Davies from the gambo. "I have read about the Llanidloes insurrection, and a bad business it was."

"And my cousin Bryn was at Merthyr Tydfil," added Will. "He barely escaped with his life, and swears that over a hundred were killed, including many who were innocent of any offence."

Collision

"So what do you recommend, Mistress?" asked Twm.

"Well, to come to my third and even more important matter. I urge you, gentlemen, to avoid violence against any persons, no matter whether they be innocent or guilty, and no matter how provoked you may be. I am not a very holy person, but that would surely be the view of our Lord, should he find himself in this predicament. Damage property if you will, if it offends you, but please do not harm men, women or children. Please resist the temptation to carry firearms. As I have mentioned before to certain gentlemen here present, goodwill and solidarity are all-important if this enterprise is to succeed and if a great victory is to be won. Once you begin to lose the sympathy of the common people, all is lost."

I could hear murmurs of approval from some, and "Amen!" from others, and I knew that my words were having the desired effect. So I decided to round off my little speech with the most important of all my points. "Finally, gentlemen, may I suggest, as somebody standing on the fringes of whatever might now transpire, that secrecy and security are all-important? There may be spies in this barn here tonight. They may go straight from this meeting and feed names and plans to the authorities. Does every one of you here present trust the man standing on your left? On your right? I have been referred to by name, as have various others. Such naming is dangerous, gentlemen, and I pray to God that during any actions which you may sanction at Efailwen or elsewhere, no man's name is ever mentioned out loud. A shout of "Help me, Tomos Ifans!" may well help Tomos Ifans on his way to the penal colonies. And might I be so bold as to suggest disguise? You all know the traditions of the *Ceffyl Pren*. They are perfect for the coming enterprise at Efailwen. Please, gentlemen, never put in writing what might eventually be produced as evidence in court. Word of mouth, passed from one to another, has to be the best and safest means of communication. At each action, please keep your numbers as low as may be reasonably required. If you live at Efailwen, please resist the temptation to smash down the Efailwen gate, and leave that to others. Those who live in the neighbourhood are much more likely to be recognized by the gatekeeper or by other onlookers who may have loose tongues. On the matter of leadership, gentlemen, I have thought long and hard. Somebody has to lead, but leaders, if they are caught, always become scapegoats. Those who lead run a very great risk of transportation or even death, in the event that things go wrong and if a magistrate or soldier is injured or

Collision

killed during a disturbance. Look what happened to Dic Penderyn. So, gentlemen, I plead with those of you who wish to lead; do it only once, or if you are foolhardy in the extreme, no more than twice. Then, if you please, retire and take no further part in the proceedings. Advise and encourage if you will, but only from a distance. And if meetings should prove necessary, call them at short notice and at different locations. That way, neither informers nor the authorities will be able to work out what is going on or when or where you might strike next..........."

There I stopped in order assess the mood of my listeners. I was met with total silence, which pleased me greatly, for I knew that every man in the barn was deep in thought. I knew then that I had probably succeeded in my mission, and I decided that it was time to retire from the meeting. "Thank you, gentlemen, for your courteous attention," I said. "I have taken too much of your time. I really have no more advice to give you, and you may take it or leave it as you will. If you will forgive me, I will now retire from the meeting so that you may make your decisions. It is not appropriate that I should be a party to them. One last wish -- please do not mention my presence at this meeting to anybody -- not even your nearest and dearest. I can help you in this great cause only if I remain in the shadows, and if my involvement is quite unknown to the authorities. From the bottom of my heart, I wish you well."

And I gave a curtsy to the assembled company and stepped outside into the dying embers of the day. "Three cheers for Mistress Martha!" shouted somebody, and they cheered and banged their booted feet onto the threshing floor, and clapped their hands. That brought me close to tears, and as I stood outside the great half-door of the barn I found that I was trembling uncontrollably. I realized that I must have used up a good deal of nervous energy, and suddenly felt as weak as a kitten. At last the tumult subsided, and the men got down to the serious work of planning the destruction of the Efailwen gate. In the quietness of the farmyard I realized then that I had probably made the most important little speech of my life, and that maybe it would lead, in some small way, to the betterment of our harsh world.

I crossed the lane and sat on a high bank on the edge of the common, with the farm below me almost lost in blackening shadow. I leaned back against a warm slab of rock. The sun was down below the mountain horizon, and as the rose-tinted glow faded in the west the last chords of the evening bird chorus faded with it. I could hear the hum of conversation down below me in the Glynsaithmaen barn. A tawny owl called from a big chestnut tree on the west side of the house. So drained of energy was I that I almost fell asleep, and was dragged back into the real world by the sounds of heavy footsteps and clattering hooves and cartwheels on gravel. The meeting had broken up, and the plotters were on their various ways home.

I wandered down and met Will in the yard, and in the deepening darkness we lit our candle lanterns and climbed aboard the chaise for the journey home.

"A satisfactory meeting, Will?"

"Yes indeed, Mistress, largely thanks to you. Do you want to know what we decided?"

"I do, but that is because I am simply an inquisitive woman. However, even though I want to know everything, it is best that you tell me nothing. If I am ever pressed by my peers I want to be able to say that I know nothing, and I want to be able to tell the truth in that regard."

"Do you mind, Mistress, if I tell Bryn and Gomer?"

"You do what you like, Will. You and the other servants may say what you like and do what you like between dusk and dawn, so long as you give me a good day's work between dawn and dusk."

"Thank you, Mistress. I will take that as consent."

We rattled along quietly on the road towards the Bellstone Quarry and the west, lost in our thoughts. Then I asked: "Will, that young man who spoke from the front of the crowd this evening, and sounded eminently sensible -- I recognized his voice. Do you know him?"

"Why yes, Mistress. That was Samuel, the youngest son of Master and Mistress Stokes. A proper gentleman, and a thinker too, by the sound of it. He was there with the two Nicholas boys from the Parrog, and your own nephew Mark from Castlebythe. And a few other young fellows known to you and me, into the bargain. *Duw Duw*, Mistress, if the discussion after you left is anything to go by, every one of them is looking for action."

At this my heart sank, and I realized that the next generation was beginning to take a hand in shaping the destiny of our little world. Should I worry about the fact that they would be placing themselves in danger? Should I inform their parents about their involvement? No, and no again.

They were, after all, grown men, and I realized that there was no need for me to look after them or even worry about them. It would be far more appropriate, in the circumstances, for them to worry about me, a lady of mature years, as I dabble in men's business, and as I slip deeper and deeper into something that I cannot control and which I do not fully understand.

ΩΩΩΩΩΩΩΩΩΩΩ

13th May 1839

Yesterday was Whit Sunday, and Will went off early in his Sunday best, riding on the chestnut pony. He was away for most of the day, and came back looking very sanctimonious.

On his return, I caught up with him outside the stable as he wiped down his faithful steed. "A pleasant day, Will?" I asked.

"Why yes, Mistress. It so happened that I was moved to go to Mynachlogddu, over the mountain. A most bracing ride it was, riding along on the mountain track before dropping down on the other side."

"So why the Sunday best?"

"The *pwnc* at Bethel Chapel, Mistress. Never before was such a big congregation seen at Bethel, and because I was late there was no room to get inside. Master Twm Carnabwth was the chief reciter."

Bryn was listening in, trying hard to keep a straight face. "Come over all religious, has our Will," said he. "He likes nothing more than a good *pwnc*, lasting three hours, on a hot Sunday afternoon. I hear that they need a new deacon at Caersalem, and he will be an excellent fellow for the job. Don't you agree, Mistress?"

"Why yes, Bryn. He might even be a candidate for the ministry. His jacket is certainly black enough, and I have seldom seen shinier boots. He does not know his New Testament from his Old, but he is a fast learner, and if we give him five or six years he will certainly be able to tell which one is which."

This went on for a little while, with a good deal of laughter and horseplay, and at last the three of us became calm enough for the consideration of serious news. "There were a good many strangers at the *pwnc,* " said Will, "and that was not a matter of chance. When it was all over, there was much talking in the graveyard and in the lanes round about. Tomorrow, Mistress, will you give me permission to get away early, and to take Gomer with me on the black cob? And Bryn, do you have it in mind to come too?"

Bryn was only too willing, but I said: "Yes, Will, for you and Gomer. But not for you, Bryn. If anything goes wrong I am not prepared to leave the Plas without a single man to look after the animals and to muck out the cowshed. I daresay, Bryn, that your time will come."

Today, not much work was done in the morning. Nothing much was said, but we all knew that the fires which would sweep across West Wales were about to be ignited, and that two of my servants would be involved in the process. Before they went, we rummaged around in the clothes chests and found some old and moth-eaten skirts, aprons and shawls which had belonged to Blodwen Owen, Will's fierce and lovely mother who had served at the Plas almost to the time of her death more than twenty years ago. That was a poignant moment, for me as well as for Will. "Are you sure that you want to use these, Will?" I asked.

"Yes, Mistress. They will rot away in that old chest. They might as well be put to some good purpose. She would have wished it. She was a large lady, and her clothes will suit me nicely when I come to change sex. And there are sufficient for Gomer too."

Now they are gone, with Will in front and Gomer behind him on the black cob. Their bundles of clothes and straw and their little bags of soot were slung across the horse's flanks. Will carried an axe and Gomer carried a sledge hammer. They looked like a pair of labourers moving from one job to another, as indeed they were.

The afternoon and evening dragged along so slowly that every minute felt like an hour and every hour felt like a day. There was not much conversation at supper, and the clock ticked away the seconds more loudly than I can ever remember. Afterwards I went outside and looked at the sky and thanked God for a fine evening. Then I went inside again, and tried to work upon my embroidery, but could not concentrate. I went outside and looked at the sky again, not knowing what I was looking for. Another battle overhead, maybe? Or a red glow far to the east, beyond the mountains, signifying distant fire and deadly destruction? There was nothing but a heavy cloud cover and a faint glimmer of moonlight, and a curlew calling in the darkness.

At last we all retired to our rooms, and I am sitting at my desk, pen in hand. I spend more time gazing out of the window than writing. I feel like a helpless mother whose small child has gone out into a storm and has not returned. Probably, at this very moment, history is in the making at Efailwen. Would that I were there! Pray God that those two dear men will return safely. I must get to bed, but I will not sleep until I hear them clattering into the yard and know that they are safe.

$$\Omega\Omega\Omega\Omega\Omega\Omega\Omega\Omega\Omega\Omega$$

14th May 1839

They are indeed safe. They came into the yard, utterly weary, at five o'clock in the morning. I was on the back doorstep to meet them as the eastern sky brightened and as the first bars of the dawn chorus were sung in Gelli Woods.

"An enjoyable and successful picnic, Will?"

"Hard work, Mistress, but successful beyond our wildest dreams," replied Will. "And thank God, nobody hurt."

"Now then, Will, you get back home to Tegwen and the two girls. They will be worried sick about you. Take the morning off, and go to bed."

Bryn appeared at the kitchen door, looking as if he had not slept either. He offered to take the tired horse and to wipe her down and feed her. Then Bessie and Gwenno appeared, and between us we steered Gomer into the kitchen, sat him down in front of a big bowl of oats and milk, and interrogated him.

"Much better than being with the *Ceffyl Pren*, it was," he enthused. "We went at it like men possessed, Mistress, and........."

"From the beginning, if you please, Gomer."

"Yes indeed. Well now, we gathered as planned, a mile up the road from the new gate, at nine of the clock. All dressed ready, with black faces and straw under our bonnets, and all looking very anonymous. No names,

Collision

Mistress, like you advised, and nobody there who lived within two miles of the gate. Twm was in charge. Determined, he was, to be the first leader, and who was I to argue with that? God knows how he found a skirt and a shawl to cover him, but there he was, as pretty as a picture. There must have been a hundred men there, although there was only supposed to be fifty. Too many angry men, Mistress, and you cannot just keep them away when there is work to be done. All of the fellows had axes and sledge hammers, and quite a few had bugles and drums and trumpets......."

"My goodness," said Bessie. "I had no idea, Gomer, that you were going off to an evening of genteel musical entertainment!"

"Entertaining it certainly was, Bessie. When we started marching, you could have heard us in Carmarthen, what with all the tootling and thumping, and fellows shouting "Away with the tolls!" and "Free passage for lime and coal!" and suchlike things. There were some shotgun blasts too, but that was not a problem since Twm had insisted at the start that the fellows who carried them should use nothing but powder and should shoot straight up into the air. Twm was mounted on a great white stallion, and he carried a ceremonial sword. God knows where he got either the stallion or the sword. What a sight that was! The rest of us left our horses behind, being looked after by two young lads, and then walked down the road to the gate. A lot of us carried flaming torches. The gatekeeper and his wife heard all the noise and came out to investigate. Did you know, Mistress, that the enemy was none other than Master Benjamin Bullin, the brother of that scabby toad Thomas Bullin? Now there's a funny thing for you, indeed!"

"Very appropriate. Are you sure you did not hurt him?"

"Oh yes. Quite certain. He and his wife fled for their lives as soon as they saw our mighty leader on his stallion and were confronted by all of us beautiful ladies. We thought that there might be some special constables there, but there were none. As soon as the Bullins were gone, we set to work on the gate, and reduced it to matchwood in no time at all. We made a bonfire of the bits. Then we took out all of the furniture from the house and piled it up by the side of the road, so as not to harm it. Very kind of us, indeed. Then we set to work on the house, reduced it to rubble and set all the timbers alight. When all was done, Twm gave a signal, and we marched back to get our horses. It was like a victory parade, Mistress! Laughing and shouting, we were. Back at the horses, Twm had a job to shut us up, but he was very hard with us. "Away, all of you!" he said. "Not a sound from this point on. We must all learn to come quietly and go quietly. If you are needed again, there will be messages." And off home we all went, one by one and two by two, in our various directions. Within a few minutes the countryside was so quiet that the only sounds were the distant ones coming from the burning house. When we looked behind us, we could see the column of smoke with red sparks in it, rising straight up into the dark sky."

That was Gomer's story. As he told it, he was almost falling off his bench with tiredness, and he was even too exhausted to eat his early breakfast. So I sent him off to bed too.

Now my relief at the safe return of the heroes is tempered by apprehension. We await the consequences of the Efailwen riot, in the certain knowledge that Master Thomas Bullin will be somewhat unhappy about the indignity suffered by his brother, and that the magistrates will be both furious and frightened.

ΩΩΩΩΩΩΩΩΩΩΩ

23rd May 1839

Today a stranger turned up at the Plas bearing a message that must have started with Twm Carnabwth or Lloyd Davies at Glynsaithmaen and was then relayed across Mynydd Preseli in the minds of three other fellows, each of whom passed it on to ten others. There was nothing in writing, and no mention of names. Having now reached the coast at Newport, it is certain that the message has also reached sympathizers all over Pembrokeshire.

Apparently the Efailwen gate has been replaced on the orders of the clerk and the surveyor of the Whitland Trust, at the insistence of Master Thomas Bullin. Work is also in hand on the rebuilding of the gatekeeper's house. Tolls are being collected again. There have been ugly scenes, and four of the small farmers who forced the gate open and passed through it without paying have been prosecuted. The magistrates have decided on a show of strength, and they have sworn in seven special constables who will work in rotation to protect the gate and Master and Mistress Bullin. According to the message, further action is planned, but those who attacked the gate ten days since are strictly banned from attending again. Others must hold themselves ready. A further message will be circulated in due course, said the courier.

I was minded to do some interrogation, so as to test the security of the system that Twm and the others had put in place. I sat the messenger down in the kitchen and gave him a jug of ale. He would not give me his name or his place of residence. I tried to extract from him the source of his information, and was delighted when he pleaded ignorance. I asked how I might send a response, and was pleased to hear that no response was expected. Then I pressed him on when a further message might be issued, but he said "Maybe tomorrow, Mistress, or maybe next week or next month. Your guess is as good as mine."

Finally I asked him how I might know that the message was genuine and was not simply circulated by a spy or a trouble-maker. "Take it or leave it, Mistress," said he. "I trust that I have not travelled all this way to pass on a cock and bull story, but in truth I believe the message to be genuine. My source was a fellow whom I would trust with my life."

When the messenger had gone, I sat down in my dressing room and thought long and hard. I was concerned that more action was inevitable, but I was greatly impressed that Twm and Lloyd had taken at least some of my warnings to heart and had put in place certain measures designed to ensure secrecy. At the dinner table I passed the message on to all of my servants, for in truth there would have been no point in excluding Bessie, Liza and Gwenno. We are in this business together, and trust is of the essence. In due course we will sink or swim together. When they heard the message, Will and Gomer were furious. "Mistress, are you sure that we are not allowed to take part in the action again?" said Gomer, with a flush upon his cheeks. "Will has a family, and must be careful, but there is work to be done, and I want to be there when that gate is removed a second time! And who decided upon this matter, anyhow?"

"I cannot be sure, Gomer. Probably Twm or somebody else from Mynachlogddu. But it is a perfectly reasonable thing that nobody should risk arrest or injury more than once. That rule, whatever its source, has my approval."

Collision

"Mistress, I do not care about risking arrest or injury, since nobody else cares about me....."

"I care, Gomer," said Gwenno softly, with a break in her voice. We all looked at her, and she blushed as prettily as a red campion blossom on a May morning. Gomer must have realized in an instant that there was some small prospect of success in his long struggle to win her affections, and he blushed too, and we all exchanged glances, and then burst into laughter.

"I care too," said I, seeking to avoid further embarrassment. "You are too valuable to me, Gomer, to run any more risks. As for you, Will, you are getting too old for these nocturnal adventures. I therefore forbid either of you to participate in any future gate removals. Bryn, you may do as you will. I would prefer you not to go to Efailwen when the call comes, but I will respect your wishes."

"Thank you Mistress," said Bryn. "I will go, and I see it as my duty. Perhaps, Will, you will lend me your beautiful party dress for the occasion, since you and I have very similar proportions......"

"You may borrow my dress with pleasure, cousin," said Will. "But on the matter of proportions I have to disagree. I declare that my waist is narrower than yours, and that my bosom is a good deal larger. Would you not agree, Mistress?"

I declined to venture an opinion on this sensitive matter, but neither Bessie nor Liza were so backward in coming forward, and from that point on the conversation deteriorated rapidly. There was a good deal of banter and horseplay around the table, which left me doubled up with laughter and with stitches in my sides. But in the midst of it all I noticed that Gomer and Gwenno were less involved in the hilarity than they might have been, and that they were exchanging the sort of glances that I normally associate with lovesick fifteen-year-olds. Not for the first time in this blessed house, love is in the air.

ΩΩΩΩΩΩΩΩΩΩ

Collision

25th May 1839

It is a mellow May evening, and as I sit at my writing desk and look out over the *cwm* I can see bats fluttering about and hunting for little flying creatures in the gathering gloom. They live in the attic, and they come and go through a barely visible hole in the eaves just above my window. Sometimes I can hear them chattering through my bedroom ceiling, and sometimes one of their number comes swooping through my open window, no doubt attracted by the light of my candle. Getting a bat out again is a good deal more difficult than letting it in..............

I am in a dreamy mood, and have no wish to sit up for half the night with my pen in my hand. Oh that David were here still, to kiss me on the back of my neck and to disturb me in mid-sentence, and to disrupt my train of thought! Thirty-four years have passed since he died, and I still miss the taste of his lips and the gentle touch of his hands. Does any woman ever recover fully from the death of a lover, a husband, and a father of her children? I fear not. And then my thoughts drift to my beloved Owain, the second great love of my life, who brought me pain, and passion, and poetry, and music, and laughter, and tears. He who was lost for fifteen long years, and who then returned to precipitate joy and tragedy. And what of those good men Ceredig, and Joseph, and Iestyn? They loved me, all three of them, but Cruel Fate conspired over and again to ensure that I could never properly give them my love and share with them my bed.

If only..... if only..... But away with morbid thoughts and useless speculations on what might have been! I have had happiness in abundance, and I must look to the future. I have to admit to myself and to my little book that I am still happy. I miss a good man at my side, and I have to say that life would be a deal easier and more pleasurable if only I could share my most secret thoughts with a husband deserving of my love and my respect. On the other hand I have a house full of angels and a heart full of love, and a family to live for and die for. I am truly blessed.

Before I close my book for the night, I must report on developments. Just now Gwenno and Gomer have the kitchen to themselves, and they are no doubt cooing like a pair of turtle doves. Gomer is utterly amazed at the change in his fortunes, for he has worshipped Gwenno since the day that he started at the Plas, more than twelve years ago. She has given him some encouragement, but she has always made it clear that her heart belongs to Bobby Morris. Now, suddenly, Bobby is frozen out. Poor fellow. I feel quite sorry for him, for he is a pleasant and good-looking young man with prospects, being currently employed as coachman to the Bowens of Llwyngwair. I know not why Gomer is in and Bobby out, but I daresay that all will be revealed to me in due course.

Dai Darjeeling has taken Bessie out to town this evening, to see a troupe of travelling players performing some silly play in a tent near the castle. I daresay they will have fun, and I daresay that Bessie will be so tired tomorrow that she will be worse than useless. Bryn has gone to the Black Lion in order to share some jars of ale with his confederates. Liza and Will are at home with their families, as they should be, and are happy enough in these hard times. And what of my prospects for the future? They are interesting, to say the least. Master Hugh Williams has sent me two letters via Havard Medical, and I have sent him two replies by the same route. I have chosen my words carefully, and it suits my purpose to play him like a heavy fish on a thin line until such time as he can conveniently visit this area again in the autumn. I cannot really respect a man with such loose morals and such a high opinion of himself, but I still think that there may come a time when we can cooperate to our mutual advantage.

ΩΩΩΩΩΩΩΩΩΩΩ

24th June 1839

A month has passed, and our hay harvest is safely gathered in. Our shearing is also done, and the wool sold for the best price I can remember. Starvation over the past two years has reduced the number of sheep in Wales, and the shortage of wool now works to my benefit. That is very strange, since animal prices are still very depressed. The cornfields have had a good start, and if we now get two months of warm and dry summer weather the barley and wheat harvests will be excellent.

Off the farm, the situation regarding the Whitland Trust tollgates continues to deteriorate. On the evening of 5th June a message came via an unknown messenger summoning the "sisters for justice" to assemble on the Login road, one mile east of the Efailwen tollgate, at ten o'clock in the evening of the following day. That gave not much more than twenty-four hours' notice to those who would participate in a "grand meeting called for the purpose of discussing certain grievances". Even if spies had passed the news of this meeting to the magistrates, they would not have been able to organize an effective defence of the gate or the gatekeeper's house in the time available to them. That pleased me, for it showed that the leaders were using their brains.

Bryn went off on the chestnut pony at six o'clock, carrying an axe and a sack full of Mrs Owen's old clothes. He returned at six o'clock on the next morning, tired but elated, and bearing news of another entirely successful operation. At the breakfast table he said that he did not know who the leader was; but he was certain that it was not Twm Carnabwth. Some of the fellows who were there had been present at the first destruction of the gate, and this caused a good deal of anger since it was in clear breach of the first message sent out. "Discipline is very difficult to impose, Mistress," he explained. "The men who live in those parts are suffering so much that they do not seem to care whether they live or die. There must have been nearly five hundred men this time, and they were difficult to control."

"Far too many, Bryn," I moaned. "Forty or fifty men are quite sufficient for the destruction of a gate and the dismantling of a flimsy house. When you have ten times that number, fellows will simply get in each other's way and start working at cross-purposes."

"Agreed, Mistress. That is exactly what happened. Some of them were drunk, too."

"So what actually happened?"

"On the way I met twenty or thirty other fellows from Newport and Cilgwyn, all heading for the assembly point. There were groups coming from all directions. When we got close to the turnpike road we all spread out so as not to attract attention, and all crossed over without being seen. We changed into our disguises behind a hedge. Amazed we were, Mistress, at the numbers of men! And what fearsome costumes! We could have been a mighty band of theatrical gentlemen on the way to perform the collected works of Master Shakespeare. The magistrates were expecting something, for we had pinned up notices on church doors and other public places calling a meeting on 6th June "for the purpose of considering the necessity of a tollgate at Efailwen". The problem was that the notices did not say where the meeting would be held, or at what time, so the magistrates were very confused, to put it mildly."

"They must have known, Bryn, that there would be action at the site of the gate?" asked Gwenno.

"Of course they did. But seven special constables had no hope of stopping us. When we all arrived with our trumpets blaring and with drums beating, just as it was getting dark, they came out of the toll house and looked like a little flock of chickens confronted by five hundred foxes. They must have seen *Ceffyl Pren* juries before, but this was on quite another scale. Anyway, we sent them packing into some of the fields round about. Master Benjamin Bullin and his family fled down the road. Down came the gate, and the new gatekeeper's house was dismantled to within a couple of feet of the ground. Then our leader on the white horse -- I think his name was Eifion -- called on us to disperse immediately. And off we went in our various directions, although some fellows were very reluctant to go, and wanted to hang about to celebrate their victory. They had to be dragged away by some of their friends. Too much to drink, I daresay. I saw several fellows who were carrying flagons of ale and cider."

"And that was that, Bryn?"

"Indeed, Mistress. It was a long and difficult journey home in the pitch blackness, but at least I had good company."

"Well done," said I, "and thank God you are safe. Now then, off to bed with you. We can manage without you until dinner time."

With Bryn off to bed and fast asleep, I took a walk on the mountain and gave a good deal of thought to security matters. I was concerned that Bryn had picked up the first name of the leader of the latest Efailwen riot, and was sure that other rioters must have heard not only his first name but his second name too. Then I was concerned about drink being carried and consumed by some of the wilder fellows involved. And some way must be found of controlling numbers, preferably by restricting the circulation of messages. Otherwise, with thousands of men wanting to take part in the destruction of gates, what was to prevent all of them turning up at the same gate on the same evening? And what then would prevent discord among the "sisters", and possibly injury and death among innocent bystanders? I was not sure whether I should intervene by contacting Twm or Lloyd; and I was not sure whether my intervention might be viewed as

Collision

unwelcome interference. I decided, for better or worse, to let matters rest for the time being. After all, I thought, we may now see an end to this trouble, and see a good harvest, and see a white dove of peace flitting across the countryside..............

No such luck. Four days since, I read in my *Welshman* newspaper that trouble had flared up again, and that the Maes-gwyn gate, some five miles north of Whitland, had been destroyed. I was not surprised. This time I received no advance message, and assumed therefore that a quite different group of men must have been involved. According to the report, only about two hundred disguised rioters were involved, but there was much firing of guns, which terrified the gatekeeper and his wife almost out of their wits. The gate and the adjacent house were utterly destroyed, and I hoped, on reading the report, that the Whitland Trust would not be so stupid as to replace them. That would certainly have inflamed passions, as at Efailwen. A couple of days after the reading of my paper, Will met one of the fellows who had been involved in the Maes-gwyn riot, and the rioter unthinkingly mentioned the names of five or six of his confederates. I was appalled by the realization that if Will had been a spy, those names would have gone straight to the magistrates, and that by now the rioters would all have been arrested and incarcerated.

Careless actions at Efailwen, and careless talk at Maes-gwyn. I decided that I had to take action. So I sent Gomer over the mountain to Glynsaithmaen with a verbal request for a meeting with Lloyd, Twm and whoever else might be providing leadership for the rioters. He came back and confirmed that a meeting would be arranged, and that I would be informed in due course as to time and location. I waited for a couple of days, and then, such was my frustration with the lack of activity that I needed to talk to someone. Not Brynach or Ioan, since I wanted them to be less involved in the troubles and was reluctant to share my concerns with them. Hugh Williams, maybe? But he was still in Welshpool, organizing the defence of those arrested following the Llanidloes insurrection. No, it would have to be Shemi, a man who knew little about politics (or so I thought) but who might help me to understand the minds of angry men and to help me to think about strategy and tactics. So without further ado I pulled on my stout walking boots and set out to walk across the common to Werndew. With a fresh breeze in my face and a warm sun on my back I felt instantly calmer, and I soon entered into a sort of walking trance the like of

Collision

which I had never experienced before. Then a strange thing happened. A little phrase came into my head: "Rebecca and her daughters. Rebecca and her daughters." Over and over again. It refused to leave me, and as I walked it took on the rhythm of my strides across the heather-clad moorland. "Rebecca and her daughters. Rebecca and her daughters......."

Suddenly I realized that I was standing at the front door of Werndew, with an arch of sweet-smelling roses over my head. I knocked, and out came my dear friend Sian. We were both delighted, as ever, to see each other, and she gave me one of her famous embraces. She insisted on providing me with a cup of tea and a few griddle cakes, and we chatted for half an hour in the shady garden before I reminded myself, and her, that I had really come to speak to Shemi. He was out on some healing mission, but at last he returned, and he and I were able to talk about toll gates and riots and the minds of men who are aggrieved. He helped me a good deal with his wise counsel, and then I told him about the strange phrase which was still going round and round inside my head.

He laughed. "I am glad to see that we are still capable of communication over a modest distance, Martha," he said, "even though we may not fully understand the import of what passes between us."

"Whatever do you mean, Shemi?"

"Well, this very morning I was moved to take up the Bible, and to go to the Book of Genesis. Chapter twenty-four, verse sixty. Nothing else was of interest to me -- and I still have no idea why."

"And what does that verse say?"

He reached down his Bible from his bookshelf, opened it at the marked page, and read as follows: *"And they blessed Rebecca, and said unto her: Thou art our sister; be thou the mother of thousands of millions, and let thy seed possess the gates of those which hate them."*

Then, in an instant, everything became clear to both Shemi and myself. It was required of us, as indeed it was required of all those involved in the riots, that we should use the scriptures in support of our campaign for justice. If the poor people of West Wales knew nothing about the revolutionary writings of Tom Paine and William Cobbett, they did know their Bibles. Most of the poor farmers and labourers were Nonconformists, and those who could read had used the Bible as their textbook. They knew many pages of it by heart, and indeed at their annual *pwnc* services they recited verse after verse in a strange and primitive chant that I found almost hypnotic. Thus far, since the first destruction of the Efailwen gate, the leaders of the Baptists and the Methodists had provided little succour for the rioters, and had indeed roundly condemned their actions in the pages of the *Cambrian*, the *Welshman* and other newspapers. But if the Bible was cited in support of a just cause, how then could these ministers vilify those who fought for justice? Even if they did not come out actively in support of the rioters, their opposition might be reduced and even silenced. In fact even the magistrates and the politicians might find it difficult to employ heavily armed troops in the suppression of a "folk protest" based upon moral and religious principles.

Shemi articulated all of this for me, and I had to agree with every word of it. "And there is another interesting matter," I added. "If the leaders of the riots are worried about violence and drunkenness amongst the rioters, the citation of Biblical sources will help them greatly in developing their arguments for moral force as distinct from physical force. The Chartists have exactly that problem, and maybe it would go away if the Nonconformist leaders could be encouraged to sign the petition which Master Hugh Williams and the others are carrying around the country."

"Agreed, Martha. But I have spoken to Brynach about this, and he thinks that that is unlikely to happen. Indeed, he says that on matters of belief and behaviour, the Nonconformists are more traditional and conservative than the Bishop of St David's. The essence of their teaching is that suffering is good for you, and that it is in any case a punishment for sinfulness. "Repent and be saved!" they cry. It is not surprising, Martha, that when confronted by such a crude and simple theology the Chartists insist that their movement should be entirely secular."

"Well, I fear that the Chartists will not make much headway in West Wales. I sympathize with them, but they do not understand the thinking of country folk. And they do not appreciate that the problems faced by our poor people are mostly of local origin, and are capable of local resolution."

"Mistress Martha for Prime Minister!" chortled Shemi. "Now that would be a fine thing."

"Not in my time or yours, Shemi. But the time will come for a woman to run this country, and when it happens I trust that she will be more than just a man dressed in petticoats."

Shemi laughed again, and then became serious. "So back to these other men dressed in petticoats who smash down tollgates. You mentioned your concerns about security and the use of names. Do you see, Martha, as I do, that there is now a resolution to that problem?"

"I do indeed, Shemi. The men are already used to the traditions of the *Ceffyl Pren*, and they already use disguise in order to maintain anonymity and to confuse the gatekeepers and the magistrates. It is but a short step from the convention of the "sisterhood" of rioters to a new convention -- that of Rebecca and her daughters."

"Of course!" said Shemi. "If the leader, whomsoever he may be, is always referred to as "Rebecca", and the rioters are always referred to as "her daughters" this would make the betrayal of individuals much less likely. And there would be an additional benefit. The magistrates will be uncertain, from one week to the next, whether they need to hunt for one great elusive leader, or whether there are Rebeccas lurking in every village and hamlet in West Wales. Confusion is a considerable weapon, if used wisely."

"Shemi, you speak as if this business is going to go on for a very long time, and that many thousands of people will be involved."

"I know it, Martha. Whatever happens in the coming days, Rebecca will not go away. She may sleep for a while, but then she will be woken by the thunder and lightning of discontent."

"I would like to disagree with you, Shemi, but I cannot. Some years ago I had a powerful premonition of violence and destruction sweeping across this land, and it has still not come to pass. Perhaps, at the moment, we are simply being given a foretaste of what is to come?"

"My feeling entirely. But I also know, Martha, that you have been given the responsibility of influencing the course of events."

"But Shemi, I am too old and feeble for such responsibility........."

"Come now, Martha. You are fishing for compliments. Very well, you shall have them. You are neither old nor feeble, and you are greatly loved and respected. You have a sort of calm beauty that has grown with maturity. You know perfectly well that men still fall over themselves in their haste to do your bidding!"

"Dear Shemi! You sound more and more like our late friend Joseph with every month that passes. Compliments will get you everywhere, and I will now give you the loving embrace which I reserve for my favourite wizards."

So I got up and embraced this big and lovely man, and kissed him on his cheek. He hugged me as a bear might hug a favourite tree, leaving me breathless. Then I said: "One last thing, Shemi, before I set off for the Plas. Joseph told me that one cannot ever change the force of destiny. You have told me the same thing, and have explained that I must accept fate. Why, therefore, should I seek to influence the actions of the rioters and the Rebeccas that might lead them, when my efforts will be doomed to failure?"

"Because, Martha, if you listen to your intuition as you walk home over the wide and hazy mountain, you will come to realise that your efforts are destined to succeed."

And as I strode home along the mountain ridge, with the wide blue sea on my left and the lush summer greenery of Cwm Gwaun on my right, and with skylarks tumbling and serenading high over my head, I knew that Shemi was right.

ΩΩΩΩΩΩΩΩΩΩ

28th June 1839

I have had my meeting with the men who are organizing the destruction of the gates. "Organizing" may not be the right word, since the protest movement is spontaneous and dependent upon local initiative and action rather than grand design. Nobody can control the small farmers and labourers of West Wales, and only a fool would try. One can cajole and place suggestions before them, but in the end they will do what they want to do.

Yesterday, and not before time, I received news of a "family meeting of certain sisters" at a place called Tufton, on the south side of Mynydd Preseli. I was to be there at eight of the clock in the evening, which hardly gave me enough time to find a bite to eat and to change into my riding habit before setting off. I travelled alone on my favourite mare, checking behind me every now and then to ensure that I was not being followed. The countryside behind me was quiet, which did not surprise me, since with hay-making and shearing still under way all available hands must have been fully occupied on the land. I arrived at the safe house with just a few minutes to spare.

Inside, in the smoky shadows, I met Twm and Lloyd, and four other fellows who introduced themselves. They were all small farmers, one from Whitland, one from St Clears, and the others from Efailwen and Narberth. They were happy enough to give me their names, and seemed to be pleased to meet me. We drank good tea, and talked with considerable intensity for two hours.

I cannot say what the results of the meeting might be. But my instinct tells me that common sense will prevail, at least in the short term, and that any future riots will be a little less riotous than the magistrates and the army might expect. All of us who were present at the meeting shared concerns about the excessive numbers of aggressive men who wished to take part in the riots, and we felt that security, tight as it was, needed to be even tighter. We agreed that all messages should be verbal, and that safe houses would never be used more than once for meetings. We were all worried about the past use of firearms and the use of strong drink, and agreed that both must be discouraged in the future. We reaffirmed the principles of harming bricks and mortar but not flesh and blood, and we agreed that all who took part in the riots should be disguised and unrecognizable. We discussed many other points too, some of them practical and others relating to ideals and objectives.

Then Lloyd asked me why I had requested a meeting. I told the men that I had two reasons. First, I had received information from a fellow tally-holder of the Whitland Trust that the Efailwen gate would be replaced for a second time, and that Master Thomas Bullin was determined to bring down the full force of the law in the protection of his rights. "His rights?" spluttered Twm, with his face almost as red as his hair. "**His** rights? And when will the full force of the law be used to protect ours?"

"That day will come, Twm. You have to believe it. But for now, gentlemen, you may assume that the Efailwen gate will need to be removed for a third time. Then I come to my other, and more important point. My information is that names were used loudly at Maes-gwyn. If that happens again, arrests will be made, tongues will be loosened by the use of money or force, and this whole enterprise will come tumbling down."

"But how, Mistress, can we prevent that? Men have to communicate if order is not to give way to anarchy."

And so I told the men of my inspiration about Rebecca and her daughters, and passed on to them the Biblical verse that Shemi had been given in his inspiration. I reported the key points of my discussion with the wizard, and watched as their faces were transformed. Furrowed brows were smoothed, and hard lips were softened by beatific smiles.

"Bless my soul!" said Lloyd. "Why did we not think of this before? It is after all a short step from the play-acting of the *Ceffyl Pren* juries to the play-acting of beautiful sisters tearing down gates. Every leader from now on should use the name "Rebecca", and all those under her command should be known as her daughters. What say you, gentlemen?

"An idea perfect in its simplicity," said the farmer from St Clears. "We must use it."

"Agreed," said Twm, with a broad toothless grin on his face. "And the words from Genesis are perfect too. I am minded to ask every minister of every Nonconformist Chapel in West Wales to preach a sermon on that verse. Even if some of them explain it away as meaning nothing in particular, it will be obvious what it means to every man and woman in every congregation, and to every farmer who has ever had to pay a toll."

"And while ours is a serious business," added the Efailwen man, "a degree of levity among the protestors at any future gate removal will tend to suppress the base instincts of those who want violence. A little play-acting and a little laughter will certainly not go amiss. If we are not careful, gentlemen, this could become a sport to rival the ancient game of *cnapan*."

"Therein lies a danger, gentlemen," said I. "Not too much levity, if you please. But the more I think about this, the more I am taken by the vision of Rebecca as an avenging angel. If we are to succeed in changing the priorities of the trusts, and even in changing the law, we will need sympathetic reporting from the gentlemen of the press. Without a label, our movement will go unnoticed amid the welter of demonstrations and riots which occur almost daily across the nation. If we have to have riots in West Wales, let them be given a name by those who report the disturbances and even by our political masters. Let the name of Rebecca become a symbol for peaceful protest and for popular resistance to the evil of the tollgates!"

The six gentlemen laughed and clapped, and I had to laugh too, and apologize to them for my sermonizing. I realized that of course they needed no sermons. They are good men and true, and they have nothing to learn from a female busybody such as me. Then I had to leave before darkness trapped me on the wrong side of the mountain. I got to my feet, gave the gentlemen a deep curtsy, and left them to their further discussions. I arrived home by moonlight, around midnight, hoping that the sisterhood of Rebecca would indeed multiply and that the female tendency towards moderation would mitigate, to some degree, the male tendency towards violence.

ΩΩΩΩΩΩΩΩΩΩ

19th July 1839

The Efailwen gate has gone down for the third time, this time smashed to pieces by a large crowd which assembled in broad daylight. The men are becoming more daring, and their contempt for the law is becoming more blatant. They put up brash notices in advance, and last Sunday there were even announcements from pulpits in the neighbourhood. According to the *Cambrian*, at least five sermons were preached on Genesis 24, verse 60. The rioters also issued an advance warning that if anybody informed the authorities of their plans or in any way hindered the work of the sisterhood, it would go ill with them. As at the previous riots, they were all dressed in female garb, and all had blackened faces, and as before they caused the constables to take to their heels across the fields. They caught one of the poor fellows, and he was severely beaten up. That caused me some concern when I read about it, as did the realization that threats and intimidation would inevitably become part of the currency of the riots.

But my concern was almost swept away when I read this deeper down in the *Cambrian* report:

"Following this latest despicable episode of disorder and destruction at Efailwen, it was reported by at least three eyewitnesses that the grotesque leader of the violent gang was addressed as Becca, who in turn addressed the rioters as "my dear daughters." We are also informed that

the notice posted on the church door at Login three days before the riot was signed by somebody calling himself (herself?) Rebecca. It has been drawn to our attention by interested parties that a certain verse from the Book of Genesis is now being cited by the instigators of the troubles as an inspiration and justification for their actions. If the criminals responsible for the disturbances are not brought to book, the disorder will continue, and the riots will come to be known as Rebecca's Riots. This must be a cause of grave concern to the civil authorities, who will have no wish to be caught up in a debate on the Holy Scriptures."

That gave me some satisfaction, and I became even more satisfied this very morning when I received a message, via Havard Medical, from Master Hugh Williams. He has been back to St Clears for a while, although most of his time of late has been devoted to the defence of the forty Chartist prisoners taken during the Llanidloes insurrection. He reminded me that he has undertaken this task entirely free of charge, and I have to admire him for that. More to the point, he passed on intelligence from the border country between Pembrokeshire and Cardiganshire, which he knows well. He talks to magistrates and gentry all the time, and he also knows a good deal about the thinking of the lower orders of society.

He reported that following the third destruction of the Efailwen gate, Thomas Bullin is not minded to waste any more money on it. Neither is the surveyor of the Whitland Trust keen to put up with further trouble in that disorderly neighbourhood. Then he reported that following the destruction of the Maes-gwyn gate the local magistrates had sent urgent messages to the Home Office begging for troops and asking for clarification on the use of the Riot Act. Could they order the troops to fire on rioters, they wanted to know, before the Act had been read out and before a reasonable time had been allowed for the dispersal of the troublemakers? Master Williams did not know what answer had been received to that question, but he did know that troops had been sent from the Brecon Barracks, and that they had arrived in Narberth on a fine Sabbath morning, where they had marched through the streets with fixed bayonets. That idiotic and inflammatory action had brought swift condemnation from the Nonconformist ministers in the town, and had followed another idiotic action by the local magistrates. Apparently they had feared a riot at the Whitland Trust's new gate at Tavernspite, and had used the Castlemartin Yeomanry to arrest a number of "suspects." At a petty sessions, two days before the arrival of the Fusiliers from Brecon, all of them had to be released because there was no evidence against them. Some poor fellows who had refused to pay tolls at the Tavernspite and other gates were fined, and Master Morris David from Efailwen, who is reputed to be eighty years old, has been hauled off in chains to Haverfordwest Gaol, charged with being an instigator of the Efailwen riots. That has caused an uproar, for the frail old fellow is known to be entirely innocent, and his neighbours fear that he will die in gaol long before he is brought before the Assize judge.

Then Benjamin Bullin, the gatekeeper at Efailwen, has made a bad situation even worse by ordering the constables to enter the houses of two farmers and to arrest them for non-payment of tolls, thus causing them to be handcuffed and held in custody overnight. Whether they are guilty or not, the constables did not have proper arrest warrants, and they may therefore be found guilty of trespass and unlawful arrest. That will lead them, in turn, to be fined and possibly imprisoned, and the Whitland Trust will no doubt have to sort the matter out. God only knows where the clerk will find the money for the payment of fines and legal costs, which Hugh Williams reckons might add up to £200.

It seems to me, after reading this latest epistle from the battlefront, that Rebecca and her daughters actually need to do very little, for their enemies -- including the idiotic Bullin brothers -- seem to have a very strong instinct for destroying themselves.

ΩΩΩΩΩΩΩΩΩΩ

25th July 1839

Suddenly, it appears to be all over. Four days since, I was summoned to an emergency meeting of the Whitland trustees at the Blue Boar Inn in St Clears. I travelled there in the company of Brynach and Ioan in the Llanychaer coach, and as we bumped along we speculated at some length as to the nature of the business to be transacted.

When we entered the upstairs room we found that there was a notice on the door announcing that this was a public meeting, and indeed some of the gentlemen of the press were there, together with assorted inquisitive townspeople. There must have been fifty people crammed into the room. Thomas Bullin and his brother Benjamin sat at the back of the room, slumped in their chairs, with folded arms and faces as black as thunderclouds. That, I thought, was very interesting. I recognized most of the trustees, but there were many other gentlemen whom I had never seen before, and as soon as the meeting got under way it transpired that they were magistrates who had previously shown no interest at all in the business of the Trust. Brynach whispered into my ear that they had every right to attend, and indeed to vote on motions properly proposed and seconded. Then the Chairman introduced a tall and elegant gentleman from the front row as Squire John Jones of Ystrad, the member of parliament for Carmarthenshire. Master Jones wished to address the meeting, said he, and he was minded to allow this unless there should be any objections.

Master Jones ensured that the meeting was mercifully short. He spoke briefly, outlining the events of the past months and laying the blame for public disorder fairly and squarely on the shoulders of the Whitland trustees. He argued that the four new gates which had caused all the trouble were of doubtful legality, since it appeared to him that inadequate notice had been given to trustees and other parties of the intention to erect them. The Chairman then allowed a short discussion, but the expected robust defence of the gates from those who had promoted them in the first place never materialized, and those of us who had travelled from far away realized that the outcome of this meeting, like so many others in West Wales, had been fixed in advance. Several magistrates urged that the four gates must be permanently removed if they were to have any chance of maintaining public order. Then Master Jones stood up again and placed a simple motion before the meeting that the order establishing the four new gates should be revoked. I seconded it immediately, and since there was no counter-proposal or amendment, it went straight to a vote. The magistrates supported it en bloc, as did about half of the trustees, and so it was carried by a considerable majority. And that was that.

As we travelled home afterwards, via Efailwen and Maenclochog, there was a distinct feeling of anticlimax in our carriage. Thomas Bullin had had his come-uppance, since he had paid out £800 for the Whitland

Collision

Trust gate contract and now had exactly the same number of gates to earn his income as the old contract holder had last year. We could hardly believe what had happened, or the speed with which the magistrates and the politicians had caved in to the demands of Rebecca. It was clear that between us we had won a remarkable victory. "What will you do now, Martha?" asked Ioan with a chuckle, as we trundled down into the *cwm* from the pass over Mynydd Preseli.

"Oh, I will think of something," said I. "I am fed up with men's business. I shall resume my interest in the dimensions and colours of the latest London bonnets, and I am minded to improve my skills in knitting and tapestry."

At this, both Ioan and Brynach slapped their knees and roared with laughter until the tears were rolling down their cheeks.

ΩΩΩΩΩΩΩΩΩΩΩ

Editor's Note: There are no full diary entries for the period between 25th July 1839 and 6th July 1842. During this interval of almost three years Martha appears to have been very happy, in spite of the difficulties facing her estate and her tenant farmers and labourers. The evidence for this comes from later diary references, and from occasional scribbled notes relating to seasonal events and to the birthdays of her grandchildren. There are also entries relating to holidays in Bristol and London in the company of her friends Mary Jane Stokes and Ellie Phillips. On nine occasions the letters "HW" appear alongside dates and times, with a different location noted for each entry.

PART THREE: 1842-1844

8. A Spark in Dry Bracken

3rd July 1842

A white-hot sun is sailing high across a cloudless sky, and although it is still early summer it is too hot for man or beast. I will not complain. After miserable summers year after year, with leaden skies and sluicing rain and failed harvests, I had almost forgotten what the month of July should be like. Shemi says that this wonderful weather will continue until the middle of September, and he is always right. Thank God for sunshine and wizards. So I am determined to enjoy summer while I can, and as I write these words I am sitting in the garden in the shade of our biggest apple tree, with a large jug of strawberry cordial close at hand. There is no wind, and the air is alive with bees and other buzzing and humming insects. A red admiral butterfly has landed on the clean white page of my diary, and shows no inclination to move on. The garden is more colourful than I can ever remember it, and at last Jac Blossom is seeing his efforts rewarded, with the cold mud and drooping foliage of earlier summers now replaced by scents and colours in profusion. Roses, delphiniums, lupins, hollyhocks, wallflowers, nasturtiums, sweet peas, buddleia and lilac are all in bloom at the same time, together with many little flowers whose names are a mystery to me and which Jac has raised from seedlings. I have a preference for wild places and mighty tumbled rocks, but I have to admit that there is a good deal to enjoy in a civilized garden on a breathless summer's day.

Brynach's little boy David, who is now seven years old, is staying with me for a few days, and he is busy building a den with two friends from the *cwm* on the other side of the garden wall. Goodness knows where he finds the energy and enthusiasm in all this heat. I can hear their giggles and conspiratorial whispering, for the den is supposed to be a secret from everybody except *Mam-gu* Martha. Gomer is clearing out the cowshed. Bryn and Will are away helping with the Trefach hay harvest, which is always later than mine. Liza and Gwenno are at work in the cool dairy, and I can hear their laughter and their chatter above the low rumble of the tumbling butter churn. Bessie is singing to herself as she works in the kitchen. It is Wednesday today, so she will be baking ten loaves of bread.

How I love this place! Its little sounds, and its colours and scents, and its blessed inhabitants, and its comfortable security. Its moods, subtle or stark, black or white, are as familiar to me and as exciting as the moods of a lover, and yet every day I am surprised by new patterns of light or little nuances that I have never noticed before. The Plas and the blue mountain which overlooks it have insinuated themselves into my soul, so that I am now a part of this place, as it is a part of me. This is my passion, and I desire no other. In Welsh it is called *hiraeth* -- I know not how it can be expressed in any other language, except maybe through the words *longing* and *belonging*. It is as much a sensual as a spiritual thing, as high as a climax in the act of loving, and as deep and terrible as the loss of a child. I have said it many times -- I will never leave this house of my own free will, and when I go I will be in a box, transported feet first.

Enough of these deep ponderings. As happens so often in my life, there is sunshine on one side and dark shadow on the other. I am moved to resume my narrative today because my inner voice told me last night that gates will soon go down again. Master Hugh Williams told me the same thing, in a letter which I received this morning. It came from London, and was delivered, as usual, via Havard Medical. Although it was brief it informed me that there have been disturbances in Carmarthenshire and that certain members of the gentry have had new hayricks burned. The reasons for the unrest are not hard to find. Over the last three years rents and tithes have gone up inexorably, and many squires have actually reduced the wages paid to their labourers. Road tolls have not gone up, because the law does not allow it; but the turnpike trusts are increasingly desperate for more income, and the surveyors have been seen out and about, assessing new gate locations. That has caused a ripple of consternation in the lower orders of society, and many are convinced that new gates are on the way. And ironically, in spite of this magnificent summer weather, food prices are high. From my visits to the farms and hovels in this area, it appears to me that there is now more suffering among the poor people than there was three years ago when Rebecca and her daughters were fighting for justice.

A Spark in Dry Bracken

Another matter mentioned in Master Williams' letter is the planned use of secret and subversive methods by the authorities in their attempts to maintain law and order. He has seen -- goodness knows how -- a highly confidential letter from the Home Secretary to the Lord Lieutenant of Carmarthenshire which appears to be the culmination of a considerable correspondence over recent months. In the letter there is a suggestion that the Lord Lieutenant might "in anticipation of future disorder, and as a matter of urgency, establish a network of individuals who might be disposed to provide sensitive information in exchange for modest remuneration." According to Master Williams, the Home Secretary suggested that such individuals might be those who are particularly vulnerable and in straightened circumstances, and who might be assumed to circulate amongst those most likely to be involved in riotous behaviour. Great sensitivity was to be employed in approaching such people, and some small sums of money might be advanced to them as gestures of goodwill. The Home Office would ensure that adequate funds were made available for this exercise. Additional funds were also to be made available for a higher scale of rewards for informers in the case of future trouble. There would be an increased willingness to deploy the army to West Wales in the event that Rebecca resumed her activities. And finally, the Lord Lieutenant was encouraged to resume his efforts to identify the "person or persons" who masqueraded as Rebecca in the troubled months of 1839.

Master Williams ended his letter thus:

Be careful, Martha. It is certain that similar letters will have gone to the Lords Lieutenant of Pembrokeshire and Cardiganshire, and we may take this development as a certain signal that unrest is on the way. Indeed, it appears to me that the Government may be intent on precipitating trouble and demonstrating its intolerance of dissension and disorder. Politicians are always looking for votes, and until our Charter is adopted the only votes that count are the votes of those who hold power. Weak governments fail; strong governments survive.

When you had your riots in West Wales some years since, I was not directly involved, but I know that you were, and you outwitted the magistrates and the constables at every turn. Riotous behaviour succeeded in forcing reform, and our leaders are desperate that such a thing should never happen again. Next time, it will not be so easy, for there will be paid spies and informers everywhere. Rewards of £10 will be behind us, and reward notices offering ten times as much for information will be posted with gay abandon. The Yeomanry and the army from Brecon were held back last time on the basis that local magistrates should suppress local disorder using local resources, but now they will be held ready and will be used.

If you see any sign of these measures being implemented, I will be interested to know of it. In the meantime, I urge you to take great care and to avoid any actions that might throw suspicion either in your direction or mine.

Your affectionate friend
Hugh Williams

This letter sent a chill to my heart in spite of the warmth of the weather and the contentment of my life. I will endeavour to follow Master Williams' advice, but for the time being matters relating to the security of our nation will have to wait, for my little grandson urgently requires my assistance in strengthening the roof of his secret den.

ΩΩΩΩΩΩΩΩΩ

15th July 1842

I have received a message from Skiff's friend Abby, who looks after some of my interests in town. Apparently three fellows who habitually drink in the Black Lion were seen to be in remarkably fine form the other evening, and each of them handed over shiny new sovereigns when required to pay for their rounds of drink. Eyebrows as well as elbows were raised as the evening went on, and ears were pricked, and Abby thinks that the three of them have received mysterious payments from the Mayor. One of the fellows is a labourer on Squire Owen's estate, and he is known as somebody who will do dirty work as required. All three of them have done duty in the past as special constables, with a little more enthusiasm than is normal in these parts. Abby and Halfpint are watching them, and will keep me informed.

My assumption that the Home Secretary's instructions are now being implemented was confirmed today when Brynach called by and joined us for dinner. Afterwards, well away from the crowded kitchen, he told me that there had been a meeting of the local magistrates at which the Lord Lieutenant himself had outlined "enhanced support for the authorities in the maintenance of good order in the community." Brynach had been there himself, and he confirmed the main points contained in my letter received from Master Hugh Williams. This is all supposed to be highly secret, but since every magistrate in West Wales now knows about it, he is going to announce the broad outlines in a column for the *Welshman*. As ever, the author of the piece will be anonymous, and there will be speculation as to the source of the revelations. There will also be fury in high places. Brynach left it to me to ensure that the details of these Home Office plans are disseminated as widely as possible, and tomorrow, although there are currently no disturbances in the neighbourhood, I will write to Hugh Williams and also call a meeting of some of those who know Rebecca and who call themselves her daughters. It is no bad thing to be prepared for eventualities.

Why has the Government decided to stir the pot of disaffection, and why now? I have mused on this at great length, sitting on my own in my dressing room as the long shadows of evening gradually consumed the bouldery slopes on the far side of the *cwm*. I cannot work it out. Chartism is no longer a threat to the Government since the ill-judged uprising of November 1839 led to the deaths of thirty people outside the Westgate Hotel in the other Newport. Out of a crowd of seven thousand men who marched on the town with the intention of setting up a brave new Chartist world, more than two hundred were arrested, and forty found guilty of assorted serious offences. The leaders, including Master John Frost, were found guilty of treason and were sentenced to death, but that sentence was commuted to transportation when it was realized by the Government that three new martyrs, whose real crime was simply to demand better political representation, could cause years of bitterness and chaos throughout the nation. The hanging of Dic Penderyn in 1831 is still seen by most people, including myself, as a heinous crime committed by the state against an innocent man. The anger felt about that death is still simmering in Wales, and the Government knows it well.

But is Chartism really dead? Master Williams claims that it is not, and that the stories of recriminations and disputes among the supporters of the movement have been exaggerated. When I recently discussed such matters with him, he said that there are many men in the Merthyr Tydfil area who are still supporters of Chartism, and that there are secret lodges in existence. The authorities know this, and they are trying to stamp out the violence, intimidation and "revenge punishments" which are still, to this day, meted out to informers and others who betrayed colleagues in the trials following the Westgate Hotel massacre. The Chartist leaders and thinkers are still free men, although they are keeping a low profile for the time being.

Then there are the Scotch Cattle, who claim to be the defenders of workers' rights. They still march about on the coalfield and in the mining districts as they have for the last thirty years or more, banging their drums and blowing their bugles, handing out beatings and other punishments to those whom they consider to be enemies, and terrifying the innocent. They specialize in threats and warnings of retribution on turncoats and traitors, and they do immense damage to property. They go about dressed in animal skins and with cattle horns upon their heads, and they are led by somebody called "The Bull". Those involved in their torchlight processions and "proceedings" mostly work outside their home areas so as to avoid recognition, and they have an elaborate support system for any of their number who may be arrested or convicted following dangerous missions. They may appear to be related to the juries of the *Ceffyl Pren* as we know them in this neighbourhood, but in their activities innocence and humour appear to be quite missing, and there is a dark and sinister side to their work. I consider them to be vicious fellows, and from what I read in the *Cambrian* and the *Welshman* their priorities appear to have little if anything to do with justice. Hugh Williams agrees with me, although he appears to be more than a little impressed with their instinct for survival over several decades, their skill in maintaining solidarity and secrecy, and their ability to organize themselves effectively as a private army.

In a recent comment in the *Cambrian* it was stated that the days of the Scotch Cattle are numbered. One of their leaders, one Edward Morgan, was hanged at Monmouth Gaol some years back, and that exemplary punishment must have frightened a good many followers. In addition, said the newspaper, the constant attendance of troops, the appointment of many special constables, the creation of a new police force, and bribes and offers of rewards "will very shortly produce the required result, namely the total extermination of the Scotch Cattle herd."

I wonder whether it is now in the mind of the Home Secretary to transfer these methods, apparently so successful in the teeming and dirty industrial districts, into the countryside where life is slower and gentler and where there is a greater respect for the law? A simple matter, he might think. Stimulate dissent, smash it down with an iron fist at very modest cost, and then enjoy the political dividends at the next election. And he might well do it soon, for if the disaffected men of the countryside join forces with the Chartists and the Scotch Cattle, a truly nationwide insurrection might be the result.

I may be wrong in all of this, but with the help of Master Williams and Brynach and Ioan, I am learning to understand the minds of our political leaders almost as well as I understand the minds of our local squires. Well, we shall see. The Chartists and the Scotch Cattle were all men, and they operated in the manner of men, with no humour and very little finesse. They have, however, taught those of us who live in the countryside a good deal about what to do and what not to do in the pursuit of justice. Rebecca and her daughters are supposed to be women, and if they are called to duty again it might be my function in life to teach them to behave as women do. Shemi the Wizard told me some years ago that I was destined to succeed in my mission, and I know that that mission is by no means over. If the time is right, let Rebecca recommence her battle, and then we shall see how well the Home Secretary and the army can cope with female wiles and female wisdom...........

ΩΩΩΩΩΩΩΩΩΩΩ

A Spark in Dry Bracken

20th July 1842

I have written to Master Williams to inform him of the implementation of the Home Secretary's directive. I have also met certain gentlemen whom I count as allies. This time I chose the location for the meeting, and with Ioan's approval I decided upon Brithdir Mawr. We met very late, at ten o'clock in the evening, so as to reduce the chances of visitors being recognized by spies or informers.

Twm Carnabwth came with Lloyd Davies from Glynsaithmaen, and I also welcomed Dafydd Ifan from Gamallt, young Squire Nicholas Lloyd Cwmgloyn, Waldo Tucker Penrhiw, Patty's sons Jack and Hubert from Parrog, my good friend Skiff Abraham, George Mathias Trehaidd, and three fellows whom I did not know from St Clears, Carmarthen and Whitland. Lloyd and Twm vouched for them, and there is no reason to doubt their integrity. Each of these men was invited verbally by a different person and by a different route, and each of them has his own constituency. Within the next few days there will be at least a dozen other meetings across West Wales, and our conclusions and suggestions will be known to at least a hundred influential men. They will include the next generation of Rebeccas. They and their confederates will decide what happens next, and if disorder returns to our country districts they will decide just how disorderly things will be.

Our meeting in the Brithdir dining room was long and detailed. There was danger in the air, and we all knew it, but I sought to introduce good humour into the proceedings, and Betsi and Ioan as hosts made the occasion a most convivial one with a constant supply of bread, cheeses and cold meats, and excellent ale on the table. Since I had called the meeting I also chaired it, and that was a new experience for me. I tried to talk as little as possible, but it appeared that I had more to say than the others, and indeed the gentlemen present urged me at the outset to report all of my intelligence. So that is what I did. I told them about the Home Secretary's letters to the Lords Lieutenant of the three counties, and about the signs coming from Newport that spies and informers are already being recruited by the authorities. At least three others around the table had suspicions about certain individuals on the peripheries of their own groups of friends, who had suddenly and mysteriously become a little wealthier than they had been before. "There are warning bells ringing inside my head," said Master Jones from Carmarthen, with a good deal of nodding from the others. "Your news is grave indeed, Mistress Martha, but it explains certain meetings of the magistrates in my neighbourhood, and the recent recruitment of special constables for no immediately obvious reason. I am also aware that our little borough police force, incompetent as it is, is on duty around the clock. And certain fellows of my acquaintance have been digging about and asking questions about Rebecca. We are watching them, but they appear very determined........."

Then I placed before the gentlemen my musings on the decline and fall of the Chartists and the Scotch Cattle, and on the lessons to be learned from the mass protests of the industrial districts. I also outlined my thinking, and that of Master Hugh Williams, on the Government's political strategy, and said that in my view the authorities were intent upon fomenting unrest simply in order to crush it and obtain some political capital from their victory.

It might have been wiser to have been less honest and forthright. A deep gloom settled across the meeting, and I felt a sudden panic in my breast, caused by the thought that the flame which had driven men to the destruction of the Efailwen and Maes-gwyn gates some years since might have flickered and gone out. But then Ioan showed his true mettle. He intervened and reminded those present that it was the right of every God-fearing man to have regular work and regular payment, and that it was the right of every God-fearing woman to go safely on her way, and to have a roof over her head, and to have food for her children. He slammed his fist onto the table and said in a voice which quivered like a steel blade: "Gentlemen, we do not want wealth or power. All we desire is justice! We know about the Charter and about the six modest requests for which hundreds of men have died or been transported to the penal colonies. We know that ten years since, Dic Penderyn went to the gallows an innocent man. Suffering, and yet more suffering. For how long, gentlemen? The Government of Lord Melbourne has blood on its hands -- the blood of poor starving people who have no vote, no rights and no pride. The law protects the rich and crushes the poor, and it is now apparent that the authorities want to extend their powers by using armed force and corruption in a lethal combination. If we are not careful, gentlemen, innocence and joy will disappear entirely from this countryside. Our community, once a thing of beauty, will become no better than a rotten corpse, riddled with maggots and picked over by the crows. Informers and spies will be our rulers, and violence, intimidation and revenge will replace friendship and trust. We will be no better than manacled black men and women in the stinking hold of a slave ship. I, for one, will never accept that. I will fight for freedom and justice, and if that fight takes me to the gallows, gentlemen, so be it!"

He sat down, shaking with emotion and with his face pallid in the light of flickering candles. There was complete silence in the room, as every person present contemplated the words of my beloved son-in-law. I was caught up in the tension of the moment, and hardly dared to breathe. At such times, I thought, are the destinies of nations decided. The old clock in the corner ticked and ticked, and became a symbol for civilization, and patience, and resolution. How extraordinary, I thought, that such words can have been uttered by a country gentleman who has food in his larder and servants at his beck and call, and sufficient resources to be a burgess of Newport and a tally-holder of various turnpike trusts! If such words had come from a starving labourer in a leaky hovel they would have been powerful enough, but they came from Ioan, who has had his ups and downs, and who is the father of three of my grandchildren..............

Then eyes were raised from the table, and met, and heads were nodded. Master Lloyd Davies Glynsaithmaen acted as spokesman. "Very well, gentlemen," he said quietly. "We thank Master Ioan for those passionate words. If he and Mistress Martha are prepared to fight for the poor and the downtrodden, we who have most to lose and most to gain cannot stand aside. I take it that we are resolved to continue our struggle?" There were solemn nods, and Twm Carnabwth said "Amen."

"More ale, *cariad?*" said Betsi to Ioan, as she appeared miraculously from the kitchen with a big jug of frothing liquid in her hand. The tension was suddenly broken, and the room erupted into laughter and conversation. I closed my eyes and listened to the hubbub, and thanked the angels of Carningli for giving their seal of approval to an enterprise which would, I knew, be dark and dangerous.

At last I called the meeting to order, for time was going on, and there was work to do. The men agreed with me, and over the course of two hours we worked with an efficiency which surprised all of us. We went carefully over the events of 1839, and discussed the successes and the failures of the campaign to defeat Master Bullin and remove his new gates. We went over the ground rules for meetings, and the passing of messages, and the leadership of demonstrations. We assumed that it would be necessary for more gates to come down, and we agreed on a code of behaviour for Rebecca and her daughters. Over and again I pleaded for violence to be kept to a minimum and to be directed at property rather than persons. We agreed that we should seek to avoid the excesses of the Scotch Cattle, and I tried to explain why the idea of a loving sisterhood should be used in place of the idea of a violent brotherhood. That was difficult for the men to understand, but they grinned and promised to pass on my pleas to all future meetings from which I might be absent. We agreed to invoke the scriptures in support of future actions, and to seek the approval of as many Nonconformist ministers and congregations as we could. And on the matter of weapons and suchlike, I accepted that they were a necessary evil but pleaded for the good humour of the *Ceffyl Pren* to be carried through into future demonstrations and campaigns. Again the men nodded and grinned, and probably thought that I was mad.

At one o'clock in the morning we got onto the business of spies and informers, and how to deal with them. We agreed that in cases of betrayal, rough justice would probably have to be dispensed by Rebecca and her daughters, and that inflamed passions would be difficult to control following future arrests, prosecutions and incarcerations of demonstrators. But I made the point again that anticipation and planning could substantially reduce the risks for all demonstrators, if they took part in actions no more than once or twice, if high levels of secrecy could be maintained, if the groups involved in actions could be kept small, and if strict rules of dress and address could be adhered to by all rioters. Master Lloyd Cwmgloyn added that where poor people were tempted to betray family or friends, or to respond to reward notices posted by the authorities, solidarity could be encouraged through the vilification and public naming of spies, informers and court witnesses, and through actions taken against them or their property. "Rebecca must look after her daughters," he said, "for they are the ones who will inherit her estate."

"That sounds like an incitement to intimidation and hatred, Nicholas," said I, with a furrow on my brow.

"I know it well, Martha," he replied. "But what is the alternative? If we can prevent treachery, by whatever means, that has to be preferable to revenge after the event. Let us call it "discouragement" rather than "intimidation", for if spies are rewarded, and get away with their activities, I foresee that beatings and even murders will follow." I had to agree with that, and I also accepted the view that letters and posters might be used freely in order to discourage treachery.

Finally, with exhaustion setting in around the table, I passed on to the gentlemen present some of the lessons learned by my beloved Owain when he was in Spain during the Peninsular War with the French. He told me once that the Spanish irregulars had become adept in the use of the spy network by the use of fellows who purported to support one side but in fact supported the other. They frequently passed false information to the French, who sometimes sent troops galloping off in one direction only to find that they had left themselves open to "hit and run" attacks in other places. Master Bonaparte lost hundreds of men as a consequence. He and his generals became utterly confused, for after the discovery that some of their spies were untrustworthy they knew not which ones were faithful and true, and which were villains. So a degree of uncertainty crept into their campaigning, and the military men found that their standard tactics of moving large numbers of men about, and planning set-piece battles, and rolling up provisions and armaments, became worse than useless. Owain had told me how he had been mightily impressed by the ability of the irregulars to set themselves limited targets, to strike quickly in unexpected places, and to melt away into the countryside before the soldiers were able to respond. I still remember his words after all these years. "I daresay that every oppressed people adopts the same tactics when faced by overwhelming military might," he had said, "and if those who act for the people have the people behind them to provide succour and shelter, they are unbeatable."

I did not need to elaborate, and at two o'clock in the morning the meeting broke up. We were all exhausted. Those who lived nearby walked home, and those who lived far away set off on their horses beneath a starlit sky with a mellow moon sinking into the west. I stayed at Brithdir for what was left of the night, although I have to admit that I slept hardly at all.

I am of the view that this meeting was far more important than the Glynsaithmaen meeting which preceded the first destruction of the gate at Efailwen. Now, we are as well prepared as we can be for the next moves that might be made by the authorities. We can only sit and wait, and I suspect that we will not have to wait for long.

A Spark in Dry Bracken

20th September 1842

We are still waiting, and that is just as well, for none of us could have coped with riots and spies and with a heavy corn harvest at the same time. It was the best harvest for many a long year, and for a few weeks farmers and labourers set aside their problems and celebrated high summer in the best possible way, with hard work and camaraderie beneath a blazing sun. There have been a good many Irish in the neighbourhood, as usual during the harvest season, and I have used ten members of the O'Connell family whom I know and trust. They brought tales of terrible hardship in the eastern parts of Ireland, and it was a salutary thing to discover that although conditions are bad in Pembrokeshire, they are even worse elsewhere.

I have omitted to report on the small happenings in my own family and household over the last three years. My dear mother Betsi died last year at the advanced age of 83. It happened, quietly and unexpectedly, in her own bed at Brawdy -- a good death after a rich and happy life. There was a big funeral in the Brawdy parish church, attended by four generations of the Howell family. My brother Morys and his family took charge of proceedings in the old family home. Catrin and her family travelled from Castlebythe, and there was a veritable procession of Morgan carriages from the Newport area. Brynach and his children travelled in one, I travelled with Bessie, Sian and Shemi in another, and Betsi and Ioan and their three boys took the Brithdir coach. Elen and her family are still in America, and after receiving a note from Morys informing her of Mother's death she immediately wrote long and beautiful letters to Morys, Catrin and me, expressing her grief and recalling the great happiness of our childhood years. When I received mine, six weeks after Mother's death, it brought tears to my eyes and caused me to offer up a prayer of thanks for the blessings brought by a good family. The only one who was missing from the funeral was my daughter Daisy, although after a stream of unanswered letters to her and to her friends I know not whether she is dead or still alive in London. That uncertainty, and the great love which I still feel for my troubled and inaccessible daughter, brings me far greater grief than that which I felt at the death of my mother. It is always there in my heart and my head, and on Daisy's birthday every year I still shed tears for her and for myself.......

A Spark in Dry Bracken

To more cheerful matters. Mistress Gwenno Philpin and Master Gomer Jenkins were married two years since, bringing to a happy conclusion their somewhat turbulent and protracted courtship. That brought me great pleasure since it brought together the family of my dear handmaiden Liza and that of my friends Shemi and Sian. It was a good wedding, and was held down in the *cwm* in the Baptist chapel of Caersalem. The ceremony was more solemn than I would have liked, and as I get older I find that solemnity is less and less to my liking. However, I threw the Plas open to the happy couple and their guests after the solemn proceedings were over and done with, and we had as good a feast as Bessie could assemble in the face of harvest failures and high food prices. Afterwards we had a *twmpath* in the barn, and I even managed to get Pastor Jacob Ifans to join me in an Irish jig. Whatever else I may achieve in this life, I count that as one of my greatest triumphs. The two young people did not have a very productive bidding, since times are tight, but they do at least have a roof over their heads. I was able to give them a cottage on the estate following the death of Jac Blossom, my occasional gardener. The Plas is quieter since they moved out, but they come in to work as regularly as ever, and they join us for most of our mealtimes.

Bryn has not been well, and he complains that the breathing problems which he developed during his time in the ironworks of Merthyr Tydfil have returned with greater severity. Shemi has been treating him, but he thinks that his lungs have been poisoned in the past by noxious fumes and that the damage is too severe to repair. Bryn does not want to stop working, and I will respect his wishes, but he cannot cope with heavy tasks any longer. I fear that whatever his wishes may be, his days of prancing about with the Daughters of Rebecca are over.

I have omitted to describe the change in my relations with Master Hugh Williams, and I must set that matter right. There is not much to say, except that he has gone up considerably in my estimation since I first met him in the spring of 1839. At that time, I played a little game with him, and having judged that his intentions towards me were not entirely honourable I decided that I would play him as a fisherman plays a large sewin. Then fate intervened, and he became somewhat involved in the court cases arising out of the Llanidloes Insurrection. I am still not sure whether I was relieved or disappointed at the time. When peace returned to the countryside following the removal of Master Bullin's contentious gates, I thought that I might never hear from Master Williams again. It came to my notice that he was working for the most part in London. But then I went to a musical entertainment at the Stokes residence in Trecwn, and who should be there, larger than life, but the gentleman himself, as arrogant and as ebullient as ever. He looked genuinely pleased to see me, and greeted me with an elegant bow and a kiss of the hand. We spent much of the evening in each other's company, and while I found his pomposity very irritating I was quite taken by his erudition and his wit. I recall that I was surprised by his knowledge of local scandals and foibles, and that I laughed more than a little.

He had to leave early, because, as he explained, his dear wife would be waiting up for him and would be worried about his safety on the dark and pot-holed roads. That caused some amusement, since it was known by almost all those present that his dear wife cared not one jot where he was, and that he was heading back in his carriage not to St Clears but to his latest mistress in Haverfordwest. When he had gone, Mary Jane took me to one side and said: "I was delighted, Martha, to observe your pleasure in the presence of an old friend here this evening."

"I would not call Master Williams an old friend," said I. "An acquaintance, perhaps. He and I have met once or twice before, and have exchanged letters on matters of mutual interest."

At this, Mary Jane giggled and gave me a hug. "Dear Martha!" she said, with a wicked gleam in her eye. "As evasive as ever. I take it that you know his reputation?"

"Only too well. As unsavoury as a pork sausage left too long on the plate and nibbled by too many children. Don't you worry about me, my dear friend. I find him entertaining, and it suits my purpose to spend a little time in his company."

"Do you find him attractive?"

"Absolutely not! His nose is too big and his eyes are too green, and I cannot abide fellows who have side whiskers and hard lips. And besides, he does not drink brandy, which means that he and I are absolutely incompatible."

Mary Jane roared with laughter. "Martha!" she gurgled. "You are blushing, as you always do when you tell lies! I will take it as read that in spite of the fact that you are old enough to be his mother, there is a certain attraction between you."

A Spark in Dry Bracken

"I am not that old, Mary Jane. May I remind you that beneath this sagging bosom there beats a heart which is as passionate as ever."

"Thinking of bosoms, I noticed earlier in the evening that when you visited my room to powder your nose, you came out with your bosom a little higher and a little more revealed than when you went in. Now that, I imagine, had nothing whatsoever to do with your discovery that Master Williams was one of our guests?"

"Pure coincidence, Mary Jane. I find that occasionally my bosom needs a little attention, purely as a matter of comfort." And my beloved friend flapped her eyelashes at me, and our eyes met, and then we both collapsed onto a sofa and had a fit of hysterics

When we had recovered, and resumed our place in civilized company, I asked Mary Jane why Master Hugh Williams had been present at her musical entertainment in the first place, since he was obviously not a family friend. She revealed to me that it was at the insistence of her younger son Samuel, who was very interested in the business of Chartism. That I found intriguing, to say the least. I recalled that young Samuel had been present at the first Chartist meeting in the Black Lion Inn some years back, and that he had also attended the big meeting in the Glynsaithmaen barn prior to the first Efailwen riot. I thought hard, but said nothing, for it is up to Samuel himself to do what he wants and to tell his mother as much or as little as he thinks fit.

Since that occasion at Trecwn, Master Williams and I have exchanged many letters. We have also met on occasions at social events organized by other people. We have never met at the Plas, or at his home in Ferryside. I have never met his wife, and nor do I have any wish to. Once or twice, for example following the destruction of the salmon weir at Felindre or following episodes of rick-burning in the Teifi Valley, we have arranged meetings at friendly houses and have discussed ways in which we might influence the actions of the rioters and the magistrates in the event of disturbances spreading and becoming more violent. But each time peace has returned, and further action, either on his part or mine, has proved unnecessary.

Nothing untoward has ever passed between us, although I am aware that certain members of the gentry and certain of his friends might assume that we are lovers. He certainly lusts after me, and I think he loves me. For all I know, he might be dropping hints around the hostelries of West

Wales that he has already added me to his list of sexual conquests. I can put up with that. For his part, he probably enjoys his social intercourse with me and other members of the minor gentry, for he is a professional man (albeit quite a wealthy one) who needs to enhance his status. And since I can be honest in the pages of this little book, I can say that I derive a frisson of excitement from the knowledge that tongues might be wagging behind my back.

Having known the fellow now for more than three years, I have come to terms with the fact that I have no desire to welcome him into my bed or to accept any invitations to enter his. And there have been many such invitations. Whether the fault be mine or his, I do not find that I am physically excited by him. But in spite of his arrogance and his irritating habits he is a generous and tolerant man, and he is driven by a fierce desire to protect the weak and to see justice done. That is why he is a Chartist, and that is why he frequently gives his services as an attorney free to those who cannot afford to pay. On that score, I think I love him a little. We both feel that we are soul-mates. We talk at great length, and when he wants to be, he is very funny. I tease him and insult him, and he pays me endless compliments. We are exceedingly comfortable in each other's company. I trust him absolutely, as he trusts me, and I think he values my counsel as I value his. And we move in different social circles and in different counties. Now that I come to think of it, that means that Master Williams and I can, if we wish it, provide very valuable assistance to Mistress Rebecca should she come knocking on our doors in her hour of need.

ΩΩΩΩΩΩΩΩΩΩΩ

20th November 1842

The bracken at this time of year is tall and brittle, and a spark has set off a fire which might yet turn into an inferno. It has been inevitable, and I have been waiting for several months for it to happen.

My own involvement was minimal, apart from a warning which I sent to my contacts in St Clears that the Main Trust, which operates mostly in the county of Carmarthenshire, had made a decision at a meeting a month ago to put up a new gate at the Mermaid Tavern, just to the east of the village. That was at the instigation of Thomas Bullin, who holds the Main Trust contract as he does the contract for the Whitland Trust gates. The man is either an idiot or an agent for the Government, but one does not have to analyze either his state of mind or his motives to see that his actions appear to the common people to be calculated to cause trouble. News came to me about a week ago that meetings of Rebecca and her daughters had been held near Whitland and Tavernspite, in order to discuss future action. According to Betsi, Ioan was frequently away at the time, in the company of two or three other fellows from the *cwm*, and she knew that something was afoot.

I know now that Ioan was involved, and that he played the part of Rebecca on the night of the first riots. Thank God that he is home safely. I went down to Brithdir to see him today, and he sat with Betsi and me in the dining room. He told us everything.

The people of St Clears knew that the gate would be put into position on 18th November, and that tolls would be charged on it with immediate effect. Within a few hours of the erection of the gate, a crowd of about one hundred men gathered outside the village. Most of them had travelled a long way to be there. They were all dressed in the approved fashion of Rebecca's daughters, and according to Ioan they all looked exceedingly beautiful, with black faces, straw hair, and puffed up bosoms. They wore the latest London fashions -- heavy flannel skirts, woollen bodices, shawls and cloaks riddled with holes, dirty cotton shirts and aprons, battered straw bonnets or floppy felt hats. On their feet they had heavy boots or clogs, and their fashion accessories included staves, axes, ropes and sledge hammers. Three fellows had drums with them, and there were two buglers who had had, a long time ago, musical training from the army. Mercifully there were no firearms in evidence. Ioan had been elected Rebecca in advance, and when he got to the assembly point, dressed magnificently in Mrs Owen's old clothes and sporting a turban of red and gold silk with ostrich feathers, he found a white stallion waiting for him. He was told that it had been "borrowed" from the stable of one of the local magistrates. Ioan says that he laid down the ground rules for the men, and off they marched towards the Mermaid Tavern with the orchestra playing soothing melodies.

There were not even any special constables in attendance, he said. The gatekeeper and his wife came out of the gatehouse to investigate the cacophony, and fled as soon as they realized that they were to play host to Rebecca and her daughters. Ioan said that as the mob reached the gate, he dismounted, and as arranged he initiated a little pantomime. He pretended to be blind, and with his staff held out in front of him he stumbled into the gate. He tapped it a few times. "Oh my dear children," he said. "There is something put here that prevents me from going upon my way. What might it be?"

"Why, it is a gate, Mother!"

"A gate? But there is no gate upon this road, and it is my right to pass back and forth, is it not, my daughters?"

"Indeed it is, Mother! Shall we open it for you and let you pass through?"

"If you please, dear children, for Becca is old and frail, and cannot see to do it herself."

"Why, there is a great lock upon it, Mother, and we have no key!"

Rebecca moaned and wailed, and finally said: "Oh, woe is me! I cannot go on. What is to be done?"

"It must be taken down, Mother, because the Bible says so, and because you must pass through."

"Down with it then, my dear daughters! It has no business here!"

And Rebecca raised her staff over her head, and the bugles blared and the drums thundered, and the beautiful daughters shouted and cheered, and smashed the gate to pieces in ten minutes with their axes and their sledge hammers.

With impressive discipline, said Ioan, the mob disappeared into the night. But the work was not yet finished, and an hour or so later Rebecca and her daughters appeared at the western edge of St Clears where they performed the same ritual and meted out the same treatment to the gate at Pwll-trap which belonged to the Whitland Trust. Then, for good measure, they completed the "cleaning" of St Clears by smashing down the side bar designed to prevent access over the River Taf bridge. Having freed the place of all encumbrances, Rebecca and her daughters then disbanded without any further delay or celebration. Ioan handed back his white stallion to the fellow who had "borrowed" it, and mounted his own hunter for the journey home. He and the other Cilgwyn men changed out of their female garb when they were a few miles clear of the village, and trotted home through the pitch blackness of the November night and through squalls of cold rain.

I had to give Ioan a hug at the completion of his narrative. "Well done, Ioan," I said. "I am very proud of you. Some months back, you changed the mood of a meeting at Brithdir and may thus have changed the course of history. Now you have taken the lead as the first Rebecca to implement the rules upon which we are all agreed. I hope that others will follow your example. It sounds to me as if your security was tight, your leadership exemplary, and your confederates well disciplined and good humoured. If no names were used in public, and if no incriminating evidence apart from horse manure was left behind, there is no way that the authorities can trace your actions back to Cilgwyn. I pray to God that you have no spies and informers among your neighbours or indeed beneath your own roof."

"I can never be sure of that, Martha," he replied. "Some people certainly know that I was away for the night, and that I came back tired and dirty, and that my horse had travelled a long way. I just have to trust to their discretion should anybody come snooping around."

"And Mrs Owen's clothes?"

"Already in the washtub."

"No finger-marks in the soot above the fireplace?"

"No, Martha. My soot was collected long since, and is in a bag behind the stable." And then Ioan burst out laughing, and kissed me upon the cheek, and gave me a great hug. "My dear Martha," he chuckled. "You sound exactly as you did when I was first courting Betsi and she was a mere slip of a girl." And to prove the point, he mimicked me with considerable accuracy. "Now then, Betsi, are you sure you are warm enough? And what if it rains? And don't take those boots, because they leak! And that is quite the wrong bonnet to wear with that red dress!"

So for his insolence I chased Ioan round the kitchen table and boxed his ears, much to Betsi's amusement. At last, when we had all settled down again, I stood facing Ioan and took his hands in mine. "Now then, my beloved and revolutionary son-in-law," I said. "I have for years worried about the fact that I have never extracted a promise from you that you would desist from involvement in riots and disturbances. Brynach gave me such a promise long ago. You have now taken the lead in smashing down not one gate, but three in the same night. Will you now promise me and Betsi that your rioting days are over?"

"I will, Martha. I have done my duty, and will adhere to the rules which we have set for ourselves. You have my word." The three of us put our arms around each other, and Betsi and I both shed a few tears.

As I walked home, I mused on the full import of the story told to us by Ioan, and of his involvement in the affairs of Rebecca. I thanked the angels of the mountain for the fact that he had come to no harm, and for the success of my strategy in leaving him to determine his own destiny. On many occasions I have been on the point of asking him for a promise to steer clear of demonstrations and riots, for the sake of Betsi and his family. That was what my head wanted. But each time I have desisted, since in my heart I knew that Ioan needed to climb a mountain and stand on the summit. He has had too many failures in his life -- in financial matters, in farming at Cenarth, and then in his attempt to manage Plas Ingli following the arrival of the Rhys family on my doorstep about ten years ago. Ioan is a proud and emotional man, and men such as he can be crushed by failure. To him, success and the respect of others mean more than wealth and status. Well, now he has proved himself with a vengeance, as a thinker, as a diplomat and as a man of action. He can hold his head up high, and I can see that Betsi is inordinately proud of him. Tomorrow there will be a new spring in his step, and though he may not be at liberty to explain its origins to those who may note it and enquire about it, he can smile enigmatically and pretend that Shemi the Wizard has given him some magic potion.

Men are strange creatures indeed, but they have their uses, and what would we do without them?

ΩΩΩΩΩΩΩΩΩΩΩ

9. A Spreading Wildfire

15th December 1842

The flames are spreading, and if the wind shifts to the east they will certainly come in this direction. Following the night of gate destruction at St Clears, the magistrates met immediately and put out notices offering a reward of £30 for information leading to the arrest of any of the rioters, and the Main Trust another £20. Rebecca was not impressed, and responded within a week by smashing down one of the Whitland Trust gates at a place called Trevaughan. According to the *Cambrian* the old lady and her daughters were in good form, and re-enacted the little pantomime that had first been used at the Mermaid gate. That looks as if it might become as much an institution as the female garb and the blackened faces.

With four gates down the authorities began to panic, and word has reached me that there is no sign of any cooperation from the public. Indeed, the magistrates are having great difficulty in signing up special constables. Even those who are pressed into service appear to have more sympathy with Rebecca than they do with the turnpike trusts or the magistrates, which means that they will not do a great deal of gate guarding. A week ago I received a note from Hugh Williams to say that there is serious disagreement among the magistrates about who should meet the costs of gate replacement. The trusts should pay, but they claim that Master Bullin should put up new gates at his own expense since he is the contractor. He claims that he cannot afford it. And the magistrates cannot allow people to pass freely, since that would be seen as a sign that the rioters have won the day. So the gates are being replaced, and will continue to be replaced as necessary, and Master Williams says that the arguments about finance will be resolved at some future date. All this is probably music to Rebecca's ears.

Today Will brought me a verbal message which he had received from somebody in Tufton, who in turn had got it from a Llanboidy man. He said that three nights since, Rebecca and her daughters had descended on St Clears again, at around midnight, and had more or less taken the place over. There were no signs of any special constables on duty. There were about eighty men in the demonstration, and they destroyed all the gates in the neighbourhood that had only just been replaced. What is more, they went through the village inviting all the residents to lock their doors and extinguish all their candles and lanterns, in effect enforcing a curfew. Any spies in the village were thus effectively put out of action. The rioters had patrols out on all six roads leading into the village, showing that the operation was well planned and executed with military precision. It was the night on which many travellers were returning towards Carmarthen from Narberth Fair, and according to the message all the drovers and farmers who passed through the village were "invited" to make contributions for the support of the poor, in view of the fact that there were now no tolls to pay. Many were happy to oblige.

One can only applaud Rebecca's intention to become involved in charitable works, and I am pleased that the latest episode of gate destruction showed meticulous planning. But this latest adventure was more like an insurrection than a riot, and I am concerned about the character of future demonstrations. Future Rebeccas might not be as restrained and as careful as Twm and Ioan, and I am certain that the magistrates will now seek the assistance of the Home Office, and the involvement of the army, before the flames spread much further.

ΩΩΩΩΩΩΩΩΩΩΩ

16th January 1843

For a month I have managed to keep away from politics and riots, and have been able to concentrate instead on Christmas, New Year and *Hen Galan*. Christmas was a white one, but not too white. Following the excellent harvest of last summer the larder and the pantry were fuller than they have been for some years, and because of depressed prices in the market place my tenants and I have sold fewer animals than usual. That meant that supplies of meat, eggs, cheese and poultry were also at a high level. We thought that we might as well enjoy the abundance of nature, and we did. We had a big Christmas at the Plas, with more than one hundred people squeezed into the old house for Christmas dinner, including all of my children except Daisy, and my five grandchildren. Brynach wanted all of us to go to Plas Llanychaer for the biggest meal of the season, on the basis that I now have enough grey hairs on my head to be a guest rather than a host, but I have my responsibilities to my tenants and my labourers, for whom times are still hard. In any case, I wanted a big Christmas and so did Bessie, and so that was that. In the event the Llanychaer and Brithdir contingents arrived from their respective homes laden with hams and joints of beef, cheeses and eggs, potatoes and carrots, apples and pears, breads and pastries and other good things, and so our over-indulgence was on a scale that would have pleased even the Patron Saint of Gluttony, whoever he might be.

With the passing of *Hen Galan*, the peace which we have enjoyed in this area has passed into history, and is now replaced by violence and discontent. I knew it would happen, for just as an easterly wind brings snow it brings smoke and flames from Carmarthenshire. The trouble was precipitated about a week ago when both the Fishguard and Cemais Turnpike Trusts met to discuss their increasingly vulnerable finances. Both had been warned of impending bankruptcy, and their clerks and surveyors had asked for increased tolls and the installation of new gates. Ioan, Brynach and I attended both meetings, but very little notice was given and several of our allies were away for the Christmas season in London and other places. We missed them greatly, and although we argued that new gates and increased tolls were illegal under the terms of the relevant Acts of Parliament, we could not sway the day. Squire Owen, Squire Jobbins and Squire Huws and their allies had prepared the ground well, and they argued that the Acts were more or less redundant and that they had assurances that no action would be taken against trusts which were simply seeking to restore the good health of their finances. We came away from both meetings convinced that certain individuals were acting on instructions from the Lord Lieutenant or even from the Home Office to stir the pot of disaffection or to test the resolve of the small farmers of this area, who have been remarkably restrained since the Christmas of 1838. So the meetings both voted for increased tolls for lime carting and for the erection of new gates and side bars.

Two days after the Cemais Trust meeting I received messages from Zeke Tomos, Dafydd Ifan and Dafydd Stokes Trecwn, quite independently asking for meetings with me. I would not meet them at the Plas, since I am holding to my principle of extreme caution in the matter of meetings and contacts, but arranged to meet them in different places at different times. I met young Dafydd Stokes in Fishguard on Wednesday and the other two "purely by chance" yesterday, on street corners in Newport and Dinas. In Newport I was sure that I was being followed and watched. This was confirmed when I bumped into my friend Abby in town. He said that the three fellows who drink in the Black Lion and who are suspected of being spies and informers have been increasingly active of late, asking questions, turning up in unexpected places, and generally interfering in other people's business. "Asking questions about you and the Plas, they are, Mistress," said Abby. "If I was you, I would watch your step. As for those fellows, I would not be too surprised if they was to get beaten up in one of the back alleys this very night, by persons unknown. A sad world it is, Mistress, with so much crime and violence about."

This morning I popped into Newport to do some shopping, and called in to see George Havard Medical. We had a brief chat about the deteriorating situation, and he told me that he had been called out late last night to treat three fellows who had received severe beatings in a street brawl. "No broken bones," he said, "but cuts and lacerations, and considerable bruising. Their assailants had used wooden clubs and staves, by the look of it. No knives, thank God. The victims would not say who was responsible, and neither would they inform the constables. I treated them as best I could, but if those particular fellows do not keep better company in future I daresay that I will be called upon to treat them again." And he gave me a wink and a wry smile. "By the way, Martha, they are not the only ones involved in observations just now. When I called in at Penrhiw the other day to treat Mistress Tucker, who has a severe chill upon the chest, I surprised one of Squire Jobbins' men who was lurking behind a hedge near the entrance to your driveway. He tried to look invisible, but when that did not succeed he looked very guilty instead. I just thought you might be interested." I was indeed, and thanked George for his friendship.

I was angry enough already, but that made me even angrier. The upshot of all these brief discussions is that the agreement which I made with Squires Jobbins, Huws and Owen more than four years ago has been broken by those three gentlemen, without any reference to me. They have raised rents for the small farms and for the labourers on their estates. Owen Gelli Fawr has started to institute proceedings against poor people who have defaulted on the payment of tithes. There have been three recent convictions through the Petty Sessions for thefts of turnips and for rabbit poaching. And Master Jobbins, who I thought had more sense, has just evicted a family from a *ty unnos* on the edge of his land and has razed their hovel to the ground, having taken no action against this family for three years. More news will follow, of that I am sure. Times are tight for the gentry just now, but they are far tighter for the small farmers, and these actions appear to be designed to inflame passions.

I have tried to control my anger as I tried to control the anger of the men to whom I have spoken. They feel betrayed, and I have promised them that I will do what I can to relieve hardship and to urge caution among the most belligerent members of the local gentry. So I have sent messages to Squires Owen, Jobbins and Huws asking for a meeting at the Plas on Monday of next week or on any date that might be convenient. I hope and pray that they will respond positively.

$$\Omega\Omega\Omega\Omega\Omega\Omega\Omega\Omega\Omega\Omega$$

20th January 1843

Now I feel betrayed as well, for my requests for a meeting with the three squires have been rejected out of hand. Of course they pleaded pressure of work, and family commitments, and prior engagements as far as my preferred date was concerned, but they suggested no alternatives, and their letters were brief and cool. They had clearly consulted with one another before writing to me. When I had recovered my equilibrium I sat down today at my desk and penned this to Squire Owen, as the senior squire:

Plas Ingli, on the 20th day of January 1843
My Dear Squire Owen,
I thank you for your response to my recent communication in which I requested a meeting for the discussion of matters of mutual concern.

A Spreading Wildfire

I have to say that I am gravely disappointed by your disinclination to meet with me. In recalling our meeting of 4th August 1838, and subsequent communications between us, it now appears to me that all the commitments which you made to me have been abandoned. I daresay that you will remember quite well those actions which you promised to take, just as I remember the things which I promised to do. I have delivered, and I have managed, through the use of various intermediaries, to restrain those in our community who might incline towards conflict.

I have said it before, and I say it again now, that I hate violence of any sort, and that I will use might and main to prevent it, and to direct men's energies into dialogue and understanding whenever and wherever they contemplate riot and disorder. As a result of my efforts, and those of many other like-minded people, this district has remained mercifully peaceful while other parts of Wales have seen death and destruction. But men who are poor and starving cannot be indefinitely restrained from taking action against those whom they consider to be enemies, and the recent inflammatory actions taken by you and your colleagues will, I fear, result in an inferno which none of us will be able to control. You and your peers have set your men to spy on me and others who are your friends. What am I to make of that? What does it tell me about mutual trust?

Any day now, the new tollgates of the Fishguard and Cemais Trusts will be put up, and new tolls will be charged. The consequences of these actions are perfectly predictable.

Our agreement is clearly at an end. That saddens me and angers me. Be that as it may, you may take it that I will continue to strive for peaceful solutions to all of the difficulties which face the rich and the poor in our district.

Sincerely yours, Martha Morgan, Mistress

I read this over many times before sending it off, but then I decided that it was perfectly suitable as a declaration of war, and that it contained nothing incriminating that might in future be used in a court of law. The letter would be passed on, for sure, but it gave nothing away regarding either my contacts or my role as a mediator, and if ever used in a public forum the letter would do more harm to the squires than to me. So I sent it off, and sent similar letters to Jobbins Holmws and Huws Bayvil. Let battle be joined.

A Spreading Wildfire

24th February 1843

New gates have gone up at Felindre, Temple Bar, Hendre and Dinas, together with five new side bars to prevent unauthorized access onto the turnpike trust roads. The new tolls are being enforced, and five farmers have been arrested and flung into the town lockup following refusals to pay. Ten new special constables have been sworn in, and while most of them have no wish at all to do their duty there are one or two thugs who are only too happy to have badges of office which they can use to legalize their thuggery. There have been ugly incidents at all of the new gates and side bars, and meetings have been held in a number of local barns and cottages over the last week. I was invited, but chose not to attend. The three Newport spies, clearly not deterred by their recent beatings, have been flung into the river near Mistress Dafis's ferry station together with three others who are likely informers, as a "gentle warning" to stay out of other people's business. They were not harmed, but involuntary swims in the river are not very pleasant at this time of year. There are rumours that the *Ceffyl Pren* jury will be out and about within the next week.

Last night Rebecca and her daughters destroyed the new gate and gatekeeper's house at Felindre, with all the traditions faithfully followed. The gate went up in flames. This was the first appearance of the beautiful ladies and their gate-removal equipment in this district. I have not yet obtained full news of what transpired, but I gather from Dai Darjeeling, who called in today, that there were no special constables in attendance, and that there were no breaches of security.

Things have also been happening further afield. According to the *Cambrian* the Pwll Trap gate went down again on the second day of the New Year, and such is the feeling in the St Clears area that no matter how many times it is replaced, Rebecca will never permit it to survive. Then at the beginning of this month, one of the Fishguard Trust's gates at Prendergast in Haverfordwest was quietly removed without trace by Rebecca, on the grounds that it was illegally located inside the town boundary and was therefore "trapping" townspeople as well as long-distance road users.

Thus far there has been no involvement from the military in Pembrokeshire, but it cannot be long in coming. When it does come, there may be lessons to be learned from St Clears. There, the magistrates got themselves into such a state, after the second destruction of the Pwll Trap gate in December, that they immediately wrote to the Home Secretary asking for troops. He declined the request, but sent them instead three Metropolitan Police officers. They arrived on 20th December, on the day after the Mermaid gate was destroyed for the third time. The fellows were worse than useless, and were so conspicuous in their strange costumes and tall hats that melting into the crowd was not an option. But the magistrates swore in no fewer than fifty-four special constables to help them, and that at least demonstrated some determination on their part. Neither the special constables nor the regulars covered themselves with glory on the second day of the New Year, for while Rebecca and her daughters were at work on the third destruction of the Pwll-trap gate they were all ensconced in the Blue Boar Inn, apparently somewhat the worse for wear. The London policemen, and the special constables, are now under the control of Inspector George Martin. I know not how efficient or intelligent he is, but he is Welsh-speaking, and that is a worry. If he has any brains inside his head, I imagine that it will not be long before his constables replace their police uniforms and dress as the locals do, for in such subterfuge lies their only hope of listening in on the conversations of Rebecca's daughters and countering their activities.

With the constables proving ineffective, the Carmarthenshire magistrates wrote again to the Home Secretary asking for troops, and when that request was also declined, they despatched a message to the commander of the Royal Marines at Pembroke Dockyard asking for a detachment to be sent. A troop of thirty men trudged wearily into St Clears on 15th January, and as soon as they arrived they found a message from Rebecca waiting for them, saying that she was minded to destroy the gate at Trevaughan, some six miles back along the Pembroke road. So the marines marched all the way back again, and when they got to Trevaughan they found that Rebecca had already completed her work and had moved on. So they headed for St Clears again, and on their way passed the smouldering wreckage of two other gates, at Pentre and Maes Oland! After only five days in the village they were ordered back to the Dockyard, since the Admiralty was convinced that an armed insurrection was on the way and that the arsenal there had to be protected. Whether this piece of false information came from Rebecca or some other source we may never know, but so seriously did the Admiralty take the rumour that additional marines were rushed to Pembroke from Bristol. Perhaps because of the same rumour, the magistrates in Carmarthen responded to the loss of marines by summoning the Castlemartin Yeomanry, which they are entitled to do without the consent of either the Home Secretary or the War Office. About thirty heavily armed troopers and officers arrived in St Clears on 21st January, and during the three weeks of their stay in the village absolutely nothing happened. The poor troopers must have been miserable indeed, for they spent their time on patrol in the dark wet lanes round about, standing on guard at the various gates, and putting up with the insults of the local populace. All these fellows had to be billeted in the village, and as soon as the magistrates realized that they would have to foot the bill for their living costs and military services they sent them packing again back to Pembrokeshire. Off they went, with the jeers of the locals ringing in their ears. As soon as they had passed through the Whitland gates on their way home, at midnight on 13th February, two of those gates were destroyed by Rebecca in an act of sheer impudence.

So Rebecca has shown as clearly as can be that she has the measure of the magistrates and the army in the western part of Carmarthenshire. She has won a stunning victory there, which will have made the magistrates explode with impotent rage. The old lady and her daughters have used considerable finesse in their operations, and they have proved very disciplined and good-humoured. Their spies have been effective, and their timing has been impeccable. I hope, however, that they do not become complacent or arrogant following this success, for if they do, it is only a matter of time before they get their comeuppance.

ΩΩΩΩΩΩΩΩΩΩ

26th February 1843

The betrayals have started, as was inevitable with large rewards on offer and with money being put into the employment of spies and informers. I heard from Master Hugh Williams today that two fellows from around Whitland have been arrested and charged with taking part in the latest destruction of the Trevaughan gate. Master Lewis Griffiths, a miller from Wiston, has come forward to Inspector Martin with a testimony and has claimed his reward for £50. It looks likely that he will get it, too. The arrests were made on the very day of the Petty Sessions in the Blue Boar Inn, so that it was well nigh impossible to organize a proper defence. According to my friend, who was in the village at the time, there was pandemonium inside the inn and outside it, and the witness had great difficulty in making his statement under oath. The attorneys who defended the charged men tried to discredit Master Griffiths under cross-examination, but the magistrates accepted his evidence and committed the prisoners for trial at the Pembrokeshire Assizes. They then sent them off to Haverfordwest Gaol under armed guard, with Inspector Martin in charge. It looked as if the crowd might lynch Master Griffiths, so he was sent off the gaol as well in the same open carriage, for his own safety! The constables had great difficulty in getting out of St Clears and onto the Haverfordwest road, so tight and inflamed was the crowd, but with the aid of their truncheons they at last managed to clear a route. The two prisoners are now incarcerated, with the traitor in an adjoining cell.

Master Timothy Powell, one of the magistrates involved at the Petty Sessions, has already had cause to regret his enthusiasm in the administration of justice, for within a couple of days of the prisoners being sent off to Haverfordwest, some of the beautiful woodlands on his estates at Penycoed and Llangynin went up in flames. He and his fellow magistrates will no doubt receive other reminders that Rebecca is displeased.

Closer to home, Brynach told me recently that the local magistrates knew last month that the Felindre gate would be attacked on the day before it happened. He has spoken to Nicholas Lloyd Cwmgloyn, who lives near the gate in question, and he says that the rioters would have been intercepted by the local Yeomanry had it not been for the mysterious nondelivery of a letter from Squire Huws to the local commander. It is reassuring to know that we have friends as well as enemies. The Squire was furious because he missed the opportunity of making arrests, but now I am even more furious, because somewhere in our neighbourhood, within our network of contacts, there is a traitor.

A Spreading Wildfire

27th February 1843

I have been giving a good deal of thought to what might have happened at Felindre. Both Rebecca and her daughters might have been taken, and that would have set our cause back by weeks, or months, or even years. We will have to find some way of unmasking the traitor in our midst.

In the meantime I have been concentrating on other matters relating to the administration of justice. It is now clear that arrests will be made and that court cases will follow. If a large riot is betrayed and if the rioters are surrounded and arrested *en masse* by troopers or fusiliers, there may be as many as a hundred men who suddenly require legal representation. They may get reasonable and sympathetic hearings from the magistrates, for some of them (like Brynach and Nicholas Lloyd) are careful fellows who will only convict on sound evidence. But others like Owen Gelli Fawr have no such scruples, and their first instincts will be to assume guilt unless innocence can be proven with utter certainty. Moreover, arrogant and vindictive men such as he would revel in the glory of catching Rebecca, who has already won some notoriety well beyond Wales.

With these thoughts in my mind I met Master Hugh Williams yesterday at my old family home in Brawdy, by arrangement with my brother Morys. That meeting was the culmination of a tour of Cardigan, Narberth, Pembroke, Haverfordwest and Fishguard over a period of three days, during which I visited a good number of attorneys who have sharp minds and reputations for the defence of the poor. I knew some of them already, having had more than my fair share of brushes with the law, and having talked at length over the years with my old friends Will Final Testament and Lewis Legal. Sadly, they are both now dead, but while they were alive they taught me whom, in the legal profession, I might trust. I needed to do nothing special to influence these legal gentlemen, other than to wear my prettiest dress, and to remind them that there were reputations to be made through the defence of poor men who were fighting the political establishment in a just cause. I told them that the Rebecca Riots, as they are now being called by the gentlemen of the press, are of truly nationwide importance, and that future press coverage of trials arising out of them will be considerable. I find that attorneys are not lacking in self-esteem, and that they will do almost anything to enhance their reputations and to find their way onto the pages of the national newspapers. They are also professional men who are seeking to enhance their status by comparison with the squires and their decrepit families who traditionally control almost everything, including the House of Commons. At least eight of the gentlemen whom I visited have already signed the People's Charter, and that says something about their political leanings and reforming zeal. At any rate, all of those whom I asked agreed that they would act for Rebecca's daughters without charge at the Petty Sessions and would provide representation for them should they be hauled before the Quarter Sessions or the Assizes. They also agreed that they would find the best possible barristers where defence before a judge was required, and that they would share information on the most effective lines of defence for those charged, whether rightly or wrongly.

When I told all of this to Master Williams and Morys, over a cup of tea in the drawing room at Brawdy, they both roared with laughter. "Martha, you are incorrigible!" spluttered Master Williams. "You have obviously found your true calling, which is referred to in the trade as perverting the course of justice. These poor fellows, many of whom I know intimately, are defenceless males who have no chance of resisting your advances. With one flutter of your eyelashes, or one delicate movement of an ankle, or one touch of your hand, you can conquer the world. You should be ashamed of yourself! And at an age when you should be tending flowers and producing samplers at a rate of ten a week............"

"My dear Hugh," said I, with pure innocence in my eyes. "Enough of insulting references to my age and personal habits, if you please. I am not aware that I have committed any misdemeanour. People talk to solicitors and barristers about legal representation every day of the week. That is what they are there for."

"Yes indeed. But here you are asking them in advance of any crime being committed, to give their services free, to agree common lines of defence, and to pool information. That, I fear, is as close as we get to corruption in our line of business."

"Come now, Hugh. You know, as I do, that attorneys talk to each other all the time about the strengths and weaknesses of rivals, about particularly striking defences or prosecutions, and about the susceptibilities and foibles of judges. When I meet socially, I talk about sheep prices. When you meet socially, you talk about the law. What I have arranged with your respectable colleagues is perfectly lawful and straightforward, and what could be more natural than occasional meetings over a jar of ale, or occasional letters and documents passing back and forth between you? Now then, brother, another cup of tea perhaps?"

When Master Williams and I left to go our separate ways, he had agreed that he would give personal representation to as many of Rebecca's daughters as possible, without charge, and that he would liaise with like-minded colleagues. He had also agreed to talk to a barrister called Master Lloyd Hall, who likes to think of himself as a knight in shining armour and who might be prepared to act in the higher courts. I do not know much about him, but I may need to pull him on board.

ΩΩΩΩΩΩΩΩΩΩΩ

10th March 1843

The traitor in our midst has struck again, to lethal effect, and I am mortified that I have not yet been able to identify him or to bring to him the rough justice that he deserves.

Last night Rebecca and her daughters attended at the Dinas gate, and reduced both the gate and the gatekeeper's house to ashes. I had no advance notification of the demonstration, or any indication of the name of the person taking on the role of Rebecca. But by all accounts the riot was a shambles, with a good deal of gratuitous violence, participation by fellows who appeared to have been drinking, and the use of firearms. Nobody was injured, and since there were no special constables in attendance there were no arrests, but this morning the gatekeeper's wife went to Squire Jobbins, who lives just up the road, and swore a statement to the effect that she heard one of the rioters being referred to as "Zeke." There are only two Zekes in the neighbourhood, one of them called Zeke Jones and the other Zeke Tomos. At any rate, arrest warrants were written out for both of them, and they were both taken in around dinner time today. Zeke Jones, the son of my old servant Hettie, had a perfect alibi in that he was ensconced in a hostelry in Eglwyswrw for the whole evening and until the early hours, with many witnesses including the landlord to attest to the truth of his story. But Zeke Tomos could not account for his movements, and so he was slapped into the Newport lock-up while further investigations were made. Three of the new constables called at his house on the Bayvil estate with a search warrant, and found a pile of old female clothes by the fireplace, with soot upon the shawl and dress collar and bits of straw adhering to a battered old felt hat. Furthermore, when they looked into the sides of the fireplace they found clear finger impressions in the soot. The stupid man had been careless in the extreme, in spite of the stress placed upon security and common sense at all of our meetings since the early days of the *Ceffyl Pren* jury in the area. I almost felt glad that such a fellow had been taken, but then I remembered that it was not his fault that his name had been used in the riot, and that he has had enough suffering in his life already. Besides, he is an emotional and hot-tempered fellow and I was genuinely afraid that he might do his own cause more harm than good when he appeared in court.

Worse was to come. This afternoon, news has reached me that there have been six further arrests in the district, with Samuel Stokes taken, and young Bobby Morris, and Jack and Hubert, the sons of Patty and Jake Nicholas, and then Shemi's son John and Will's son Gerallt. I have yet to discover what charges might be levelled against them, and indeed whether they were all actually involved in the destruction of the Dinas gate, but already I have had urgent messages from their distraught parents, and the trouble associated with Mistress Rebecca is coming uncomfortably close to home.

I have sent a message to Hugh Williams via Master Havard Medical asking for his help, but I doubt that he will receive it and act upon it before the Petty Sessions are over and done with.

ΩΩΩΩΩΩΩΩΩΩ

A Spreading Wildfire

11th March 1843

I fear that Hugh Williams may not have received my letter, since Rebecca has also been at work in the destruction of all the gates at Narberth and at Robeston Wathen. There are reports that the gatekeeper's wife at Robeston Wathen has given a testimony that the leader of the rioters who destroyed her home and her gate was a person who spoke and acted as a gentleman might. If a squire's son is being accused of involvement, Master Williams will certainly be involved at the Narberth Petty Sessions and will be impossible to reach. On the other hand, he might be in London.

I have enough on my hands without sending messages to my friend at all of the points of the compass in the hope of finding him somewhere. I have been visited by a host of desperate parents -- Shemi and Sian worrying about John, Will and Tegwen concerned about Gerallt, and Mary Jane and Dafydd frantic about Samuel. No doubt I would have been equally worried if Brynach or Ioan had been arrested and incarcerated, and I have thanked God several times today that their involvements with Rebecca are over and done with. As a result of my meetings, and with messages coming in all day from my spies, I have now ascertained that apart from Zeke Tomos, none of those taken into custody was actually involved in the attack on the Dinas gate. They have been charged with unlawful assembly and plotting criminal activity, since they were all involved in a meeting in a barn at Tregynon last week. Will was there as well, and he says that there were at least thirty fellows present. He went down to see Zeke and the others in the lock-up this morning, and Zeke is prepared to swear on pain of death that he has not betrayed his colleagues. That means that someone else who was at the meeting has passed names to the authorities, and it is now a matter of the gravest importance to find out who the traitor is. Will has some thoughts on the matter, and will follow these up with the assistance of Abby, Halfpint and other faithful fellows in town. In the meantime, the Petty Sessions are planned for tomorrow afternoon in the Royal Oak Inn, and I have persuaded Jenkins Legal from Fishguard to act for the prisoners. This afternoon, he held private meetings with the prisoners, as is his right, and decided upon the main lines of his defence. I want nothing to do with that, and I will not even attend the court, since I can only work effectively if I am away from the public gaze.

A Spreading Wildfire

My most difficult meeting this morning was with Mary Jane and Dafydd Stokes, dear friends for many years and now, as members of the gentry, caught up unwittingly in criminal activity. Dafydd is a squire, a substantial landowner and a magistrate, and although he and I have campaigned together as tally-holders of the Fishguard and Cemais Trusts, and although we share common ground on the People's Charter and other matters, he is in some ways naive about the ways of the world, and his dear wife seemed genuinely surprised about Samuel's involvement in the Rebecca Riots. They pressed me hard and asked whether I was aware of their son's support for Rebecca, and I had to admit that I did know of it. I have had other difficulties with Mary Jane in the past, particularly relating to the disappearance of her brother Owain, the last great love of my life. Now, once again, she reacted very emotionally and said that I had betrayed her by not warning her at an earlier stage of the danger confronting her son. Then I too became very emotional, for if there is one thing I hate above all others, it is mistrust between friends. And Mary Jane is truly the friend whom I love best. With my voice quivering with emotion, and barely able to contain my tears, I had to remind her that Samuel was now more than thirty years old, and that it was no business of mine to report on his actions to his mother. He was quite old enough to decide for himself, said I, on those matters which he wished to share with his parents and those which he wished to keep secret. Dafydd thought hard and agreed with me, and said that he had suspected some involvement on his son's part, and might even have unwittingly encouraged it through his broad support for the activities of Rebecca in conversations over the kitchen table or in the drawing room at Trecwn. Mary Jane calmed down at last, and we agreed that this was no time for recriminations, and that we must concentrate on getting Samuel and the others out of the lock-up and safely home. But when she and Dafydd left for home I was saddened to discover that her embrace was less warm and spontaneous than usual.

This evening I called an emergency meeting of the local daughters of Rebecca, and it was held in the barn at Fachongle Isaf. Brynach, Ioan, Gomer and Will came with me and supported most of the points which I made. I am afraid that I was very upset, and I must have sounded very ferocious, for afterwards some of the men said that they had seen steam coming out of my nostrils. That is probably an exaggeration, but during the discussions it transpired that the Dinas riot had been organized by a group of rascals who had shared a few jars of ale together and who had thought it would be a jolly thing to smash down the Dinas gate. They had done no proper planning, and had had no proper leadership. They had followed some of the conventions of Rebecca, but were ignorant of others, and so once again I had to enunciate the principles of security and solidarity. They were a rough group of men, and so I thought there was no great point in trying to explain to them the differences between a sisterhood and a brotherhood, but by the end of the evening they were rather more aware of their responsibilities than they had been at the beginning. Some of them actually apologized to the assembled company for their carelessness and their drunken behaviour, as a result of which Zeke might well end up in the penal colonies. At Will's insistence, all the men present swore oaths that they would adhere to a strict code of behaviour in future, that they would commit nothing to writing, that they would take part in a maximum of two riots and then retire into the shadows, and that they would not squeal if arrested. Some of the fellows were very worked up, and wanted to grasp hands and mingle blood in the creation of a brotherhood bond, but I thought that would be a messy business and would not necessarily increase the trust between one man and his neighbour. Then it was agreed that any persons who appeared as witnesses in court cases, or any other spies and informers, would be punished without mercy, and that the word would be put about in the neighbourhood to that effect. Special constables would also be picked on and informed that it was their duty to melt away if they should be guarding a gate that was subject to any future attack.

All those present knew that one of their number had betrayed his colleagues, so there was a good deal of suspicion in the barn. But nothing could be done which made his identity any clearer, for every man present swore the oath of allegiance, and in my judgement a man who is a traitor will have no scruples about falsely swearing an oath of solidarity. The only thing that might deflect a traitor from his corrupt course is the fear of what might happen to him if he is found out, and I have ideas on that matter which I might implement before many days have passed. But first there is the matter of the Petty Sessions, and the small matter of a good night's sleep, for it is now one o'clock in the morning and I am utterly exhausted.

A Spreading Wildfire

12th March 1843

The Petty Sessions have been held, and all the men except Zeke Tomos have been freed. This evening I have had a detailed description of the proceedings from Jenkins Legal, and from his description, and from the assessments of others present, the occasion was something of an anticlimax. The first cases to be dealt with by Squire Owen from Gelli Fawr, Squire Bowen from Llwyngwair and Squire Gittins of Tredrissi were those of the six accused of attending an illegal and treasonable meeting. Master Jenkins did not dispute the fact that the six prisoners had been at a meeting, but he argued that there was no law to the effect that fellows could not meet together socially for one reason or another. Furthermore, nobody had produced a shred of evidence that anything in the meeting was treasonable or threatening to the interests of others. "Where is the witness who will attest to this court that something nefarious was going on at the meeting?" he asked. "And if we do not have a witness, we must surely expect a sworn and signed statement instead. Where is it, sirs? The truth is that it does not exist. And since it does not exist, there is not a shred of evidence on which these six innocent men can be convicted. I therefore ask the court to throw out the charges against them, and to release them immediately." The magistrates had to agree to that, in spite of Squire Owen's scowls, and the six were released without further ado, to scenes of great jubilation.

The case against Zeke Tomos was another matter. The Dinas gatekeeper's wife would not appear as a witness, because she was not prepared to run the gauntlet of a furious crowd, but there was the little matter of her sworn and signed statement, and that was presented to the court. Master Jenkins had hoped to argue that there was doubt about the identity of the Zeke whose name was called out at the riot, but then the landlord of the hostelry in Eglwyswrw appeared to give evidence, and attested to the fact that Zeke Jones had been on his premises at the precise time of the riot. The finger was thus pointed very firmly at Zeke Tomos, and Squire Huws from Bayvil popped up as a witness and attested to his violent nature and his propensity for getting into trouble. Master Jenkins objected to this, on the grounds that the Squire was an unreliable and biased witness who was involved in a long-running dispute with Zeke and who had an interest in seeing him behind bars. At this, Squire Huws exploded, and shouted "Sir, I take the strongest exception to that remark.

I am a magistrate myself, and would never allow personal considerations to influence my evidence as a witness, given on oath!"

The case was slipping away from that point on, said Master Jenkins, and it became irretrievable when the constables' notes relating to the visit to Zeke's house were read out by the Clerk of the Court. Not one of the constables involved was able to appear as a witness, since they had all three disappeared in mysterious circumstances, but their notes made a considerable impact on the magistrates. Master Jenkins argued that the notes were inadmissible as evidence, since they could have been written long after the visit or could be complete fabrications. In any case, he said, he wanted the opportunity of cross-examining the constables, and he was denied that right. There was no sworn statement and no name, he said, and so the evidence must be dismissed.

The magistrates considered the case made for the defence, but the evidence against Zeke was strong, and in all conscience they could not release him. So after a short discussion between themselves, they found the matter proved, and committed him to Haverfordwest Gaol to await trial at the Quarter Sessions. In the midst of angry scenes out in the street, the poor fellow was taken in chains to a cart manned by six special constables, and away it went in the dim light of the early evening, up the Cilgwyn Road, heading for Mynydd Preseli and the county town.

I am recording all of this late at night, as the moon sails high and bright and as the owls call to each other in Gelli Wood. After their close shave with the law, six good men are back in their own comfortable beds, but I daresay that Zeke Tomos has a hard bed to lie upon in the cold heart of Haverfordwest Castle.

ΩΩΩΩΩΩΩΩΩΩΩ

13th March 1843

I was very much mistaken in the matter of Zeke Tomos's bed. Last night he slept in a barn in Brynberian, and tonight he is fast asleep in the hay above our cowshed.

A Spreading Wildfire

Rebecca's daughters are more organized in this area than I had realized, and when the cart bearing Zeke and the special constables towards Haverfordwest was on the highest part of the mountain it was ambushed by about twenty beautiful sisters. They did not carry torches, and in the moonlight they must have looked like demons emerging from the pit of Hell. The constables were beaten with staves and ran for their lives, leaving Zeke and the horse and cart unprotected in the middle of the road. So the vehicle was commandeered and its occupant was taken to a friendly house near Brynberian. Zeke's chains were cut off and thrown away. This morning the horse and cart were delivered to a farm near Puncheston by an innocent fellow who claimed that he had come upon them by the roadside and who thought it to be his civic duty to hand them over to somebody responsible. No doubt when the hue and cry has died down the horse and the cart will be identified and will return to Newport.

This morning, with the constables back in town and telling wild tales about the violence meted out to them by Rebecca's daughters on the mountain top, the release of the prisoner is the one and only topic of conversation. The Mayor and the magistrates immediately put out a notice offering a reward of £50 for information leading to the apprehension of the "violent escaped prisoner" Zeke Tomos or to the capture and conviction of any of those involved in the ambush. A search party went galloping off to Mynydd Preseli and spent much of the day searching for clues. Of course they found nothing, and when they got back to Newport they found that there was a notice nailed to the church door which read:

Take Notice
I give you notice, you squires and townspeople that when injustice is done and when poor innocent men are taken in chains to rot in the dungens I will have my revenge. They shall be freed, and those held to be responsiball shall be named and shall suffer in their sted. And take notice that if any of you shall betray my children it will go ill with you. We will know who you are, and I shall visit you in the night and you and your kind will see all that you have go up in conflaggeration. So I tell you not to go after my child who is freed, and to leave him in peace, for he have had enough of sufferin.
Faithfull to Death with all poor people
Becca and daughters

272

A Spreading Wildfire

That was enough to cause a shiver of fear to run up and down the spines of all the constables and special constables in town, and also to give the magistrates some cause for thought, but they persisted with their searches and most of the properties in the neighbourhood were visited during the day. The Plas, and all its outbuildings were searched, not very effectively, during the morning, on the assumption that Zeke was most likely to be hiding out in the attic or the barn of somebody known to be sympathetic to Rebecca. But Rebecca is no fool, even if she is not very good at spelling, and during the afternoon a rumour started to circulate around town that Zeke had been seen in Puncheston and that he was heading for Fishguard with money given to him by Rebecca and with the intention of catching a boat across to Ireland. Off the constables galloped towards Puncheston, and half an hour later Zeke Tomos turned up at the Plas, disguised as a sack of flour on the floor of a cart driven by Dic y Felin. He is now hidden in the hay in the loft above the cowshed, and I have to work out what to do with him.

I am deep enough into this Rebecca business already, without having a fugitive with a price on his head hiding in my hay-loft. He cannot go home to his wife, that is for sure. In addition to my servants, there must be at least six other people who know that he is here, and that exposes me to the possibility of betrayal. If the authorities turn up and find him at the Plas it would be virtually impossible for me to plead innocence, and I could end up in gaol myself as an accomplice of Rebecca. That would prejudice the whole of the noble enterprise in which we are engaged. I have no wish to hand Zeke over or to facilitate his recapture, for I do not look on him as a criminal; but I wish that he could hide somewhere else.

ΩΩΩΩΩΩΩΩΩΩΩ

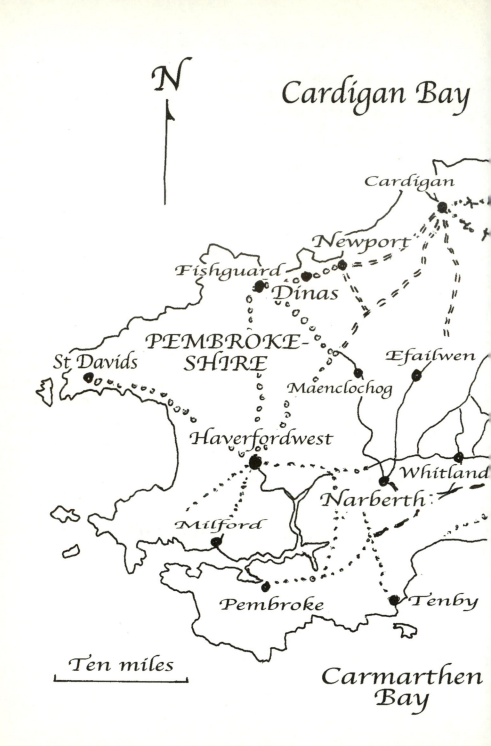

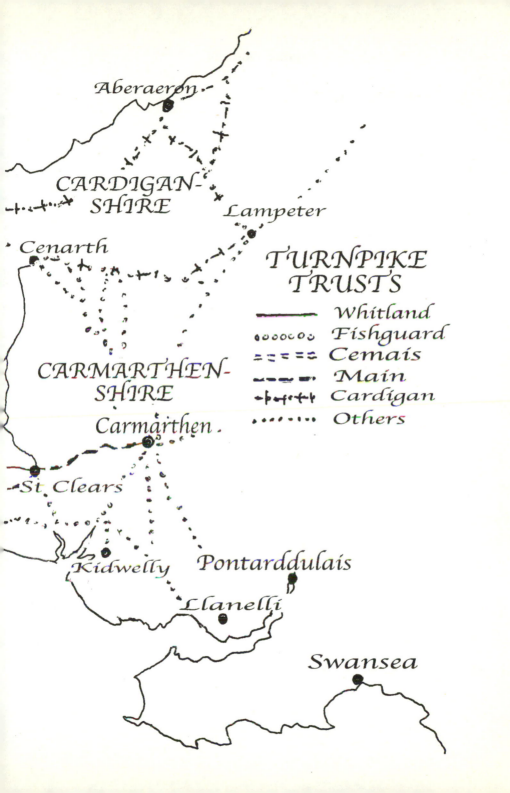

Aberaeron

CARDIGAN-
SHIRE

Lampeter

Cenarth

TURNPIKE
TRUSTS

―――――	Whitland
₀₀₀₀₀₀	Fishguard
‒ ‒ ‒ ‒	Cemais
‒ ‒ ‒ ‒	Main
‑+‑+‑+‑	Cardigan
·····‥	Others

CARMARTHEN-
SHIRE

Carmarthen.

St Clears

Kidwelly

Pontarddulais

Llanelli

Swansea

10. Smoke Signals

3rd July 1843

A young man called Thomas Campbell Foster has been to see me. He turned up this morning, quite out of the blue, when I was in the middle of a discussion with Will on the labour we are still owed by our tenants and neighbours now that the hay harvest is over and done with.

"Mistress, there is a young gentleman at the door," said Gwenno. "Very apologetic, he is, about not writing in advance. But he wonders if you might have time for a brief conversation?"

"Who is he, Gwenno?"

"Master Tom Foster, Mistress. He says he is from the *Times* newspaper."

My heart sank, for I was not sure that I wanted newspaper-men prying around the Plas, especially since Zeke is still hidden in the hay-loft above the cowshed. But I could not very well send him away, and I was intrigued to find out what he wanted. So without further ado I terminated my meeting with Will, and asked Gwenno to show Master Foster in to the drawing room.

He bowed deeply when he entered, and I immediately liked the look of him. He is quite short, with a sturdy build and a barrel chest. He has tousled blonde hair and sparkling blue eyes, chubby cheeks and unruly side whiskers. He has fine teeth, and a good-humoured mouth. The lines on his youthful face are associated in my mind, at any rate, with smiles rather than scowls, and when he talks he does indeed grin a good deal. His dress was respectable but somewhat wrinkled, and I deduced on meeting him that he travelled a lot, slept often in his day clothes, and was more concerned about his work than his appearance. His breeches were well-worn and had that sheen on the inside legs that showed him to be a man who spends more time in the saddle than in the comfort of a coach. Even before he opened his mouth, I judged him to be both intelligent and strongly opinionated.

"Mistress Martha Morgan of Plas Ingli," he said, "it is a very great pleasure to meet you at last! I have heard so many good things about you and your beautiful residence, from so many quarters, and it appears that all of them are true."

"I thank you, sir, for your kind words. I am not sure that I should be pleased by my apparent notoriety, for I try to remain out of sight."

"I venture to suggest that it is well nigh impossible for an elegant lady such as yourself to do such a thing, madam," said he, without explaining further.

We spent a few minutes chatting about this and that, and Gwenno brought in some tea and griddle cakes, since it appeared that Master Foster was hungry and thirsty, having breakfasted early in Haverfordwest, and having been in the saddle for three hours. He told me that he had been sent by the owner of his newspaper to investigate the causes of the troubles in West Wales and to report on any further happenings for his readership of more than twenty thousand influential people. The fact that his newspaper was read by the gentry, magistrates and members of parliament placed a considerable burden of responsibility on his shoulders, he explained, and for this reason he was intent upon finding the best possible sources for his reports and for his examinations of the roots of rural discontent.

"These are early days, Mistress Martha," said he. "I have been here only since midsummer, and my first dispatch for the newspaper appeared only a week ago. But I am already getting a feel for what is going on. I have met a good many people, including those in authority, the military, and disaffected poor farmers, and over and again, people have said to me "Go and talk to Mistress Martha Morgan. She knows what is going on." I have also come to the view that you are trusted to a remarkable degree by the rioters, by the tally-holders of the trusts and by the magistrates. I am intrigued, to say the least, that in the midst of all this chaos and violence, you appear to have very few enemies."

"I am not sure that you are correct in that, Master Foster. Your visit here this morning will have been observed and recorded, and since there are spies at work behind assorted walls and hedges I assume that they have been put there by my enemies. They will not have recognized you, but they will soon find out who you are."

He nodded. "I will have to get used to surveillance," he said. "For my part, I am probably watched by both the authorities and the rioters. Like you, I will have to try and win their trust through the accuracy of my reporting and the consistency of my printed comments. I have sent in four reports thus far, and have received kind words from readers who know the situation in the troubled districts."

"And what are your initial feelings about the justice of the cause espoused by Rebecca and her daughters?"

"I have to say that those beautiful ladies already have my sympathy, for the deeper I dig the more I discover about the hardships which they have to endure. They are facing a combination of poverty and starvation that appears to be more cruel than in any other part of our nation. I am not surprised that the oppression exercised by the turnpike trusts has proved to be the last straw, and that the gates themselves have been given the status of symbols or icons by the rioters."

"I think you read the situation well, Master Foster. And what do you think about the conduct of the riots? Are you impressed?"

"Questions, questions, Mistress Martha!" laughed the man from the *Times*. "I am the reporter, and I am supposed to be interviewing **you**! No matter. I am flattered that you should seek my opinion. Not many of my informants do that, and I conclude that you have more than a passing interest in what is going on. May I also conclude that you have more than a little knowledge of where the riots have occurred thus far, and who has been involved, and how the rioters have behaved?"

"I will admit to nothing, Master Foster. Secrecy and security are my watchwords. In any case, I have a natural suspicion of reporters, their motives and their methods."

"Now that is unfair. There are men of integrity in every profession, just as there are charlatans. In any case, your son is a reporter for the *Welshman*, and I assume that he is sincere and as honest as his mother?"

"How did you know that, sir? My son never uses his name, and his identity is a closely guarded secret."

"Come come, Mistress Martha! I am a man of integrity, and I never reveal my sources."

"*Touché*, sir!" I replied, and I had to laugh too. We talked on, mostly about the riots and the root causes of rural discontent, and I decided that I liked this fellow Foster. I liked his sharp wit, his directness, and his appreciation of subtleties and nuances. I also judged, as we talked, that he was honest, and that he liked me. Having been initially suspicious of him, I found that I was gradually moving towards a position in which I might take him into my confidence, and give him certain information which might, if properly publicized, help the cause of Rebecca and her daughters.

In any case, I was getting tired of all the secrecy which had surrounded me for a good part of the last five years and which had shut off an important part of my life even from my nearest and dearest. Even Betsi, my own dear daughter, and my beloved servant Bessie were not fully informed of my movements or my contacts. They knew a certain amount about my dealings with Rebecca and her daughters, but for better or for worse I had chosen to keep certain things from them. Other things -- but again with notable exceptions -- were known to Will and Gomer, Brynach, Shemi and Ioan. In maintaining this secrecy, it is not as if I mistrusted any of them. But secrecy can become obsessive, and I have been pondering recently on the manner in which it can be used to build up a sort of arrogance. Those who know only a part of what is going on are destined to remain weak, but those who are in possession of the full facts are the ones who can exercise power. They can manipulate information at will, let drop little titbits for those who scrabble about under the table, withhold information which others might want or even need, and give knowing nods when others feed them with material which was already in their possession. Power, for good or ill. Was I enjoying myself so much, in my pivotal role in the Rebecca Riots, that I was becoming an insufferable bore, puffed up with my own self-importance? If that was happening to me, surely Bessie would have taken me to one side, as she has done so often before, and given me a good ticking off?

Then again, was there a danger in so much information residing in one person? As Brynach reminded me once, being alive is a precarious business, and it is all too easy for life to be snuffed out in an instant by a fall from a horse, or by a fire in the house, or indeed by a highway robber with a bludgeon in his hand. How much would this great enterprise be set back if I was to die suddenly, or if I was to be flung again into that dark dungeon in Haverfordwest Castle following betrayal by a traitor?

"Mistress Martha, I apologize for breaking into your reverie, but we were talking about the activities of the Fishguard and Cemais Turnpike Trusts........."

"Were we really? Oh my goodness, Master Foster, I do apologize. My mind does tend to wander sometimes. That is what comes with being a grandmother, and with grey hairs and declining eyesight."

"A penny for your thoughts?"

"That is a very impudent question, sir. But I am minded to give you a truthful answer, since I judge you to be an honest man. I am in possession of a good deal of confidential information, and I was wondering whether I would be wise, or possibly very stupid, to entrust some of it to you, in the full knowledge that you might use it in your newspaper or in some future Commission of Inquiry, should there be one."

"In my estimation you would be very wise to pass on to me information that should be in the public domain. But other things might be best kept inside your heart and your head, at least until you know me better and until I have earned your trust."

"Those are honest words, Master Foster, and I respect you for uttering them. And what assurances can you give me as to confidentiality?"

"As I have already stated, Mistress Martha, I never, ever, reveal my sources without permission. If you wish your statements to me to be confidential, with no clues given as to their origin, I swear to you on the Bible that I will respect your wishes."

"Very well. No mention of my name or my place of residence in any of your reports or other written submissions? No hints to show that your respondent is a woman? No acknowledgements of any sort to the help that I may give you? No direct correspondence between us, and no further meetings after today at Plas Ingli?"

"I agree to all of those conditions. You may trust me absolutely." Master Foster smiled infectiously, with his eyes sparkling. Then he added: "Nonetheless, I am intrigued as to why you should desire such strict anonymity. Most of my contacts are only too happy to see their names in print, and to bask in the imagined glory that that brings."

I laughed. "I understand that. We are all vain creatures at heart. But I am a woman, and women do not meddle in politics. Revelations as to my identity would not be good for me, or for your newspaper, or for women generally, or for the cause which I espouse, for we would all attract ridicule and disapprobation. No, Master Foster, in these circumstances secrecy and anonymity must be maintained."

Then I asked Gwenno to serve us a light dinner where we sat, in the drawing room. When all was laid out before us, on side tables, I thanked her and asked her to ensure that we were not disturbed for the next two hours. And so, as we ate and drank, I talked and he wrote a good deal in his notebook. I told him about the root causes of rural discontent as I saw them, and about the actions of the local gentry and magistrates which appear to have been calculated to cause trouble. I told him about the activities of the *Ceffyl Pren* jury in and around Newport some years since, and about my attempts to mediate on behalf of the squires and on behalf of the poor people. That, I said with some pride, had led to a period of relative calm in Newport when there had been trouble elsewhere. Then I related the effects of the five terrible harvest failures during the last eight years, which had brought the poor to the edge of starvation and the rich to the edge of bankruptcy. I told him of my efforts, and those of other concerned squires, to restrain the activities of the local turnpike trusts, and of my failure to prevent new gate construction and increased tolls. I told him of my sympathy for the Chartist cause and of my deep conviction, borne out by events at Llanidloes, Merthyr Tydfil and the other Newport, that large demonstrations involving thousands of men on the streets were doomed to failure. I expressed my anger at the events of 19th June, when a big meeting in Carmarthen had attracted 6,000 people and had gone out of control, leading to the attempted sacking of the Workhouse, a charge from the horsemen of the 4th Light Dragoons under Major Parlby, and the arrest under chaotic circumstances of more than sixty of the rioters. I explained my fascination with the "hit and run" methods of radical groups in other parts of the world who were intent upon fighting injustice with maximum effect and minimal loss of life, and I told him of my attempts, at various secret meetings with disaffected small farmers and labourers, to adapt the theatrical methods of the *Ceffyl Pren* juries to a greater cause -- the reform of the laws relating to poor people, tithes, and the turnpike trusts.

Master Foster asked me about the origins of the charade involving Rebecca and her daughters, and I told him where the idea had come from, and of my attempts to promote it among those who were intent upon the destruction of gates and gatekeepers' cottages. I told him how messages were passed among groups of men across West Wales, and how nothing was ever put in writing. I told him of some of the other rules agreed to by the rioters, and of my attempts to enforce them and to maintain discipline.

"From now on, Mistress Martha, discipline may be very difficult to maintain," said Master Foster. "These riots are going to spread, of that I have no doubt. Thousands of men will be involved, and you can only reach a small proportion of them with your messages and your appeals for restraint."

"I know it, sir, and that saddens me."

"But my enquiries thus far, mostly among the gentry and the merchant class, show a degree of puzzlement about the secrecy and the skills of the rioters, their good humour, their appreciation of the need to attack symbols of oppression and to create strong images in the minds of newspaper readers and politicians, their skilful use of Biblical sources, and their determination to avoid harm to individuals while meting out destruction upon property. Do I see your influence in all of this?"

"I will admit to it, sir. But I find it very difficult to teach muscular and hairy men what the differences are between a sisterhood and a brotherhood."

At this, Master Foster roared with laughter. "Do not be too surprised by that, my dear Mistress Martha! From my limited observations, a sisterhood is almost impossible to create, even among sisters. And among men who are both angry and starving, utterly impossible. It seems to me that what you have achieved already is quite remarkable, with maybe a hundred gates down, some of them destroyed repeatedly, with hardly any injuries and very few arrests. You can, I think, take pleasure in the knowledge that without your restraining and organizing abilities, matters will have been far worse."

"Thank you, sir. But you will, I think, now understand why I want, and indeed insist upon, anonymity."

"Agreed. And in years to come, when people ask me "Who was Rebecca?" I will know the answer, but will say nothing."

"There is no Rebecca, Master Foster. Perhaps I may be called one of her daughters. Rebecca is an icon associated with a just cause, just as a trust gate is a symbol of injustice and exploitation. There are a hundred others who deserve to be called Rebecca far more than I, for they are the ones who ride out at night with blackened faces, and smash gates and set fire to gatekeepers' cottages, and in the process risk transportation or even death. I am too much of a coward for such activities."

"I doubt that, Mistress Martha. Cowardice does not appear to be a part of your makeup. Now, I have taken up too much of your time, and I have arranged to speak to your son Brynach this afternoon. But before I go, can I ask you four direct questions?"

"Ask me, sir. I will answer if I can."

"Thank you. First, are these riots motivated by a desire to cause insurrection, or to bring down the government?"

"Absolutely not. In spite of everything, there is great loyalty to the government and the crown in this area. The causes of disaffection in West Wales are local, although they may also be symptoms of a nationwide malaise. The solutions will also be local, although they will require government intervention to implement them."

"As I thought. And are the riots orchestrated in some way by the Chartists?"

"Again, I can place my hand on my heart and say that they are not. It might suit the government to find a link between the Rebecca Rioters and the Chartists, and indeed there are some Chartists who would like to forge an alliance, but the rioters are simply angry and starving, and most of them know absolutely nothing about Chartism."

"That confirms my early impressions. And is there a link with Ireland?"

"No, sir. Whatever claims may be made to the contrary, the large number of Irish who are in the countryside just now are here for the harvest, as they are every year. They are starving and disaffected too, but in my estimation they are politically naive and have no wish to interfere in Welsh affairs. In any case, people in this area do not like the violent Irish way of doing things. There may be one or two Irish agitators about, but nobody listens to them or takes instructions from them."

"Very well. And finally, is there in your opinion a government plot to stir up unrest in West Wales for political reasons?"

"The Home Office is too clever to place anything on the record, but I do believe that to be the case. Messages have gone to the magistrates and the Lords Lieutenant encouraging them to take a hard line in their dealings with Rebecca, and funds have been made available for rewards, for the protection of witnesses, and for the payment of spies and informers. I think that some of the tally-holders of some of the turnpike trusts take instructions from London, and they want trouble more than they want extra income. There is a readiness to use the army, and I anticipate that there will be a thousand armed soldiers in West Wales by the end of this month. I have other indications, too. If the government wants trouble, it will get it. But the army is already showing itself to be not very clever at dealing with the likes of Rebecca and her daughters........"

"And some of the military commanders already have mud on their faces, thrown up by the trusty steeds of Rebecca's daughters as they disappear into the darkness. The whole scenario is indeed intriguing."

Then Master Foster stood up and thanked me for my frankness and my willingness to share with him material which would certainly land me in prison should it ever be repeated in court. I smiled and said: "I have no regrets, sir. That material was weighing heavily on my shoulders. You are welcome to it. But please do not let anybody else look at your notebooks!"

"I promise it, Mistress Martha. And I trust that when you read my reports in the *Times* in the weeks to come, you will be able to think "Ah yes, I told him that!" while remaining happy about my discretion and your anonymity. May we meet again?"

"Of course, sir. But not here. If you want to talk again, write to me via Master George Havard Medical in Newport, with one envelope inside another. He will see that I get your letter. I will reply, and suggest a friendly venue."

Master Foster bowed, and I curtseyed, and he thanked me for my hospitality. Then he called for his horse and went on his way, following the mountain track towards Llanychaer.

Have I been too honest with Master Foster, and has my trust been misplaced? If he betrays me that will be the end of Mistress Morgan and the end of the Plas Ingli estate.

ΩΩΩΩΩΩΩΩΩΩ

15th July 1843

Zeke has been here for four months. He is still in the hayloft, hidden during the daytime and emerging sometimes at night, dressed as one of Rebecca's daughters, to take part -- against all the rules -- in more episodes of gate demolition. When he goes as far as Newcastle Emlyn or Carmarthen he stays away for a full day, returning to his bolt-hole twenty-four hours later under cover of darkness. He has become adept at avoiding the spies who are stationed on the Cilgwyn Road and on the mountain, and it is now easier for him to travel about since he has a heavy beard and long hair. We have given him some old clothes, and he has changed his name. He calls himself Thomas Evans in case anybody meets him, accuses him of being a vagrant, and asks for his name. When the hay harvest was under way I had to get him out of here, so one cloudy black night he made his way over the mountain to Shemi and Sian's house and hid there until the Plas Ingli harvest was in and the harvesters all gone. Then he returned to his nest in the hay, utterly dependent upon the food and drink provided for him at regular intervals by my servants.

He cannot return home to his little farm on the Bayvil estate, since it has gone up in smoke. As soon as he had been convicted by the Petty Sessions and been released from his chains by Rebecca's daughters, Squire Huws evicted his wife Myfanwy and let their property at a far higher rent to somebody else. Rebecca posted a notice on the church door warning the Squire that it would go ill with him if he did not relent, but he was determined to face down the mob, and he issued a very belligerent notice of his own. Rebecca was as good as her word, and three nights later a gang of about forty beautiful sisters turned up on the Bayvil estate, evicted the new tenant, and burnt the house to the ground. So now the Squire has to make do with no rent at all. I hope he is pleased with himself.

Myfanwy has gone to live with her mother in Crymych, and although that house is watched by opportunists who know that Zeke will turn up there sooner or later, they have contrived so far to meet a few times in friendly houses. There is a rumour in the Crymych area that since Zeke has disappeared, Myfanwy has taken up with a wild fellow called Thomas Evans. The chapel elders are very disapproving, but she can probably deal with that. As for me, I had better refrain from any involvement in Zeke's marital affairs. I have quite enough problems to be going on with.

Zeke is as angry and as unpredictable as ever, and while he is eternally grateful for the shelter and the sustenance which I provide for him, his insistence on joining as many riots as possible is causing me grave concern. One day he will be captured, and his crimes will be compounded. Alternatively he will be betrayed, and that is my main worry since more and more people know that he is here. His wife certainly knows, and he has probably told some of his "sisters" during the riots that this is where messages will reach him. Just now he has a chill, and yesterday Dai Darjeeling was passing the cowshed when he heard sneezing from the hayloft. He assumed that it must have been either Will, or Gomer, or Bryn, but then on entering the kitchen he found all three of them there, tucking in to their dinner. He wondered aloud who might be in the hayloft. We did not tell him, but he is not stupid, and from our furtive glances he might well have guessed that we were hiding the famous fugitive. He will not tell anybody, but others who might make a similar discovery will not be so discreet.

So Zeke must go. I told him as much this morning, and although he was initially angry with me he had to accept my point that too many people now know that he is here, and that a betrayal becomes more and more likely with every day that passes. Tomorrow, after dark, he will move on, and he will find refuge in a number of safe houses and barns in the Maenclochog and Efailwen area. He has many friends in those parts, and the authorities on that side of the mountain have so many riots to cope with that they have little or no time to go hunting for fugitives.

I do not know why, but I smell treachery in the air, and I will be glad to see the back of this fellow.

ΩΩΩΩΩΩΩΩΩΩΩ

17th July 1843

Zeke has gone, but he has had a very close shave, and he is lucky that he still smells the fresh air of freedom in his nostrils. He went last night, shortly before midnight, with no great ceremony. He took with him enough food for several days and the women's clothes which he uses during his outings with the daughters of Rebecca. When he had gone, we issued a corporate sigh of relief, and Bessie said: "Thank God he is out of here, Mistress. I never liked the fellow, and tonight I will sleep sounder in my bed than I have for some months past. So will Gwenno, I daresay."

"Oh? Has she had difficulties with him?"

Smoke Signals

"She is a very pretty girl, Mistress, and when a fellow has been shut up in a hay-loft for four months I daresay that female company is one of the things that he misses most. A couple of weeks ago, when you were away somewhere, he tried to grab Gwenno when she was delivering his dinner. She gave him a black eye and a kick in the groin, and that caused his passion to subside. We women decided after that that the men could deliver his meals from then on, and although they grumbled, that is what they did. We never told Gomer about the incident. If we had, he would have beaten Zeke up, sure as omelettes is eggs."

I laughed, and went to bed in a good humour. I was woken shortly before dawn by a thunderous knocking. By the time I got downstairs Bessie had already dragged herself out of bed and had opened up the back door, to find three special constables there. Constable Lewis was waving two pieces of paper in his hand. One was a search warrant for "all of the buildings within the curtilage of the house known as Plas Ingli", and the other was an arrest warrant for "the violent escaped criminal known as Zeke Tomos, who has a price of £50 on his head." The documents were duly signed by two magistrates, Squire Owen of Gelli Fawr and Squire Laugharne of Pengelli Fawr. I would have sent the fellows packing if one of the signatures had been that of Squire Huws, in view of his personal feud with Zeke, but I could find nothing wrong with the procedure followed, and so, having given the constables a piece of my mind for their insolence in waking up the household at such an uncivilized hour, I had to let them in.

"I will not forget this outrage," said I, "and a complaint will go to the Lord Lieutenant. The fugitive is not here, and when you search the house you will confirm what I say."

"Thank you, Mistress," said Constable Lewis, "but the house is of no interest to us, indeed. We will now search the hayloft above the cowshed." And that is what they did. They climbed up the steps and opened the trapdoor, and because it was barely light they stumbled about in the sweet-smelling hay with their candle lanterns, while I shouted at them from below to be mindful of the risk of a conflagration. There were curses and yells from the three elderly constables as they floundered about and banged their heads on the low beams, and having found nothing they resorted to prodding the hay with pitchforks in the belief that Zeke might have burrowed down and made himself invisible. They emerged with scowls on their faces and with their clothes covered with hay.

"What did I tell you, gentlemen?" I said, maintaining the fierce and outraged expression on my face.

"The bastard have gone," said Constable Lewis. "But we could see where he have been sleeping, Mistress, for there was a cosy little bed in the hay. He must have had a warning we was coming."

"Nonsense, gentlemen. The cats sleep in the hay all the time, and some of my young haymakers use the loft occasionally at the end of the harvest for purposes which I shall refrain from describing. I do not encourage it, but I cannot, alas, prevent youthful high spirits or cosy beds in the hay. Now kindly go back to the magistrates and tell them that Mistress Morgan is not amused."

So the traitor has been at work again, and I have spent a considerable part of today trying to work out who he is. I have drawn a blank, for there is virtually nothing to work on. Will and his friends in town have not got very far with their inquiries. Our enemy may be a man or a woman -- but is most likely to be the former, since the betrayal which led to the arrests of seven men back in March appears to have been based upon inside information about a meeting of Rebecca's daughters in the barn at Tregynon. The only people who can be eliminated from my enquiries are the seven men who were arrested and charged. How many others were at that meeting? I have been unable to find out, since those whom I have questioned say that there were thirty or forty fellows present, some of them known but others unknown, and many lurking in the shadows. I have about twenty names, but I cannot arrange spies to follow all of them around, and neither do I have the resources to question them personally or investigate their activities over the last few months. Suspicion might also fall upon the wife of the farmer at Tregynon, or one of the other Tregynon servants, or indeed upon any of the other wives who may disapprove of the nocturnal activities of their husbands. But surely that disapproval would not extend to betrayal, with the attendant risk of imprisonment or even transportation for those found guilty in the courts? And what about Zeke's wife Myfanwy? Does she love him and support him, or hate him and reject him? In spite of all the misery she has had to put up with over the years, she appears to have accepted his rare and secretive conjugal visits to her new residence in Crymych with good grace, and Bessie, who knows her, says she would never betray her husband or anybody else. But with rewards on offer, and further payments being made beneath the table from the magistrates' "espionage fund", who knows what the most loyal of poor people might do?

I have to admit to being confused. I have now decided that I might as well forget about the Tregynon meeting and concentrate instead on this latest betrayal relating to Zeke and the Plas Ingli hayloft. Who knew that he was here? All my own servants and their wives and husbands, for sure, and Dai Darjeeling, and the daughters of Rebecca who released Zeke on the mountain, and Dic y Felin who delivered him here with his horse and cart. I trust my own servants and their families absolutely, and neither Dai nor Dic would support the magistrates since I know their sympathies well. Tonight, while I have been thinking and writing, I realized that I have been mistaken in concentrating on the lower orders of society and that I should have been looking much higher up. The person who was responsible for the arrest and search warrants held in the grubby hands of Constable Lewis when he came to the Plas would, I thought, lead me to the traitor. The warrants were signed by Squire Owen and Squire Laugharne. One of them -- probably the former -- must have had direct contact with the person who knew that Zeke was in my hay-loft. It is well known that Squire Owen is my enemy and an enemy of Rebecca, so I will concentrate on him to start with. My spies have been watching him for some time. Tomorrow I must ask for their reports and work out whether they have come upon anything significant.

ΩΩΩΩΩΩΩΩΩΩ

18th July 1843

This morning I talked at some length to Will, and then I went to town and managed to find Abby, Halfpint, and two or three of my other spies. They told me a good deal about Squire Owen's movements over past months, and they gave me lists of names of those who have been seen visiting Gelli Fawr or who have been seen in the Squire's company of late. His tenants, his servants, his labourers and his drinking colleagues figured prominently, as did various business contacts and legal gentlemen. There have been one or two social events at Gelli Fawr involving the members of five or six of the local gentry families, and of course those families were attended by their own coachmen and servants. I could see no pattern or no evidence of repeat visits or contacts with somebody who might be an informer. The trail was as cold as that of a fox on frozen ground. I had absolutely nothing to go on.

So I decided that I should find out who had requested the search warrant and the arrest warrant which had been signed by the two squires. I made my way to the house of Master Henry Eynon, once a bailiff and recently elevated to the position of Clerk to the Justices. He is the very fellow to whom I sold that horrid chest some years back and who later had it removed by the gentlemen of the *Ceffyl Pren* jury. I hoped that he would not mention it or embark upon a conversation about Italian furniture and master craftsmen. I found him at his desk, filling in some records.

"Oh, it's you, Mistress Morgan," said he, making it obvious that he was not pleased to see me.

"Good morning, Master Eynon," I replied. "I am delighted to see you, and to have the opportunity to congratulate you on your recent elevation to a position of great responsibility."

"Thank you, Mistress. No less than I deserve after all those years of putting up with public hostility and uncooperative debtors, not to mention potato peelings and rotten eggs. What can I do for you?"

"You will recall that I was recently visited by the constables who were intent upon searching for Zeke Tomos at the Plas and arresting him. That was an outrageous action which caused me great distress. Somebody provided you with false information in the hope of obtaining the reward on his head. I am minded to initiate a prosecution of the person responsible, and I will be grateful, therefore, if you will provide me with his or her name."

Master Eynon suddenly looked like a rabbit confronted by fifty hungry ferrets. "As I recall, Mistress, the warrants were signed by Squire Owen and Squire Laugharne," he said, with his face red. "I trust that there was nothing wrong with my paperwork?"

"Not at all, Master Eynon. All was in order, so far as I could see. But I daresay that the squires were not the ones who asked for the warrants. If I may, I should like to see your records so as to establish the identity of the person who seeks to destroy my reputation."

"My records are private and confidential, Mistress. They are available for examination by the magistrates and the Lord Lieutenant, but certainly not by any Tom, Dick or Harry who comes in through my door. If my records were to be available to all, I fear that law and order would be replaced by chaos."

"I doubt that, sir. I am not any Tom, Dick or Harry. I have the greatest respect for the law, and indeed I have some knowledge of it. Openness and confidence are essential for its implementation. Are you saying that you refuse to show me your records?"

"Correct, Mistress," said Master Eynon, with his eyes bulging and his hands writhing.

"Very well, sir. You will very shortly receive a visit from my attorney, who has every right to look at your records. Neither he, nor I, will forget this piece of nonsense, and when this matter comes before the justices at the next Petty Sessions I fear that your suitability for the post of Clerk will be brought into question. Good day, Master Eynon!"

So I swept out of his scruffy office, looking as imperious as I could. As I went up the street, I nodded to my friend Abby, who was stationed on the corner opposite the Royal Oak awaiting instructions. He nodded back, and I made my way home. Later on, he sent me a message via a little boy who lived on the Parrog. It told me all that I needed to know, and confirmed my suspicions. Apparently, within a few minutes of my departure Master Eynon sent a written message to Squire Owen of Gelli Fawr. The messenger was seen galloping along the Cilgwyn Road, and it is clear that Master Eynon wanted it delivered at high speed. Then the Clerk had slipped out through his back door, and had set off on foot along the Cardigan Road. Abby had followed him at a safe distance, and had seen him turn left into the entrance of the Llwyngwair estate. There he had lost sight of him, but after half an hour the fellow had come out onto the main road again. Then, said Abby, he had walked home with a countenance as black as thunder.

I was puzzled by this. It was now clear to me that there was a conspiracy going on, and that Squire Owen and Master Eynon were involved in it. But who else was involved? Surely not Squire Bowen of Llwyngwair or any other member of his family? They were all good Methodists who also had radical political views, and I could not imagine them conspiring with Squire Owen or anybody else to suppress freedom and justice. I knew that they visited Gelli Fawr socially on occasion, but I knew that relations between the two families were cool rather than warm. I have now written to my good friend Ellie Phillips of Ambleston, who is the sister of Squire William Bowen, in the hope of finding enlightenment. She is close to her brother, and they share a good many confidences. I have also asked my attorney to pay a visit to Master Eynon with a view to investigating the warrants issued prior to the attempted arrest of Zeke Tomos.

My instinct tells me that I am about to discover something interesting, which will drag me far out into the murky waters of intrigue and betrayal. I hope that I will not drift so far from the shore that I will be unable to struggle back into a safe haven.

ΩΩΩΩΩΩΩΩΩΩΩ

25th July 1843

I have taken out a subscription to the *Times* newspaper, in order to follow the reports of my new friend Tom Foster. I am impressed, and I have already discovered in his words a good many of the things which I told him at the beginning of the month. His sympathy for the rioters is undoubted, as is his sense of outrage at the behaviour of the turnpike trusts. I am also very impressed by his discretion, for there is no hint in any of his reports that some of his most precious information has come from me. I know what is going on locally, but his reports are of great value to me in keeping abreast of developments further afield. And those developments are spectacular indeed, with riots taking place almost daily across the length and breadth of West Wales. Many gates have gone down in the remote areas around Llandeilo, Newcastle Emlyn and Lampeter, and every time the gates are replaced around Whitland and St Clears they are removed within a few days. There have been riots on the coalfield area around Kidwelly, and although the problems faced by poor people in that area are very different from those of the open countryside, it is interesting to see that the gates of the turnpike trusts have become the main targets of the disaffected. Many of the rioters there spend their time underground, and have probably never paid a toll in their lives. Closer to home, the gates around Cardigan and in the lower Teifi Valley have gone down over and again.

I have tried not to be too involved in these latest developments. For a start, I am watched too closely for comfort, and even with the invaluable assistance of Havard Medical it is difficult and risky for the daughters of Rebecca to get letters to me, or for me to get letters out. I have contrived to meet Master Hugh Williams twice during the past month in friendly houses far away from Newport, but he is increasingly busy with the defence of those who have been arrested, and he is aware that his movements are also closely monitored. I have received many verbal messages from various parts of West Wales, as a result of which I have contrived to attend half a dozen meetings as far afield as Cynwyl Elfed and Kidwelly, but so many men are now involved in the riots that orchestration and control are impossible. I fear that what happened at the Dinas gate in the spring has been repeated elsewhere, with groups of reckless daughters acting against the advice of their older and wiser sisters and initiating actions which are ill conceived and poorly executed. Some thugs and petty thieves have also become involved, and that causes me particular concern, since their motives will be very different from those of the poor farmers. They will be looking for revenge against their enemies, and intimidation and extortion will accompany thieving and thuggery. I had a message from Tom Foster via Havard Medical yesterday, and he has identified this trend too. He is worried by it, since it could lead to a loss of public sympathy, but he considers that those responsible for petty crimes will most likely be the ones to be betrayed to the authorities. In turn they will most likely be the ones who are given stiff exemplary sentences by the courts, since the magistrates will know that the punishments set are broadly supported by the public. So Rebecca and her daughters, if and when they are caught, and if they have acted with due restraint, may continue to enjoy public approval. That means that witnesses will not appear against them, and that the justices may have to release them for lack of evidence. Complicated matters indeed.

I suppose I should not worry too much about the fate of those who dress in the clothes of Rebecca and who drift into petty crime. I should be much more worried about the manner in which the forces of law and order are now assembling in West Wales. If the Home Secretary wanted widespread discontent and rioting, he and his tame magistrates have certainly achieved that objective, and they are now embarking upon the second phase of the Home Office plan -- namely the demonstration of government resolve. Tom Foster and Hugh Williams are both close enough to the authorities to confirm what is happening. We have already seen the dragoons at work in Carmarthen, and the cavalry has now been joined there by Colonel Love and a detachment of 150 infantrymen from the 73rd Regiment. The said Colonel has the reputation of a butcher, for it was he who commanded the soldiers in the bloodbath at Merthyr Tydfil in 1831 and in the bloodbath at Newport in Monmouthshire in 1839. He appears to be a fellow who believes in the merits of brutality and overwhelming force, but now that he is in charge of military operations in West Wales he is also showing himself to be aware of the peculiar challenge facing him in the country districts. In addition to his army detachments he has control of various detachments of Royal Marines, and he also instructs the men of the Castlemartin Yeomanry, who know the country well. He has over a thousand heavily armed men under his command, and he has sent small detachments of them to be stationed in sensitive places all over West Wales. They patrol very visibly, and that has an intimidating effect upon local people. They are guarding many gates and workhouses, and some weeks ago another attempt to burn down Narberth Workhouse was foiled by the Yeomanry. There are rumours that soldiers will shortly be billeted in Fishguard or Newport. There are also rumours that Colonel Love has asked the Home Office for field artillery and for a large detachment of Metropolitan Police who will work with the local constables.

Whatever may be the truth behind these rumours, I am worried that Rebecca's tactics thus far may now be matched by quite subtle tactics on the part of the authorities. The soldiers are visible enough, and are generally easy to avoid, but if Rebecca loses the tacit support of the special constables under the influence of the policemen from London, she will have problems. She will also have to cope with the increasing infiltration of her ranks by informers, some of them controlled by Master George Martin, the Welsh-speaking policeman from Carmarthen, and others under the control of Captain Napier who is the Chief Constable of Glamorgan. Some of their men have already abandoned their uniforms, and I have received three messages suggesting that constables operating outside their home areas have attended meetings with the daughters of Rebecca and have even taken part in riots in the knowledge that they are immune from prosecution. Indeed, these traitors stand to win substantial rewards in the event of successful prosecutions of rioters. The only thing that is likely to restrain these fellows is the threat of instant retribution from Rebecca.

Another messy development is the interference of this strange fellow from Newcastle Emlyn called Edward Crompton Lloyd Hall, to whom I have already referred. He is a barrister and a landowner who seems to be out to make a reputation for himself as a "Pacificator". I met him briefly once, in the spring, and did not like him. According to Hugh Williams, he privately professes great sympathy for Rebecca and her daughters, and indeed he has received deputations of poor farmers and has promised to act on their behalf in the reform of the trust laws. At the same time he publicly denounces Rebecca through letters to the newspapers and through public notices, and it is rumoured that he writes almost daily to the Home Secretary, Sir James Graham. He may be a spy, and Master Williams does not know whether the good Sir James instructs him or finds him a considerable irritant. At any rate Master Lloyd Hall has his mail intercepted and opened, just as Master Williams does. The authorities clearly have suspicions that either of them, or both of them, may provide the brains behind Rebecca. I suspect that each of them enjoys notoriety, and thrives on accusations that he is the real Rebecca. They will do nothing to discourage rumours and may even encourage them. Such is the way with vain and puffed-up gentlemen. That suits my purpose very well indeed, for with the government and the army concentrating on hunting for big fish, little fish such as I can swim about without undue molestation.

ΩΩΩΩΩΩΩΩΩΩ

3rd August 1843

Yesterday I was very irritated, since my attorney reported that on visiting Master Eynon and demanding a sight of his records, he claimed that they had "been lost". Then I got a letter from Ellie which said that she had no doubt at all about the loyalty or the steadfastness of the members of her family at Llwyngwair.

But in spite of these setbacks there has been progress at last in the matter of the traitor who operates in our midst. Last night there was a very productive meeting in the barn at Llanychaer, which Brynach allowed at considerable risk to himself. If accused or pressed on the matter, I suppose he can always say that he knew nothing about it. I was there, along with about sixty fellows, most of whom I recognized. Plans were laid for the destruction of twelve gates in North Pembrokeshire, all on the night of 6th August. The meeting broke up about half an hour after midnight, and I knew as soon as I had stepped outside the great oak door that we would be betrayed.

I had taken the precaution of placing a watch on the houses of Master Henry Eynon, Squire John Owen and Squire William Bowen, in the conviction that something of interest would happen after the meeting at one or another of them. I had asked my spies to remain in position at least until dawn, and if necessary to make innocent enquiries of servants as to comings and goings. This morning, at various times and in various places, I met Abby, Halfpint and Master Jacob Jones. They told me some interesting things. First, Abby told me that Master Henry Eynon had received a visit from Master Bobby Morris at about two o'clock in the morning. A few minutes later the pair of them jumped up onto Master Eynon's pony, one behind the other, and went trotting off up along the Cilgwyn Road as fast as the poor beast's legs would carry them.

"Bobby Morris!" I spluttered. "Surely, Abby, he cannot be the traitor? He is one of the heroes of the campaign! Are you sure that you were not mistaken?"

"No mistake about it, Mistress," said Abby. "My eyes are not as good as they were, but I think I know everybody in town. The figure I saw was well muffled, but Master Bobby has a sort of shuffling walk that I know well. And the fellow I saw was shuffling, indeed."

When I met Halfpint, who had been stationed behind the hedge near the entrance to Gelli Fawr, he said that two fellows arrived on a pony at about three in the morning. They were well wrapped up, and he did not recognize them. But after their arrival he saw candles being lit in the Squire's room, and they stayed lit until dawn. The fellows on the pony stayed for about an hour, and then they left and headed back towards

Newport. Shortly after that, Halfpint saw lights in the stable, and he knew that a horse was being made ready. Then, as the first glimmer of dawn started to spread across the eastern sky, a messenger galloped out of the yard and headed not towards Newport but the other way, taking the road towards Puncheston and Haverfordwest.

And when I met my old friend Jacob Jones, who was stationed outside Llwyngwair Manor, he said that shortly before dawn a pony with two fellows on board came wearily along the road from Temple Bar. The man on the pony's rump hopped off at the gatehouse, said farewell to his colleague, and walked towards one of the workers' cottages to the east of the big house. The fellow on the pony trotted off towards Newport.

"On the pony, Master Henry Eynon, and his passenger Master Bobby Morris?" I asked.

"Precisely, Mistress. How did you know that?"

"I have my sources, Jacob. Now then, here are two shillings. I am greatly indebted to you. Now go home and get some well-deserved sleep."

At first, I could hardly credit the fact that Bobby Morris was the traitor I had been hunting for. He had been a friend of the Plas for many years. He had courted Gwenno with a rare passion and had enjoyed the hospitality of my kitchen for more evenings than I cared to count. He had also worked for me during many harvests and shearing times prior to his employment as a coachman for Squire Bowen, and had been on the best of terms with Will and Bryn. His relations with Gomer had always been frosty, but that is the way with rivals for the affections of a beautiful maid. He was angry when Gwenno finally declared her love for Gomer, but was he really angry enough to finally try to wreak some sort of revenge on me, and the Plas, and Rebecca, three years after the happy couple were wed? But then again, I know well enough what unrequited love can do to a man, having had to cope with the likes of Moses Lloyd, John Fenton and Ceredig ap Tomos in my time. Two villains and one good man, all three dead because they loved me and because I could not return their love. I should not really be too surprised if the pain in Master Morris' heart had turned into an incurable disease.............

But I had no time to speculate endlessly about motives. I was sure that a message had gone from Squire Owen to the Lord Lieutenant or even to Colonel Love, containing full details of the gate removals planned for the night of 6th August. If I did not act quickly, ambushes would be laid and there would be wholesale arrests if not wholesale slaughter. I needed to share my terrible information and to seek advice -- and quickly. To whom should I turn? Not to Ioan or Brynach, I decided, since they had already been too close to the action and since I had extracted promises from both of them that they would desist from further involvement with Rebecca. So I decided to keep the matter secret and away from men. Gomer, Will and Bryn had already had their fingers burnt, and I did not want any of them to spend the period of the corn harvest languishing in gaol. I had enough problems to cope with as it was.

So with the men away working in the fields I called in Gwenno, Bessie and Liza, and we held a female Council of War in the dining room. I told them about Bobby Morris' betrayal. Bessie and Liza were amazed, and could hardly believe it. "But Bobby Morris has himself been in prison, Mistress, betrayed by somebody else," said Bessie. "Surely that means that there must be two traitors at least, who are not working together?"

"One might assume so, Bessie, but I have been giving this some thought. I think that Bobby has been working alone, and has been given the task of feeding information to Master Eynon and Squire Owen. If there is a traitor among Rebecca's daughters, what better way could there be to confuse all of us than to slap him into prison along with a few others, in the sure knowledge that he would be released in a few days to thunderous applause from the public? Bobby Morris, martyr, hero and traitor. No, the evidence is incontrovertible. He is our man. What say you, Gwenno? You know him a good deal better than the rest of us............."

"I can hardly believe this myself, Mistress. But he was very bitter when I married Gomer, and he has not spoken to me since. He wrote to me once or twice, in a very threatening manner, and about a year ago he insulted Gomer in the Black Lion and would not retract his insults even after Gomer had taught him a lesson in fisticuffs."

"Oh, indeed?" said Liza. "This is all news to me."

"I saw no need to tell you, Mother. This was a matter of importance only to Bobby, Gomer and me. I thought it was all over and done with."

"Do you think that he still loves you?" asked Bessie.

"Yes, I believe so."

"Now then, my dear friends," said I, "much as I would like to continue our debate about the furies that reside in men's breasts, we had better do something quickly if a disaster is to be avoided."

And so we talked, with a degree of discipline and resolution that surprised all of us. At the end of our discussion, the four of us left the house and headed in different directions. Gwenno went off to talk to Shemi and Sian and to some of our friends in Dinas. Bessie went up to the top fields to consult with Bryn, Will and Gomer. Liza went to talk to the men in Cilgwyn, and then walked over to Brynberian. Finally I took my pony and went to Newport and then to Fishguard. By tomorrow every one of Rebecca's daughters in this district, except for Master Bobby Morris, will know that there has been a change of plans.

ΩΩΩΩΩΩΩΩΩΩ

4th August 1843

With one mission accomplished, I have turned to another of even greater importance. Bobby Morris has now been informed, through his regular contact, that the twelve local gates will go down on the night of 7th August, that is, one day later than the date fixed by the recent meeting of the daughters of Rebecca. I have had to ensure that he does not suspect that his treachery has been uncovered, so the message was a matter-of-fact one, justified simply on the grounds that with the corn harvest now starting, it had been difficult to get messages to all of the potential rioters in the short time previously allocated. When he received the message, Bobby simply grumbled about inefficiency, but within a few minutes of its receipt, as soon as he was on his own again, he abandoned his work in the Llwyngwair stables and set off for town, where he told Master Eynon of the change of plans. In turn, that beloved fellow sent a message at high speed to Squire Owen, and then the Squire passed it on by sending one of his men off at the gallop towards Haverfordwest. I know all of this from my spies.

By tonight, the authorities will all know that they have one extra day to assemble their forces, and we can no doubt expect a good turnout of fusiliers and dragoons at all of the designated gates on Thursday night. They will not be amused, for if all goes according to plan they will arrive to find that the gates are not there any more.

8th August 1843

Thank God that we have achieved our objectives, and that our enemies have been routed. Rebecca and her daughters turned out in great force on the night of 5th August, assembling at agreed points all over North Pembrokeshire. Simultaneously, groups of beautiful sisters smashed down the gates at Fishguard, Dinas, Cilgerran, Letterston, Maenclochog, Puncheston and Newport. All of the riots were led by somebody called Rebecca, dressed in the usual exotic and delicate fashion and riding on a fine horse "borrowed" from one or another of the local gentry. Two of my horses were used, supposedly without my knowledge, causing me to complain bitterly in town on the following morning to all who were prepared to listen. "*Duw Duw*," they will now be saying, "did you know that two of Mistress Morgan's horses were stolen by the rioters for the attacks on the Newport gates? There's terrible for you!" So now I am Mistress Morgan, innocent victim of a local outrage. The horses are safely back in the stable, and I am learning that confusion is a valuable weapon.

At each of the riots the little charade involving Rebecca and her daughters was enacted, and at each one the gatekeeper and his family were invited to leave their premises and to remove their belongings before house demolition began. Blazing torches and musical instruments were much in evidence. There were minor incidents at the Dinas East gate and in Puncheston, where gatekeepers became belligerent and refused to cooperate. In one case the offending fellow was trussed up and left in a roadside ditch, and in the other he was beaten up and then "encouraged" to take part in the work of demolition. There was no opposition anywhere from the special constables, since they followed the usual convention of fleeing for their lives at the first sound of Rebecca's bugles and drums. In three or four places, constables were captured and were required to set fire to the piles of smashed timbers which had previously been turnpike trust gates and flimsy gatekeepers' houses. Half an hour after midnight all the Rebeccas and all of the daughters had disappeared into the warm August darkness, leaving behind them twelve blazing bonfires

So far as I can gather, no names were used at any of the riots. There was no use of firearms, nobody was drunk, and nobody was seriously injured. Where there were other houses and hovels close to the scenes of the action, residents were encouraged to lock their doors, put out all candles and lanterns, and to remain out of sight. In each case, patrols of beautiful daughters were sent out to all of the approach roads in gate neighbourhoods to ensure that there were no military ambushes and to give warning of any military movements. If the cavalry had come galloping to the assistance of any of the gatekeepers, Rebecca and her daughters would in all cases have been able to take evasive action.

On the morning of 6th August there were a good many tired farmers and labourers in the cornfields of Pembrokeshire, and I daresay that in spite of the perfect weather not much harvesting was done. There was only one topic of conversation in town and country, and when my reports came in from the various groups of rioters, I was well pleased that their actions had been exemplary. My only concern was that all of the riots had been executed with too much precision and too much discipline, and that the authorities would conclude, in North Pembrokeshire at least, that there was some person or small group organizing and orchestrating events. That conclusion would not be too far wide of the mark, and I knew that from now on I would have to act at all times with the utmost discretion and concern for detail.

On the same morning I took the precaution of asking some of my friends from town to pick up the four spies who had been keeping me and the Plas under close observation for the past few weeks. I was getting irritated with their interference, and knew that there would be many messages during the day. So Skiff and Abby organized a posse which picked up all four of the fellows at the crack of dawn, before they were properly awake, carried them down to the Parrog, and flung them into the sea. There was no great ceremony involved, and for this occasion at least, the traditions of the *Ceffyl Pren* were set aside. One of the spies had to be rescued because he could not swim, and that caused considerable amusement. I hope that the wretched fellows will have got the message that Mistress Morgan does not like being spied upon, and that their time would be better spent in helping with the corn harvest.

This morning, as the towns and villages of North Pembrokeshire stirred themselves into the activities of the day, news started to circulate about notices nailed to all of the church doors in the communities affected by the night's rioting. I daresay -- in fact I know -- that the notices were all very similar, although they were written by different hands. The Newport one read as follows:

Smoke Signals

Take Notice
Ye good people of Newport, that Becca and her children will not any
longer suffer the grievous harm inflicted by the gates at Newport which
are put there without her permission. She is greatly inconveenyenced
when going about her business indeed. Therefore she and her children
have removed these abominutions. Take notice that if any should seek to
put them up again, or if any should give help to the magistrates and the
constabules, it will go ill with them, and they will burn in Hell. All shall
be in conflaggeration. And if any should be spies and informers, we shall
know who they are and we shall take our revenge.
Faithfull unto death
Becca and children
Aug 5th 1843

The repercussions of the "night of infamy" were many and varied, and I daresay that it will be some while before I can assess their full effects. As news of the riots reached the authorities, a sort of panic set in, for the military commanders and the magistrates realized that more than a thousand men had taken part simultaneously in completely successful actions, executed with military precision. That was more of a threat to law and order than they had ever faced before, for in the past, actions had been restricted to two or three locations per night. Emergency meetings were called by the Fishguard and Cemais Trusts, and by the local magistrates.

Brynach attended the magistrates' meeting, as is his right, and reported that it had been utterly chaotic. Squire Laugharne of Pengelli took the chair, and found it difficult to follow any sort of agenda or to control his fellow justices who were outraged by the insolence of Rebecca and who sought to blame each other for the failure to anticipate her latest attacks or to infiltrate the ranks of her daughters. Some of the magistrates had been informed by Squire Owen that the attacks would come on 6th August, and some of them had further been informed that the date had been changed to 7th August, so now there was wholesale confusion. The said Squire was accused of incompetence and of depending upon unreliable informers. Master Henry Eynon was there, and there was very clearly bad blood between him and the Squire, for they squabbled incessantly and blamed each other for the fiasco. It was clear that they had both been fed false information from somewhere, and the conclusion had to be that they had been betrayed by their own informant. So much for the past. But the magistrates had another problem, for at the very time of the meeting Colonel Love and the Lord Lieutenant would be assembling troops for the ambushes which they would be mounting at twelve locations in Pembrokeshire, with a view to achieving the demise of Rebecca and her daughters. Some detachments of soldiers would already be on the march. If messages did not get to the authorities quickly, they would find out through local gossip that the twelve gates were already destroyed. At the same time the credibility of the local magistrates would be destroyed and might be impossible to rebuild. Brynach said that he listened to all of this with a good deal of amusement, and in due course his notes will be incorporated into another report for the *Welshman*. When I asked him what action the magistrates then took to rescue the situation, he said that after an hour of squabbling they sent express messages to the Lord Lieutenant and to Colonel Love and Major Parlby to inform them that the gates were already down, and to apologize for the fact that they had acted upon false information. They had also written to the Home Office to complain about the fact that they were outwitted at every turn by Becca and her daughters, and to request permanent garrisons of soldiers and Metropolitan Policemen in all of the towns and villages of North Pembrokeshire. There was not much hope of their request being acted upon, said Brynach, and they knew it.

As for me, I attended the meeting of the Cemaes Trust in the upstairs room of the Royal Oak. That was attended by another bevy of babbling squires, and was equally chaotic. With four of the Cemais gates replaced over recent months and now destroyed yet again, everybody appeared to be intent upon blaming everybody else for the fiasco and for the failure of the Trust's own efforts at gathering intelligence. The Trust's clerk was vilified for his incompetence, and Squire Owen, who had set himself up as the guardian of the Trust's affairs, was attacked in his absence with such gusto by some of his erstwhile friends that I could hardly believe my ears or my eyes. I sat silently at the back of the room, pondering on the strange ability of women (and in particular Rebecca and her beautiful black-faced daughters) to rouse normally placid gentlemen to a state of great agitation. I must have had a grin upon my face, for Squire Huws of Bayvil, who was sitting in the chair and trying to keep order, suddenly cast a fierce glance in my direction. "Mistress Morgan of Plas Ingli," he snarled, "you appear to find all of this very amusing. I know that you have argued before for lower tolls and fewer gates, and you appear to know more than the rest of us about what is going on. Perhaps you would care to enlighten us and advise us as to what to do next in order to avoid the loving attentions of Mistress Becca?"

That wiped the smile off my face, and I felt the colour rising in my cheeks. I stood up. "Sir, I resent that insinuation," I said. "I have never hidden my concerns about the activities of this Trust, and at one meeting after another I have followed a consistent line, seeking better management, more careful accounting, removal of some gates, and greater sensitivity in toll collection. My advice, and that of a minority of other squires, has been disregarded. On a personal level, Master Chairman, you asked me some years ago to mediate with the poor farmers with a view to removing the causes of conflict. I did as I was asked, in a perfectly open and honest fashion. Together, we did achieve a degree of harmony in our community. Then, sir, you went back on our agreement, in spite of my pleading. Do you deny it, sir?"

I paused for effect, and Squire Huws squirmed in his seat. There was complete silence in the room. So I continued. "If you sow the seeds of discontent, gentlemen, you should not be too surprised when you have to reap a miserable harvest. If I was smiling a moment ago, it had nothing to do with the predicament of this Trust, which is truly appalling. Forgive me, but I was smiling because I do not often hear thirty gentlemen all talking at the same time."

Squire Nicholas Lloyd Cwmgloyn stood up with a grin on his face. "Master Chairman, I should like to say that Mistress Morgan is quite justified in allowing herself a wry smile. She has never hidden her views, and she has argued forcefully at past meetings. And when she has been defeated at the vote she has accepted the decisions of this Trust with good grace. In my estimation she deserves our respect."

"Agreed," said Squire William Bowen Llwyngwair. "She understands the poor people of this region a good deal better than I do. So I, for one, would appreciate her advice on what to do next." There was a murmur of approval from the other gentlemen in the room, and the Chairman had no option but to ask me for a proposal.

I stood up again. "Thank you, sirs, for your expressions of confidence.

In the present circumstances, with inflamed passions on all sides and with the consequences of the latest gate destructions not yet fully apparent, it would in my view be unwise to take any precipitate action. Quiet reflection and careful consideration would be more appropriate. Therefore I suggest that the Trust does not immediately replace the four gates that have gone down, and that we should ask the Clerk for a study of the effects of reduced tolls in the future. The Newcastle Emlyn Trust has already reduced its tolls, and that has more or less put an end to the activities of Rebecca in that area. We should advertise our decisions very widely, in the press and in local notices. Then perhaps we should meet again in three months to consider the matter further, in the light of developments."

"Master Chairman, I second all of that," said Squire Lloyd. "If Mistress Morgan's motions are adopted, we will lose nothing, and the Trust will go up considerably in the estimation of the travelling public."

There were no amendments, and so the matter was carried unanimously. All of a sudden, a room full of squabbling enemies was transformed into a room full of smiling friends. Afterwards, while Gomer was getting the chaise ready for me to travel home, I took advantage of the amiable atmosphere in the bar by taking Squire Huws to one side. "My dear Madoc," I whispered into his ear, "I will be only too happy to spread word of this decision through my contacts. But I cannot help effectively while I am bothered by silly fellows lurking behind hedges and boulders. I have had promises before that they will be removed, but they are still there. Get rid of them, please, before somebody gets seriously hurt."

I curtseyed, smiled sweetly and went on my way, leaving the Squire spluttering into his ale. I do not know whether he has any say in the activities of the spies, but I thought that my dark warning would certainly find its way to the man in charge of their deployment. Perhaps it is time to place it on the public record who that man is.

ΩΩΩΩΩΩΩΩΩΩΩ

11. Too Close to the Flames

14th August 1843

I never cease to be amazed by the stupidity of gentlemen who are well educated and who should know how to react to changing situations and how to provide leadership. They start off as sensible and likable young fellows, and then off they go to Oxford, where they learn how to be stupid. When they are warned as to the likely consequences of their actions, their reaction is to flex their little muscles or to strut about like bantam cocks, squawking to the world that they know best and that nobody tells them what to do.

Squire Huws is more stupid than most, especially when he has Squire Owen alongside him. Two days since, with the spies still on duty in spite of beatings and involuntary swims in the estuary, and in spite of my polite request for their removal, I thought that serious action was required. So I let it be known in certain quarters that I would not be too displeased if they were captured and taught a little lesson. I daresay that Will and Bryn might have been involved in organizing things, but without my knowledge five of the spies were suddenly picked up this morning from locations around the Plas by the members of a *Ceffyl Pren* jury. I heard this from Gwenno. She says that this time the men were not taken to the estuary or given the ducking stool treatment, but they were taken to the ford at Trefelin, trussed up and sat in the middle of the cold river, with the water up to their necks, while they were questioned by a black-faced "female" and her beautiful friends as to the name of the person who paid them. Over and again the spies refused to give the name, but then some of the locals turned up and joined in the fun by throwing rubbish and food scraps at them. They could not take evasive action except by ducking their heads under the water. While this was going on, the bugles blared and the drums thundered, and nobody thought of summoning the constables. It was all very cruel, but after about half an hour it was effective, for one of the spies blurted out "Master Henry Eynon pays us and tells us what to do!" This same name was elicited from the other four as well, within the hearing of at least twenty locals who were lining the banks of the river.

"Enough, enough!" cried the foreman of the jury. "Now then, you bastards have caused quite enough trouble to be going on with. We hereby accuse you of spying upon Mistress Morgan of Plas Ingli, trespassing on her land, and causing her great anguish and distress through your harassment. Guilty or not guilty?"

"Guilty as charged!" shouted the crowd over and again. So the five fellows were dragged out of the river, still trussed up like the wild inhabitants of a lunatic asylum, and transported on a gambo to the Plas, where they were deposited unceremoniously into the dung-heap at the bottom end of the yard. Will and Bryn were kind enough to drag them out and to sluice them down with a few bucketsful of water from the cattle trough. Then they were deposited on the floor of an empty stable to await the arrival of the constables. The foreman of the jury told me that all five of them had been trespassing on my land and that they were suspected of stealing blackberries, potatoes and damsons in addition to all their other crimes. He then confirmed that the name of the Clerk to the Justices had been given by all five of the men under "polite questioning", in the hearing of many independent and reliable local persons. Then Master Dafydd Ifan (for it was he) gave a passable imitation of a curtsy, turned on his heel, and waddled off down the road, swinging his hips quite seductively. Bessie and I laughed and decided that these fellows were becoming so expert at being females that we women had better look to our laurels.

Within ten minutes I was on my way to Newport. I walked, for it was a beautiful afternoon, and I wanted to think. I decided to extract my revenge upon authority by easy stages. So when I arrived at Master Eynon's office I simply said that five fellows had been apprehended on Plas Ingli land, and that they were now held in custody in my stable. He realized at once that I was talking about his spies, and all of the colour drained out of his face. "Master Eynon," said I, "you are the Clerk to the Justices. I hereby request that you despatch the constables to the Plas, that they then charge these fellows with trespass, harassment, theft and spying, and that they then arrest the villains and place them in the town lock-up until such time as a Petty Sessions can be arranged. I will give you, here and now, a sworn statement, and I expect you to act upon it. There are, by the way, a good many witnesses who will no doubt be happy to appear in court to attest to the appalling crimes which have been committed."

Master Eynon tried at first to become invisible, and then he tried to slide past me so as to effect his escape, but I can become quite wide when required, and in the end he had to accept that he was trapped. So he got out his pen and took down my statement, which I then swore on the Bible and signed. I watched over him while he wrote out the arrest warrant for the five spies. Then I bade him good day and left him to find a magistrate or two who might sign the warrant. That would be difficult, I knew, for most of his gentry cronies were involved in the spying conspiracy and would stand to lose a good deal if these fellows started to babble under cross-examination. With my parting words I reminded him that the spies were still on my premises without authorization, and that if they were not out of my stable and in the lock-up by milking-time, I would have to feed them on humanitarian grounds and would have to send him a bill for the supervision and maintenance of criminals. I would hold him personally responsible for the failings of the justice system.

When the constables finally arrived at five o'clock this afternoon to· take the spies away, I had already fed them and allowed them to change out of their sodden clothes, but since I was feeling benevolent I decided not to charge for these services. I inspected the arrest warrant and discovered that it was signed by Squire Collyer of Tredafydd and Squire Edwards of Llwyngoras. That was very interesting, and suggested to me that maybe half a dozen of the more senior squires, including Owen Gelli Fawr, Huws Bayvil, Jobbins Holmws and Laugharne Pengelli had been asked to sign the warrant but had refused. That was something for me to mull over.

With the spies gone, and the milking over and done with, I sent Bryn down to Cilgwyn with a brief to assemble the names of those who had witnessed the confessions of the spies as they sat in the river at Trefelin. He came back not only with fifteen names but with eight signed statements to the effect that each of the spies, when gently asked who paid them for their activities, had replied "Master Henry Eynon pays us and tells us what to do!" None of the locals looks upon Master Eynon with any affection, and neither do they have any respect for Squire Owen and his cronies, for all of these gentlemen have been responsible for great distress locally. So all of the witnesses said that they will happily appear in court if required. Their statements will have to be rewritten and sworn, but for the moment they will do, and they will assist me in my task of getting rid of the corrupt Clerk to the Justices and the corrupt magistrates whom he serves.

Too Close to the Flames

16th August 1843

The Petty Sessions have been held in the Llwyngwair Arms, and Master Henry Eynon has disappeared. In truth it was the other way round, for he went missing only two hours before the magistrates were due to gather to hear the cases against the five spies. So in the event, with no Clerk to organize things and no papers for the magistrates to look at, proceedings were more than a little chaotic. There were three magistrates on duty, with Squire Bowen of Llwyngwair chairing the sessions. He did his best to maintain some sort of order, and dealt with each case in turn. I appeared as a witness, as did Bryn and Will, and five of the local people who had witnessed the rough justice of the *Ceffyl Pren* in the river at Trefelin. I would have liked to employ Master Hugh Williams to prosecute my case against the five prisoners, but I could not get a message to him in time, and had to use young John Wilkins Legal from Newport instead. He is a bright fellow, still learning his trade, but he performed with great skill. The magistrates tried to restrict his questions to the matters referred to on the arrest warrants, but he cleverly moved from spying and trespassing to the manner in which the five fellows had been apprehended by the *Ceffyl Pren* jury and to the interrogations at Trefelin. I gave my evidence, as did the witnesses. Then, before the magistrates could stop him, Master Wilkins asked the first prisoner, one Arwel Coggs, what questions he had been required to answer while he was trussed up in the river.

"Sir, you may not ask that," said Squire Bowen. "We are seeking to establish whether this fellow trespassed, and harassed Mistress Morgan, and stole items of her property. What he said while bathing in the river is immaterial."

"With respect, sir, it is not. I have already established without a doubt that these fellows were trespassing. That has not even been questioned by the defence. We have to establish whether their trespassing was a random matter, with these five prisoners all happening to wander onto Plas Ingli land and to lurk about behind hedges at the same time purely as the result of chance, or whether their activities were directed and coordinated. I will prove that the latter was indeed the case, that they were trespassing because they were paid to do so by Master Henry Eynon, and that they were on Plas Ingli land specifically in order to gather information about the movements of Mistress Morgan and her servants and acquaintances. In other words, sir, they were paid spies who were at work when they were apprehended. That is a very serious matter, and if proved will show that Mistress Morgan has had her rights and privileges as a free citizen very seriously interfered with. Sir, I await your permission to proceed."

Squire Bowen could not argue with that, and neither could his colleagues, and so Master Wilkins obtained from all five of the prisoners confessions that they had indeed admitted to the *Ceffyl Pren* jury that they were paid to spy on Plas Ingli by Master Henry Eynon. That, said my lawyer, was tantamount to an admission from all five of the defendants that they were involved in a conspiracy to harass innocent citizens as they went about their lawful business, and indeed to pervert the course of justice. In comparison he said that trespassing and eating a few of the Plas Ingli potatoes were minor matters, deserving only some nominal punishment. Then he asked for an arrest warrant to be issued for Master Henry Eynon, who was a part of the conspiracy and who probably took his instructions from somebody in authority. "Who is that person?" he asked, and gazed meaningfully into the eyes of each of the magistrates in turn. With that, he rested his case.

The magistrates retired into their little back room and pondered for well over an hour. Then they emerged and passed judgement. "We find all five of the defendants guilty as charged of trespass and harassment," said Squire Bowen. "They will each pay a fine to this court of two pounds plus costs. We do not find the case relating to the theft of assorted foodstuffs proved, and we dismiss that particular charge. On the matter of conspiracy and spying, we are unsure of the law and require guidance. In the absence of our Clerk, that guidance will have to be obtained from the Lord Lieutenant. However, the case appears strong and we therefore remand the prisoners on bail to appear at the next Quarter Sessions in Haverfordwest. Squire Owen of Gelli Fawr has already agreed, in advance of these Petty Sessions, to put up a surety of £5 for each of the prisoners. They will therefore be released on bail as soon as the £25 is received. The money should be received and acknowledged by our Clerk, who has apparently absconded, so I will receive it instead. The prisoners are warned that if they abuse their freedom and go anywhere near Mistress Morgan or her estate, they will be immediately rearrested and imprisoned, and their sureties will be forfeited. Their fines and costs must be paid within four days. As for Master Eynon, there is strong evidence that he has been involved in a misdemeanour of a most serious kind, which ill befits a man in such a position of authority. He is therefore dismissed from his post with immediate effect, and Squire Collyer and I will now issue a warrant for his arrest. Court dismissed!"

Before going home, I borrowed pen and paper from Master Wilkins Legal, and wrote out a note which I nailed to the church door. This is what it said:

Take Notice.

Mistress Morgan of Plas Ingli wishes to thank the unknown gallant gentlemen who recently apprehended five disreputable fellows who have been causing her great distress and interfering with her lawful business. They will be interested to know that the five fellows have now been found guilty of trespass and harassment, and have been suitably punished according to the laws of the land.

It is to be hoped that no further episodes of harassment and trespass will occur in the months to come, and that all good citizens will be allowed to live their lives in freedom, according to the dictates of their conscience.

Martha Morgan

Mistress, Plas Ingli

16th day of August 1843

That was all this morning. Now it is late in the evening, and I am sitting at my desk with moonbeams competing with the light from my candles. I have spent the greater part of the day in a sort of daze, caused no doubt by the speed at which matters are developing. Master Bobby Morris and Master Henry Eynon have disappeared, and I hope that I have finally seen the last of the spies and prowlers who have caused me so much aggravation. Arwel Coggs and his friends are free to wander about, but they are silly fellows and I really have no wish to see them incarcerated in prison. Most important, by putting up the sureties for their release on bail, Squire Owen has given me the clearest possible signal that he is the one who has been orchestrating everything, including the activities of the two fugitives. I think I knew that already. But how much higher does the chain of command go? To the Lord Lieutenant, or even as far as the Home Secretary?

17th August 1843

The corn harvest is in full swing, and I thank God that Will is here to take charge of it. I have to admit to being singularly ineffective this year as a decisive manager of the estate, since I have been so preoccupied with spies and meetings and riots and politics that my mind has been elsewhere. But with eight fields to harvest and the weather currently dry and sunny, Will has asked me for twelve men with scythes and I have given them to him by calling in my tenants and various labourers. I have given work to ten of the travelling Irish, but had to turn at least another thirty away. Three barley fields have been cut today simultaneously, and the place has been crowded with more than forty men, women and children all selling their honest labour beneath a high golden sun. Bessie, Liza and Gwenno have been maintaining a miraculous supply of food and drink out into the harvesting fields, and since last autumn's apple crop was a good one Bryn's special brew of cider has been hugely popular. Between drinking times the men swing their scythes for an hour at a time, protected from the sun by their straw hats but working bare-chested and with their lean brown bodies burnished by sweat. Gomer, a little over thirty and in his prime, has the body of a Greek god, and has a similar build to my dear departed David. I could watch Gomer, and the rest of them, for hours, and I derive much pleasure from it. I suppose that that means I have still not lost my appreciation of the male form in spite of my advanced age.

This morning, as I sat on a shady bank overlooking Parc Mawr, supervising the gathering and the sheaf binding by eighteen women, I found that my mind was wandering off onto the questions which preoccupied me for much of yesterday. Where are Bobby Morris and Henry Eynon now hiding out? What mischief are they up to, now that they are presumably under the protection of the authorities who have been paying them? And how did Bobby Morris know that Zeke was hiding in the hayloft of the Plas? He has not been anywhere near the place for many months, so does that mean that somebody else beneath my roof has been indiscreet, or possibly even feeding information to him? Questions, and more questions, and no answers.............

"*Mam-gu*, can we go for a walk on the mountain?" said a little voice behind me. I turned round, and there was David, my youngest grandson, and his father Brynach. They were both laughing, and Brynach teased me because they had both been standing behind me for five minutes, observing me in my trance, and trying not to giggle.

"Now then, Mother," said Brynach. "Your grandson, who is nine years and one day old, has come all the way to the Plas to thank you for the beautiful new shoes which you gave him as a present, and to tell you all about his birthday party. Is that not right, *bach*?"

"Yes, Dad," said David, and proceeded to fling his arms around me and to give me a big kiss on the cheek. Then he thanked me very politely, and launched into a detailed description of his presents and his birthday celebration at Plas Llanychaer. He did not get very far, for his father stopped him by holding up his hand. "Patience, child," he said. "Your grandmother was thinking of other things when we arrived, and you must not tell her everything at once."

He stood in front of me, held out his hands, and drew me to my feet. Then he embraced me and kissed me on both cheeks, as he always does when we meet. "I am reliably informed, Mother, that you are miserable company these days," he said. "You cannot even concentrate on the harvest properly, let alone giving time to your family and friends. You are apparently utterly obsessed with spies, to the point of suspecting everybody and trusting no-one."

"Oh, indeed? And who says that about me?"

"Your servants, and my sister Betsi, and even some of the people in town. The latest rumour is that you are suffering from some terrible ailment, so frequent are the messages that seem to fly back and forth between you and Havard Medical."

"But that is preposterous, Brynach......"

"I know it, Mother. But people notice, and people talk. There are things that we must talk about too, but not now. David requires your assistance in examining the summer flowers on Carningli."

"But I am keeping an eye on the harvesters, and if I were not to be here they would soon enough be spending more time gossiping than working."

Brynach laughed. "Mother, you are talking rubbish. You need a walk on the mountain, and the instructions of a nine-year-old grandson must be obeyed. Now, off you go. I will keep an eye on things, and what is more I will give the women a hand. I will enjoy it, and might even find time for a little flirting!" And he winked, threw off his shirt, and strode out into the shimmering field of cut barley.

I had no option. David took my hand and led me out of the field and into the lane which runs to the top fields and the open common. It was uncommonly hot, but as we climbed we picked up a gentle breeze, and we cooled ourselves down by having a splashing contest in the pool at Ffynnon Brynach. David is now getting too big for such frivolous games, but he probably participated just to please me. We followed sheep tracks through the great expanse of yard-high bracken which covers the lower slopes of the mountain, and then we came to the scree slopes where the bracken gives way to furze, heather and bilberry and dry grasses. David talked incessantly about his birthday party, and his latest friends, and his presents, and the delights of currant cake with sugar icing, and I was transported from the world of spies and intrigues into the world of innocent childhood. I did not object, and indeed I realized that such transportation was long overdue. Was this precious time with my grandson not really the most important thing in my life? The hard world beyond the mountain would probably not suffer all that much if I delayed until tomorrow what I might have done today, and indeed I realized that Rebecca and her daughters would probably get on perfectly well without me next week, next month and next year.

So little David and I gathered bilberries, and ate them by the handful, and got our hands and our faces covered with purple juice. We watched the old raven and his mate, and marvelled at the fact that they had reared a brood of six young ones this year. They sat in a row on their favourite rock near the stunted rowan tree, nonchalantly preening their jet-black feathers. The young ones looked to be even larger than their parents. A kite flew overhead and was attacked by four mewing buzzards who gave us an exhibition of acrobatics in the high blue sky. We lay on our backs in a grassy hollow and watched the white clouds over the summits of Mynydd Preseli as they tumbled and expanded and shrank with infinite slowness. We closed our eyes and had a competition to determine which of us could identify the largest number of different birdsongs. I counted ten, but David counted twenty-five, and although I did not believe him it was too hot to argue with him. And anyway, when you are nine years old, and brainy to boot, you are always right. We walked onwards and upwards, marvelling at the wild August colours of golden furze and purple and red heather and white grass. We climbed among the huge bluestone boulders and crags on the south side of the mountain, and played hide and seek. I showed my young grandson a thing or two about climbing techniques, even though I was encumbered by skirts and petticoats, and he was amazed that I was able to reach the summit without half a dozen servants to push me up. He said as much, with a cheeky gleam in his eye, and so I grabbed him and put him over my knee in order to teach him a lesson. He squealed and I giggled, and soon the pair of us were rolling about in the heather, having hysterics.

When we had calmed down we sat side by side on the topmost summit crag and surveyed our kingdom, with the sun still high and a southerly breeze just strong enough to keep flying insects at bay. From our vantage point we could see the work going on in all of the Plas Ingli cornfields, and a good many other cornfields as well. We sat there for a long time, talking about the white sailing ships out in Cardigan Bay and about the mountains of North Wales faint on the far horizon, and about distant islands and faraway lands. I did not articulate it, but I wondered what my sister Elen was doing at this precise moment, far away over the western horizon in the United States of America. She, after all, was David's real grandmother, the mother of Brynach and the lover of Iestyn Price the Nightwalker. One day, I thought, David must know all of this, but not yet. I put my arm around the little fellow's shoulder and drew him close. I kissed the top of his head. We sat there in silence, comfortable in each other's company.

Then we heard the sound of cowbells tinkling, and when we looked down at the Plas we saw that Bryn was leading the animals from Parc Bach back to the cowshed for the evening milking. "Time to go down, David," I said. "Your father will be wondering what has happened to us, and we must not be late for supper." So down we went, scrambling and sliding, and hopping from rock to rock. As we descended we chatted fourteen to the dozen, and David wanted to know the name of this plant and that bird, this rock and that butterfly, this mossy crag and that distant mountain peak. It was a joy to give him his answers, for he was thirsty for knowledge, and I knew that one day this world would be his.

ΩΩΩΩΩΩΩΩΩΩΩ

19th August 1843

Thirty Light Dragoons from the 43rd Regiment have been brought in to Newport, and twenty new special constables have been sworn in. In addition, there are two Metropolitan Policemen in shiny new uniforms, brought over from Carmarthen to assist in the suppression of dissent in our tiny town. This seems to me to be an extraordinary and disproportionate action to take in a place of no more than a thousand souls, and there is huge local resentment. The soldiers have been billeted out in ten lodging houses in town, and although nobody wanted to take them the officer in charge showed all of the women concerned an official piece of paper which made refusal to cooperate into a criminal offence. So they are now installed, patrolling the streets, guarding the two gates left on the west side of town, and being generally ostentatious. They are spat at and sworn at, but they are well trained, and they do not react to even the most abusive of taunts.

By all accounts this deployment is part of a new plan of action by the Home Secretary. He is greatly displeased with Colonel Love, whose soldiers inevitably arrive at riot sites at the gallop on the day after a riot has occurred. Now he has increased the size of the military presence, and wants small troops to be billeted in virtually every town and village.

The officer in charge of the Newport detachment is Lieutenant Richard John Rice. Now there is a name to conjure with, for he is none other than the cousin of Joseph Rice, now deceased, one of the murderers of my husband David. He is also the nephew of Squire Benjamin Rice, the monster who was responsible for my scourging through the streets of Newport, and for my incarceration in Haverfordwest Gaol, when I was a young woman. The squire was transported for his sins, and died many years ago. Lieutenant Rice is a sallow youth with narrow eyes and a high opinion of his own abilities. He called on me to pay his respects. I gave him tea, but he is probably out to get me.

Of course, while the soldiers are here nothing much will happen, and they will soon get bored. More to the point, having asked for the soldiers the magistrates and the Town Council will have to pay for their keep, and there are already complaints from townspeople on this score. I estimate that within a week or a fortnight the accumulated bill will be so high that the soldiers will be relieved of their duties and sent elsewhere. They may well end up in Fishguard, for the activities of the Fishguard

Trust are causing great resentment locally, and trouble is brewing.

I have given up any hope of discovering how Master Henry Eynon or Master Bobby Morris discovered that Zeke was hiding out in the Plas hayloft. Zeke may well have been guilty of loose talk himself, and if people knew how to get messages to him they must have known he was here. More likely, the spies who have been watching the Plas from quite good vantage points including the summit of Carningli must have seen and reported on meals being carried from the kitchen door and across the yard and into the hayloft at regular intervals. It would have been a simple matter for anybody receiving these reports to conclude that Zeke was the man being fed.

So that is water under the bridge and out into the sea. All three of the fellows concerned are now in hiding, and are being hunted by people who want them dead or alive. In fact, any one of the fugitives would probably be only too happy to catch up with the other two in order to wring their necks. Master Eynon probably thinks that he has been betrayed by Master Morris, and vice versa. Squire Owen is probably hiding one or other of his accomplices, but he probably wishes them dead too. Colonel Love and the Lord Lieutenant want them alive, for they are in possession of valuable information and they might well be required as witnesses in forthcoming court cases. But if Rebecca catches up with them and manages to loosen their tongues, that will be the end of the Owen family and the Gelli Fawr estate. The scenario is intriguing.

ΩΩΩΩΩΩΩΩΩΩ

28th August 1843

The mounted soldiers are still in town, and in order to relieve their boredom my friends and I have been playing little games with them. Through the use of our spy network it has been a simple matter to set decoys and lay false trails, and in the last week hardly a day has passed without some innocent diversion. On Monday they went galloping off to Eglwyswrw on a tip-off, in order to arrest Zeke Tomos, who was supposed to be hiding in the barn of the Rector of the parish. Of course Zeke was not there, and neither the Rector nor Lieutenant Rice was amused. On Tuesday a note was found on the street indicating that Rebecca and her daughters would take down the gate at Robeston Wathen that very evening at ten of the clock. Off they galloped, to find that Rebecca was nowhere to be seen and that the said village was as peaceful as may be imagined. While they were away, the stable in which they keep their horses in Newport went up in flames. On Wednesday, within half an hour of their weary return to base after their wild goose chase over the mountain, they received a whispered message that a meeting of Rebecca's daughters was planned near Pandy in Cwm Gwaun for three o'clock that very afternoon. So off they thundered on their sweating and straining steeds under the full glare of the harvest sun to find, when they got there, that Squire Owen was sitting by the cool pools and cataracts, enjoying a picnic with certain of his gentry cronies and their families. They were not amused either, and by all accounts there was a heated altercation between Master Rice and the Squire, with the former accusing the latter of a total breakdown of his intelligence operations. And so it has gone on -- frivolous maybe from my point of view, but serving the noble purpose of creating great ill-will among the forces of law and order.

In recent weeks I have received great help in the provision of information from my friends Mary Jane Stokes and Ellie Phillips. Ellie has been particularly helpful. She long since fell out of love with her brutish husband Walter, and since he is close to the squires who take their instructions from the Home Office she knows who meets whom, and where, and why. She comes to Newport often, to see her family at Llwyngwair and to attend to the illness of her sister-in-law Mistress Jane Bowen, and when she does come we meet for tea at the Plas or in Master Dai Darjeeling's new tea-room. We have to be careful at all times, but I never send messages via the postal service and when I move about I try to ensure that I give no advance warnings and leave no trails. The spies who are currently on remand have probably been replaced by new ones, and Jacob Jones tells me he has suspicions on that count. In the middle of all this intrigue, Will told me the other day that I am now referred to on the communications network not as Mistress Martha Morgan but as *"Mam-gu Becca"*. I do not know whether to be flattered, amused or worried.

30th August 1843

I thought that trouble was coming on the territory of the Fishguard Trust, and so it has happened. Brynach has just written a report for the *Welshman* concerning the illegal gate operated by the Trust in Prendergast, just inside the boundary of Haverfordwest. Last time that gate was quietly removed, but its replacement has caused a simmering anger. The other day three hundred Rebeccaites met at Corner Piece Inn to the north of the town and marched on Prendergast after getting very drunk and rowdy. It is rumoured that they drank the inn dry. An informer got a message out to the authorities. The rioters were so disorganized and took so long to get to the gate that when they arrived an ambush was waiting for them. One horse was killed in the chaos which ensued, and two young rioters were arrested. The rest of the beautiful daughters scattered and managed to escape, but the gate remained intact.

When I read this appalling news yesterday I was seated at the kitchen table with Bessie and Liza, who were both cleaning silver cutlery. I thumped the table and exploded: "Another idiotic episode, with drunken rioters, no proper leadership, and more men in prison! How on earth can we win the war if battles are lost in this way, through incompetent leadership and poor discipline? We must call a meeting at once, and take action before these wild elements destroy all the hard work done thus far........."

"Don't you dare, Mistress." The words came from Bessie, and I could hardly believe my ears. There followed a long silence, during which I could feel my colour rising. I looked at both Bessie and Liza, who continued to polish away at the silver with tense fingers and exaggerated arm movements. I looked at their faces, and saw that their lips were tight and their jaws set firm.

"What did you say, Bessie?"

"I said, Mistress, that you would be very unwise to call a meeting of Rebecca's daughters."

"Do you presume, Bessie, to tell me, your Mistress, what to do?"

"I simply advise you, Mistress, because I love you and have no wish to see you come to harm."

"I am grateful for your love and your concern, Bessie," I said coldly, "but I am quite capable of making rational decisions and quite capable of

319

looking after myself. Is that not so, Liza?"

"I sometimes wonder, Mistress, whether you are acting for the best," said Liza, confirming that I had a rebellion on my hands.

I sat back in my chair and closed my eyes. I breathed deeply. Not for the first time, my beloved handmaidens appeared to be intent upon teaching me a lesson about myself. Did I want to hear what they wanted to say? If I stormed out of the room and slammed the door, this business would gnaw away inside me until it got out into the open anyway. If I was to reprimand them for their insolence, what good would that do to our loving and intimate relations? If I was to disregard them and go my own way, I might for ever lose their trust. In the end, the prospect of a dark and suspicious kitchen was too miserable to contemplate. So I opened my eyes and looked at Bessie. "Very well," I said. "Tell me the worst."

After taking a moment to compose herself, Bessie did tell me the worst. "Mistress," she said softly, "Liza and Gwenno and I, and the men, are seriously worried about the extent to which you are becoming involved with Rebecca and her daughters. What started as a pleasant diversion, or as an effort on your part to do something for the poor and hungry, has turned into an obsession. An unhealthy and dangerous obsession. You eat and drink Rebecca. You talk of little else, Mistress. You neglect this household, and you appear oblivious to the needs of your servants and your tenants and labourers where once your concern and your awareness were exemplary. You have hardly any time for your grandchildren, and this is upsetting for both Betsi and Brynach. The little ones are growing up before your eyes, Mistress, and you appear hardly to notice them!"

"But Bessie, this is a great cause, and personal sacrifices have to be made.........."

"That may be, Mistress, but have you not already done enough? Your influence upon the activities of Rebecca and her daughters has been immeasurable. Without you and your restraining influence, God knows what might have happened. But advice is one thing, and interference is quite another. It seems to me, Mistress, that you are now so obsessed with this business that you are seeking to orchestrate and direct things, and to lever yourself into situations which are really none of your business. What if the rioters at Corner Piece do stupid things? Is that really your concern? They are grown men, and if they are idiotic enough to get caught, is that not a matter for them?"

Too Close to the Flames

"But in the great scheme of things their actions are gravely damaging to others, Bessie."

"The great scheme of things!" exploded Bessie, with her eyes flashing. "Whose great scheme of things, Mistress? You mean **your** great scheme, do you not?"

"I have no scheme, Bessie," I said weakly and without any great conviction.

"Oh, I think you do, Mistress. Since I am being both honest and brutal today, I think I see a great scheme in all that you do. Nobody doubts your sincere desire to help both the poor and the starving, but above and beyond that you are driven by a desire to show that a mere woman can manipulate and control angry men and change the course of history. Do you deny, Mistress, that you love every minute of this war? Do you deny that you are stimulated, almost in the manner of female arousal, by the triumphs and the climaxes of your campaign? And do you deny, Mistress, that what you love most of all is control, and direction, and power?"

Then Bessie stopped, probably sensing that she had said a good deal more than she intended. I opened my eyes and looked at her, and saw that she was shaking with emotion. I was shaking too, with a mixture of anger and guilt. I did not know what to say. There was a long silence, and then Liza gave a little cough and said: "Forgive me, Mistress, but I agree with all that Bessie has said. If you dismiss her for her insolence, dismiss me too. You may not have noticed, Mistress, but life in the Plas is not great fun any longer, in spite of our efforts. We cannot get letters in or out. Every move that we make is watched by spies, and we have to think about every word and every action. You gave succour to that wretched fellow Zeke Tomos, when you should have sent him packing........."

"I did not have much choice in the matter, Liza. He was simply dumped on me."

"That is a matter of opinion, Mistress. You are away more often than you are here, and when you are at the table with us your mind is elsewhere, planning and scheming and trying to work out who is doing what, and why. We do not know who to trust and who might be a traitor. The Plas, which was a place of light and laughter, is feeling more and more like a prison, and we servants feel like prisoners.........."

Her voice cracked, and she stopped speaking, even though she might have had more to say. I thought that she was about to weep, but she held

321

herself together, as did Bessie, and with the tension of a drawn longbow in the air the three of us looked at each other. There was another prolonged silence, as I tried to collect my thoughts. Then I managed a weak smile and found my voice. "Enough, enough, the pair of you," I said. "Thank you for being so honest with me, my dear friends. Thirty years ago I would have dissolved in tears under such an assault, and twenty years ago I might have sent the pair of you packing for insolence and insubordination. But I am now older if not wiser, and I will go to my room and think on your words and your loving advice. Excuse me, but I need to retire for an hour or so."

I got up, unsure as to whether my legs would hold me, and walked unsteadily out of the kitchen and up the stairs. I went into my bedroom and closed the door carefully behind me. Then I flung myself onto my bed. I did not weep, but I hammered my pillow with my fists and kept on beating and hammering it until I was exhausted, and until my rage subsided. Then I turned over and lay on my back, and gazed at the ceiling, with my mind racing. No matter how much I wanted to protest against the harsh words which had been thrown at me, and no matter how much my mind told me to defend myself, I knew that Bessie and Liza were right. I reminded myself that I had seen it coming, several weeks back, this mad obsession with conducting an unruly orchestra instead of being a fiddle player. I got up and looked back through the pages of my diary. There it was, in my entry for the third day of July, in the middle of the recollection of my conversation with Tom Foster. I feared then that I might become an insufferable bore, puffed up with my own self-importance, and now I had become just that, to the point of losing my humanity and causing acute distress among my servants and my family.

Suddenly I felt that the walls and the ceiling were pressing in on me, and I had to get out into the fresh air. I rushed downstairs and went through the kitchen like a whirlwind, pausing only to tell Bessie and Liza as I passed that I was minded to take a walk on the mountain. I dragged on my walking boots and threw a cloak over my shoulders, as protection against a cool westerly wind. Then I rushed up the mountain, as fast as my legs would carry me, with my hair and my cloak blowing about me and probably with a wild look in my eyes. I remember nothing of my walk, but then I found myself at the entrance of my cave. I scrambled inside and threw myself onto my little bed of sheepskins in the furthest corner. Then I let myself go and wept until there was no more weeping to do.

Too Close to the Flames

After that, I composed myself and sat upright with my back against the wall of blue rock. I managed to still my mind and to listen to my intuition. I knew that I still had work to do, for both Joseph and Shemi had told me of it. I also knew that there would be victory, and that the time for it was not far off. But in the meantime I had to renew my contract with humanity, and I had to relearn the meaning of humility. There were dear people from whom I required forgiveness, and I knew that I had to go home in the red light of evening, and ask for it.

So I left the cave and walked back down to the Plas, arriving just in time for supper. Bessie and Gwenno were serving up boiled beef, potatoes and cabbage and carrying things to the table. As they glanced at me they looked sheepish. But I smiled at them and got smiles in return. Bryn, Gomer, Liza and Will were seated in their usual places, and I was surprised to find Shemi and Sian there as well. I should not have been surprised, and realized at once that they had come because the wizard had sensed the turmoil in my breast and could not stay away.

It was obvious to me that my ferocious handmaidens had already given the assembled company a detailed report of the afternoon's proceedings, for expectant eyes were directed towards me from every side and corner of the big oak table. I felt no hostility, but a great upwelling of love and support. I was in no mood for a long speech, and we were in any case all hungry, so I simply said: "My dear friends, we all know what has happened today. Mistress Martha Morgan, *Mam-gu* Becca, has been brought down a peg or two, and not before time. For that, I have to thank my beloved Bessie and Liza from the bottom of my heart. My instinct tells me that I should kneel before each one of you in turn, and anoint your feet with my tears, and dry them with my hair. But that would be presumptuous of me, and would probably put all of us off our supper. So I will simply say that I am sorry for my neglect and my mad obsession with putting the world to rights, and instructing others in the manner of doing it. Please forgive me, my dear friends. I hereby give each and every one of you permission to kick me hard if at any time in the coming weeks I act above my station or forget my humanity. Now, may I please have a warm embrace from each one of you in turn? I think I need it."

And I did embrace each of my angels in turn, and a good many tears were shed. I went and fetched half a dozen bottles of my best Portuguese wine from the cellar, and for all I know I might have fetched some bottles of brandy too. In truth my memories of the evening are a little hazy, but I do recall considerable noise and laughter, and from the state of my head this morning I can safely say that a most enjoyable time was had by all. Shemi and Sian were incapable of finding their way home at the end of it, so they slept in the old nursery. I am a changed character, as gentle and humble and harmless as a little brown mouse, and I promise in the pages of this diary that I will never again do anything silly.

ΩΩΩΩΩΩΩΩΩΩΩ

8th September 1843

The Light Dragoons have gone back to Carmarthen, and good riddance to them. And I have spent a week on jolly social visits, feeling so benevolent and kind that I have even given jovial greetings to the spies at the bottom of my lane every time I have gone past. I have apologized to my children and grandchildren for my recent arrogance and neglect, and have promised to be a reformed grandmother. When he heard that promise, Benjamin, my oldest grandson, said "Bravo, *Mam-gu*. You had better take up knitting!" with a grin which stretched from ear to ear. I have even spent time picking ten baskets of apples in the orchard and twenty pounds of blackberries around the late summer lanes, with nothing in my mind but beautiful thoughts.

I have to admit to feeling considerably refreshed. But after a week of abstinence from messages and intrigues, I am also a little bored, since I cannot spend my whole time being benevolent, and since my servants and friends cannot devote all of their time to the admiration of my virtues. They have their own lives to get on with. So perhaps just a little involvement in the affairs of Rebecca might be appropriate, so as to get me out from under the feet of my servants, to keep my mind active, and to ward off the effects of old age.

I keep on getting messages, whether I like it or not, and some of my contacts are aggrieved that I have failed to respond to them. News has come of a battle between Rebecca's daughters and the army in

Pontarddulais in Glamorgan. According to Brynach, who seems to know almost everything that goes on, far and wide, about a hundred Rebeccaites attacked the gate and destroyed it, but were then ambushed by policemen and magistrates who captured seven of the daughters. Soldiers galloped about in a state of some confusion. There was hand-to-hand fighting, and much bloodshed. Then, to crown a disastrous occasion for Rebecca, the police shot and captured the leading lady herself, who was dressed in her usual high fashion and who was later identified as John Hughes or Jac Ty-Isha. He will surely be transported.

The other big news concerns a meeting in the open air on the slopes of Mynydd Sylen near Llanelli. It was widely advertised "with a view to consider the riotous circumstances of that part of the country, and to discuss the best ways of restoring peace and removing complaints." According to reports, there were at least 8,000 people present, including many women and children. Eight thousand! I am truly amazed. The gathering was organized by my friend Master Hugh Williams, who also acted as one of the main speakers. He condemned violence, as did the other speakers, and all pleaded for lawful and peaceful protest. A petition to the Queen (somewhat along the lines of the old People's Charter) was prepared, and its wording was discussed and amended. The meeting was not in the least seditious, and on the surface it had nothing to do with Rebecca or the Chartists. It was even chaired by Squire William Chambers, one of the local magistrates, to give it an aura of respectability. The *Times* was thanked for its role in bringing crucial issues to the attention of the nation, and Tom Foster was accorded a warm welcome. The meeting ended with three cheers for the Queen before the crowd dispersed in complete silence and good order. When I read about this grand and loyal occasion in the *Welshman*, I could not resist a wry smile. Master Williams is no fool, and next time I meet him I will give him a little pat on the back, and maybe, if he behaves himself, a kiss on the cheek.

ΩΩΩΩΩΩΩΩΩΩΩ

12. Burnt Fingers

25th September 1843

I am still trying to resist any further involvement in the affairs of Rebecca, but it is not easy to remain on the periphery when great events are unfolding. On the very day of my last diary entry, Fishguard was thrust into national prominence, probably for the first time since the French Invasion of 1797. I knew it was coming, for the Fishguard Trust has been utterly insensitive to the needs and aspirations of the local farmers, and in the face of threats and warnings against the hated gatekeepers in and around the town, two new gates have gone up and a harsh regime of toll collection has been instituted. So on Friday 8th September, having given due warning, Rebecca and her daughters arrived in the town and smashed down and burned the two offending gates. The gatekeepers were publicly warned that if they continued to collect tolls, Rebecca would return on the following Monday and burn down their houses as well. But on Saturday the silly fellows started to repair the gates, with Trust approval, and insisted on collecting tolls as usual. So Rebecca summoned all of her daughters to the town on Monday, and they turned up in huge numbers. Six hundred of them took part in the formal proceedings, but thousands more came to join in the carnival. The constables and the magistrates were nowhere to be seen, and for three hours Rebecca was the queen of the town. She and her daughters paraded around the streets, with bands playing and crowds cheering. All of the gates and tollgate houses were destroyed and burned. Master Henry Collins attracted the ire of the protestors and had his house blasted by gunfire, and the Trust's surveyor John McKenna had his garden wall levelled to the ground.

According to my newspapers, this open insurrection sent a shockwave to the heart of the political establishment, not only because of the brazen and open manner of Rebecca's occupation of the town, but also because of the abject surrender of the forces of law and order. In 1797 the army and the magistrates had abandoned the town and left it to the tender mercies of the French; now they had done it again, and left the town in the warm embrace of Rebecca. The Lord Lieutenant was furious, and letters have

326

certainly gone to the Home Secretary. Sir James must be thoroughly sick of letters from the magistrates of West Wales, and with sending off troops to look after places where damage has already been done. The government is a laughing stock, and the soldiers are greeted everywhere with taunts of "Out to catch Becca today, boys?"

One thing which is not a laughing matter is that the first death of the Rebecca Riots has occurred. I met Tom Foster when he came to Fishguard a week ago, and he told me about it. On 9th September a crowd of Rebecca's daughters gathered at Hendy near Pontarddulais, and destroyed a gate there. They were probably the same fellows who were involved in the rout nearby just a couple of days earlier. They also set the gatekeeper's house on fire. Sarah Williams, the gatekeeper, had been put in at Hendy to supervise the collection of increased tolls, so she was hated as much as the gate itself. When her house was going up in flames, she became hysterical and started to rush about, in and out of the inferno, trying to save her furniture and other possessions. What happened then is unclear, but she was warned to keep away. Shots were fired in the air, and the old lady was then peppered with gunshot. She died in the house of her neighbours. Whether her death was an accident is still not clear, but Tom Foster thinks that her injuries were the result of a direct shot from somebody with murder on his mind. If they catch him, he surely deserves to hang. In the following days the newspapers -- including the *Times* -- carried bold headlines such as *"Cold-blooded Murder of Toll Collector"* together with graphic descriptions of the victim's injuries and outraged editorial comments.

One would have thought that this event would have turned people against Rebecca in Carmarthenshire and Glamorgan. But that is not what has happened, and Tom says that many people simply shrugged and said "Mistress Williams had it coming to her." More amazing still, at the Inquest on 11th September, a jury of a dozen respectable local people listened to all the evidence of doctors, eyewitnesses and police, and then recorded a verdict that "the deceased died from the effusion of blood into the chest, which occasioned suffocation, but from what cause is to this jury unknown." In other words, they could find no evidence of a crime having been committed.

That reluctance to point a finger of blame may have something to do with the involvement of very rough fellows in that part of Wales in the riots, with intimidation and coercion coming more and more to the fore. The magistrates and the police constables are personally threatened and singled out. They are losing hayricks and barns and other property, and Tom thinks that it is only a matter of time before some of the grand houses of the gentry go up in flames. He also has it on good authority, from talking to frightened farmers, that Rebecca is subjecting them to a sort of blackmail. Some of them are threatened with violence if they do not turn up for gate destruction work when they are summoned. Others are required to pay out two shillings and sixpence per riot, which they have to pay out at secret meetings. If they refuse, they have their ricks fired. The money is supposed to be used to help the poor, but in fact it goes to the purchase of powder and shot.

Then Tom tells me that there is a ferocious gang at work in the Llanelli and Pontyberem area, led by two thugs who call themselves Shoni Sgubor Fawr (John of the Big Barn) and Dai'r Cantwr (David the Singer). The gang is based at an inn called the Stag and Pheasant, where they drink and plan campaigns of terror and intimidation. They dress up in the garb of Rebecca's daughters, and Shoni goes about proclaiming to all and sundry that he is Rebecca. They are heavily armed, and they know all about threatening letters, the extraction of protection money, blackmail and intimidation. People are terrified of them, and the army and the magistrates are in the process of combining forces in order to hunt them down. They will probably be betrayed, says Tom, for they have far more enemies than friends, and the rewards now on offer for their capture are very tempting as far as the criminal classes are concerned.

When I heard all of this from Tom, my heart sank. I told him as much, and he placed a kind hand on my shoulder by way of consolation and encouragement. "This is not your fault, Martha," he said as we parted. "We both anticipated this turn of events, and we can but hope that across the three counties common sense will get the better of insanity."

Rebecca has changed, and where she once had a smile upon her face, she now shows a scowl. I am not sure that I know her any longer, and not sure that I want to have anything more to do with her.

ΩΩΩΩΩΩΩΩΩΩ

Burnt Fingers

13th November 1843

It may have been my ambition to part company with Rebecca, but it appears that she has no wish to part company with me.

We have suffered a terrible defeat at the hands of the authorities, and I am furious that even with our spy network in place we had no wind of what was coming. Maybe, with relative peace in this neighbourhood and with the wildfires of insurrection burning uncontrollably elsewhere, we all allowed complacency to replace vigilance......

At two o'clock this morning, in pitch blackness and driving rain, special constables and Light Dragoons descended on households across North Pembrokeshire and arrested many of the men who have been involved thus far in the riots. I am still trying to put together the full picture, but as far as the Plas is concerned, we were all awakened by thundering hooves in the yard, and by the flickering lights of torches as men surrounded the house. There was a great hammering at the door, and when Bessie opened it two terrifying figures in oilskins came in out of the pouring rain and demanded to know where Master Bryn Williams might be found. Bessie told the fellows, quite truthfully, that Bryn was fast asleep in bed, and that he was indisposed and currently unable to work because of a chest ailment. At that point I appeared and demanded to know what was going on. I immediately recognized one of the fellows as Lieutenant Rice of the Dragoons, and he said that his colleague was a special constable designated to affect the arrest of Bryn Williams on a charge of participating in riotous assembly and other dastardly crimes in the company of Rebecca and her daughters.

"And where is your warrant, sir?" said I.

"Here it is, Mistress," said the constable. "You will find that it is entirely in order."

He handed it to me, and I sat at the kitchen table and examined the soggy document in detail. It did appear to be in order, and it was signed by Squires Owen and Jobbins. "And who instructed you to come here?" I asked.

"The new Clerk to the Justices, Master Richard Lord."

"And who has brought charges against my man Bryn Williams?"

"The Mayor of Newport, Mistress, on the sworn testimony of Master Bobby Morris."

I knew at once that this was part of a large-scale operation, and that many men would be taken, all betrayed by Bobby Morris. I cursed myself, not for the first time, for allowing Master Morris to slip through our fingers when we first discovered that he was an informer. Now he was embarking on his campaign of revenge, and he would pick up his tidy reward for his treachery. I was surprised that I was not under arrest myself. But my immediate concern was Bryn, whose health was declining fast and who needed constant medical attention. So I said: "Gentlemen, I refuse permission for you to take Master Williams from this house. He is a sick man, and cannot be moved."

"With all due respect, Mistress Morgan," said Lieutenant Rice with a happy smile on his face, "we do not need your permission." And he gave orders for the soldiers to search the house. They very quickly found Bryn in his room, and allowed him to dress. Then they arrested him, and took him away. He was very stoical, but he looked very ill, and I feared that we might never see him again. He looked at me with pleading in his eyes, but there was nothing that Bessie and I could do to resist the forces of law and order, so I said: "Don't you worry, Bryn. Do not say anything while you are in custody. I promise that we will soon have you free, and I will ask Master Hugh Williams to advise us and come to your defence."

Then I gave one last blast to the constable and the military officer. "This man is sick," I said, "and you gentlemen are utterly irresponsible in taking him from this house against my wishes and against all the rules of human decency. I wish it to be recorded that if anything happens to him, I will hold you personally responsible. Is that clear?"

"Yes, yes, it is perfectly clear," sneered Lieutenant Rice. "We will look after him as if he was a newborn babe, and I will personally tuck him up in bed each night."

So I wrote out a note containing my protest and referring to Bryn's state of health, and copied it, and then insisted that Lieutenant Rice and the Constable should sign both copies. I gave one to the officer, and he stuffed it into his pocket. Then they dragged poor Bryn away and went out into the wild wet darkness.

When they had gone, Bessie and I stoked up the fire, and made some tea, and spent the rest of the night sitting in the kitchen feeling exhausted and miserable. Before dawn, people started to arrive at the Plas with messages about other arrests. Will was taken from his cottage, and Gomer from his. The two Nicholas boys from the Parrog are under arrest, as is

Dafydd Ifan from Gamallt, George Mathias from Trehaidd, Shemi's son John, and Squire Collyer's young son Justin.

I had little time to assess the scale or the import of what had happened in the night, for there were cows to be milked and animals to be fed, and all of my men were gone. Gwenno came early, but she was greatly affected by the trauma of having Gomer dragged from their bed in the middle of the night, and she sat in front of the fire, hardly capable of speaking. Liza came and was a tower of strength, and she ran down into the *cwm* to get help from some of my tenants and labourers. We coped, but the animals were restless and uncooperative, and it poured with rain incessantly. It was eleven o'clock before we all managed to sit down and have some breakfast.

Then more news arrived. Young Thomas Laugharne from Pontfaen is taken, as are Samuel Stokes, Will's son Gerallt, my nephew Mark Bowen, my tenant Waldo Tucker, and even Skiff Abraham. I was amazed when I heard that Skiff was in custody, for he is the most astute of men, protected by a network of spies and allies and always careful to keep clear water between himself and breaking waves and rocky shores. Then, just as the ten of us around the kitchen table had finished breakfast, my son-in-law Ioan arrived. "Martha," he said in a voice hollow with despair, "Benjamin is taken. He was at Castlebythe at the time, but they found him there and arrested him, at five o'clock this morning. The constables appear to have been very well informed. Bobby Morris?"

I nodded. I could hardly reply, for I had a band of cold steel wrapped around my heart. My oldest grandson under arrest for participating in the Rebecca Riots! And not just him, but the sons of some of my nearest and dearest. These arrests affected not only the labouring and farming classes, but the gentry too. The repercussions did not bear thinking about. I embraced Ioan, and we held onto each other, and tried to give each other strength.

ΩΩΩΩΩΩΩΩΩΩ

14th November 1843

We are trying to come to terms with this disaster, but it is not easy. Arrests on such a scale are unprecedented, and it is now clear that 35 men have been taken into custody, presumably all on the basis of a sworn statement from Master Bobby Morris. His location is a closely-guarded secret, but there is fury throughout the county concerning his treachery, and his poor parents, who live near Brynberian, have been abused and ostracized by their neighbours. I have sent messages to Tom Foster and Hugh Williams. I want them both here as soon as possible, since we need maximum press coverage and also a good defence when the men are hauled before the magistrates at the next Petty Sessions. We still do not know when that will be, but it will certainly be within the next few days. Probably the venue will be Fishguard Town Hall, which is something to be grateful for, since the local magistrates are generally benign and even weak. It is widely assumed that the likes of Squire Alexander Williams of Langton and Squire Tom Vaughan of Castlebythe are honest fellows who are secretly sympathetic to the aspirations of Rebecca and her daughters. After all, did they not quietly leave the town of Fishguard recently to the tender mercies of Rebecca, when they could have stood their ground and fought it out with their constables alongside them? If Squire Williams is one of those on duty when the cases are dealt with, I have some hope of a successful outcome, since he was, as a young man, a tutor for my children at Plas Ingli. He knows many of the accused, and knows them to be good people. A faint hope maybe, but one must hold to it...........

This morning, when I woke up, I was as close to despair as could be, and was minded to go rushing off in order to apologize to the wives and parents of those taken into custody. But Bessie absolutely refused to let me out of the house, and told me to pull myself together. "How many times must you be told, Mistress, that you cannot take upon yourself responsibility for the actions of others? All of those taken are grown men. They all took risks, and they knew what the penalties might be if they were caught. Instead of wallowing in misery. Mistress, you will serve them best by ensuring that they are free men again by the end of the Petty Sessions." She was quite right of course. I should have ticked her off for her insolence, but my beloved handmaiden is becoming as fierce as old Mrs Owen was when she ruled the roost here at the Plas, and I thought it best not to resist her instructions.

I am greatly concerned about Bryn's health. His breathing problems have been getting worse and worse, and of late he has only been able to do the lightest of tasks around the garden and the dairy. Before his arrest he was in bed for three days, and both Shemi and Havard Medical have been attending to him. His lungs are so poisoned from his time in the iron industry that Shemi thinks he may not ever recover his full strength. On that basis, I have already started to look around for a new cow-man. That is a minor matter for the future. For the present, I am still not sure where Bryn is incarcerated. Some of the prisoners are in the Fishguard lock-up, and others are in Haverfordwest Gaol. That is a terrible place, and the prisoners will probably be crammed inside the cells, at least six to a cell and with precious little warmth or care. I have asked Havard Medical to find out where Bryn is, and to insist on seeing him so as to assess his condition and to give him medication. He went off on his pony this morning, and since then I have had no report of his whereabouts.

Of equal concern is the attempt by the authorities to find witnesses who will appear at the Sessions in order to support the charges made by Bobby Morris. Notices offering rewards of £100 "for information leading to the conviction of any of those persons currently awaiting trial for the unlawful destruction of toll gates" have gone up all over Pembrokeshire. They are torn down as soon as they are put up, but times are hard, and I am greatly afraid that some of those who know the details of certain nocturnal activities will be tempted to come forward. Rebecca has herself put up notices threatening revenge against any informers, so there is a battle in progress for the hearts of both the rich and the poor.

ΩΩΩΩΩΩΩΩΩΩ

16th November 1843

The tragedy of the arrests and incarcerations was terrible enough. But it has now been overtaken by a tragedy even more terrible. Bryn is dead. He died this morning, in Haverfordwest Gaol, shortly before the prisoners were taken to Fishguard for the Petty Sessions. Even now, as I sit at my desk and recall the events of the day, I am numbed and horrified, and find it difficult to concentrate on anything but the memory of that good and brave man. He was an exemplary servant, loyal and hard-working, and although he was never in perfect health since the day of his arrival at the Plas he never complained of his suffering, and never sought to pass his tasks over to any of his comrades. He was well educated and well-spoken, and he knew how to enjoy life. Even in the midst of my grief for his passing, I can manage a little smile at the recollection of his tales of wild events in Merthyr Tydfil in the sordid streets around the iron works. He was a bachelor who lived a good and useful life, and who made many people (including me) grateful for the blessings which he brought to us through his smiles and his wit. Now he is gone. Another good man dead. Another funeral to arrange.

We knew nothing about Bryn's death until the start of the Petty Sessions. Outside the Town Hall, before they started, there was pandemonium. The Royal Marines from Pembroke Dockyard had been called in to provide protection for the authorities and for Master Bobby Morris, and they stood in front of the hall, three ranks deep and with fixed bayonets. Somehow or other they hustled the magistrates inside, with insults and screams from the crowd and with rotten fruit and other missiles being flung at them. I was pleased to see that Squire Jenkins of Cilciffeth was the senior magistrate on duty, and knew that he would chair the bench. Then Bobby Morris arrived, with an armed guard of Dragoons led by Lieutenant Rice. I though that they would never get him in through the door, such was the hostility and abuse from the crowd, and there was so much pressure from angry citizens that several people actually got injured on the line of fixed bayonets. At last the prisoners were led through the crowd, all of them in shackles and all showing tension and exhaustion on their faces. I recognized all of them, and counted them in to cheers and applause and shouts of "Long live Rebecca!" and "Three cheers for Becca and her daughters!" I did not see Bryn, and I felt fear and apprehension in the pit of my stomach.

At last, inside the hall and with the public gallery packed and noisy, Squire Jenkins commenced the proceedings. "Silence in court!" he thundered. "The court is now convened, on the sixteenth day of November in the year of our Lord 1843. There is but one matter before us today, relating to charges brought against thirty-five men in the sworn testimony of Master Bobby Morris of Llwyngwair. Master Morris is here to read out his testimony and swear it before the court?"

"Yes, sir," said the Clerk to the Court, to the accompaniment of furious chants and abuse from the public gallery.

"Silence in court! If I do not have it, I will have the court cleared! Now then, are all the prisoners present to face the charges?"

"No, sir. Thirty-four are present, and one is missing."

"Oh indeed? And why might that be, Master Clerk?"

"Sadly, sir, Master Bryn Williams of Plas Ingli died this morning while being held in custody."

At first, this statement was greeted by a shocked silence. Then somebody started shouting from the gallery, and more joined in, and soon there was a veritable cacophony of screams and wails and shouts from the members of the public, with feet banged on the floor and pieces of paper and other missiles hurled onto the floor of the courtroom. I was with Bessie, and she and I sat silently in the midst of the maelstrom, holding hands and with tears rolling down our cheeks. No matter how he tried, Squire Jenkins could not silence the crowd, and at last he had to clear the court. We were all bundled out into the street, and it was not until the prisoners emerged into the light of day some twenty minutes later that we found out what had happened during the formal deliberations.

According to Benjamin, who later told us everything, the proceedings were mercifully short. Since Master Hugh Williams could not be found in the time available, some of the prisoners were defended by John Wilkins Legal and others by Robert Morris Legal -- both local men and both very clever. Benjamin said that after the formalities of identification, Master Bobby Morris had to stand in front of his former friends and read out his statement. He looked like a haunted man, and as he spoke his voice dropped to a whisper and perspiration poured from his brow in spite of the coldness of the winter air. Three times Squire Jenkins had to say to him: "Speak up, man! We must hear what you have to say!" When he had finished his catalogue of betrayal, and sworn his statement on the Bible, the prisoners were charged and asked to plead. All answered "Not guilty." The prosecuting lawyer declined to question any of the prisoners, and simply asked for a few matters in Bobby Morris's statement to be amplified and clarified.

Then the defending lawyers were given the opportunity to cross-examine Master Morris. They carved him up with a surgical knife, said Benjamin, and spent just a few minutes highlighting inconsistencies, assumptions, possible cases of mistaken identity, and bits and pieces of secondhand and thirdhand information. Master Morris, already a bundle of nerves, was now reduced to a gibbering wreck of a man. After five minutes, Morris Legal stopped his cross-examination, and turned to the magistrates. "Sirs, I have had enough of cruelty. I submit that it is obvious to all of us in this room that Master Morris's evidence is utterly unreliable. He may have sworn it to be true, but his case is no more robust than a moth-eaten blanket, and there are so many holes in it that the truth shines through it like a golden dawn....."

"To the point, please, Master Lewis."

"Ahem. Quite so, sir. The essence of my case, and that of my colleague Master Wilkins, is this. We have not a shred of evidence on which to convict these men who have so cruelly been dragged from their beds on a cold winter morning. The authorities have placed notices and offered rewards, but they cannot produce a single witness to attest to the truth of anything that Master Morris has placed before this court. I submit that what we have heard is fabrication, from beginning to end...."

"Be careful, Master Lewis. What we have is a statement sworn on the Bible. Are you accusing the witness of perjury?"

"Heaven forbid, sir. But what I suggest is that he is under such great pressure, and feels such a great weight of public disapprobation pressing down upon him, that his memory is playing tricks with him. He is confused and frightened, and in those circumstances no statement from his lips can be considered safe. The situation will not be improved if you find these men guilty, or if you remand them on bail or in custody for trial at the Assizes before a judge. With the passage of a month or two, Master Morris will become an even more unreliable witness, and the acquittal of all of the prisoners on all of the charges will be inevitable. Just think what Lloyd Hall Attorney might do to him! Gentlemen of the bench, I submit that you will save all of us a great deal of aggravation, and quite properly serve the cause of justice, by throwing out the charges against these men, and releasing all of them forthwith."

And after a ten-second deliberation, that is what the magistrates did. The shackles were removed from the prisoners, and they were allowed to walk out as free men into the cold fresh air of Fishguard Square. They were greeted with scenes of wild elation, and embraced and carried away in triumph by their nearest and dearest. But there is deep fury in the community about the death of my servant Bryn Williams, and the Dragoons are being accused of murder. It is already common knowledge that Bryn was seriously ill when he was taken from the Plas, and that he was arrested in spite of my specific request for compassion on medical grounds. In due course, I will find out what happened in the prison, and how he died. There will have to be an inquest before the funeral, and I will be required to attend.

Now, late at night, as I sit in a shaky pool of light and stare at a guttering candle, my mind is buzzing and I feel that my heart is being pulled apart by conflicting emotions. Ecstasy at the release of Benjamin, Will, Gomer and the others. Deep, deep grief at the loss of Bryn, one of my angels. Relief, in some small degree, that Bryn's suffering is at an end, and that he is now at peace. Pleasure, at the recollection of Bryn's tall tales around the kitchen table. Apprehension, for I know not what will follow from this episode, or what might lie in store for Master Bobby Morris, traitor and enemy of the people, who once laughed with Bryn and counted him as a friend. He knows, as we all know, that but for him Bryn would still be alive and sleeping comfortably in his warm bed at the Plas.

ΩΩΩΩΩΩΩΩΩΩ

20th December 1843

I have been in no mood for diary writing, but with Christmas approaching I must seek to put dark events behind me and get on with my life. My chronicle of events is miserable indeed, but I must steel myself and bring it up to date even though I would prefer to go down into the kitchen and help Bessie with the manufacture of our rich currant cake.

The inquest into Bryn's death took place in the Shire Hall in Haverfordwest exactly one month ago. I had to attend in order to give evidence, as did Bessie, Shemi and Havard Medical. Will and Gomer did not see their friend in prison, since they were held in Fishguard, but my grandson Benjamin shared a cell with him, and he was also required to make a statement to the jury of twelve men. Like all inquests, it was a painful business. The prison doctor, who undertook a postmortem, pronounced the cause of death as suffocation arising from a severe blockage of the lungs and from the inhalation of noxious substances. Shemi and Havard Medical agreed with some of that, but stated that prior to his arrest Bryn was receiving treatment and was by no means close to death. Master Havard, who was refused consent to minister to Bryn in prison, was especially strong in his opinion that maltreatment and lack of medical care was the trigger which caused Bryn's sudden death. Bessie and I described the process of the arrest, and told of our concern, and Lieutenant Rice's cynicism, before Bryn was taken away. I also produced for the jury the protest note which I had written out at the Plas, and which had been duly signed by Lieutenant Rice.

But Benjamin's testimony was the most powerful of all, and he told of the manner in which he and thirty other prisoners were shackled and then taken in open carts across Mynydd Preseli through the pouring rain. The journey took four hours. There were at least twelve soldiers in the escorting party. He said that on the journey Bryn was coughing and shivering uncontrollably, and that when he drew the attention of Lieutenant Rice to his condition he simply laughed and accused Bryn of play-acting. The men pleaded for blankets or covers, but were left soaking and shivering while the escort of dragoons all wore full oilskins. On arrival in the county town, the prisoners were flung into filthy cells in Haverfordwest Castle. Bryn and Benjamin and four other men were put into cell number five, where they were denied any opportunity to change into dry and warm clothes and where they were given only one thin blanket each to cover themselves. The dragoons remained on duty at the castle, and appeared to treat the prisoners as their special charges. By dusk on the first day of their incarceration Bryn's condition had deteriorated, but still Lieutenant Rice would not call a doctor in spite of Benjamin's pleading. By the middle of the next day Bryn was vomiting and could not stand, and then, on the insistence of the jailer, the prison doctor was called. He examined Bryn, ordered some warm clothes for him, and insisted that he should be given an extra portion of soup for supper. Bryn managed to get it down, but vomited it all up again within a few minutes. During the night he became unconscious, said Benjamin, and in spite of his calls for help it was left to him and the other prisoners to look after him, and he died early in the morning.

When Benjamin had finished his narrative, I looked at the faces of the jury members. I could see that they were appalled by what they had heard, and their obvious anger was not at all mitigated by the smooth and self-satisfied statement that came from Lieutenant Rice immediately afterwards. As he droned on, my mind wandered to a strange coincidence. Cell number five in Haverfordwest Castle was the very cell in which Joseph Rice, the lieutenant's cousin, had met his death at the hands of one of his own accomplices while awaiting trial for the murder of my husband. That was in the year 1806, almost exactly thirty-seven years ago. At that time, Richard John Rice would have been but a child. I wondered if he was aware of the connection, and of the manner in which his evil cousin had met his end, covered in gruel and strangled by another evil monster named John Howell.   If he did know, perhaps he saw the death of Bryn Williams, under his care, as part of a campaign of revenge against the Plas and its inhabitants...........

I was jolted away from my dark train of thought by the Coroner, who summed up succinctly and then asked the jury to consider their verdict on the cause of death. It did not take them long. When the jurors returned to the court the foreman read out the following short statement: "We find that the cause of death was suffocation, brought on by ancient damage to the respiratory tract and greatly accelerated by wilful neglect." All who were present in the room gasped, and I saw that Lieutenant Rice's face was suddenly drained of all colour. That was not exactly a verdict of unlawful killing, but it was as near as may be imagined.

That gave us some small comfort as we travelled home over the mountain in the light coach, but we had a *Gwylnos* and a funeral to plan, and that gave us no comfort at all. On the next day, Bryn's body was delivered to the Plas in its coffin with permission to proceed to burial, and he was laid to rest in Caersalem graveyard on the 23rd day of November. We thought that the *Gwylnos* and the funeral would be small affairs, since Bryn had no local relatives, but we were overwhelmed with the sheer press of people and with the sense of outrage felt by everyone at the manner of his death. In the minds of almost everybody, Bryn is the first martyr of the Rebecca Riots, and Lieutenant Rice is labelled as his killer.

Burnt Fingers

A week after that, I met Hugh Williams at a friendly house, and he told me that Richard John Rice is facing a court martial, and that he and his detachment of dragoons have been moved out of Wales so as to avoid retribution or any further trouble. It is almost certain that Rice will be dismissed in disgrace from the army. "And good riddance to him," said Master Williams. "The army does not need fellows like that, for it has an almost impossible job already. But this affair has had one further consequence, in that Colonel Love has now taken all army detachments out of the Newport area, in recognition of the fact that feelings are running so high that even the smallest incident could escalate into a disaster. I sense that the butcher colonel is coming to realise that it is impossible to deal with this unrest with the resources at his disposal, and I also think that he is more than a little sympathetic to the case being made by Rebecca and her daughters."

"Oh, do you really think so, Hugh?"

"I know it, Martha. Remember that I move in the right circles, and that like you, I have a tidy little network of spies. We are winning. You may take my word for it."

He grinned, and I smiled back, having almost forgotten what it was to smile. Then I recalled that I had promised myself that I would congratulate Master Williams on the cleverness of the Mynydd Sylen meeting, that I would pat him on the back, and that I would kiss him on the cheek. So I did all three. And much to my surprise, Master Williams, the arrogant master of all that he surveys, the Don Juan of Kidwelly, blushed as sweetly as a fifteen year old boy who has just been kissed for the first time.

There is one further matter to report before I can draw a line under this miserable affair. Master Tom Foster came to Bryn's funeral, quite openly, and I invited him to stay at the Plas. He wrote a long report for his newspaper, which was published in a prominent position with a large headline. In spite of all that had to be arranged, we contrived to spend several hours in earnest conversation, as a result of which my respect and liking for him increased even more. He had an abundance of news to give me, but the most important item concerned Master Bobby Morris. He said that after the Petty Sessions in Fishguard, after my return to the Plas, a large crowd hung about on Fishguard Square, baying for the blood of the traitor. They would have lynched him too, said Master Foster, in spite of the presence of Royal Marines with fixed bayonets. At last the soldiers smuggled him out of the back door, and took him to Haverfordwest under armed guard. For his own protection, he was kept in solitary confinement overnight in a small cell in the gaol. Over the next few days, with the agreement of the Lord Lieutenant and the Home Secretary, he was given a new identity, paid the sum of fifty pounds, and escorted out of the county under cover of darkness to make a new life elsewhere.

That might have been the end of the matter, said Master Foster. But Mistress Rebecca does not allow her enemies to escape that easily, and according to his contacts a watch was mounted for him all over Wales. He thinks that at least a thousand men might have been involved. Then, a fortnight later, a small item appeared in the *Welshman*, as follows:

UNFORTUNATE DROWNING IN ABERYSTWYTH HARBOUR
The body of a young gentleman was recovered from the water in Aberystwyth Harbour on the morning of Wednesday last. He was identified as Mr Elwyn Simpson, recently moved to the town from Cardiff. It was confirmed that he had died from drowning, and according to the authorities foul play is not suspected. We extend our deepest sympathy to the family of the deceased man.

Within a few days, said Master Foster, the daughters of Rebecca throughout the three counties knew that the dead man was Bobby Morris, and that his throat had been cut before he had been flung into the icy water of the harbour. The authorities will take no action, for that would serve no purpose whatsoever.

Two days ago a notice was pinned to the church door in Newport. This is what it said:

Take Notice,
You people of Newport, that Judas Morris have gone to his maker, and have had his just reward for his treachery. So it will be with any other who informs upon Becca & her daughters and who brings the English army into the houses of innocent people at dead of night. The gates must go, and the army with them, or else all will be distruction and conflaggration.
Faithfull unto death,   Becca and daughters

341

Burnt Fingers

So is the tragedy of Rebecca compounded. I had nothing to do with either the hunt or the killing. But two men who broke bread with me at my table are dead, and I have to accept that without my involvement in this Rebecca business they would both still be alive. Tonight, as I sit at my desk just a few days before Christmas, jollification is the last thing I want to think about, for I am tired, and sad, and numbed by the ice which has penetrated my heart.

ΩΩΩΩΩΩΩΩΩΩ

13. Inferno

4th January 1844

Another Christmas has come and gone. It was as cheerful as we could make it in the circumstances. Since it came so soon after Bryn's death I was in no mood to organize a big Christmas, and Betsi and Ioan made life easier for me and my servants by inviting us to Brithdir for Christmas Day and Boxing Day. That was eminently practical, since Brithdir Mawr and Plas Ingli are so close that there was no danger of us neglecting the animals.

Tom Foster has been in London for Christmas with his family, but he is a very enthusiastic fellow who does not know how to relax, and he is back in Pembrokeshire ready to file more reports for his newspaper. I met him today, at the home of Mary Jane in Trecwn. He feels comfortable in Pembrokeshire, and he declares that he likes it better here than in Cardiganshire, where all the innkeepers and lodging-house keepers are grasping villains, or in Carmarthenshire, where he spends most of his time. He told me that he is looked on in certain quarters in that county with unallayed suspicion and hostility, and some of the leading members of the Carmarthenshire gentry have done their best to keep him out of meetings and have orchestrated attempts to undermine him in some of the smaller Welsh newspapers. He was physically assaulted by two squires shortly before Christmas, and he has a powerful personal enemy in the Vice-Lieutenant of Carmarthenshire, one George Rice Trevor, son of Lord Dynefwr. I have encountered this fellow before, at a meeting in Carmarthen. He is a puffed-up dandy who has a very inflated opinion of his own abilities and who appears to be utterly insensitive to the real causes of distress in the countryside. He has written to the Editor of the *Times* and to the Home Secretary complaining that Tom's reports are biased and inflammatory, and he has accused him of "fomenting discord and discontent" by writing of things other than the tollgates and turnpike trusts! When Tom told me this, he laughed and so did I, but I was relieved to hear that his Editor has given him a complete vote of confidence and left Master Rice Trevor with a flea in his ear.

Another thing that Tom did was to remind me that while we have a strengthened military presence in West Wales, with more than 2,000 troops now stationed here, and while we still have gates going up in flames, great battles have already been won. In July and August last, I was so preoccupied with traitors and spies and with my own personal problems that I almost failed to notice that two fellows from London were dispatched by the Home Secretary to the Three Counties in order to evaluate the causes of rural discontent. Master Thomas Hall, who is a barrister, and Master George Ellis, who is a solicitor, held many meetings and interviewed many aggrieved people over a two-week period and reported to the government at high speed. The Home Secretary was clearly impressed by their evidence of corruption and maladministration within the trusts and by the wide range of other grievances which bubbled up to the surface, and he immediately instituted a full Public Inquiry or Royal Commission. The Commissioners (Squire Frankland Lewis and Messrs Clive and Cripps) started work in Carmarthen in October, and must have visited more than twenty places during their expedition. They were on the road for seven weeks, and took evidence for 35 full days. Then they retired to London in order to ponder and draw their conclusions. Hugh Williams and I were invited to give evidence but declined, but almost everybody of importance on the gentry side and the poor farmers' side gave evidence, and Tom Foster was in attendance for the whole time. He thinks that the Commissioners' Report will appear in about two months' time, and he hopes that while it will not exonerate Rebecca and her daughters it will argue that they were suffering terrible injustices and that the root causes of their pain must now be addressed as a matter of urgency.

"And do not forget, Martha," said Tom, "that that was not the end of the matter. Many side-bars have been removed by the Trusts which put them up illegally, some gates have quietly been removed, and the Aberystwyth and Cardigan Trusts have even reduced tolls. That is a cause for celebration. Master Hall's report on the grievances, and the searching questions asked by all of the skilled gentlemen involved, have caused even the Whitland Trust to relocate gates, to make agreements on the use of tickets for passing through second and third gates, and on new exemptions from toll charges."

"Better late than never, Tom. But I cannot help feeling that if only the trustees and tally-holders had listened to the likes of Ioan, Dafydd Stokes, Nicholas Lloyd and me five or six years ago, we might all have been spared a good deal of trouble."

Now Tom has gone back to Carmarthen to deal with those who want to wipe the look of bright-eyed anticipation off his ruddy face. We two have become the firmest of friends, and we share virtually everything. However, there is one thing that I will never share with Tom. When I have spent a morning walking on the mountain and thinking it through, I may commit it to the pages of this diary.

ΩΩΩΩΩΩΩΩΩΩΩ

5th January 1844

I have been up on the mountain, walking back and forth rather aimlessly in bitterly cold weather, with a leaden sky and with flurries of snowflakes whirling about me. Miserable weather, and Mad Mistress Morgan, you might think. But no -- this sort of weather is wild, and powerful, and it is capable of freezing the thoughts inside your head if you are not careful. When I come out in this weather I am reminded just how small I am and just how enormous and implacable are the forces of nature. If Cruel Fate was to decide upon it he could snuff me out with a snip of his bony fingers. He could bury the Plas from doorstep to chimney pot, as he has almost done once or twice before. He could block every road, pull down every tree, level every mountain and fill in every valley......... We cannot doubt that such things happen, for are we not familiar with the evidence of Noah's Flood, and of great volcanic outpourings, and earthquakes which have levelled whole countries?

I sat on a rock near Ffynnon Brynach, warm enough in my winter dress, and coat, and cloak. I let the snow pile up around me, and I thought of Bryn. I thought of that terrible occasion five years ago, when Bryn had joined us on our desperate search for Brynach and the children in the midst of a mighty snowfall on the mountain. He was certainly a sick man at the time, but he worked with us like a man possessed, and never once complained although, in retrospect, he should never have come out and should never have indulged in such exertions. And why had he done it?

Because I had asked him to -- without any thought of his own health or his own safety.

This appalling thought confirmed something that has been going round in my mind since Christmas -- that in my arrogance and in my pleasure in manipulating and instructing others, I have asked them to undergo the most terrible hardships and risks while I have slept safe and warm in my bed. Throughout this business of Rebecca, and throughout the episodes which preceded it and involved the *Ceffyl Pren* jury, I have taken delight in dreaming up mad schemes and in persuading others to do my bidding in order to change dreams into reality. As a result of this, many of my nearest and dearest have been arrested and have had close shaves with the law. And Bryn, poor kind gentle fellow that he was, would never have got involved with Rebecca but for me, and would almost certainly be alive today.

I got up from my frozen armchair, and stumbled and slid back down the slope to the Plas. Once inside, I stamped my feet and shook the snow off my outer garments. "My goodness, Mistress," said Bessie. "You look like a monster recently descended from the highest and snowiest mountain in the world. But you have a rosy glow on your cheeks, and I daresay you are ready for a good dinner."

"Thank you, Bessie. Yes, I daresay I am." So we sat around the table -- Bessie, Liza, Gomer, Will, Gwenno and me. We tucked into our turkey broth. Six of us, the best of friends, as comfortable in each other's company as the oldest and gentlest of married couples. We did not need to say anything, but Liza saw that there was something on my mind, and so she said: "Are you minded to share your thoughts with us, Mistress?"

I looked up, swallowed hard, and placed my spoon on the table alongside my wooden soup bowl. "Very well, Liza," I said. "I think that would be wise. I have been thinking rather deeply lately, and have been making decisions. I will tell you about these decisions in a moment, but before I do that I want to beg of you not to ask me to change my mind. I will not be shifted from my course, and I do not wish to enter into an argument or a dispute with you, the dearest of my friends. Neither will I ask you for your involvement. I am about to face grave danger, and I have no right to expect that you will be involved in any manner whatsoever."

"Mistress, this sounds very mysterious and not a little ominous," said Bessie. "What eccentric plot have you hatched up this time? Please tell us at once, and put us out of our misery."

"Very well. I have decided that I will take part in one episode of gate destruction with Rebecca and her daughters. And if it is decided that the gate or the toll-collector's house should be burnt, I wish to be the one who starts the fire."

At first, my announcement was met with a stunned silence. Then they all started to talk at the same time. I grinned, and held my hand up, and at last the hubbub subsided. "I understand your reactions perfectly well, dear friends," I said. "You probably think that I was mad enough yesterday, and that the full moon has now brought me to such a state of derangement that I should be shut away in the lunatic asylum. So far as I can tell, I am still in full possession of my faculties. Now then, let me explain. This whole business started by chance, five years ago, when I encountered a *Ceffyl Pren* jury going about its lawful business and when I expressed rather more support for its endeavours than was wise. From that point on, I effectively became a part of a shady and subversive movement of poor men trying to remove injustice and to provide food for their starving children. My own growing political awareness pushed me further and further into this business. You know most of what has happened within the last couple of years, and indeed I have been reprimanded more than once, by you and my family, for my obsession with Rebecca and her daughters and for my role in writing tunes and conducting the choir. Yes, I agree that to some degree this role was thrust upon me, but that is a feeble justification, and so I also agree that I have enjoyed it more than was seemly for a respectable lady. But with my willing involvement a great fire has been ignited across the counties of South Wales, and it still rages. Hundreds of gates have been reduced to ashes, and thousands of men have been sucked into the inferno. And they and their families have suffered because of it. God knows how many will be transported to the living hell of Australia. Some men have died, and one old female gatekeeper has been murdered. Two of the men who have died used to sit with us around this table, summer and winter................"

I felt a break in my voice, and I had to stop for a moment. But Bessie, who was sitting at my side, placed her hand upon mine. I breathed deeply, and found the will to continue.

"I feel, dear friends, as I imagine a general must feel after he has sent his cavalry and his infantry into a long and bloody battle, during which he has sat upon some distant hill summit and watched them die. Well, Bryn and Bobby are dead, one of them brave and steadfast to the end, and the other a good man led astray by dark emotions. I cannot help it, and do not ask me to explain it, but I feel a heavy sense of responsibility for both deaths. I have to do something, particularly as a practical gesture in honour of Bryn's memory. And I never want it said of me, on Bryn's behalf or anybody else's, that I asked others to take terrible risks while I sat among the old blue rocks of Carningli in total safety, listening to skylarks and gazing at distant horizons. It may sound arrogant or presumptuous to you, Will and Gomer, but the feeling in my breast as I speak is perhaps something that only a woman can feel. Perhaps it has something to do with motherhood, or with the turbulence of female emotions. I doubt that it has anything to do with logic, or with the rules of rational behaviour......... Enough, enough. I will say no more. But please, all of you, respect my wishes for no dispute."

There was complete silence in the room for a very long time. The air was charged with a strange sort of raw energy, and I hardly dared to breathe. Then I realized that I was weeping, and so were all of the others. Even Will, the hardest of hard men, was dabbing his eyes with his neckerchief. At last, noses were blown, and throats were cleared, and eyes met, and we all managed to exchange feeble smiles.

"Why are we weeping?" I asked in a voice that was so husky that I hardly recognized it myself.

"Well, Mistress," explained Bessie, "I do not have any idea why you are weeping, but as for the rest of us, we are weeping because we love you. Is that reason enough?"

"Thank you, Bessie," I croaked. "Yes yes, I do believe it is."

ΩΩΩΩΩΩΩΩΩΩ

26th January 1844

Hen Galan was a strange occasion this year, celebrated in effect under the watchful eye of a military occupation force. Lieutenant Bodkins and his dragoons did their best to appear benign, but it will be a long time before they are forgiven for what happened to Bryn Williams, and there were a number of tense incidents in which I had to play the role of mediator. The lieutenant and I do not trust one another, but from my point of view it is no bad thing to seek to understand the enemy.

We have been coping as best we can with the winter weather, and with the extra tasks required to compensate for the fact that we are still one man short. I will employ a new cow-man within the next few weeks, but before doing that I have a certain mission to fulfill. For three weeks the excitement has been mounting in my own breast, and in the breasts of my servants. But within the last few days it has not been easy to keep my intentions secret from my own family, and if Brynach or Betsi find out what I have in mind either one of them would certainly truss me up in a straitjacket and keep me prisoner in some dark attic until such time as this Rebecca business is over and done with. That would indeed be a fate worse than death, and would subject my servants to quite terrible pressures.

So secrecy is the watchword. Yesterday I attended a meeting of Rebecca's daughters in a remote barn in the hills near Trecwn. Will and Gomer came with me. It was a packed meeting, with euphoria in the air since all the men in attendance knew that victory was now within Rebecca's grasp. But there was also apprehension, since the dragoons and Royal Marines are patrolling everywhere these days and since three more informers have recently fled the county after being named in public notices pinned to church doors. False messages about a meeting in Johnston found their way into the hands of the military officers earlier in the day, so they and their troops were far away and effectively out of action -- but with £500 rewards now on offer we could never be sure that the barn was free of traitors seeking to follow the path of the late lamented Bobby Morris. Everybody who went in through the door knew the password, and all necessary precautions were followed to the satisfaction of the leaders. I did not enter the meeting, but sat outside in the cowshed, where it was warm, with my face blackened and my body covered with my thickest woollen dress and muffled in heavy cloaks and shawls. I did not want to be recognized by anybody.

Plans were laid for the burning of a particularly troublesome gate at Scleddau, not far from the estate of Squire Alexander Williams. This gate was there against the wishes of the Squire. It belongs to the Fishguard

Trust, whose tally-holders and trustees appear to be incapable of learning lessons that would not challenge a two-year-old. If it takes five large bonfires to teach them that a gate at that location is not popular with the local people, said the chairman, let them have bonfire number five! That brought cheers, but according to Gomer an atmosphere of calm efficiency then prevailed, and detailed plans for the attack were drawn up. Then Will asked for the floor, and it was given to him. According to Gomer, he spoke with great passion, and he was respected because he was one of the very few men who had been taken into custody not once but twice by the constables on charges of participating in the riots. He said that he had made a special journey on that very evening in order to pick up *"Mam-gu Becca"*. She had attended many previous meetings, he said, but this evening she had come because she had a special request. She wished to assist in the destruction of the Scleddau gate.......

At this point, said Gomer, the meeting became chaotic, with fellows shouting "Impossible!" and "This is men's work!" and "Disaster will surely follow!" But most of those shouts came from fellows new to the campaign, and gradually other voices became stronger, shouting such things as "We have no rule to ban her!" and "If she wants to risk her neck, so be it!" and "If she is mad enough to do it, we should admire her and not condemn her!" I heard the clamour from the barn as I sat in the cosy cowshed, and assumed that some such altercation was in progress. Then, according to Gomer, some of the most senior of the men present reminded their confederates of the contribution which *"Mam-gu* Becca" had made, in the background, ever since the first riot at Efailwen. Some of them argued that I was the real Rebecca, and that it would be ungracious and ungentlemanly of those assembled to refuse my request. Then Will asked whether I might enter the meeting and speak for myself. They agreed to that, and Gomer came to fetch me. I gave the password and entered the barn.

I remained close to the great oak door adjacent to the threshing floor, and spoke from the shadows. I told them of my guilt for the deaths of honest men and women, and said that I wished to honour the memory of one man in particular through sharing the risks to which he had been exposed, and contributing in exactly the same way as all of the other daughters of Rebecca towards the ultimate triumph that was not far off. The men heard me out, and as soon as I stopped I knew that I would gain their approval. The barn with its massive high beams and barley sheaves piled against the walls buzzed like the inside of a giant beehive. Then they agreed formally to allow my participation, on condition that I followed the instructions of Rebecca to the letter. "And one last thing, *Mam-gu*, if I may," said the Chairman. "A few thousand people know about you, even if very few of us know your true identity. You are spoken of with the same reverence accorded to King Arthur in England and Llewelyn Fawr in Wales. The authorities know about you too, and would give anything to discover who you are, or to capture you red-handed. If word gets out about your participation in the gate destruction at Scleddau, you will become the greatest prize since this disorder began five years ago. If any of us is worth £500 to the authorities, the price on your head must be at least five thousand. You know that, *Mam-gu*?"

I nodded, and he continued. "That means that this disturbance will be for the highest ever stakes. There will never be a greater risk either for you or for any other of the daughters attending. Are you deterred?"

I swallowed hard, and said, in a shaky voice: "No, I am not. I will go through with it."

"Amen," said the Chairman. "We reconvene, dear daughters, at eleven o'clock, at the place agreed, on the evening of Thursday, the day after tomorrow. The password is Charlotte, and if there is any change you will hear of it. The meeting is closed."

So the rough fellows with their gaunt faces streamed past me out into the cold night air, and I was touched because many of them smiled and bowed as they passed me. We had the chaise parked around the corner, and soon we were on our way home. We did not talk much as we clattered along in the faint pools of light shed ahead of us from our candle lanterns. I knew now that I was into this business so deeply that it would take a miracle to get me out unharmed.

Ω Ω Ω Ω Ω Ω Ω Ω Ω Ω Ω

27th January 1844

It is late at night, and with twenty-four hours to go to my appointment with destiny, I am both terrified and exhausted. The terror might be understood by those who read these lines, but the exhaustion comes from a quite unexpected turn of events.

I have spent much of the day in meticulous planning with my servants -- regarding clothes, the best way to disguise my sidesaddle mount, the time required to reach the meeting point, which horse to use, which escape route to use in the event of an ambush, and so forth. Then a good deal of time and effort has gone into disposing of unwelcome visitors, including my own daughter Betsi and Dai Darjeeling, who has never before received such short shrift from his beloved Bessie. I have pretended that I have been suffering from a chill and a severe headache, and have promised all and sundry that they will be only too welcome on Friday, when I expect to feel much better. People are not stupid, and they must know that something is afoot, but my family and friends understand the need for discretion.

Things were going as well as might be expected when my dear friend Patty, from the Parrog, came running up the driveway. She was told that I was ill, but she would not accept that, and she pushed poor Gwenno aside, climbed up the stairs, and burst into my bedroom. I was sitting there beside my dressing room window, trying, with precious little success, to calm my nerves and compose my thoughts. "Why, Patty, how good to see you!" I mumbled, without much warmth.

"Mistress Martha," said she, still puffing from her exertions. "Please forgive me for this intrusion. It is unforgivable to arrive unannounced, but this is quite literally a matter of life and death. May I give you a message from one of your most implacable enemies?"

"I have rather a lot on my mind just now, Patty, and I am not sure that I could cope with hate and vilification..........."

"I will give you the message anyway. It is from old Constable John Wilson, a man who has always been your enemy and mine. He is currently on his death bed, and is not expected to survive the night."

"Good gracious, Patty. I did not even know he was still alive. Are you sure of this?"

"I have come straight from his cottage. It is best described as a hovel, and it is located on a patch of rough land at the bottom of the garden belonging to his son Samson."

"Another special constable, and too keen by half, according to my friends Abby and Halfpint."

"Never mind about him, Martha. The message is this: Samson is gone. Come at once, or you will die."

"Oh my God! What can this mean, Patty?"

"I am as mystified as you, Martha. But Samson is certainly gone. He rode out of town, along with Constable Lewis and all the other special constables, just as I received the message asking me to call on old Master Wilson."

I groaned and buried my face in my hands. "This gets worse and worse, Patty. Which road did they take?"

"The Fishguard Road. At least thirty of them, riding together."

"They never were very good at secrecy, Patty."

"I beg your pardon?"

"Never mind. I will explain some other time. Now then, we had better pay a compassionate visit to Master Wilson's hovel."

We rushed downstairs, and I asked Gomer to make the light chaise ready as quickly as possible. It took longer than I would have liked, since the ponies were all in one of the top fields, and by the time we got down to the Cilgwyn Road the dark shadows of dusk were prowling across the landscape.

When we arrived at the smoky and damp hovel which the ancient law officer called home I was surprised to see Shemi's white pony tethered outside. "Dad has beaten us to it, as ever," said Gomer with a grin. We knocked and entered, and found that the interior was lit by a cluster of candles on a low table near the far wall. There was a little box bed which contained a frail figure draped in blankets. Shemi was kneeling at his side, holding his hand and pronouncing some strange words which I did not recognize. He raised his head, gave us a faint smile, and said to the dying man: "Master Wilson, Mistress Martha has come at last. I will move away now, and let her hold your hand. That will be pleasant, will it not?" The figure nodded.

So I took Shemi's place at the side of the bed, and held Constable Wilson's little bony hand in mine. It had the coldness of death about it. I looked at his face, and it had the pallor of death about it. I was amazed that he was still alive. He managed to squeeze my hand, and whispered: "Come close, please, Mistress. I fear that even whispering is a mighty task for me............."

"Of course, Master Wilson. I am pleased to be here, and to bring you some comfort at this difficult time."

"Difficult? No no, Mistress. Dying is easy, I can assure you." And he managed a little grin. I smiled back. "I have things to say to you, and will try to stay alive until I have finished. Water, please."

I gave him a few sips of water. Then he breathed deeply and continued. "You may not remember it, Mistress, but I was one of those who scourged you through the streets of Newport when you were but a slip of a girl, and I was one of those who enjoyed the task. That was the most cowardly thing I ever did, Mistress, and it has gnawed away at me over all these years. When I came to realize, as the years passed, that you were truly a fine and honourable lady I tried over and again to apologize to you directly, but I never summoned up the courage. I always was a coward. So I swore to myself that one day, if I could, I would heal the stripes on your back and make full recompense to you. The stripes are still there, Mistress?"

"They are, Master Wilson, but the pain has long since gone."

"Will you forgive me, Mistress?"

"Of course. I have learnt how to forgive over the years, and I do it now, with all my heart."

He sighed, and was silent for so long that I thought he had breathed his last. But then his whispering continued. "You know, Mistress, that my son Samson is one of those sworn in as special constables in these difficult times?" I confirmed that I did know it. "Well, he and I have been estranged for many years. He is not a very nice man, Mistress, though I say it myself. But this morning, when he heard from somebody in town that I was dying, he tried to make his peace with me. He came blustering in, and said that he would make me the proudest father in the world and would show everybody in Pembrokeshire that the Wilsons of Newport are not people to be tampered with. I asked him what on earth he was talking about, Mistress, and he said that he would shortly deliver to the magistrates the greatest prize since the beginning of the Rebecca Riots, and would receive as a reward several thousand pounds. He whispered in my ear: "Father, I will deliver Rebecca herself, and I believe her to be

Mistress Morgan of Plas Ingli." I said that I did not believe it, but then he said he had been at a meeting near Trecwn last night, and had heard all the plans laid out for a riot at the Scleddau gate tomorrow, Thursday. He said that somebody called *Mam-gu* Becca had been there, and had asked permission to take part in the riot. This was granted, he said, and after the meeting the mysterious woman had set off for home in a chaise with Will Owen and Gomer Jenkins.........." The poor man coughed, and then managed to ask: "Was Samson right, Mistress? If not, I will stop."

I nodded. "Pray continue, Master Wilson."

"Well, your life is now in danger, Mistress. Samson went straight from here to tell the magistrates, and to send a message to Major Parlby in Haverfordwest. If there is a riot tomorrow at Scleddau, there will be an ambush by the military, and I fear that there could be great loss of life. I hope, Mistress, that in telling you all of this, I might save you and other good men from a miserable fate."

I squeezed his hand. "I think you have done that already, Master Wilson, and I thank you from the bottom of my heart. Yours has been the action of a brave and honourable man."

"Do you really think so? That brings balm to a troubled soul, Mistress. One last thing, if I may. Watch out for Nathaniel Evans Waunbayvil. Do you know him?"

"Why yes, Master Wilson. A poor and honest fellow, so I believe."

"Not so honest as you might think, Mistress. The chinking of golden sovereigns is too much for him. He was at the meeting in Trecwn, and got Samson in by giving him the password. He is a traitor who will sell his friends."

"How do you know all of this?"

"Samson told me everything, Mistress. He was in a very bragging and expansive mood, and intent upon impressing me. He assumed that I would take all his words into my grave. He was not a bit interested in my state of health....."

"Come now, Master Wilson. He is your son, and of course he loves you and is concerned about you."

"If only, if only, Mistress Martha........." Then the poor fellow coughed again, and a shadow passed across his face. His breathing was very shallow, and getting shallower with every breath. I asked if I might give him some more water, or anything else, but he shook his head. "I am slipping away, Mistress," he murmured. "Bring my son to justice. You have my consent in that. Have I done a good thing today, besides healing some ancient wounds?"

"Yes, and yes again, Master Wilson. It is not in my power to confer blessings or to bring peace to those who need it, but I have love in my heart, and that is mine to give away, to those who have won my respect and my affection." So I leaned over him and kissed him on the cheek, and Constable Wilson smiled faintly, and passed away.

We three old friends sat where we were for some minutes. There were no tears, for the dead man was very old, and I suppose he would have died long since had it not been for the ministrations and companionship of Shemi and a few others. But then Shemi put his hand on my shoulder and said: "May he rest in peace, Martha. I heard some of what he said to you. By the sound of it, you have work to do. Go and do it. Patty and I will take care of arrangements here. And do not worry about either Samson Wilson or Nathaniel Evans Waunbayvil. I will look after them." I looked at my dear friend the Wizard of Werndew with questions in my eyes, but he simply pulled me to my feet and pushed me out through the door.

Gomer was still there, sitting patiently in the hedge and in the darkness while the pony nibbled at assorted herbs and grasses a short distance away. He lit the candle lanterns, and we trotted home as fast as we dared. On the way we made five stops, and at each one I gave the following message of six words: "Parlby knows. Boncath instead. Password Delilah." I trust that this message will go through the usual channels to all of the men who are likely to turn out tomorrow. Others will already have realized that a betrayal has occurred, simply from the sight of special constables galore rushing off in the direction of Fishguard, where they will no doubt be given a full briefing tomorrow by Major Parlby and other officers. I now have to place all of my trust in the efficiency and effectiveness of our system for passing messages. Now I will try to sleep, but in truth I feel like a prisoner in a condemned cell, on the night before an execution. I daresay that I will spend the night staring at the ceiling, listening to the moaning wind and longing for the dawn..............

ΩΩΩΩΩΩΩΩΩΩ

Inferno

29th January 1844

Friday afternoon. A winter gale is raging outside, but here in my bedroom it is warm enough, and I am well contented with life, for I have been to the top of my mountain and have returned relatively unscathed.

Will, Gomer and I set off at different times and by different routes, heading tortuously towards Boncath. I did not want their company at the Boncath gate, and indeed I specifically forbade it, but they refused to follow my orders, and insisted on coming. In truth I was glad of it, for I was very nervous indeed. As my horse trotted along the rough lanes around Eglwyswrw and Pantyderi at dusk I went through our plans over and again, seeking to consider every possible eventuality but knowing full well that nothing would work out quite as planned. I was greatly relieved when I came to a lonely cottage at the roadside near Blaenffos and saw three candle flames in the darkness, one of them shining through red glass and the other two white. The three of us met inside the cottage, which belonged to one Bowen Owen, who was yet another distant cousin of Will's. Between them, my two servants had carried some bread and cheese for our supper, a flagon of fruit cordial (since I had placed a strict ban on alcohol consumption for the first time in my life), all the old clothes needed, a bag of soot and a small sack of straw, some pitch and tallow for our torches, and the tools required for gate destruction. We ate our supper in silence, such was the tension in the air, and as we did so we saw through the filthy smoke-stained window adjacent to the roadway a succession of faint lights, some of them carried by men riding horses and ponies, and others moving on foot. All were heading towards Boncath

Then we took off our outer garments and transformed ourselves into the daughters of Rebecca. Petticoats and skirts, shawls and jackets, aprons and cloaks were dragged out of the clothes bag. They were so filthy and ragged that even a vagrant would have been ashamed to appear in them. After one more wearing, I thought, these things are fit only for the bonfire. I wanted to wear a very beautiful red silk turban with golden ostrich feathers on my head, but Will would have none of it, and said that he would not allow me to wear anything that might attract attention. So he wore the turban instead, and told me to wear a very battered grey felt hat. That was the first time in my life that I have accepted the fashion advice of a gentleman, but in retrospect it was the soundest advice I ever got.

Gomer wore an old straw bonnet that once belonged to his mother Sian. Then we stuffed straw beneath our hats, blackened our faces and necks with soot, and made ready our torches. I took a light axe and strapped it to my back, and Will and Gomer carried sledge hammers on the basis that they would be far more useful in the event that the toll-keeper's cottage had to come down as well as the gate.

We were ready. Will looked me in the eye and held my hands in his. "Are you still sure you want to do this, Mistress?" he asked. "If you want my opinion, I would still prefer you to wait here in cousin Bowen's cottage until we return."

"I still want to do it, Will. So, shall we set off? We do not want to be late."

"Very well, Mistress. We will do our best to protect you. But from this point on, not a single word from you, if you please. Can you go two whole hours without speaking?"

I grinned, and nodded, and we set off. By half past ten we had joined forces with many others heading for the gate, and as the crowd of beautiful daughters increased I felt less and less self-conscious about the fact that I was the only rider mounted sidesaddle. So voluminous and grotesque were the costumes of many of my "sisters" that many of them could have been riding in female style as well. I recognized a good many of those heading for the gate, in spite of their disguises. Some of them met my eye, and nodded in acknowledgement. Will and Gomer stuck close to my side, but occasionally they entered into deep conversations with other fellows, and I saw a good deal of gesturing and glancing in my direction. I knew that they were making arrangements for my safe delivery, and I loved them for their loyalty and their gentlemanly concern.

Suddenly we were at the assembly point, and two daughters took each new arrival to one side and asked for the password. "Delilah," I said, in something approximating to a bass whisper. Then I was swept into the wild euphoria which must have characterized every riot since the first destruction of the gate at Efailwen. Rebecca was there, resplendent upon her white stallion, dressed in silks and satins and wearing a magnificent red and green turban upon her head. She wielded a heavy sword in her hand, and as she waved it over her head it glinted and gleamed in the light of sixty candle lanterns and a faint moon. She had around her four sisters whom I took to be her lieutenants. I did not recognize her, but I knew her voice as that of the chairman of the Trecwn meeting which I had addressed. That having been said, his identity is still a mystery to me, and that is as it should be.   I looked around, and estimated that there were maybe twenty sisters on horseback, and around forty on foot. There would certainly have been twice that number, had it not been for the betrayal and the change of plans. But that was a blessing, I thought, since large numbers of men always seem to walk into trouble or create trouble for themselves.

Rebecca held her hand up, and her daughters became quiet. "Welcome, my children," she said in her deep bass voice. "We have work to do, and will do it here if we cannot do it at Scleddau. Some of us know the traitors, and they will be dealt with. That is for the future. As for tonight, is the orchestra present?" Several musical instruments were waved in the air, and a ripple of laughter passed through the crowd. "Good, good. You may play when I give the order. Now then, our plan of action. The gate is about half a mile ahead of us, on the west side of the village. I have been through it today, and it will come down easily. The gatekeeper is a miserable fellow, but he has a wife and two young children and I want them unharmed if possible. If any of you, my dear children, are carrying firearms, I want them to be left here and collected afterwards........."

"But Mother, we always carry our shotguns. No shot. Just powder, you understand......"

"Silence!" hissed Rebecca, with menace in her voice. "I will not tolerate dissent, and for this evening, I make the rules. And I make all my rules with good reason. Leave all firearms here. Now! In a pile in the hedge, if you please."

And she said not another word until all the shotguns and pistols had been deposited, with a good deal of grumbling, close to where her white stallion stood at the roadside. Then she detailed four of her daughters to mount guard over the weapons. They grumbled too, since they wanted to smash down a gate, but they obeyed. "Now then," continued the leader, "we have wasted time. And we are in danger of losing our greatest weapon, which is surprise. Is the western watch in place, and equipped with signals?"

"Yes, Mother."

"And the eastern watch, with signals?"

Inferno

"Yes, Mother."

"Very well. Finally, no gratuitous violence. We hurt timber and stone, not flesh and blood. No names, whatever happens. Faithful unto death?"

"Faithful unto death, Mother! Faithful unto death!" rang out the shout from the beautiful daughters, as they cheered and waved their axes and their billhooks and sledge hammers in the air. "Light torches and leave candle lanterns here," shouted Rebecca. We all obeyed instructions. "To the gate!" said she, and off we went, with the riders in the middle of the road and with the walkers on the flanks of the procession. "Orchestra, commence serenade!" said she, and somebody started thumping a heavy drum while others tootled on their bugles and trumpets, and somebody even started crashing upon a pair of cymbals. It was a truly tuneless serenade, but not devoid of a certain grotesque charm.

So the weird and noisy procession proceeded to the gate, and as we rounded the last bend in the lane and brought it into sight we saw that the gatekeeper was standing in the middle of the road, flanked by two special constables. He looked very belligerent, and they looked frightened. I noticed, from my position some way back in the host of protestors, that there were lights in the windows of the little cottage adjacent to the gate, and that there were children peeping out with frightened eyes. Rebecca rode right up to the gatekeeper, and demanded to be let through. He refused, and after a short altercation he was seized by Rebecca's sisters and trussed up with a rope which somebody miraculously produced. The two constables fled off along the road into the village, and Rebecca let them go.

"Now then," said Rebecca. "Ask your wife and children to come out, and they will not be harmed." At this, the gatekeeper spat in Rebecca's face. This would have stirred most Rebeccas into a fury, I thought, but not this one. She simply shook herself, and said "Oh my daughters, my beautiful complexion is destroyed. What shall I do?"

"Leave him to us, dear Mother, while you proceed upon your lawful way," said a particularly well-built daughter, who then proceeded, with several others, to take the fellow to one side and to give him a severe beating. It was not pleasant to watch, and caused the wife and children inside the cottage to start screaming uncontrollably. Without any further instructions from Rebecca, several of the daughters then entered the cottage and escorted the wife and two children out into the street. They were marched, gently enough, fifty yards down the street, and were told to sit at the roadside. Two of the daughters watched over them while other daughters carried furniture and belongings out of the cottage and piled them up at the roadside. This took maybe ten minutes, and I could see that Rebecca was getting agitated as time slipped through her fingers. Throughout this part of the protest, Gomer and Will stayed very close to me. Then Rebecca went up to the gate and raised her sword. "No time for pantomimes tonight, dear daughters, but what has to be done?"

"Away with it, Mother!"

Then, much to my surprise, Rebecca turned to me, and said *"Mam-gu, the honour is yours."* There was a great cheer, and Gomer and Will helped me off my horse and led me up to the gate. They allowed me to take the first strike at it with my axe. I made no impression on the stout oak timbers whatsoever, but the daughters laughed, and suddenly they were all at work with their saws, axes and sledge hammers. Even the stoutest of gates could not have withstood the assault, and in about fifteen minutes the gate was in splinters and the gateposts were sawn through at ground level. I was exhausted and covered in sweat, and realized that my black face was seriously smudged as a result of my exertions. The fragments of wood were piled high in the middle of the road, and then Rebecca surprised me again by saying: "All will be in conflagration, and *Mam-gu* will light the flame." She handed me a burning torch, and without thinking I tossed it onto the pile of wood. Soon the wax and tar spread onto the oak splinters, and ignited them, and in a few minutes the mighty fire was ablaze. The daughters cheered, and the bugles blared, and the drums thundered, and I started to enjoy myself.

Suddenly there was a shout from one of the daughters. "Mother!" she cried. "A signal, to the north!" We all looked up into the sky, and saw the last sparks of a red signal rocket, in the sky and far away.

"Than means troops have been spotted, probably approaching over Llechryd Bridge," said Rebecca. "Never fear. They are still several miles away. Still time to deal with the house. Are all of the possessions out?"

"Yes, Mother."

"Very well. Collapse the roof, and then ignite the timbers when they are down. Quickly now!"

And her daughters, considerably hindered by their beautiful gowns, clambered all over the flimsy structure, sending slates flying off the roof and at last levering off the joists and the rafters. But before they had finished the task, another shout went up. "A second signal, Mother! This time from the eastern watch!" I looked up and saw another red rocket arching across the night sky, leaving behind it a trail of white smoke and red sparks. It was very much closer than the first rocket. "*Diawl!*" swore Rebecca, registering concern for the first time in her voice. "That must mean dragoons at the gallop. If they had been fusiliers or yeomanry they could not possibly have come so far at such speed. We have two minutes. Decoy group, remain in place and execute our plan. *Mam-gu* and the rest of you, follow me!"

Our intrepid leader spurred her horse and trotted up the road for fifty yards, and then turned off into a dark lane overhung by ancient trees. There was pandemonium as assorted daughters sprinted after her or looked for their horses. At first I could not find mine, and as I cast my eyes around the scene of our devastation I saw that the cottage had still not been set on fire. So with my left hand I grabbed a burning timber from the bonfire that had once been a gate, and flung it in through the space where there had once been a front door. I was vaguely aware of a terrible pain in the palm of my hand. Then I was swept off my feet by Gomer and flung across the front of Will's horse. I was utterly confused, and lost my felt hat in the process. Will galloped off after Rebecca, with me dumped across the horse's neck like a sack of potatoes. I was aware of Gomer galloping alongside. We got round the corner into the cul-de-sac just in time, as a troop of dragoons appeared in the distance at the gallop, with sabres drawn. I slipped to the ground and peeped round the corner with many others, protected by the darkness. At a signal the mounted daughters who were milling about close to the site of the burning gate whipped up their mounts and galloped off along the Blaenffos road, heading for the location of our assembly point. The dragoons followed them helter-skelter, although their horses were clearly very tired. When I saw this I moaned, fearing a total disaster, but Will grinned and said: "Never fear, Mistress. We have planned for almost all eventualities."

Then I winced with pain, and Will noticed it, and I had to admit that my left hand was burnt. He knew what do do, and ran out onto the main street. He grabbed a bucket from the pile of possessions belonging to the toll collector and his family, filled it up with ice-cold water from the cattle trough forty yards away, and ran back to me, spilling half of it all over the road. There was still enough left for me to submerge my hand, and that brought blessed relief. Will swore when he realized that his actions had been observed by the toll-collector's wife and children, and when he realized that injured rioters are liabilities, certainly until they are back in the safety of their own homes and probably later on as well. "I am sorry, Will," I moaned. "It was stupid of me to pick up that burning timber..........."

"Well, Mistress, we all do stupid things in the heat of the moment. You will at least be pleased to know, at any rate, that the cottage is well and truly alight."

Then I heard two gunshots in the distance. My heart sank, but then a green rocket went up into the sky. Immediately Rebecca, who was sitting patiently on her stallion awaiting just such an occurrence, spurred her steed out into the street again. We all followed, with me among the walking daughters since I had lost my horse. "Right, my daughters, home with you! You have done a good night's work, and deserve to sleep well. But take care, look out for lights and keep your ears skinned. Other soldiers could be coming from other directions. Those who have things at the assembly point, follow me!"

I spotted my horse further up the main street, and was amazed that she had not bolted into Carmarthenshire, what with all the fires and bugles and drums and galloping dragoons. Gomer fetched her for me, and helped me to mount. Then we followed Rebecca back along the Blaenffos road. As we trotted away, I looked back and saw the gatekeeper's wife in tears, with two wailing children in tow, running across the road to where her battered husband lay, trussed up and bleeding, in the roadside ditch. It was an image of such desperate poignancy that it did not leave me for the whole of our journey home, and it has still not left me. Perhaps it will be burnt into my soul just as a burning timber has burnt itself into the palm of my hand. More scars, as if I do not have enough already.

When we got back to the assembly point, an extraordinary sight met our eyes. Eight dragoons, looking very battered and sorry for themselves, sat in the middle of the road, trussed up like Christmas turkeys. Their sabres were stuck into the roadside turf. Two dead horses lay not far away, but the other six military mounts were tethered at the side of the road, with their heads down, drinking dirty water from the roadside ditch.

They looked utterly exhausted. Soon everything became clear. Rebecca had scouted out this assembly point earlier in the day, and had chosen it because it was ideal for an ambush. A heavy trip rope had been laid across the road by the daughters who had been left behind to look after firearms and lanterns. The decoy group had galloped across it, but then it had been pulled up just as the dragoons arrived, causing a gigantic tumbled mass of horses and men to come crashing to the ground. It was a miracle that nobody was killed. Almost all of the soldiers lost their sabres as they fell, but when they looked up they were confronted by a group of beautiful daughters armed to the teeth with shotguns, rifles and pistols. They had no option other than to surrender, and in any case they were too dazed to fight. So they were tied up tightly and all of their weapons were confiscated as souvenirs. Two of the horses were so badly injured as they fell that they had to be shot. Then the green rocket had been fired to signify that all was well.

We all gathered up our belongings from the pile at the side of the road. Rebecca, having ascertained that none of the soldiers was badly injured, and having ensured that they were as comfortable as trussed up men can be, requested that eight of the daughters might donate their straw bonnets to a good cause. They obliged, and she then placed a pretty bonnet on each of the soldiers' heads, and tied each one neatly beneath each stubbly chin. The fellows looked perfectly charming, and we all played the fool and squealed with admiration. Then Becca waved her sword in the air for one last gesture. "Enough of tomfoolery," she shouted. "Goodnight, my daughters! Sleep well, and forget everything!" And she galloped off with her lieutenants along a little lane heading, I assumed, towards Cilgerran. Within a few minutes every trace of her occupation of the site, and of her impeccable ambush, was gone. Will, Gomer and I trotted off by the faint light of the new moon towards cousin Bowen's cottage, in a thoroughly good humour. But we were almost too complacent. There was one last scare for us, for on one of our frequent listening stops we heard heavy hooves coming towards us and knew that this could only be another troop of dragoons or yeomanry cavalry. We immediately extinguished our lanterns, and Will found a field gate and opened it. We tried to get our horses into the field, but for some reason mine became excited, and as the sound of the hooves became closer I slid out of the saddle with the intention of leading and cajoling her through the gate. As

Inferno

I hit the ground with my right foot I twisted my ankle over, and fell with a cry of pain. I let go the reins, but luckily Will grabbed them while Gomer grabbed me and bundled me into the field. That was not a moment too soon, for a large troop of maybe twenty soldiers immediately galloped past within a few feet of our hiding place. Our horses became restless and difficult to hold, but by then the soldiers were past and we were safe.

There is not much more to tell. We left all of our fashionable costumes and headgear -- apart from my lost hat -- in Bowen's cottage, and by now they will have gone up in flames on his garden bonfire. He is a kind fellow, and strapped up my damaged hand and my swollen ankle. Our soot and remaining straw was dumped. We each had a thorough wash with hot soapy water. When we arrived home, again by different routes, shortly before dawn, Gomer and Will went to their own cottages and I turned up at Brithdir since I needed an alibi. When I rattled Betsi and Ioan up out of bed they were both furious, and they were even more furious when I told them what I had been up to and showed them what sort of a state I was in. Anyway, they gave me a bed for what remained of the night, and will probably forgive me in due course.

Now I am too tired to continue, and my battle injuries are both proving to be very painful. I must try to catch up on lost sleep, and have given Bessie and Liza strict instructions that I must not be disturbed.

ΩΩΩΩΩΩΩΩΩΩΩ

14. Smouldering Embers

30th January 1844

I have felt thoroughly miserable throughout the day. I have had a drumming headache, I have felt cold and drained, and I have been sick several times. That makes me angry, since I take pride in hardly ever falling ill. Bessie tells me that I should not be surprised at the screams of protest coming from my body, since I am sixty-five years old and have had to cope with more exertions than a circus tumbler in the last few days and since my emotions have been shaken up as never before. Shemi has been to see me, and has started work on repairing the damage. While he treated my hand and foot injuries with strange poultices and potions he insisted on hearing all about the adventure at Boncath. I told him everything, since there is no point at all in trying to hide things from wizards. Now he has gone off to treat two others who suffered injuries during the same disturbance, and he has promised to come back later and cheer me up.

To some degree my spirits have been lifted by the good news which has filtered in from various quarters. Not one of Rebecca's daughters was taken by the authorities, and there were no serious injuries. The Light Dragoons of the 43rd Regiment have become a laughing stock, since most of them spent a fruitless night lying behind hedges near the Scleddau gate, while eight of their comrades were captured by Rebecca at Boncath. What is even more distressing, with respect to army morale, is that those poor fellows were found and released from their trussed-up elegance not by their own regimental comrades but by the amateur soldiers of the Cardigan Yeomanry. They will never hear the last of that, and I am cheered up considerably by the thought of the conversations which must be taking place in officers' quarters throughout West Wales at this very moment. I am cheered up even more by the recollection of what happened yesterday on my return to the Plas, and I must put it down in writing.

I wanted to get back to the beloved place by ten in the morning, since if I had left it any later Bessie and the other servants would have been sick with worry. I left my own horse at Brithdir for the moment, and was given a lift home by Ioan in his chaise. As we entered the driveway we saw that we had visitors. There were about half a dozen soldiers standing in the yard, and two others stood to attention on either side of the back door. A group of magnificent horses was tethered outside the stables, and I was relieved to see that both Will and Gomer were assisting a couple of army grooms in the business of feeding and watering them. This looked like an important visit, and Ioan wanted to turn round and take me straight back to Brithdir, but I was still filled with a mad excitement in spite of my lack of sleep. After checking that no soot was visible on my face or neck, I decided to confront the enemy.

Bessie was looking out through the kitchen window, and saw us arrive. She came rushing out, and although we were closely observed she could not resist throwing her arms around me. "Oh, Mistress Martha, thank God you are safe," she gasped, in Welsh. "Will and Gomer were not sure............."

I admonished my beloved servant, again in Welsh. "And why on earth should I not be? Little visits to friends are perfectly safe these days, now that the roads are so well guarded by our friends in the army. And some of them are so intent on looking after us well that they have even learnt the language of heaven. Is that not correct, gentlemen?" Most of the soldiers looked blank, but one of the door sentries caught my eye. He smiled and nodded. "Indeed, Mistress," he said, in perfect Carmarthenshire Welsh. "Some of us were even born in Wales, and are proud of it!"

Having thus encouraged Bessie to be more careful in future, I asked her who my visitors were. "Colonel Sir James Frederick Love, Mistress, and Major John Parlby. They are in the drawing room drinking tea, and wish to see you the very moment that you arrive home."

"I will have to deprive them of that pleasure, Bessie. I have been travelling, and these old injuries of mine have caused me a little bother. I need a bath and a complete change of clothes. Kindly inform them that I will be with them in approximately half an hour."

She curtseyed, and while she conveyed my message to my guests I trotted upstairs with Liza hot on my heels. She filled up a bathtub for me, and I soaked myself for ten minutes while she washed my hair and scrubbed soot off my neck and face. I even had soot on my bosom, even though I could not imagine how it might have got there. The injury on the palm of my hand was giving me excruciating pain, and on the site of the burn there was now a blister the size of a sovereign. But I had to disregard it, for my mind was buzzing with speculations. I assumed that the two officers were not in possession of either a search warrant or an arrest warrant, or they would have made that plain from the beginning. I assumed that they had probably come straight from the abortive ambush attempt at Scleddau, and were in possession of information fed to them by Samson Wilson. I also assumed that they were in possession of hard material provided to the magistrates by Henry Eynon and Bobby Morris and also some speculative nonsense provided by Squire Owen and others. They will have done their homework well, and they will probably seek confirmation from me, through loose words or unguarded comments, that I am *Mam-gu* Becca. I also assumed that they would not yet have caught up with what happened at Boncath, since the army's communications network is much slower than mine.

When I hobbled into the drawing room wearing my favourite red velvet dress and with my hair freshly washed and pinned up high, I began to feel nervous. I gave as deep a curtsy as my swollen ankle would allow. The gentlemen's uniforms were far more colourful than my dress, and as they bowed their spurs chinked and their medals and buttons gleamed like the midsummer sun. We introduced ourselves with due formality.

I was determined not to be intimidated by either the stout Colonel, with his white hair, his ruddy complexion and his abundant side whiskers, or by his slim and pompous junior partner. "Gentlemen, I bid you a warm welcome to Plas Ingli," I said in my sweetest voice. "I must apologize for my absence when you arrived here this morning, but since I was expecting no visitors over these few days I took the opportunity of a visit to an old friend of mine. I might have stayed away longer, but an old injury to my hand proved unexpectedly bothersome, and then I twisted an ankle on dismounting from my horse. So I decided to return home for medical treatment and a few days of peace and quiet."

Having thus made my excuses, and having encouraged my visitors to feel both guilt and sympathy for me in my painful predicament, I showed them my bandaged hand and smiled benignly while their apologies and excuses came tumbling out. In truth I heard nothing of what either of them said, for I was thinking three steps ahead. "Colonel, you must be hungry. Have you breakfasted, and has my wonderful Bessie kept you supplied with tea?"

Smouldering Embers

"Do not worry about us, Mistress Martha. We had an early breakfast, at a place called Scleddau. You know it, perhaps?"

"Of course. A pretty little village, but too far from the sea for my liking............."

"And encumbered by a very inconvenient tollgate, so they say," added Major Parlby, with his eyes gleaming.

"They do say that, sir. But its presence makes no difference to me. I am a Fishguard Trust tally-holder, and I go through without any cost whenever I pass that way."

The two military gentlemen exchanged glances, and I saw at once that the Colonel did not like the crude approach favoured by the Major. "Quite, quite," said the old fellow. There was an awkward silence, and I took the opportunity to fill up their tea-cups from the fine china tea-pot on the stand near the fireplace. There appeared to be a reluctance to get to the point, and both of these senior military men appeared to be intimidated and even shy. I concluded that they were not very used to dealing with women. So I took the initiative, and directed my attention towards the Colonel. I looked him straight in the eye and said; "Sir James, you must forgive me, but I am tired and I will appreciate it if you will tell me the purpose of your visit. You have not come all this way simply to enjoy my tea. I will ask you a straight question. Are you here because you are following up on certain nonsense fed to you by Constable Samson Wilson?"

The poor fellow spluttered into his whiskers and became red in the face, while the Major's previously inscrutable expression was transformed into a scowl. Just then an angel must have flown across Carningli, for a miracle happened. There was a clatter of hooves in the yard, and all conversation came to a halt. The three of us got up and went to the window, and we saw a soldier dressed in the blue and grey of the Light Dragoons leaping down from his horse. There was a good deal of gesticulating and pointing, and the messenger banged on the kitchen door. Bessie opened it, and from our place in the drawing room we could hear him asking for Major Parlby. Then there were heavy booted footsteps on the passage floor, followed by a knock on the door.

"Come inside!" said I.

Bessie opened it, and announced that there was a messenger, come to see Major Parlby. The young fellow stepped inside, clicked his heels, saluted most beautifully, and said while staring straight ahead, out through the window: "Good morning, Mistress! Good morning, Colonel, and good morning, sir! Excuse this rude interruption of your meeting, sir, but there is an urgent message from the Cardigan troop, sir! Becca took down the Boncath gate last night and burnt the cottage, sir! No arrests and no serious injuries, but eight dragoons were captured and their weapons all taken, sir! They were trussed up, and left in the middle of the road, sir! With pretty bonnets on their heads, sir!"

I was so utterly fascinated with this young fellow's staccato style of delivery, with his voice rising at the end of each sentence, that I was quite unprepared for the final line of his wondrous message, and although I pride myself on my delicate manners and restraint, I could not prevent a loud guffaw. I saw that the Colonel was himself fighting like the devil to suppress a fit of the giggles, and he had to fight even harder when he saw that the Major's face was like thunder. "Damn it, man," hissed Master Parlby, "what is the situation now? Am I needed?"

"Yes indeed, sir! The Cardigan Yeomanry rescued our men and took possession of the bonnets, sir! They are claiming them as military trophies, sir! Lieutenant Bodkins requires your assistance in their recovery, sir! As soon as may be convenient, sir, at Cardigan Camp, sir!"

At this, Major Parlby groaned, and I thought that the poor fellow might burst into tears. But the Colonel patted him on the back and said: "You had better go, Major. You will seldom have a more interesting military mission, I daresay, and your diplomatic skills will be tested to the limit. I will see you back at Carmarthen HQ. Good day to you, sir!" And the Colonel saluted smartly, and received a salute in return. For my part, I received a rather grudging thanks for my hospitality, and a stiff bow, before the wretched fellow went rushing off with his messenger. Five of the other soldiers were his, and he summoned them to join him in the yard. A couple of minutes later, all of the soldiers of the 43rd Regiment were gone at the gallop towards Temple Bar and the Cardigan Road.

The old Colonel shook his head more in sorrow than anger as he watched them go. "The major has not had a good twenty-four hours," he said. "First of all, he dragged me and all the other senior commanders off to Scleddau, together with two hundred soldiers, in order to witness the apprehension of the most precious prize yet in the campaign against Rebecca. And now this bonnet business at Boncath. The reputation of his regiment is at stake, Mistress Martha. At Scleddau, he promised that he and his commanders would catch a certain *Mam-gu Becca*, who was the real organizing brains behind the disturbances. A woman, Mistress Martha! Can you believe such a thing?"

"Quite extraordinary, sir. I can hardly credit it."

"Quite so. At any rate, there we were behind this hedge for the whole night, in the freezing cold. The most exciting thing to happen was an argument between two tawny owls in some distant wood. So he got a good ticking off for yet more appalling intelligence. In his defence, he brought forward this fellow called Constable Simpson Samson, or some such thing..........."

"Samson Wilson, sir."

"Quite, quite. This fellow claims to have been at the very meeting where the plans were laid, some days since, and where this woman put in an appearance and pleaded to take part in the destruction of the Scleddau gate! Can you believe that, Mistress?"

"Unbelievable, Colonel. Only a woman suffering from some strange derangement would ever contemplate such a thing."

"Never was a truer word spoken, Mistress. So I sent Sumpson Simpson packing, and told him to keep his intelligence to himself in future."

"I do happen to know the fellow, Colonel. He suffers from wild delusions and fantasies, and is entirely untrustworthy. His old father, who died just a few days since, said this to me with his dying breath."

"Most unfortunate. The son is a double agent?"

"He probably thinks so. But his messages are fit only for books of fairy tales, and not even a little child should take them seriously."

There was a long pause, and to my astonishment I saw the old Colonel grow visibly older before my eyes. His shoulders became slumped and round, and he hung his head. I was surprised to see that he had a massive burnt area on his bald pate, and I knew that he had done his fair share of fighting.

"Intelligence has always been our problem, Mistress Martha. We -- and by that I mean the army -- are beaten. We have already lost this war with Becca because our intelligence has not been intelligent. Much of it has been stupid, stupid! We do not have the people with us, and without the people we cannot win, no matter how many troops we have on the ground. I have said this repeatedly to the Home Secretary, Mistress, and I pray to God that some day he will listen to what I am saying. The grievances of the poor farmers are deep and terrible, and every day I am supposed to try and suppress these men as they try to get their deaf and blind political leaders to receive their messages. I am not surprised that they attack gates and try to burn down workhouses........"

"Be careful, Colonel. Your words are safe with me, but you are too kind a man to be a soldier, and I am worried for you."

He laughed. "Don't you worry about me, Mistress Martha. I am already put out to grass, and soon I will be retired. I cannot do much harm to myself." He shook his head and said quietly, almost as if he was talking to himself: "Good intelligence is the key. Now that was a messy business, the War on the Peninsula, but the intelligence was exemplary, and our double agents were better than those working for the French, and so we won. It was touch and go, but we made it in the end because we knew more about their deployments than they knew about ours. There was this fellow who worked for me...... fluent Spanish and French speaker........ badly injured in some shipwreck or other, and abandoned by his woman in Wales. From somewhere in West Wales, as I recall. Bravest man who ever lived, Mistress. Now what was his name? Damn it, age is a terrible thing, and it eats away at the memory........."

"Owain Laugharne, Colonel," said I, suddenly as weak as a day-old kitten, with tears streaming down my face.

"Yes indeed, Mistress! That is it! He had several names, but that was his real one! How did you know.........."

His voice trailed away as he looked at me and saw my tears. I tried to control myself, but I could not. So the old soldier, whom I once referred to in the pages of this diary as a butcher, and whom I had never met before, came and put his arms around me and let me weep onto his medalled breast. Bessie heard me wailing and came rushing in to the drawing room in order to effect a rescue, but the old man stopped her in her tracks with the gentlest and most compassionate of looks, and she let me weep. At last I came up for air, and gave Bessie a feeble smile. The Colonel gave me his kerchief, and I wiped my red eyes.

"Please forgive me, Colonel," I said. "And forgive me, Bessie, if you will. I was certainly not assaulted by this gallant military gentleman. I fear that I was overcome because I suddenly realized that we have shared one particular friend, long ago. Master Owain Laugharne, double agent and love of my life."

Bessie's eyes widened, as did those of the Colonel. Then she demonstrated why civilization would collapse without her. She curtseyed and said: "Sir James, I perceive that you and my Mistress have further talking to do. I have a light dinner prepared, and if it is my Mistress's wish, I will shortly serve it in the dining room."

"Of course it is my wish, Bessie. The Colonel cannot go outside to face his soldiers with all that wetness on his breast in any case. Pretty bonnets, and now tears! My God, what is the world coming to?"

The Colonel laughed, and protested, but we overruled his protests, and then convinced him that there was enough in the oven for four soldiers as well. So he and I sat in the dining room and talked of old times, while the soldiers and the servants ate in the kitchen. We talked of my beloved Owain, and I discovered a good deal about him that he had never articulated to me himself. We talked of politics, and protests, and social change, and of the pending disaster in Ireland, and of a good deal else besides. At last I was so exhausted that I could hardly keep my eyes open, and he reminded me that he had not slept either during the previous night. We both laughed, and before he left the dining room he asked: "Mistress Martha, I am going to ask you to trust me. That old injury on your hand. Not a burn, I hope?"

"Yes, Colonel, as it happens."

"Just you take care of it, and keep it well covered. Domestic accidents are all too common these days. And your recent visit to a friend -- in a pleasant part of the county, I trust?"

"Yes indeed. The Boncath area has very pleasing rolling country, and I like it well enough. But it lacks decent mountains, and I am minded to stay at home from now on."

"I am relieved to hear it, both for your sake and mine."

He grinned, thanked me profusely for my hospitality, and kissed my hand. As the light of late afternoon faded away, we exchanged farewells as a pair of lifelong friends might have done, and he and his escort trotted away down the driveway towards Newport on their magnificent military horses. I waved, and pondered on the stupidity of the labels "friend" and "enemy". I have been betrayed by friends and befriended by enemies, and I am not quite sure any longer what this world is coming to.

3rd February 1844

The strands which go to make up Rebecca's shawl are being woven together in a most extraordinary way, but I am too close to the weave to fully appreciate the pattern.

Following the visit of Colonel Love and Major Parlby there was a cascade of speculation locally about what their intentions might have been. It was widely assumed, when news first began to circulate about the visit at 8 o'clock on the morning of 29th January, that I would be arrested and taken from the Plas in chains and under an armed military guard. The Colonel had never before been seen in this area, and the Major only very rarely, and it was argued that the top military men in Wales would not have come to the Plas other than on a top military mission. As the morning wore on, with no further comings and goings, some of my friends in Newport imagined that I was probably being subjected to some grotesque form of military torture, and they started to organize a mass demonstration. Abby, Halfpint and Skiff even started to plan an heroic rescue, which included an intention to kidnap the Colonel and the Major and to hold them to ransom. These loyal and touching plans were abandoned when the messenger from Cardigan galloped up to the Plas and when Major Parlby and his men shortly afterwards went galloping off with such determination that they might have been intent upon saving that quiet town from insurgents. When I heard this, I did not have the heart to tell people that the real purpose of their mission was to rescue eight pretty straw bonnets. After that, with only the Colonel and four of his men left at the Plas, local concerns subsided somewhat, and when Sir James and his escort finally left after eight hours of occupation, with extremely jovial farewells on the doorstep, the cascade of speculation turned into a veritable maelstrom.

How should we deal with all of that? On the following morning, when I had recovered from my lost sleep and when Shemi's potions had worked their magic, I consulted with all of my servants around the kitchen table. It was my first opportunity to review the events at Boncath with Will and Gomer, and my first opportunity to hug those two heroes, to thank them for acting as my guardian angels, and to bless them for pulling me out of at least two situations that might have led to disaster. "Too enthusiastic by half, this daughter," said Will. "Not only did she strike the first chunk out of the gate, but she threw the torch to light the bonfire, and then she fired the house timbers too. If we had let her, she would probably have gone up in flames like Joan of Arc....."

"No chance of that, Will. One little burn on my hand is more than I can cope with. Anyway, I am done with rioting. Too many things to think of, like patrols and watches, signal rockets and guns, contingencies and deployments, and decoys and traps. Men's business, and best left to men."

Gomer roared with laughter. "It is called military planning, Mistress. There are several thousand poor fellows in Pembrokeshire alone who know all about it, having learnt a thing or two under arms from General Picton and the Duke of Wellington. Anyway, most of what Rebecca and her daughters have done over these few years is a direct result of your exhortations and your instructions, is it not?"

I held my hand up in surrender. "I give in, Gomer. I am tired of military matters. I want to know how we should deal with the rumour about Colonel Love's visit. Any ideas?"

"Treat it as a strictly social visit, Mistress," said Bessie. "Be honest with people and tell them that Master Owain Laugharne, to whom you were betrothed long ago, was once under the Colonel's command, and that the realization of this common link lay behind his natural desire, as a gentleman, to call and pay his respects since he was already in the neighbourhood."

"Perfect, Bessie!" I said, giving her a kiss on the cheek. "Your thinking is a good deal more nimble than mine at the moment. Will you put this about, dear friends?"

They agreed with that, and that is the story we all gave to friends and neighbours and even to Betsi and Brynach when they called with all the torture devices of the Inquisition to interrogate me shortly afterwards. I hope that they have now forgiven me for my night of madness, but under their merciless prodding I was forced to promise that I would never do such a thing again. Strange that, since some little while ago I had to extract similar promises from Brynach and Ioan. Now I really had better start behaving like a respectable old lady, for the sake of my own health and the health of my nearest and dearest.............

When I was left to myself again, after dinner, I retired to my room and started to mull over my conversation with Sir James, my new-found friend. I judged him to be a genuine, kind gentleman with a fund of compassion in his heart and a respect for good Christian values -- but I suddenly feared that on this occasion my instinct might have led me astray. He had encouraged me to weep in his company. Tears can be a woman's greatest weapon, but as I have discovered before, to my cost, they tend to wash away inhibitions and discretion and can leave one utterly at the mercy of cynical and manipulative gentlemen. His bumbling and mumbling -- had that been a ploy to put me off my guard? He had got me to admit, in effect, that I had been at the Boncath riot and that I knew about the planned Scleddau ambush. I had said too much about Samson Wilson. A cold sweat broke out on my forehead when I realized that I had probably been the silliest woman ever to be interrogated by a sophisticated military officer, and that he now had more than enough information in his head both to confirm that I was *Mam-gu* Becca and to condemn me to transportation.

I felt myself spiralling into a state of panic, and forgot about everything which Joseph and Shemi had taught me over the year about trusting my heart over my head. I slumped onto my bed, with my heart beating wildly. Then I heard the pounding of galloping hooves upon the frosty turf of the driveway, and assumed that this was the beginning of the end. I froze, and tried not to hear what was going on downstairs, but there was a heavy knocking on the back door, the echoes of a brief conversation, and then the sound of horse's hooves going off in the direction from which they had come. I heard Bessie's footsteps on the polished timbers of the passageway and the stairs. She knocked, and came inside.

"Why, Mistress," she said when she saw me slumped on the bed. "Are you not well?"

"Tired, Bessie. So, so tired."

"There is a sealed message, Mistress. From Colonel Love, delivered by his special man. He does not require a reply."

It was written in a tidy hand on heavily embossed paper, and this is what it said:

From Colonel Sir James Frederick Love
Officer Commanding, Wales

To Mistress Martha Morgan, Plas Ingli, Newport in Pembrokeshire
3rd day of February 1844

Smouldering Embers

My Dear Mistress Martha,

First, I must apologize for descending upon you so early in the morning the other day, for failing to give you advance warning, and for staying so long when you were clearly very tired. Not the actions of a gentleman who has his wits about him, but then warfare and social unrest both have the effect of dulling sensibility and bringing brutality and vulgarity to the fore. I have lived with such things since I was fourteen years old, and to be honest with you, I am weary of the whole wretched business of using British soldiers -- instead of intelligent laws and political reform -- to maintain good order in the British countryside.

There -- I have already given you enough to have me hanged for treason. But I trust you and you will not betray me.

In my defence, I came to the Plas because Major Parlby wished you to be intimidated by the sight of our broad chests and gleaming medals, and planned that you should be interrogated without mercy. Then, he thought, you could be arrested for your involvement with Rebecca and her daughters. He wants more medals and more glory. Feeble fellow that I am, I went along with him. He assumed you to be Mam-gu Becca, and I suspected it too, but you have left no footprints, and your attention to detail has been exemplary. You have been protected by such loyalty and such walls of silence as I have never experienced before, in any of my theatres of military activity. Not a single spy or paid informer -- and there have been many -- has been able to provide anything that might stand up in court relating to your activities. And I have been amazed, more than once, to discover how you have dealt with your enemies through the use of humour rather than violence.

So, my dear Martha, I was intrigued to come to the Plas and to discover the basis for the almost universal esteem accorded to Mam-gu Becca. And whom did we meet? Not some fierce and scheming crone with hate in her heart and vengeance in her eyes, but a beautiful and elegant lady in a red velvet dress, with the figure of a twenty-year-old, with black hair with scarcely a trace of grey in it, and with eyes to die for. And what of our welcome? Not a hostile gesture to be seen, and not a cold word spoken. Hospitality, in short, which lacked nothing in sophistication or gentility and which was a good deal more friendly than that of many a fine mansion of my acquaintance. The house which you have built is a friendly house inhabited by angels, Martha, and that tells me a good deal about why you are widely loved and respected.

When I returned to HQ I obtained a full report on the Boncath riot. The only error committed was the use of the word "Mam-gu" by various people on a number of occasions. That was foolish, and the toll-collector's wife has sworn to it, but it was not your fault. Otherwise the organization was utterly magnificent, and if you know who Rebecca was, and who her lieutenants were, I will appreciate it if you will pass on my congratulations. The army cannot win against such skill and such commitment, and is already defeated. You know that anyway, with the likes of Major Parlby spending his time rushing about in order to recover eight missing pretty bonnets and to rescue the reputation of his regiment...........

I thank you for confirming, quite knowingly, your awareness of the plans for Scleddau and Boncath. You have entrusted me, on the basis of your own intuition, with the knowledge of your role as Mam-gu Becca in these riots since they commenced some years ago. I will respect that trust, and I will never betray you. I suspect that I will never even be tempted to betray you, since within a month the Royal Commission will report, and Rebecca will have won a great victory for the people. I suspect that there is no need for any further rioting.

On the matter of your actions at Boncath I suspect from my reports that you were the one who first struck the gate, who ignited the bonfire, and who sent the house timbers up in flames. You are not used to lighting fires, Martha, and I am not surprised that you burnt your hand. Kindly keep away from fires in future. I can only express my total admiration for your determination and your courage in what must have been the strange and even alien environment of a riot involving angry and violent men. I know that Bryn Williams, the man who died in prison because of the idiocy of Lieutenant Rice, was one of your beloved servants. I also know what it is like, Martha, to plan and orchestrate campaigns and battles, and to stand well back while foot-soldiers and cavalry are sacrificed in the cause. In other words, I understand perfectly why you did what you did at Boncath, and I salute you for it.

And finally, my dear friend, I return to your beloved man Owain Laugharne. I promise you that prior to my visit I had no knowledge whatsoever of any relationship between you and him. The manner in which he came into my mind was due to serendipity, or maybe to the intervention of angels. I thank you for sharing with me over our charming lunch the story of your short but blessed time together. He was a truly great man, loyal to his country and loyal to his commanding officer. Your role in Wales, Martha, has been not dissimilar to his in Spain, and has involved no less dedication, no less skill, no less patriotism, no less doggedness, and no less heroism. You deserved him, as he deserved you.

Destroy this letter, if you please, Martha. That is the only request I make of you.

Your affectionate friend,
James Frederick Love

PS. Rest assured that neither you nor any of your friends, servants or family will ever face prosecution in the matter of Rebecca and her daughters. I have asked the Lord Lieutenant to discourage any further investigation into your affairs, and I have received an assurance that from the date of this letter all spying activity relating to you and Plas Ingli will cease. If you receive any aggravation in future from Major Parlby or any other member of our armed forces, that will be contrary to my instructions, and I shall be pleased to hear of it.

I have wept a great deal lately, and when I had finished this letter I wept again, and then laughed, and then cried and laughed at the same time in the manner of a six-year-old child. At last sleep covered me with its blessed blanket. Liza tells me that I slept for fourteen hours, as calmly and gently as a new-born babe which has not a care in the world.

ΩΩΩΩΩΩΩΩΩΩΩ

5th February 1844

The first snowdrops are peeping out in the cold damp hedgerows, and there is a little more warmth in the sun, and the breeze from the west has the freshness of spring about it. The spies have gone. I know it because Abby called here in person today, having received his own reports that they had abandoned their stations, and having had it directly from the mouth of Billy Coggs that there would be no further surveillance of Mistress Morgan or the Plas. Brynach has picked it up from his fellow magistrates as well -- even from the mouths of those who have previously denied any knowledge of secret activities. I received a letter from Richard Lord, the Clerk to the Justices, to say that all files and documents relating to me and the Plas have been destroyed. The Lord Lieutenant is behind all of this, and there is little doubt in my mind that Sir James stands behind him. Suddenly I can meet my friends and contacts openly at the Plas. Suddenly I can receive and send mail via the mail coaches, and suddenly Master Havard Medical is relieved of his onerous duties as an intermediary. His garrulous neighbours will be intrigued that henceforth I will no longer visit him several times a week, and that the correspondence between his surgery and the Plas will suddenly cease, and they will be convinced that I have been miraculously cured of some chronic ailment.

Not everybody will be amused by the orders which have in effect given me immunity from prosecution and the protection of the army, and I daresay that Squire Owen, Squire Huws and Squire Jobbins will be grumbling into their breakfast porridge and muttering darkly about betrayal and corruption. Major Parlby, who was angry enough already, will now feel that he has been belittled by his commanding officer. And a group of spies and informers will suddenly have nothing to do. I suppose I need not worry too much about them, for they have probably been paid well enough, and on balance I should be pleased that the new circumstances will result in a considerable reduction of the National Debt.

Tom Foster has been to see me, and we spent a pleasant morning together. He thinks that he is still under surveillance, and he thinks his mail is still tampered with, but he seems remarkably relaxed about such things and says that he has done nothing illegal. In any case, he knows from his other contacts that Rebecca's victory is won, and he knows that once the Royal Commission has reported and once Parliament is charged with enacting new legislation, there will be no appetite for further prosecutions. He visited Colonel Love in Carmarthen on his way to Pembrokeshire, and was amazed to hear him speak of me as a friend and ally in the campaign to bring peace back to the countryside. "I understand that you and he have met, Martha," he chuckled. "I daresay that he came as an enemy and left as a friend, as is the way with all your other enemies. Did you wear your red velvet dress for the meeting?"

"Yes, Tom, as it happens. It was the first one that came to hand."

"And your emerald necklace -- the one which draws the eye inexorably down towards two of your greatest assets?"

"You are a very crude fellow, Tom, just like journalists in general. But yes, now that you come to mention it......"

Tom roared with laughter. "Mistress Martha, you are quite priceless! The poor Colonel must have been utterly defenceless against such weaponry. He probably hung out the white flag of surrender within ten minutes of his arrival, and decided from that point on that his mission in life should be to act as your humble servant."

"He is a good deal too tough for that sort of thing, Tom. But we did talk at length, and not just about Mistress Rebecca. He is tired of her attentions, and so am I."

Then I had to tell Tom about the Boncath riot, and about my part in it. He had already worked out that I had been there, since he went to Boncath on the day after the disturbance and talked to the gatekeeper and his wife. They both referred, in their testimonies, to Rebecca as the leader of the riot and to the presence of somebody else called *"Mam-gu* Becca". They assumed that she was a woman, because she rode sidesaddle and because she was carefully guarded and assisted by two other of Rebecca's daughters. They told Tom that she had burnt her hand on setting the house on fire. Then Tom reached down into his bag and pulled out a battered felt hat. "Yours, Martha?" he asked. I looked at it carefully. "Why yes, Tom, I do believe it is," said I. "Yet another of the essential items from my wardrobe which I use in my charm offensives against innocent gentlemen. But according to the *Times* felt hats of this sort are no longer in fashion, and I am minded to get myself something more appropriate for the new era." And with that, I tossed it onto the burning coals in the fireplace.

Tom has written his report of the Boncath riot in terms which will enrage the politicians in London. He showed it to me, and in it he expressed admiration for Rebecca's meticulous planning and poured scorn and ridicule on the pathetic and ill-coordinated attempts by the army to get to the gate and to save it. He described the manner of the capture of the eight dragoons, and enjoyed himself greatly in describing the pretty bonnets which they had on their heads when they were found. He made no mention at all of *Mam-gu Becca,* and for that I thanked him. He also described, in another column, the abortive ambush attempt at Scleddau which led the two most senior military commanders in Wales to spend a night behind a damp hedge while Rebecca and her daughters were having fun twenty miles away to the east.

"Enough is enough!" he thundered at the end of his report. *"Even if the military commanders in West Wales had ten thousand troops at their disposal they would not make the slightest impression on Becca and her daughters, who are supported by almost all of the local populace. Whenever she wishes, that tough old lady will lead them a merry dance, calling the troops to one place when she is at another, and taking increasingly audacious and impudent actions designed to bring ridicule upon the very soldiers who once saved this country from Master Bonaparte. The only thing that will stop Madam Becca is a transformation of the turnpike trust laws and legislation designed to address all of the grievances of the rioters. The Prime Minister and the Home Secretary must take those actions NOW which they should have taken five years ago. If they do not legislate, there will be fresh blood on the streets and on the hands of those who presume to call themselves our political leaders."*

When I read this, I said: "Oh my goodness, Tom! This is strong stuff, and sounds treasonable. Will your Editor print it?"

"He will print it, Martha, for it is a true and accurate representation of the situation."

As we sipped our tea, Tom and I talked of our understanding of the current situation. I said that I was not aware of any further actions planned for this area, and promised that I would put out a message urging restraint from this point on, on the grounds that assurances were coming from far and wide that political action designed to resolve all outstanding issues was imminent. For his part, Tom told me that there were now very few pockets of discontent in the three counties of West Wales, and that the current waves of riots were breaking on the shores of North Wales and the Welsh Borders. He said that the thugs belonging to the Stag and Pheasant Gang each now had prices of £500 on their heads, and that both the military and an assortment of bounty hunters were after them. Shoni Sgubor Fawr and Dai'r Cantwr had been seen the other day in the country north of Carmarthen, he said, but the dogs were closing on them all the time, and he predicted that they would be flushed out and apprehended very soon, and probably within three days.

Now Tom has gone. I daresay that we will meet again soon. I hope that by the time of his next visit I will have recovered enough energy to take part in a modest celebration of Rebecca's triumph.

ΩΩΩΩΩΩΩΩΩΩ

6th February 1844

I have been tying up more of the loose ends hanging from the weave. I have written a letter to Colonel Love, thanking him for his kind remarks, his refreshing honesty, and his instincts for compassion and discretion. I tried not to be too specific, since I thought that my letter might be opened and inspected by others before it reached him. I also said that he would be very welcome to call at the Plas should he find his way to North Pembrokeshire again in the future, and I said that I had acted upon his request. And I have indeed burnt his letter, as he asked.

Then this morning I sent Will to Boncath with a large bundle of things intended for the wife and family of the gatekeeper who recently lost his house and his gate. There was nothing for him, since he is a surly and aggressive fellow, and deserved his beating. But since the time of the riot I have been haunted by the image of his weeping wife and his screaming children running across that dark roadway, their faces illuminated by flames. I have been forced into a realization that when there is conflict there are victims on all sides. I have done my best to hide away from this fact, but now I cannot evade a recognition that when social disturbances occur on this scale we are all brutalized, and we all suffer. Neither can I escape from some personal responsibility when men, women and innocent children are hurt. A bundle containing children's clothes, shoes and toys, and foodstuffs including bread and butter, cheese, smoked joints and potatoes does not go very far in salving my own conscience; but it is a gesture, and from the point of view of the recipients, it is better than nothing. Will found the toll-collector's family being sheltered by neighbours. He gave them the bundle of supplies, and said it was from a lady who wished to do some small thing to alleviate their distress. *"Mam-gu* Becca?" asked the oldest child. Will smiled enigmatically and went on his way, with their thanks ringing in his ears.

This afternoon Gwenno came back from a shopping expedition to town with some hot news. She told us in the kitchen that there had been a fire in a cottage called Clyn, in a small and remote valley on the estate of Squire Owen Gelli Fawr. The cottage had been utterly destroyed, in spite of attempts by some of the estate workers to put it out. But when at last it had been possible to get into the smouldering ruin, the men had discovered two bodies inside. There had not been much left of them, but they had just been recognizable as the bodies of Nathaniel Evans and Samson Wilson, the traitors who had attended the meeting at Trecwn where the Scleddau gate attack had been planned. On the wall of the burnt-out cottage the following message had been daubed: *So die another pair of traitors. None such shall escape my wrath. Signed, Becca and daughters.*

So death and retribution continue to stalk across the face of this once-innocent and quiet landscape. And Rebecca has shown, yet again, her capacity to find her enemies and to deal with them.

Or has she? And are these murders quite what they seem? The constables have accepted the popular version of events at face value, and the local people have simply sighed and said "Good riddance!". But when I became aware of the details there were some things that did not ring true. For a start, there had been no prior message from any of Rebecca's daughters locally that these two traitors had been found, or that they would be executed. Neither had any of my contacts admitted responsibility, via our network of communications, for the killings, or for any knowledge of them.

I was mystified by all of this, and was still too tired to try and work out what was going on. But then I recalled that Shemi had told me some little time ago that I should not worry about Nathaniel Evans and Samson Wilson, and that he would deal with them. So, since it was a pleasant enough afternoon, I walked over the mountain to Werndew and was lucky enough to find the wizard at home. I asked him about the burnt corpses at Clyn, and asked him what he knew of the matter. "There is more to this then meets the eye, Shemi, is there not?" I asked.

"Indeed there is, Martha," said Shemi. "Let me explain. I said that I would deal with these two fellows, and I immediately started to make investigations as to their whereabouts. After a good deal of sleuthing I traced them to Clyn, where they were being kept alive by Squire Owen. He did not want them there, and he had urged them to flee to Ireland or some such place. I walked in on them a few nights ago, in my full regalia, and gave them the shock of their lives. They were very frightened indeed, both of Rebecca and of the Squire. They also seem to have convinced themselves, Martha, that they were being hunted down by Henry Eynon and Zeke Tomos, and they seemed to fear that every shadow on the common or in their dark valley would turn out to be one or other of them, armed with some fearful weapon of execution."

"And were they being hunted down by those fellows, Shemi?"

"It is quite possible, Martha. Sad to say, I have lost track of them. They are probably out hunting for each other! At any rate, when I spoke to our friends in the wood, there was clearly bad blood between them, and I was also interested to hear that they were both scared to death of Squire Owen, their erstwhile employer."

"Do you mean that the Squire employed them too? I assumed that he controlled Master Morris and Master Eynon, but did his control or his patronage extend across a whole network of informers?"

"I am convinced of it. To return to the matter in hand, I was not sure that either of the fellows in the cottage was all that wicked, and they appear never to have actually caused any deaths or major injuries to others. So I put the fear of the devil into them and told them to get out of Pembrokeshire at high speed, never to return. They promised that that was what they would do, on pain of spending the rest of their lives under a wizard's curse."

"That seemed like an eminently sensible conclusion to the matter, Shemi, and I congratulate you on it. But then...........?"

"But then their charred bodies were found in the cottage, with Rebecca given the blame. I knew that something was wrong, so I went up to the place at high speed this very morning and examined the corpses. They were dead before the cottage was set on fire. My theory is that Squire Owen has done this terrible thing, and has dressed the murders and the fire up so as to cast the blame on Rebecca. He assumed that nobody would question that, since it was commonly assumed that Rebecca wanted both Nathaniel and Samson dead."

"And what about Henry Eynon?" I asked. "Could he be involved?"

"I doubt that, Martha. It was clear to me from my conversation with the men in the cottage that they did have contact with Squire Owen and Gelli Fawr, but that the Squire was also desperate to find Henry Eynon and was indeed afraid that the fellow might try to kill him."

I buried my head in my hands. "Of my God," I moaned. "What a tangled web! Two more villains dead, but two others still on the loose. What will you do now, Shemi?"

"Well, I have spoken to some of the servants at Gelli Fawr, and to certain others. I will shortly go and speak to magistrates whom I can trust. In the meantime, I am following a trail which will lead me to Squire Owen, and which will lead him to the gallows.

I gave Shemi a hug before setting off or home. "Dear Shemi!" I said. "You sound more like our dear departed Joseph all the time. God help the criminal classes in general, and Squire Owen in particular."

"They need no help from God, Martha, or from me. In my experience they always incriminate themselves, and guilt inevitably addles the coolest of brains."

Now I am back at the Plas, waiting quietly for the remaining tangles in this weave to be sorted out by Shemi's delicate fingers. There is nothing more for me to do, and for that I am eternally grateful.

ΩΩΩΩΩΩΩΩΩΩΩ

15th February 1844

Complacency always was one of my greatest failings, and now I have had to pay the price for it in a most appalling fashion. Two days since I had to cope with one of the worst days of my life, and afterwards I was so shocked that I could hardly speak, let alone communicate with my diary. At last I think I am coming through the tunnel and into the first glimmer of daylight, and Bessie tells me that I must record what happened, and move on into the full glare of the sun.

The day started well enough. Shrove Tuesday, the day of the annual *cnapan* contest on Berry Sands, was a day of celebration in the local

Smouldering Embers

community. The labourers and small farmers of the district have few enough opportunities for social intercourse and sporting activity, and on this day, every year, they meet in their thousands, with most of the able-bodied menfolk participating in the strange and brutal game on the beach and representing one or other of our local parishes. The men of Plas Ingli have always represented Newport against Nevern, and this year was no exception, with Gomer and Bryn well prepared and eager for the play. As servants, they have to play on foot, but Brynach and Ioan are allowed, in view of their landowning status, to ride with the other gentry, and this year they were joined by my young grandsons Benjamin and Abel from Brithdir. There was great excitement all round, even though the day is always difficult for me since it is the anniversary of the black day in 1805 when my dear husband David was killed on the beach by four vicious and cowardly enemies. But that was long ago, and nowadays I am adept at holding my emotions under control and at joining in the jollification among the stalls and sideshows, even if I still do not understand the game and do not mind particularly who wins.

The day dawned bright and crisp, and perfect for the fellows who would be rushing around on the beach in their thousands in pursuit of a hard wooden ball boiled in tallow. It was not so bad for the rest of us either, and at about eleven in the morning I walked down to Brithdir to join Betsi and two of her female servants on a trip down to the Parrog where the stalls and entertainers would be much in evidence, and where the crowds would be gathering. We took the Brithdir chaise, and had not a care in the world as we trotted along down Greystones Hill into town.

We left Bessie, Liza and Gwenno behind at the Plas since somebody had to keep an eye on the animals and since there was a mountain of pancakes to be manufactured. All being well, the rest of us, including filthy and hungry players and satisfied and dissatisfied spectators, would arrive back at the Plas towards the end of the afternoon for the traditional pancake feast. We expected at least six men, four women and three children to arrive, all hungry and intent upon comparing the Plas Ingli pancakes with the Brithdir pancakes which we had consumed last year. My three female servants were all looking forward to the feast, and since Bessie still uses the old pancake recipes taught to her by the wonderful Mrs Owen long ago, she knows that her pancakes are lighter and crisper and tastier than anything else in Wales.

Smouldering Embers

When I left the Plas in the morning, the three women were in the best of spirits, singing and fooling around in the kitchen as they measured out quantities of flour and spices and other secret ingredients for the sweet and savoury pancake mixtures. Then, at about one o'clock, in the midst of the jollification on the Parrog, and with the crowds cheering on the crowds of half-naked men rushing about on the distant parts of Berry Sands, a little worm of worry started to nibble away inside my head or my heart -- I could not tell which. I was with my grandchildren David, Rose and Owain at the time, watching a silly juggler doing extraordinary things with china plates. I tried to concentrate on having a good time and amusing the children, and tried to banish worries and dark thoughts, but I became more and more tense, and at last I had to hand the children over to Betsi and say that I was not feeling well. Betsi immediately became concerned, but I explained away my furrowed brow and flushed cheek as something to do with the noise and the smells of cooking and the crush of people, and said I simply needed space and fresh air in order to recover. I said that I would walk home over the mountain. "No no," said Betsi. "I will not hear of it. Take the chaise, Mother, and we will walk home later." But I wanted to walk, and somehow I knew that I had to go home not on the road but over the mountain. So I said my farewells, and said that I would see them all later on back at the Plas for the pancake feast.

I hurried back through the town and made my way towards the mountain by the lane leading from College Square. That led me up onto the northern side of Carningli, with the track at first gentle but then steepening inexorably towards the summit. My heart pounded as if it wanted to burst, and my legs burned with the effort of climbing, but there was a sort of desperation within me which I was at a loss to understand. I had to stop several times to catch my breath, and cursed the fact that I was not as fit and strong as I used to be. But the weather was good, and so was the visibility, and I knew that as soon as I reached the summit I would be able to look down onto the great scree banks which were piled against the southern slopes. More to the point, I knew that I would be able to look down directly on the Plas, and pick out any small details that might be of interest. Not for a moment did I doubt that there was something wrong in that beloved place, or that my intervention was desperately required.

At last, gasping for breath and with perspiration streaming off me, I reached the summit. I had the presence of mind not to stand up on the

388

skyline, but I slithered between two rocks to a position which afforded a good view. At first I could see nothing untoward. But then I strained my eyes and looked harder. I noticed that the gate between the yard and the driveway was open. That meant that something strange was going on, since no member of our family or circle of acquaintances would ever leave a farm gate open. Then I noticed that all of the breeding ewes in the bottom paddock were clustered round the feeding trough, making a considerable noise. That meant that they had not been fed. It was now, according to my little pocket watch, two of the clock, one hour later than their usual feeding time. Then I noticed that the dogs were barking in their kennels, as if something had disturbed them. My sense of foreboding increased, although there was nothing which I could identify as the obvious cause of it. I looked about me, and saw that the family of eight ravens was in occupation of the mountain's highest crag. They sat in a row, but they were not in their normal nonchalant mood. They were all looking at me intently, as if they had understood the turmoil in my breast. Then a strange thing happened. The old male, whom I have always thought of as the King of the Mountain, suddenly took off, and after wheeling in the wind forty feet above the summit, turned to the west and sped off over the common with rapid powerful wingbeats. He made no sound, and neither did his mate or his offspring. Within a minute or two he was just a speck in the distance, and I knew that he was going to fetch my friend the Wizard of Werndew.

With just a little encouragement in my heart, I thanked the other ravens and decided that I had better get down among the rocks so as to approach Plas Ingli. I had now recovered my breath, but my heart was still pounding so loudly that I thought it must be audible from the yard below. I knew that I must descend while remaining invisible from the Plas. If there were intruders in the house they would certainly keep an eye open for anybody approaching along the driveway from the Cilgwyn Road. They would not expect anybody to come down from the mountain summit, but I must take no chances. Luckily I knew this side of the mountain better than I knew the back of my own hand, and I knew that if I followed a line between boulders and craggy outcrops which prevented me from seeing the house, the occupants of the house would not see me. So in spite of the fact that I was dressed in my rather elegant winter town outfit, I slid and slithered and crawled my way downwards. I cut my hands and knees in the process, and cursed the fact that the blister on my left hand was still not fully healed, and that my twisted ankle was still giving me pain.   But in my desperation I forgot about pain and concentrated on controlling my movements, for there are more than a few places among the rocks where a lost foothold or a misjudged leap can lead to a painful and possibly catastrophic tumble into a dark chasm. Today, of all days, I dare not fall...........

At last, towards the base of the area covered by fallen rocks, I dared to peep out at the Plas. Nothing had changed.   The sheep were still demanding their rations, and the dogs were still barking, but the house itself seemed to be afflicted by an eerie silence, as if it was quite deserted. It occurred to me that maybe it was deserted, and that Bessie, Liza and Gwenno had been abducted, and on this basis I was almost stupid enough to stand up when I suddenly spotted a man with a gun walking out of the yard and around the back of the house. He stopped, and looked up towards the mountain, as if he was scanning the rocky slopes for any signs of life. I thought for a moment that he was looking directly towards me.   I froze, and was terrified that he had spotted me. But then he resumed his patrol, wandered past the front door and re-entered the yard. It was obvious to me now that he was stationed outside the kitchen door, and that he would undertake an occasional more extensive patrol just to check that the coast was clear. I had never seen this man before. He was dressed in the rough clothes of a working man. Who was he, and what on earth was he doing at the Plas?   How many comrades did he have?   Not many, I surmised, because if there had been, there would have been other watchmen and other patrols. And I knew that since he had just done a circuit of the house, he was not likely to do another within the next few minutes.

Frantically I resumed my descent, not worrying too much whether I was visible from the house. I cursed the fact that the bracken was now broken and battered by wind, rain and occasional snowfalls, and provided me with no cover whatsoever. But I reached Ffynnon Brynach safely, where I stopped and anointed myself and prayed for the assistance of the angels of the mountain. Then I continued to slide and crawl until I was behind the topmost wall that separates our cultivated land from the open common. I stopped to regain my breath and to control my thumping heart, and watched the house for several minutes. Nothing moved, and there was no further sign of the watchman.

Smouldering Embers

Suddenly there was a most terrible scream from the house, followed by a fearsome commotion of more screams, and shouting, and struggling. That was Liza's scream, I was sure of it, and my blood froze when I thought of what might be going on at that moment within my blessed house. I was so terrified that at first I did not react, but then I realized that I had to try to do something, so I crouched down low and ran towards the house, always staying on the blind side of one or another of the stone walls or hedges that bounded the fields. At last I reached the back wall of the cowshed, without any clear idea of what I was going to do. I sidled across the narrow passageway to the back wall of the dairy, and then dared to peep out to see whether the watchman was still near the kitchen door. He was still there, no more than twenty feet away from me, a very rough-looking fellow with a straggly black beard and ragged clothes. He looked more like a vagrant than a farmer or a labourer, but he held a shotgun in his hand, and he looked much more alert than I might have hoped.

Now everything was quiet inside the house again, and I thought for a moment of trying to get in through one of the windows or through the front door. But I knew not how I might get through a heavy sash window without making a frightful noise, and I knew that the front door would be locked. In any case, I had no idea how many rooms were occupied, and how many men I might have to deal with, and I assumed that I might immediately be apprehended by a man with a gun. I dithered, and that might have been my undoing, for when I then peeped around the corner I saw the man stir, and stretch, and stamp his feet. I withdrew at once, and pressed myself back against the wall, and as I did so I heard the fellow's heavy footsteps coming towards me. I knew that I was going to be discovered and captured. But then an extraordinary thing happened. The seven ravens who had watched me on the summit of the mountain suddenly appeared, and started to swoop down and attack the watchman. I heard, but did not see them as they wheeled and dived at him, one after another, making noises which I had never heard from ravens before. I heard the man swearing and shouting at them, and then I heard his gun clattering onto the ground. The intensity of the ravens' attack increased, and the fellow started to sound not just angry but frightened. Ravens are big heavy birds, and they can do great damage with their beaks, their wings and their claws. I knew this was my opportunity. I looked around for a weapon, and saw that the broad shovel which Gomer uses for cleaning out the cowshed was leaning against the wall just a few yards away. Without thinking, I ran out and grabbed it, and ran to where the watchman was still trying frantically to fend off the birds. Luckily he had his back to me, and with all the force I could muster I brought the flat of the shovel down on the back of his head. He crumpled to the ground, and I thought that I might have cracked his skull or broken his neck.

There was a sort of mad energy in me, driven by a mixture of mortal fear and animal fury. I was in no mood to worry about my victim's state of health, so I turned him onto his front, pulled his arms behind him and tied his wrists up as tightly as I could with the woollen scarf which I had around my neck. Then I grabbed the gun from the ground, flung open the kitchen door and ran into the kitchen.

The scene which confronted me was truly appalling, but before I could take it in properly there was a wild struggle at the far side of the room. I saw Bessie fighting with a man who had been holding her captive. I saw a knife flashing, and she screamed in agony, and then I saw the man falling to the floor. "Damn you, woman!" he shouted. Bessie ran towards me, passing the kitchen table, and as she passed it, with great presence of mind she grabbed a pistol which had been resting upon its battered, scrubbed surface. She had blood pouring from a serious wound on her arm. "Oh, thank God you are here, Mistress," she gasped, as she reached me and turned to face her captors. "I had almost given up hope." She pointed the pistol at the man who had cut her as he struggled back onto his feet.

"Put your hands above your heads, all of you!" I shouted. "Or God help me, I will shoot you this instant!" I had not yet worked out how many men were in the room, but then I saw that on the table there was a kneeling man, with his breeches down around his knees and with his white buttocks exposed. He had his back to me, and he was kneeling between the opened legs of one of my servants. It could only be Gwenno. Her undergarments had been pulled off, and had been thrown onto the floor beside the table. Her petticoats, and her dress, had been pushed up over her waist. "And you, sir," I hissed, with a white rage flooding through me, "get off her and away from that table! If you have harmed her, I swear that I will kill you with my own hands!"

I turned to Bessie and asked "Has he........?" She shook her head, and relief flooded through me. The man on the table, whose passion had already subsided, pulled up his breeches and stepped down onto the stone flags of the kitchen floor. He still had his back to me. Then he tightened his belt, and turned to face me. I saw his face, weatherbeaten and almost hidden behind a heavy unkempt beard. It was Zeke Tomos, the man whom I had saved more than once and whom I had hidden in my hay-loft during his months as a fugitive from the law officers. He laughed, in a manner which sent a chill into my heart. "So we meet again, Mistress Martha," he said, "and once again under difficult circumstances. That was not very kind of you, depriving me of one small moment of pleasure in a life of misery............" He smiled menacingly, and took a step towards me.

"Back off, Zeke!" I shouted. "One step more, and I will shoot you. Get back against the wall!" He stopped, and shrugged, and then shuffled back to join the man who had cut Bessie with his knife. As he passed the table, he felt with his hand for his pistol, having remembered where he had placed it. "It has gone," said Bessie. "Now it is in my hand, and I am minded to shoot you with it if you give me the slightest reason."

All this happened within the space of a few seconds, and now my concern was directed towards Gwenno, who lay as if she was dead on the kitchen table. Still pointing the shotgun at the intruders, I shouted: "Gwenno, now you are safe. You are safe!" She did not move, so I said to Bessie: "Help her please, Bessie, and bring her here towards the door." Bessie went and helped the poor girl, who was in such a deep state of shock that she could hardly move, let alone walk or talk. She was as white as a sheet, and was shivering uncontrollably, and made strange little noises as she gasped for air. With infinite tenderness and patience Bessie helped her to arrange her clothing, and put her arm around her, and helped her to the floor. Then she supported her across the five yards between the table and the sanctuary of the kitchen door. She sat her down on a chair and then turned to help me in the task of keeping the intruders under surveillance.

Only then did I notice that Liza was lying on the floor, close to the door into the scullery, trussed up with rope and with a gag in her mouth. Her eyes were open, and although she was clearly terrified she seemed to be unharmed. "Are you all right, Liza?" I asked. She nodded. Then I noticed that there was another man in the room -- a huge fellow with wild hair, cauliflower ears and a nose that appeared to have been broken more than a few times. He had a long beard, and he was dressed in rough corduroy trousers, a flannel shirt and a red woollen waistcoat. A jacket, which was probably his, was thrown onto the settle by the fire. On the floor I could see a pile of dirty plates, and the bowls which we always used for pancake mixtures. These fellows had eaten well. They had also been drinking a good deal, for on the cupboard near the scullery door was the heavy enamel jug which we used for serving ale to the harvesters in the fields, and several pint mugs. . "Are they drunk, Bessie?" I asked.

"Don't count on it, Mistress. But they have certainly been very thirsty."

"And how many are there?"

"Just these three, Mistress, and the fellow outside. I presume you have dealt with him?"

"I have. He will not trouble us again."

"Any more weapons?"

"I do not think so. Apart from the knife.........."

I realized that the knife could cause us trouble, so I turned to the man who had cut Bessie. "You, sir!" I shouted. "That knife. Place it on the floor in front of you. Now!" He had hidden the knife away in his clothing, and shrugged his shoulders as if he was ignorant of its presence, but I was not going to be defied by this fellow, whoever he was. So I said: "Sir, I will count to five. If the knife is not on the floor by the time I reach five, I will shoot you. One, two, three, four............"

The knife clattered onto the floor. "Just in time, sir. I am not playing games. Now kick it towards me. He did as instructed, and the knife came spinning across the floor towards the place where Bessie and I stood with our firearms. Bessie picked it up. "Now then, Bessie, cut Liza free, if you will," I said. "I will keep you covered, and if any one of these fellows moves a muscle I will pull this trigger and shoot one or another of them. I do not mind which."

So Bessie cut away Liza's ropes, and removed the gag from her mouth. She then helped her to her feet and guided her towards the door. Once she had reached safety, her first instinct was to enfold her daughter Gwenno in her arms, and her second was to burst into tears. That was not a lot of help to me, so I said: "Liza, take Gwenno outside. She needs fresh air, and we all need assistance. Check that the watchman is still incapable of causing us trouble, and then please go and get help. But first, take that towel from the behind the door and bind Bessie's injury. I have seen enough blood for today." She did that, while Bessie continued to point her pistol at the men on the other side of the room.

Then Liza dragged Gwenno outside, leaving Bessie and me facing the three intruders. They were too far apart, and I realized that that made it difficult for us to cover them with our weapons. So I shouted to the big fellow near the fireplace; "You, sir! Keep your hands above your head, and move across to join the other two. Slowly, if you please. Any violent movement might frighten me, and cause this thing to go off........" Reluctantly, he moved away from the fireplace, moving so slowly and unsteadily that I was sure he was drunk. When I was satisfied, I said: "Right, stop there! Now then, all three of you, stand side by side, and each of you place your hands on top of your heads!" They obliged, with a great deal of scowling and mumbling. "Now that is better," I said. "If any one of you does anything stupid, I will press this trigger, and all three of you will die. Shotguns are very good for killing more than one person at a time, and you all deserve to die like dogs."

Still, not more than a minute or two had passed since I entered the kitchen. Everything had happened so quickly that I had had no chance to feel fear, and had had no chance to think about what was going on. Now there was a strange situation, with three desperate men lined up on the far side of the room and Bessie and I standing near the open kitchen door covering them with a shotgun and a pistol. I hoped that Bessie knew what to do with her pistol, for I had no idea what to do with a shotgun, and indeed did not know whether it was primed for firing. If any of our prisoners picked up on any uncertainty in our behaviour or in our words, all might be lost. So I tried to hold our advantage, such as it was, with aggressive words. "Zeke Tomos," I said, "I have seen enough today to convince myself that you have been transformed from a man into a wild animal since last we met. Who are these other men? You, sir, with the red waistcoat, what is your name?"

"I thought you would never ask me, Mistress," he said in a rough voice, with his words slurred. "John Jones, or Shoni Sgubor Fawr to my beloved friends."

"And you, sir, the one who cut Bessie with the knife?"

"David Davies, called Dai'r Cantwr by some because I sing with the voice of an angel."

"And what are you doing here? I thought that you two were being hunted down by constables and dogs in the woods near Carmarthen?"

Smouldering Embers

"So we were, Mistress," said Dai, who appeared a little less drunk than his massive and fearsome-looking partner. "Escaped, we did, under cover of darkness. Then we met this fellow Zeke near Login, and he encouraged us to come over this way where we could hide and have the chance to meet some of his friends."

"Do not count me as one of Zeke's friends, sir. He is no less a traitor than Henry Eynon and Bobby Morris and the rest of them who have been tempted by a few pounds from the English Queen." Then I turned to Zeke, who stood between the two Carmarthen thugs with a smile on his face. That made me think that he was probably insane, and that he was by far the most dangerous of the three. "Zeke, why did you bring these fellows to the Plas?"

"Matters to attend to, Mistress. I had a certain amount of unfinished business with Miss Gwenno that I wished to complete.........."

"You are worse than an animal, Zeke Tomos. She is a respectable married woman, as you know full well."

"Come come, Mistress. You must know that I never was greatly taken with respectability. Gwenno, on the kitchen table at the Plas, was a dream that I have had for many a night as I slept under hedges and in barns. She is very pretty, and very demure. We men have certain needs, Mistress, that have to be met. Anyway, it was my turn......."

I looked at Bessie with a question in my eyes. She shook her head. "Not here, Mistress. But before you came they boasted to us that they have had four other women in various other cottages this very morning, on the way to the Plas."

"How can that be, Bessie?"

"It is quite possible, Mistress. Remember that every able-bodied man in the neighbourhood is at the *cnapan* play today, and that virtually every house and cottage in our two parishes, and further afield, is unprotected."

"Oh my God," I moaned, wondering which of our neighbours might have been defiled by these monsters.

Suddenly Dai piped up, in a high tenor voice. "Do not blame me for the excesses of my friends," he said, with his eyes darting around the room. "I am a good Christian gentleman, and never approved of such things. Ale and pancakes, yes, but women, no, except in desperate circumstances."

Smouldering Embers

At this, Shoni gave a great guffaw. "Don't listen to him, Mistress. Ale and pancakes, indeed! He enjoyed that juicy wife near Brynberian just as much as we did. Is that not right, Zeke?"

That almost tipped me over the edge, and I felt a wild rage rising within me. Almost involuntarily, I felt my finger tightening on the trigger of the shotgun. Zeke saw what was happening, and sought to buy more time. He was the only one of the three who seemed to have his wits about him. "Enough of that, Shoni!" he said. "Tell Mistress Martha why we really came to the Plas."

The big man blinked and shook his head, as if he was trying to concentrate. "Yes indeed," he said at last. "Mistress Martha and the Plas. Yes yes. Well, you may be surprised to know this, Mistress, but I am the real Rebecca, and I am the brains behind this whole Rebecca business from start to finish. There now! The truth is told!" He opened his eyes widely, and paused for effect, and it was clear that he expected Bessie and me to break into spontaneous applause. When we did not, a shadow came over his face, but he continued, speaking very slowly. "There is more to me than meets the eye, indeed. Among my confederates, in Carmarthenshire, before I was forced to take to the road some weeks back, I heard word of some woman in Pembrokeshire who was calling herself *Mam-gu Becca*, or some such thing, and I thought that it would be a pleasant thing, indeed, to meet her some day, for social reasons, so to speak. So when Zeke said that he knew this *Mam-gu*, he kindly offered to arrange for a sociable visit, Mistress. And a good thing it is, for............"

Suddenly, in the midst of this protracted monologue, Zeke dropped his hands and launched himself across the room, presumably having made a calculation that I was listening so intently to Shoni that I would react slowly rather than quickly, and having made another calculation that I would not use the gun even if it was primed and ready for use. I have no clear recollection of what happened next, except that I screamed, and so did Bessie. Then there was a ferocious explosion as I pulled the trigger of the shotgun, which I had been holding at waist level. It kicked back out of my hands. I fell to the ground from the force of the blast, and then, after what seemed like an age, I opened my eyes and saw blood. Blood everywhere, splattered onto my clothes and my hands, and onto the wall behind me. Zeke Tomos was dead, spreadeagled on the kitchen table where he had been thrown by the force of the blast. He had taken it full in the stomach, and I cannot begin to describe the damage that had been done to him. At that point I must have collapsed, because all I can recall is more screaming, presumably from Bessie, and then hysterical shouts from her: "Out, you bastards! Get out! Get out now, or I will shoot you too!" I heard heavy stumbling footsteps, echoing inside my head, and I have a blurred recollection of two men rushing past me and through the kitchen door. I heard the rustling of Bessie's dress as she followed them out.

Then it was silent. Such a silence as I have never heard before and never wish to hear again. Then the silence faded, and I was aware of three sounds -- the pounding of my own heart, the gentle crackling and sparking of the burning logs in the fireplace, and the drip, drip, drip of blood from Zeke's right hand, splashing down into a bright red pool on the kitchen floor beneath the edge of the table.

"Martha, are you all right?" It was Shemi. I opened my eyes and nodded, although I was incapable of words. He lifted me up as if I had been a small baby, and carried me upstairs. He placed me gently onto my bed, lifted my head, and placed a glass to my lips. "Now then, drink this down, Martha," he said. I followed his instructions without question, and was overcome by drowsiness, and then slipped into blessed unconsciousness.

When I came to, it was quite dark outside, but my room was brightly lit and a fire was glowing in the grate. There was a hum of conversation, and it sounded to me as if the house was full of people. I felt very drowsy, and as I tried to work out where I was and what time of day or night it might have been, Liza came up the stairs and into my room. She smiled when she saw that I was awake. She came over to my bed, sat at my side, and held my hand.

"Tell me that that was all a terrible nightmare, Liza," I moaned, "and that none of it really happened.........."

"I am afraid, Mistress, that it did happen. But thanks to you, we are all relatively unharmed. I have some rope burns where I was bound up, and some bruises where those monsters kicked me and punched me. Bessie's cut arm looked more serious at first than it really is, and Shemi says it will heal in no time. She is deeply shocked too, and is asleep next door. Gwenno, who came within an inch of being ravished by that monster Zeke Tomos, is all right. Gomer has taken her home, and with his tender love she will feel safe and rested by the morning. Our main worry is you, Mistress. How do you feel?"

"Truly terrible, Liza. My limbs are aching, and my head is bursting with pain."

"That is not surprising, Mistress. You are covered with cuts and bruises from your climb over the mountain. You also appear to have crawled through assorted furze and bramble bushes without noticing it, with the result that you have scratches and thorns all over your hands and legs, and on your face too."

"Oh my God, Liza. That sounds terrible. Please keep me away from a mirror for the next fortnight."

"I will do my best, Mistress."

Then I noticed, as my head continued to clear, that I had been washed and changed into my prettiest white cotton nightdress. "That dress, with all the blood on it, Liza....?"

"Soaking in cold water, Mistress. In half an hour it will go into the boiling washtub."

"And Zeke Tomos, Liza?" I asked, gripping her arm and with terror in my eyes.

"Don't you worry, Mistress. They have taken him away. By now, he is in the mortuary down on the Parrog, awaiting inspection by the Coroner and Havard Medical."

"But all that blood! We must clean up the kitchen, Liza, before all the others come for their pancakes!" I made to get out of bed and rush downstairs, but Liza pressed me back gently onto my pillow.

"All done, Mistress. The kitchen is wiped and scrubbed. The table is cleaned with sugar soap and is as white as snow. There will be no pancakes today, for the intruders consumed most of the mixture before you arrived, along with a good few quarts of ale. They were very hungry and thirsty. Mistress. One might have thought that they had not seen food or drink for a week."

Then I suddenly remembered the fellow outside the kitchen door, whom I had hit with the heavy shovel. "That other fellow, Liza, is he all right?"

"I cannot lie, Mistress. He is not all right. He is dead too."

Then my composure entirely disappeared. I do not know what I tried to do, but I think that I tried to get up out of my bed and fight my way past Liza. I think I became hysterical, for running round and round in my head was the terrifying thought that whatever the provocation might have been, and whatever the danger faced by me and by my servants, I had on that very day murdered two men.

ΩΩΩΩΩΩΩΩΩΩ

16th February 1844

I could not continue my narrative of events last night, for the recollection of them was so appalling that I could not cope. But I have had one more night of fitful sleep, and I am strong enough to continue. There is not very much more to tell.

When I became hysterical, following my realization that two men had died at my hands, Brynach and Shemi came rushing up from the kitchen to try to calm me down, and Shemi had to give me another dose of his blessed sedative. That worked, and I slept through the night with Liza at my side. In the morning I was a good deal calmer, and I was able to have a good wash in the tin bath in front of my bedroom fire before going down on Liza's arm to breakfast. The kitchen was still full of people, and it looked to me as if they had been there all night while I had enjoyed the luxury of sleep. Shemi was there, having refused to go home until he was quite sure that Bessie and I were well enough to cope with our recollections of our day of terror and the events of the new day. Brynach, Ioan and Betsi were there, as were Will, Gomer and Gwenno. As soon as she saw me Gwenno got up from the table and ran into my arms. We said nothing to each other, but we embraced for a long time and wept together. Then, when I had recovered my equilibrium, I sat down to enjoy some toasted bread and orange marmalade. Before I could take my first bite, Bessie appeared, walking somewhat unsteadily and looking very much the worse for wear. That started me off again, and the two of us embraced and wept for so long that Liza had to remind us that our tea was getting cold. At last, with all of us seated round the table, and with tears wiped away, I was able to piece together the last bits of the puzzle.

Shoni, Dai, Zeke and Barti (for that was his name) had burst into the kitchen without warning at about twelve noon. My three servants had been thoroughly involved in making the pancake mixtures, without a care in the world, and they were taken entirely by surprise. The intruders had their weapons, and threatened to use them. Bessie and the others tried to talk to them and to find out what they wanted. It was clear from the beginning that Zeke wanted Gwenno, but it seemed that Shoni wanted me, in spite of the fact that I was twice his age. Since I was not there, he said that he was prepared to wait. The men were nervous, and they seemed to be resigned to the fact that their days were numbered. Zeke, in particular, was convinced that he was going to die very soon. Shoni and Dai, who were the two in charge, realized that they had more than enough time at their disposal for over-indulgence of all sorts, since nobody was likely to appear at the Plas until the *cnapan* game was over and done with. So they demanded ale and pancakes. Bessie said that she and Liza and Gwenno had no option other than to fetch ale in great quantities from the pantry for the men and to serve it to them as they lounged about around the kitchen table. They also cooked up pancakes on demand, trying to stretch the process out so as to use up time. According to Liza, they thought that if they could keep the men occupied with food and drink for maybe two hours, they might somehow escape from their captors. They also thought that if they could get the men drunk enough they risked violence and violation, but they also gave themselves a chance of escape.

As the minutes ticked away, and as the ale began to affect the men's behaviour, Shoni became more and more brash and argumentative, and Dai started to become tearful. All of them became more talkative, and Dai started to weep because, in spite of being a good Christian gentleman, he had been involved in the execution of a traitor that very morning. Bessie said that when she heard that her blood froze, but Zeke was happy enough to fill in the details. He said that the four of them had been watching Gelli Fawr on the previous night, in the hope of seeing Squire Owen either coming or going from his mansion. He was Zeke's main enemy, and Shoni and Dai had promised on oath that they would help Zeke to shoot him. But while they had been watching the front entrance from the roadside, who should they see coming up the track from Pandy but Henry Eynon, the other man whom Zeke wanted dead rather than alive. So they had grabbed him and slit his throat, and had draped his body across the mansion's entrance gate as a warning to the Squire. Then they had disappeared into the woods, and had decided that Plas Ingli would be an appropriate port of call, after a few intermediate stops at lonely cottages and farmhouses where they might find women who were on their own .

I could hardly believe the cold-blooded and callous nature of this narrative, and I asked Liza whether Bessie was making these men appear more like animals than human beings, just to make me feel better about my role in their deaths. "No no, Mistress," said Liza. "Bessie has got it exactly right. Zeke showed no more concern about slitting the throat of Henry Eynon than he might have done about killing the Christmas pig. He was cold, Mistress -- as cold as ice."

"And the other three?"

"Hardened criminals, all three, Mistress. Dai had a bit of sensitivity about him, but Shoni was the roughest and most brutish fellow I have ever met. And as for Barti, he was a thug and a petty criminal. When he had got a few jars of ale inside him, be boasted that he was the one who shot Mistress Sarah Williams during the riot at the Hendy gate."

"That cannot be true, Bessie!"

"Indeed it is true, Mistress, so far as we can tell. Shoni and Dai both confirmed it, for they were both involved in that riot. Barti seemed to think that that was his single greatest achievement in life."

"And how many innocent women and girls have they violated during this reign of terror in the community?"

"It is difficult to say, Mistress. At least four yesterday, and several others on the day before, by the sound of it."

Liza then took up the story, and described a sudden change in the mood of the men. Shoni started to get violent, and for a moment it looked as if he might start fighting with Zeke. But Zeke calmed him down and told him what pleasures there were to be had from a room occupied by three pretty ladies. "They got to thinking of the practicalities," said Liza, with her voice breaking and her face pale, "and had the idea of dragging us one by one into one of the servants' rooms. But Dai said that would mean splitting their resources, and would make them vulnerable in case anybody turned up unexpectedly. So they decided on using the kitchen table and on enjoying us one after the other. I think the four of them were near enough mad from the effects of the ale, Mistress, and were prepared to throw caution to the winds."

"But they were not entirely stupid, Liza, if they had the presence of mind to send Barti outside as a watchman?"

"Quite so, Mistress. That was on Zeke's insistence. He was always thinking a good bit clearer than the others."

"And the terrible scream, Liza, which I heard when I was coming down the mountain?"

"That was me, Mistress. They decided on Gwenno first, and grabbed her and threw her onto the table. She fought with every ounce of strength that was in her, but Zeke is a strong man, and Shoni is twice as strong as him. She had no chance, and was soon exhausted. Then I got mad with rage, and attacked them with my bare hands............"

"She was quite heroic, Mistress," said Bessie, "and to protect her daughter she fought like a cornered she-cat. But at last they beat her into submission, and tied her up, and stuffed a gag into her mouth to keep her quiet. I was held at the far end of the room, by Dai, who held a knife to my throat and said he was minded to keep me for himself. Then as Zeke started to climb on top of poor Gwenno, on the table, we heard the sound of beating wings and strange noises outside, followed by Barti swearing and getting frightened. We heard the thud when you hit him on the head with the shovel, Mistress, and then you burst in with the shotgun in your hand. You know the rest as well as we do."

When my servants had finished their narrative, there was complete silence around the kitchen table. Then Shemi, who becomes wiser and more decisive with every passing year, said: "So now we have the aftermath of this miserable affair to deal with. The two bodies have gone to the mortuary, and inquests will have to be held within the next day or two. I have examined both bodies, as has George Havard Medical, and we will probably give identical evidence. We may have criminal investigations to cope with............"

"I know, I know," I moaned, as my eyes filled with tears. "Two murders, and not a shadow of doubt as to the evidence. When will the constables come for me? Will you help me, all of you, and ask Master Hugh Williams if he will defend me?"

"Dear Martha!" laughed Shemi. "Why must you always see the blackest of the options before us? Have you learnt nothing from all of your brushes with the law? There is not the slightest chance that anybody will bring charges against you. You killed Zeke in self-defence -- you have three witnesses to attest to that, and all of the evidence from the kitchen points to it."

"But Barti Richards?" I asked, with my voice little louder than a whisper. "Surely I cannot argue that that was self-defence too?"

"The evidence is incontrovertible, Martha. When I examined Barti's body he had cuts and scratches all over his face, head and hands. When I examined you, after the incident in this kitchen, you too had scratches and wounds on your legs, hands, arms and face. It is perfectly obvious that this fellow, who was very drunk, attacked you viciously, and that you defended yourself with your finger nails and any other weapon you could find, until at last you prevailed and hit him with a shovel. If you had not done that, he would surely have killed you, for he was also in possession of a shotgun. Then, thinking him to be still alive, you tied his hands up so as to keep him from further mischief. Nobody could possibly bring a charge of murder or manslaughter in the face of such evidence, Martha. Take it from me that you are quite safe, and may sleep soundly in your bed tonight."

"But what about the ravens which attacked him and diverted his attention?" I whispered.

"Ravens?" said Shemi. "What ravens?"

ΩΩΩΩΩΩΩΩΩΩ

23rd February 1844

The inquests have been held, and I am still a free woman. I have gradually come to terms with the realization that nobody is interested in arresting me or charging me, and as news has spread of the terrible events in our kitchen there has been a great upwelling of support from all segments of the community. Flowers, gifts and letters of support have come from far and wide, and we have received an endless stream of visitors, all of them wishing us well and congratulating us on coping with the most dangerous criminal gang ever seen in these parts. Even my erstwhile enemies among the gentry have been glowing in their praise, for they wanted the world to be rid of Zeke Tomos and the Stag and Pheasant Gang just as much as the magistrates and the army did. Tom Foster has paid us a visit, and he published a graphic account of the Plas Ingli incident in the *Times*, under the headline: *Hostages held by Violent Criminals in Pembrokeshire -- two die as heroic women fight back.*

I could not face the inquests into the deaths of Zeke Tomos and Barti Richards, but Bessie and Liza were strong enough to attend, and they gave harrowing accounts of what had happened. Shemi and Havard Medical gave evidence as to the injuries of the deceased men, and although it was strictly the task of the jury simply to identify the cause of death in each case, they went a good deal further. They recorded their findings that Zeke Tomos "died from shotgun wounds to his abdomen, occasioned by a headlong attack on a helpless woman while he was in an inebriated state," and that Barti Richards "died from a combination of excessive alcohol and a blow to the head from a blunt implement held by a woman who was defending herself from a frenzied attack." As Shemi said afterwards, the members of the jury could not have been much kinder or more understanding, and he was well pleased with them.

There were three further inquests in Newport on the same day. In the investigations into the deaths of Nathaniel Evans and Samson Wilson, the jury decided that both men "had been shot in the head at point-blank range by a person or persons unknown, who had then sought to destroy the evidence of their crime by burning the bodies of the deceased." And finally it was decided that Henry Eynon "had been killed by loss of blood and shock, occasioned by a knife cut across the throat by a person or persons unknown." So the magistrates and the constables are now conducting three murder inquiries, with few resources and very little skill to call upon. I daresay that Shemi will be required to bring matters to a satisfactory conclusion.

As to the two fugitives Shoni Sgubor Fawr and Dai'r Cantwr, when they fled from the Plas on the day of the incident in the kitchen they can hardly have expected to get very far. They were much the worse for wear, and they did not know the territory in which they now found themselves. As news of the tragedy spread, they suddenly found that not only did they each have a price of £500 on their heads, but that they were hunted by Rebecca and her daughters, and by the constables, and by the army. In addition there were many bounty hunters out and about, keen to find them and apprehend them. Then there were the husbands and families of the eight poor women whom they had terrified and violated prior to their arrival at the Plas. If any of them had found the fugitives, they would have been strung up from the nearest tree, with not even the formality of a mock trial.

In the event, Rebecca found them, after a series of tip-offs, in the woods near Aberfforest. Her revenge was as merciless as it was grotesque. Without any further ado, the pair of them were castrated and were then dumped on the roadside not far from Dinas. They were found there, purely by chance, or so we are told, by a farmer who was passing by with his horse and cart. He just happened to have some ropes with him, so he trussed the fellows up, transported them to Newport and delivered them to the house of the Clerk to the Justices. He claimed his reward of £1000, and he will get it in due course when the two of them are tried and convicted. He has already announced that £200 of his prize money will go to Zeke Tomos's widow, and that the rest will be used to alleviate suffering and to prevent local people from being thrown into pauperism. Seldom before can there have been such a generous farmer in North Pembrokeshire, and it is probably safe to assume that he has been taking advice from Rebecca in matters of financial management.

The castrated monsters lost a huge amount of blood, but Havard Medical was called to the Long Street lock-up as soon as the pair were shut away there, and they will probably survive. As soon as news of their capture started to circulate, a violent crowd assembled in the street, and feelings were so strong that the constables feared that the prisoners would be dragged out and lynched. So the magistrates had to call in the army and organize a special armed guard, and they were then transported to Haverfordwest Gaol by a troop commanded by Major Parlby. A Petty Sessions has already been held, and the pair have been remanded in custody on charges of murder, rape, riot, theft and various other charges. It is widely expected that when their cases come before the Quarter Sessions judge, they will be condemned to hang.

ΩΩΩΩΩΩΩΩΩΩΩ

15. And the Smoke Drifts Away

6th March 1844

Spring, blessed spring, and I am learning once again how to love this place. That process is helped by the exuberant birdsong which washes up the slope from the *cwm* every morning, come rain or shine, and by the freshness of the air and the golden warmth of the sun. With my foolish obsession with Rebecca, I had forgotten to look at my world, and to smell the delicate scent of hedgerow violets, and to listen to the wild sounds of kites and buzzards wheeling high overhead. But now Rebecca, like King Arthur in the days of Welsh heroes, can go to sleep in the knowledge that her task is done, ready to be wakened should she ever be needed again. King Arthur is said to be asleep with his warriors around him, in some mighty cave in North Wales; Rebecca, if she wishes, can sleep in my cave on Carningli, although there is no room for all her daughters.

Within this blessed house, the last three weeks have not been easy. All four of us women have been trying to come to terms with what almost happened and with what did happen, and poor Gwenno has had a particularly tough time of it. She is pretty and vivacious and is normally full of the energy and optimism of youth, but she was so deeply affected by the brutality of Zeke Tomos and Shoni Sgubor Fawr that on some days she has been terrified to leave her cottage and to come to the Plas, even with Gomer walking alongside her and holding her hand. Liza has spent a lot of time with her, and so have Bessie and I, and our dear friend Shemi has been as strong as the mightiest oak and as sensitive as gossamer. He has enfolded Gwenno in a magical cocoon of caring and tenderness, and although he is a man (and a big strong man at that) he seems to have an instinctive appreciation of what is in her mind and what is needed by way of healing. And she is getting better, thank God, with every day that passes. As for us older women, each one of us has had difficult days, and each one of us has wept a great deal; but somehow we have avoided corporate dark days, and by some miracle of the human mind when one of us has been low the other two of us have contrived to be as chirpy as sparrows. So we have come through it.

407

And the Smoke Drifts Away

Gomer was at first profoundly affected by the incident in the kitchen, and was afflicted by rage and guilt in equal measure -- rage at the brutality of his fellow men, and guilt that he was away at the *cnapan* play when his wife was being subjected to all the terrors of Hell. If Zeke had not been dead already, he might have rushed off, hunted him down and killed him with his bare hands. But he had to support Gwenno and forget about himself, and he did all that a good husband should do in such appalling circumstances, and more. Will was a great support to him, and Ioan and Brynach also stood by his shoulder and helped out around the farm when, for whatever reason, he failed to turn up for work. Thankfully, it has been a quiet season on the land, and we have had wonderful support from my tenants and labourers, to the extent that on some days we have had more people here offering their services than I could find jobs for. Speaking for myself, I thank the bright stars in Heaven that I have an estate to run, and grandchildren to care about, and friends who love me...............

Tom has not been to see me of late, but today I read one of his excellent reports in the *Times*. It said that the Royal Commission which has been looking into the Turnpike Trusts and the grievances in West Wales has completed its deliberations and has written its report. That lengthy and detailed document, containing a verbatim record of the testimonies of hundreds of people, will now be considered by the Government with a view to the introduction of new legislation. An uneasy truce exists between Rebecca and the authorities, and new episodes of gate burning and gatehouse destruction are few and far between. That is not surprising, since there are few gates left standing in West Wales! Most of the incidents that do occur are not really initiated by Rebecca at all, but are opportunistic actions by petty criminals or the working out of little feuds between one family or another. These incidents do not have much public support, but they still worry Tom as they worry me. Neither of us will be happy until new laws bring real peace back to the countryside, at which time the public will start to work with the constables and the army to suppress the activities of lawbreakers and thugs and nuisances.

Today Master Hugh Williams called to see me, quite openly since neither of us is worried any longer about spies and informers. Tongues may still wag, but I have coped with that before and can cope with it again. He called some weeks ago, soon after the incident in the kitchen, but that was not an easy visit since I was still suffering from nightmares and was in a very strange mood. He tried to cheer me up on that occasion, and indeed succeeded to some degree, and I was grateful for his concern and for his gentlemanly insistence in helping me with practical matters relating to inquests and so forth. But this time I have to admit that I greatly enjoyed his visit. I felt much more like my old self, and we walked together on the mountain, talked of family and friends, and laughed together. I count him now as a good friend. He is still arrogant and insufferable in many ways, and I still do not find him particularly attractive, but he is witty and well-informed, and as Bessie keeps on reminding me, companionship is a valuable commodity, not to be rejected out of hand. As for him, now that he has got the message that I have no wish to invite him to join me between my sheets, he is more relaxed and more natural in his manner of behaving. And of course, since he is not dreaming about hidden treasures the whole time, he is a good deal more attractive because his priorities have changed. I think -- and indeed he tells me this -- that he greatly values my friendship, my conversation and my hospitality. I am sure that those sentiments are honestly expressed.

There is one other matter to report. Squire Owen of Gelli Fawr has been arrested and charged with the murder of Nathaniel Evans and Samson Wilson. He currently languishes in Haverfordwest Gaol, and his case may well come up for trial at the next Quarter Sessions, possibly on the same day as the cases against Shoni Sgubor Fawr and Dai'r Cantwr. He may hope that he will escape the gallows on the grounds that he is a squire, but the evidence against him is very powerful. And in some ways he deserves the rope more than the others, for he has abused his position of power and responsibility to spy on others, to corrupt the workings of the legal system, to promote self-interest, and indeed to pervert the course of justice. More to the point, it is now clear that he has killed two men with his own hands and then tried to pin the blame on Rebecca.

The constables did little enough to bring the fellow to justice, but Shemi showed exactly the same devotion to the truth as my beloved Joseph Harries did all those years ago, and he dug about and kept on digging until he found it. He was encouraged in his endeavours by the findings of the inquest jury which pointed towards murder, and then he was supported by some of the honest squires from the neighbourhood, including Nicholas Lloyd Cwmgloyn and Stephen Prosser Frongoch. They wanted justice done, in spite of the crude pressure placed upon them by Squire Owen and his cronies to stay well clear of dirty business. In the end, by patient work, Shemi demonstrated that the paint used to daub the cottage at Clyn came from the Squire's own carpentry shop, and that there were traces of it upon an old pair of breeches which he wore around the estate. How he obtained access to the breeches is a mystery to me, but wizards move in mysterious ways and clearly have privileged access to the wardrobes of the gentry. Then, while the corpses of Masters Evans and Wilson lay in the Parrog Mortuary, he managed to extract the balls which had killed them from the wounds in their skulls. Then he matched those to one of the pistols in the Squire's armoury and showed from little scratches on them that they were fired from that weapon and no other. He interviewed the Squire, who became very belligerent and frightened, and although he personally did not collapse under questioning it was a different matter with his servants. They have always feared him and hated him, and Shemi has now obtained sworn statements from a number of them which show that on the night in question the Squire went out late, having extracted his pistol from his gun cabinet and having put it in his pocket; that on the same evening he took a can of paint and a brush from the carpentry shop, and a large can of turpentine oil; that he was seen returning to Gelli Fawr in the early hours, shortly before the alarm went up concerning the burning cottage; and that the clothes which he subsequently thrust into the washtub in the laundry had both soot and turpentine on them. Circumstantial evidence, maybe, but Hugh Williams is of the view that a strong prosecuting attorney will batter him with it to such an extent that a confession becomes almost inevitable.

ΩΩΩΩΩΩΩΩΩΩΩ

20th May 1844

About a week ago my dear friend Tom Foster wrote to me from London to say that the response from the Government to the recommendations of the Royal Commission has been almost entirely positive, and that legislation has now been drafted. If all goes well, it will come before the Queen for her signature before the end of the summer. The most interesting thing in Tom's letter was the information that John Frederick Campbell, otherwise known as Earl Cawdor, is the man entrusted by the Prime Minister with the task of seeing the new Act through Parliament. He had been asked originally if he would act as chairman of the Royal Commission which has recently reported, but had had to decline that invitation. But Tom is now greatly encouraged. He has met the great man, and he says that he knows West Wales so well, and has such a deep sympathy for the plight of the poor farmers, that he will be more than capable of dealing with any of the defensive ploys that might be employed by conservative squires and members of parliament to preserve the status quo and to resist reform.

Now it so happens that Earl Cawdor is the son of Lord Cawdor, the man who was saved from disaster at the time of the French Invasion by my husband David. The old Lord Cawdor was also the man who extracted me from prison many years ago and who subsequently saw that my enemies were brought to justice. That was in partial repayment of the debt that he owed to David, but when I met him in later years, on two or three occasions, he never failed to remind me that I should call upon him if ever I required assistance in the future. If there is one thing above all others which preoccupies the members of the Pembrokeshire gentry it is the calculation of indebtedness; and I am certain to this day that Lord Cawdor, in his own estimation, had repaid only a part of his debt to the Morgan family of Plas Ingli when he died in 1821. With this in mind, I made some inquiries as to the current whereabouts of the Earl, and discovered last Tuesday that he was currently at his country seat at Stackpole for a short break between parliamentary sessions.

After considerable thought I sat down and penned the following brief letter:

Plas Ingli, Newport, Pembrokeshire
Tuesday 14th May 1844

My Dear Lord Cawdor,
We have not met, but if you are as knowledgeable and curious as your late father you will know at least a little about me. I am Mistress of the Plas Ingli estate, beneath the shadow of Carningli and not far from

411

And the Smoke Drifts Away

*Newport, which I hold for my lifetime although it is owned by my son
Brynach Morgan, Squire of Llanychaer and Plas Ingli.*

*You are a busy man, and I am reluctant to write to you in this fashion,
but many years ago your father promised that if I should ever need help in
any matter, he would do his best for me so long as it was in his power. That
kind assurance was given following the French Invasion of our beloved
country in 1797, when my late husband David was able to provide some
assistance to your father which then enabled him to avoid a French
ambush. That was a long time ago, and you probably know nothing about
it, but it provided a little bond between your family and mine which I
value to this day.*

*Might I pay you a brief visit at Stackpole on the afternoon of Friday
next? I must return to Plas Ingli on the same day, but an interview of
perhaps thirty minutes would be greatly appreciated if that does not
conflict with any other appointment in your diary. I seek assistance not for
myself but for many others, and I dare to hope that it may be within your
power to provide it.*

I send my warmest greetings to you and your beloved family.
Yours truly
Martha Morgan
Mistress

I sent it to Stackpole with Gomer, on our fastest horse, and I was
more than a little surprised when he returned ten hours later with a note
written in the Earl's own hand. It gave me a great deal of encouragement,
for this is what it said:

Stackpole
Tuesday 14th May 1844

My Dear Mistress Martha,
*It gave me great pleasure to receive your note written this morning.
You are in luck that I am currently in residence, since I spend most of my
time in London these days, deeply involved in affairs of State. But here I
can breathe and be happy, and my happiness will be increased by a visit
from you on the afternoon suggested at two of the clock.*
I know a good deal more about you and your family than you might

412

imagine. My father told me more than once of the heroic action of your late husband in saving him from a certain catastrophe during the French Invasion; and he swore that that heroism saved both his career and the fortune of our family. He spoke of you too, in glowing terms, as a brave and independent lady who has had to cope with personal tragedy on a scale which would have led most of us into the depths of despair. But, dare I say it, your beauty and your indomitable spirit have made you into something of a legend among the members of the Welsh gentry. How could I have been ignorant of your name and your reputation in such circumstances?

You might be interested to know, Mistress Martha, that in recent weeks there has been a good deal of talk about you here in London. For that you can blame your friend Thomas Campbell Foster, a great admirer, who has taken it upon himself to publicize the disturbances in Wales in as forthright a manner as may be imagined, much to the disgust of some of my fellow members of parliament! He has told me of your role as a conciliator, and of your promotion of the principles of peaceful protest, and on both counts you deserve the gratitude of the nation. And then I have read Master Foster's recent account in the Times of that appalling incident in the kitchen of Plas Ingli and of your fortitude in conditions of great personal danger.

It will be my pleasure to welcome you to Stackpole, and I look forward to the occasion.

With affectionate greetings
John Frederick Campbell, Earl Cawdor

So on Friday last I travelled to Stackpole with Gomer in the chaise, on a bright and beautiful May morning. It was a long journey, since Stackpole lies on the south coast of the county, a very long way from everywhere and on the other side of the great waterway of Milford Haven, but Gomer and I enjoyed ourselves as we trotted along, and for my part I saw a good deal of pretty countryside that I had not seen before. We passed through at least twenty places where toll gates used to be located, and saw not a trace of a tollgate or a toll-collector. We passed assorted troops of soldiers here and there, and they all seemed considerably more relaxed than they were three months ago. Indeed, the tension, fear and suspicion which have disfigured this blessed county now seem to have fled away, to be replaced by a degree of confidence and ease.

Stackpole is a most extraordinary place, set in verdant pastures and perched high above a long and narrow lake said to have been formed by Lord Campbell through the damming of a little valley. The sea is not far away. There are woodlands and parklands, and the buildings on all parts of the estate are made of grey and white limestones the like of which we never see in the north of the county. The mansion must be one of the grandest in Wales, and one of the most gracious. I admired it enormously as we trotted towards it along the entrance driveway; but it would not suit me, for it must have cost a veritable fortune to build and it must require another fortune every year just to keep it in good order. Neither would I like to employ a staff of more than a hundred, since I have problems enough with five.

My meeting with the Earl was a delight, and it quite restored my faith in the Pembrokeshire gentry. Although I did not seek it, I spent two hours in his company, walking around his walled garden, and along the shores of his lily ponds, and through his leafy parklands. He is an affable and amusing gentleman who appeared only too happy to talk with some honesty about the intrigues and the strange ways of Westminster, and when we got onto the subject of the Rebecca Riots he proved to be even more knowledgeable than I had anticipated. And he knew more about me than I had guessed from the contents of his letter. As we talked, I looked beyond his diplomatic turn of phrase and his careful use of words and saw quite clearly that I had been intensely observed by the Home Office. It was clear that he had been briefed by Colonel Love, and I hoped that that briefing had been selective rather than comprehensive. The Earl certainly knew more than I had appreciated about *Mam-gu* Becca and about the manner in which Rebecca had organized her daughters over the past five years. But he grinned, as I did, when we discussed the ease with which the army had been defeated and the problems encountered by the magistrates in making arrests and in obtaining convictions on the key personalities behind the riots.

This brought me to the reason for my journey to Stackpole. I did not need to remind the Earl of the debt which his family owed to mine -- that would have been crass in the extreme. But I asked him in the politest possible way to leave no stone unturned in his efforts to bring the Turnpike Trusts Bill onto the statute book. I urged him to devote all his attention to improving the draft Bill so as to address as many as possible of the grievances of the poor farmers of West Wales, many of whom he counted as his tenants. "Sir, I ask this not for myself but for the people of Wales," I said. "I have a good life, as I daresay you do, but there are many who do not, and if you can obtain the Queen's signature on this piece of legislation it will be the thing, above all others, which will show that when the people make demands which are just and farsighted, our political leaders have the wisdom and the generosity of spirit to respond. I trust, sir, that this Act may become a more lasting memorial to you and your family than the wonderful mansion built by your father."

"You are a very persuasive woman, Mistress Martha, and I am greatly relieved that I can count you as an ally rather than an adversary. I have many items to deal with in parliament over the coming months, and in truth I was minded, before today, to leave the Turnpike Trusts Bill in the hands of junior colleagues. But I will do as you ask. I will place the papers relating to this Act at the top of the pile which plagues my desk, and I will give this matter my personal attention and my highest priority. I can guarantee nothing, for there are many doughty opponents who fear change as much as they fear the onset of old age. Some of them, I know, are already well past any understanding of what this is all about. But leave it with me if you will, and we shall see whether we cannot do something here of which we can all be proud."

So I took my leave of this gracious gentleman, and waved to him as he stood at his grandiose front door and watched us go. "You have got a good and faithful friend there, Mistress," said Gomer, as he gave the pony a flick of the whip. "I daresay that he will move Heaven and Earth just to make you happy."

"Rubbish, Gomer! What makes you think that?"

"Oh, just his eyes, Mistress," grinned my faithful manservant. "He is a very grand fellow, and when you arrived he had the eyes of a gun-dog, bright and sharp. But when you left, he had the eyes of a sheepdog puppy, keen to earn a lump of sugar for fetching a stick. Personally, I put it down to the red dress and the emerald necklace, but maybe there is more to it than that.............."

I boxed his ears for that piece of insolence, and we laughed so much that I almost fell out of the chaise as we went round a sharp corner at breakneck speed.

3rd June 1844

A miracle has happened, and I declare myself to be the happiest woman on earth. I have still not properly come to terms with it, and my emotions are so disturbed just now that my nearest and dearest must think me mad. I trust that they will forgive me, and that I may at some stage return to normality.

Yesterday morning, with a strong wind buffeting the house and with summer rain sweeping in from the west, we were getting on quietly with what appeared to be a perfectly normal day. I was upstairs, sitting at my desk and gazing out at the sodden landscape, trying to concentrate on the estate accounts. Liza was tidying up my bedroom, humming a little tune as she worked. Bessie was preparing vegetables for our dinner, and Gwenno was in the dairy, turning over the butter churn with as much energy as she could manage. Gomer was dressed in his oilskins, cleaning out the cowshed, I daresay with the shovel that I had used to hit Barti Richards on the head. Will was pottering back and forth across the yard, similarly covered up against the weather, feeding the horses and no doubt cursing the rain.

Then, in the distance, I saw the chaise belonging to Tom Transportation coming up the driveway from the Cilgwyn Road. I knew it was his, because it had a red hood with "Elegant Conveyances for Hire" painted on it in large letters. There were several large bags and bundles tied to the back, on the luggage rack. Who on earth could this be? I was mightily intrigued, and said so to Liza, and so the pair of us stood in the window, with our arms around each other, and watched as the elegant conveyance came closer and closer. It did not stop at the front door, but proceeded through the gate into the yard, indicating that the passenger was intent upon entering the house through the kitchen door. More and more intriguing. Liza and I rushed out onto the landing and looked out through the window at the top of the staircase, which afforded a better view of proceedings.

The chaise was halted, and the passenger or passengers remained out of sight under the hood while Tom braved the drenching rain and carried all of the baggage into the kitchen. I heard a snatch of conversation between him and Bessie. Then he helped down a single figure onto the glistening black flagstones of the yard, and she paid him his fee.

It looked as if she was intent upon staying, maybe for a long time. She opened up a small and colourful urban umbrella, and held it over her head. Then Tom doffed his hat, climbed up into the driving seat, and drove off down the driveway back towards Newport. The lady stood in the rain for a few moments, as if unsure what to do, and then she took a deep breath and made for the kitchen door.

Liza and I looked at each other and shrugged, and then went downstairs to see who this mysterious visitor might be. I came into the kitchen and saw a large woman wearing a wide-brimmed and very fashionable straw bonnet, with her body draped in an elegant green cloak. I remember looking at her feet, and thinking that those delicate blue boots were not intended for use in farmyards. She looked at me, and then she said: "Mother......?"

I knew in an instant that the woman before me was Daisy, my long-lost and beloved daughter whom I had wished above all else in the world to be alive, but whom I had feared to be dead. My prodigal daughter had returned to Plas Ingli. From that point on, on that morning of miracles, my recollections are hazy. I recall shouting "Daisy! Oh, Daisy! Is it really you?" and rushing into her arms, and weeping. Then she wept too. Liza slumped onto the settle by the fire, with tears streaming down her face. Bessie stood with her eyes wide and her face white, as if she had seen a ghost; but then she smiled too, and was overtaken by emotion, and wept tears of joy. Then Gwenno came in from the dairy, wondering what all the fuss was about, and stood there with a bemused look on her face, wiping her hands on her apron. For some reason that caused me to behave even more strangely, for I abandoned Daisy and grabbed Gwenno, and dragged her in a sort of wild Irish jig around the kitchen table, shouting at the top of my voice "Oh Gwenno, Daisy has come home! Daisy has returned!" At last I had to stop and catch my breath, and I saw that Bessie and Daisy were embracing like long-lost sisters. There was a big difference in age between them, of course, but I should not have been surprised at this show of obvious affection, for Bessie had been a maid at the Plas during Daisy's childhood and had seen the seemingly unending conflict between mother and daughter that had finally resulted in her departure for London in the year 1821.

Then Gomer appeared in his disgusting oilskins, covered in dung and bits of straw and dripping polluted rainwater, and so did Will, looking not much tidier. Our tears turned to laughter, for seldom had any of us observed a scene of greater incongruity, featuring two grizzled and filthy farm servants confronting a portly lady dressed in the most elegant and expensive of London fashions. Daisy smiled at the two men. "Will?" she asked. "Is it you? I think I recognize you and remember you from those good old days of long ago........."

"Indeed it is, Mistress. But I fear that I do not recognize you."

"Will, I am Daisy, the horrible child who walked out of this place more than twenty years since and swore never to return." She turned to Gomer. "And you must be Gomer? I think that you were just a child when I left, but I do remember you as a mischievous little fellow with a hatred of small girls. I know a good deal about you, of course, from all those letters written by my mother. I would love to embrace both of you kind gentlemen, if you would be so considerate as to get out of those oilskins......."

And there was more laughter, and more embracing, and more tears, and we spent the morning all talking at once. Not a lot of work was done for the rest of the day, and of course I sent messages at once to Brynach and Betsi, and to Shemi and Sian who had both loved Daisy dearly when she had been a little child. The Plas became even more chaotic when Betsi and Ioan arrived, followed closely by Brynach and the children from Plas Llanychaer, and the Wizard of Werndew and his dear wife. Of course we had to kill the fatted calf, and Betsi and Liza produced a mountain of good things for the table. We used the dining room, for I took a sudden dislike to the kitchen table. Will, whom I trust a good deal in the management of my cellar, produced two dozen bottles of my most expensive French and Portuguese wines, and a few bottles of brandy and porter, and I am ashamed to report that at the end of the evening they had all disappeared.

I gave Daisy the room next to mine, which used to be the nursery, and she settled in with Liza's assistance. She was very tired, and once our wild homecoming party had broken up she slept for a long time. As the house settled into quietness I lay awake and gazed at the ceiling in the warm darkness, euphoric and slightly drunk, but with my mind buzzing. I knew that there was a good deal of territory to be covered with Daisy over the weeks and months that lie ahead, for while I had written her a stream of letters she had never once replied, and I knew virtually nothing about what had been happening in her life. I hoped that she would be honest with me, but I braced myself for some very uncomfortable revelations. I was also realistic enough to know that we were now strangers to each other, and that she was even a stranger to her sister Betsi and her brother Brynach. How would they react to her arrival in our midst, and to the obsessive attention that I would now lavish upon her? Would jealousy, resentment and even anger come bubbling up to the surface? And how would she adapt to life in rural West Wales, a place where, in her estimation, nothing ever happens? Questions, questions, and more questions, spinning round and round in my head. They were still tumbling and spinning when I drifted into sleep.

Today, with the rain headed for England and with Carningli and the *cwm* bathed in mellow sunlight, I was able to spend some time alone with Daisy. She is very unfit, and does not appear to have walked anywhere for the last twenty years, but I dragged her, puffing, up to the rocky bank adjacent to Ffynnon Brynach, where we sat down with our arms about each other and surveyed the world.

"Oh Mother," she sighed. "This place is so, so beautiful that I can hardly bear to look at it. How was it that I ever chose to leave it? I must have been mad. Indeed, I believe I was mad, tipped over the edge of reason by stupid dreams of glamour, and fame, and unmeasurable wealth..........."

She spent a long time staring across the misty *cwm*, watching the mist swirling and rising after yesterday's rain. "Now then, Daisy, there are a million things that I need to know. First, the children. You said last night, in the middle of all that chatter in the dining room, that you have three children. Where are they, and how old are they, and what are their names? I have to know everything........"

Daisy laughed, and her eyes gleamed as I remember them gleaming in the years of her childhood. "Dear Mother!" said she. "You will know everything, all in good time. In fact, I fear that you will have to wait until tomorrow, for today I have work to do."

"Whatever do you mean, Daisy?"

"Well, in answer, Mother dear, let me ask you another question. Why do you think that I have suddenly returned home?"

"Could it be because you love me, and love the Plas?"

"Of course. Both of those things. But there are other things too. I have led an utterly useless life, Mother, self-centred and hedonistic to an extent which you, in your wonderful innocence, could never imagine. I will spare you the sordid details. Suffice to say that when I was young and beautiful the world of London society was at my feet. Gentlemen swarmed around me like wasps around a juicy apple. I appeared at all of the great social occasions, sometimes on the arm of one gentleman and sometimes on the arm of another. For a while I was kept by the Prince Regent, and when he became respectable I flitted from one grand house to another, from one apartment to another, wanting for nothing. I was on terms which we might describe as "intimate" with more gentlemen than I care to mention. I was at the centre of more than one scandal, and I daresay I was responsible for the destruction of more than one marriage. My three children were born, of three different fathers, and they are the real blessings of my life. They have good allowances, all three, and they are happy enough. I am not proud, Mother, of that phase of my life........."

Her voice broke, and I saw that tears were welling up into her eyes. I squeezed her hand, but said nothing, for I sensed that she wished to continue.

"But then, Mother, as I became fat and old, I realized that my place on the arm of my latest patron could no longer be assured. I found that I was not invited to the great social occasions any longer, and that young ladies the same age as my daughter were taking my place in society. Not to put too fine a point on it, Mother, I was put out to grass. I did not want for comfort, for it is the rule in London that ex-Mistresses are well supported so long as they obey the first rule of polite society -- discretion. So I was discreet, and humble, and got on with my life as best I could, in conditions of increasing loneliness."

"Oh Daisy, I am so sorry."

At that she laughed. "Mother, you are truly not of this world! Why should you be sorry for me, when I have always been the captain of my own destiny, and when I have richly deserved every punishment that life may now choose to throw at me? But I must move on. In recent years I have read your letters with increasing emotion, although I was too frightened, always, to reply to a single one of them. I think I wanted you to believe me to be dead, since I thought that that would be preferable to meeting you again and having to tell you what I am telling you now. I always was a coward, Mother. Then in the long hours spent in my own company, I took to reading the *Times*. Some years back, I read of the disturbances in the three counties, and wondered idly whether you might have any knowledge of them. Then, last year, I suddenly saw the reports sent in by a man called Thomas Campbell Foster.........."

"Why, how wonderful, Daisy! I count him as a dear friend."

"I thought as much. His reports were so vivid and so terrifying that I bought the newspaper every day, looking for his latest dispatch from the troubled districts. I read that the troubles were flaring up around Newport and Dinas, and then that somebody called Rebecca was organizing a campaign of resistance against the army and the magistrates. I do not know why, Mother, but I knew of your concern for the poor, and I knew in the depths of my stomach that you were involved in the riots. I felt on several occasions that you were in grave danger, and that I must come home and help you. But as cowardly as I was, I resisted. Then I read Master Foster's account of the truly appalling episode in the kitchen of this blessed house. I was so terrified, Mother, that I was physically sick. Then I walked round and round in my apartment for hours, thinking and thinking as I have never thought before. I decided to seek advice, and went to see my old friend Sir James Love on one of his visits to the city.........."

"Good God, Daisy, you cannot be serious! I know him too, and have a great respect for him. He never mentioned that he knew you."

"And why should he, Mother? He did not know, until I met him a few days ago, that my real name is Daisy Morgan and that I was born and bred in Plas Ingli."

"Daisy, I am getting old," I groaned, "and I am now very confused. Please will you tell me what this is all about?"

"My pleasure, Mother. I think I knew it already, but Sir James confirmed to me that you have been intimately involved in these riots from the very beginning, and that you have placed yourself in appalling danger as a result -- not once or twice, but continuously, year after year. Take it from me, mother, that he is a very great admirer of yours. I asked him what I might do to help your great cause and to ensure your safety. More to the point, I asked him what I might do to keep you out of mischief in the future. He thought for a long time and then said that in his estimation the thing that you wanted most passionately in life was not a new dress or even a small fortune, but the passage of the Turnpike Trusts Bill and the removal of the burdens borne by the poor people of Wales. If those things could be achieved, he said, he thought that you might be truly happy. So before I abandoned London and headed west, Mother dear, Sir James and I talked well into the night about what might be done."

"Daughter, I am still confused."

"I decided, Mother, that I should deliver the Turnpike Trusts Act to you, in the hands of a new daughter."

"But Daisy, the Act is not yours to deliver. It has to go through parliament, and even Lord Cawdor is not certain of it..........."

"You fail to appreciate, Mother, what leverage a courtesan has over those gentlemen who have enjoyed her hospitality. Lord Cawdor is an honourable man, and I have never had any dealings with him, but there are forty or fifty others, in positions of great responsibility both within the government and the opposition, about whom I know too much for their indefinite comfort..........."

"Daisy! You do not mean to say that you plan to blackmail them? That would be a wicked thing to do!"

Daisy laughed. "No no, Mother. Nothing so crude. You are as cunning as a vixen, says Sir James, but he also loves your naivety, and I begin to understand why he is your devoted servant! This is a wicked world, and I would not have survived in it if I had not learnt its wicked ways. I have given all of these gentlemen favours in the past, and favours must always be returned. This afternoon, when we have anointed ourselves in this crystal spring and have returned to the Plas, I am going to write at least fifty letters to the most famous men in the land. I will not mention their names to you, for that would be indiscreet. I will gently remind each one of these gentlemen of a particular debt that I am owed, and I may, if I am so moved, mention certain facts which are in my possession and which are best kept out of the public domain. Then I will ask them for one favour -- namely the easy passage of the Turnpike Trusts Act and support for legislation reforming the Poor Laws, the Corn Laws and the collection of tithes and church rates. They will do this for me, and their reward will be my silence."

Then I laughed too, and with so much mirth that I had to hang onto Daisy in order to avoid falling into Saint Brynach's sacred spring. "Oh Daisy!" I spluttered. "You are quite incorrigible! Where on earth did you learn how to manipulate innocent gentlemen in this quite outrageous fashion?"

"From you, Mother, if truth be told."

So we laughed, mother and daughter, as if we had been two small girls giggling over the foibles of a first boyfriend. We anointed each other with sacred water from the spring, and then, hand in hand, we skipped back to the Plas. When we got there I gave Daisy a pile of paper and envelopes, and a pen and a full ink-pot, and left her to write her letters.

ΩΩΩΩΩΩΩΩΩΩΩ

10th August 1844

Almost three months have passed, and life at Plas Ingli has entered a new phase. Daisy has settled in and is proving to be a delightful companion. She has to relearn the ways of the country, and she has to rebuild her relationships with her brother and sister, and with my servants, and with a good many others besides. But she is trying, and I love her dearly. She has thrown away her blue boots and her patterned umbrella, and has taken to wearing rough clothes and to walking on the mountain. She has a bloom upon her cheek and a new sparkle in her eye, and whenever I look at her I am reminded that she was once the prettiest young lady in the *cwm*, and the one lusted after by every red-blooded male within a radius of twenty miles. She has lost a stone already as a result of her new spartan diet, and she becomes more attractive with every day that passes.

As for those letters, they must have had a miraculous effect, for according to messages which I have received from Tom Foster the legislation which we all desire has had a remarkably smooth passage. He can hardly believe it, and neither can the Government. The signs of a successful outcome were good, and we all knew what was coming, but this very morning I received a letter by express messenger from Lord Cawdor himself. It was short and to the point, and read as follows:

House of Commons, 9th day of August 1844
My Dear Martha,
I have wonderful news for you and for the whole of Wales. This very morning the Queen graciously gave her Royal Assent to the Turnpike

And the Smoke Drifts Away

Trusts Act, which will have the effect of reforming and regulating the trusts and ridding the poor farmers of many of the huge burdens that they have had to bear in past years.   In the event there was virtually no opposition from my fellow members of parliament -- a thing which is in my experience unprecedented.   Even my most implacable enemies across the floor of the chamber appear to have been bewitched on the occasions set aside for discussion of the details of the Act, and I am at a loss to understand the extent to which peace has broken out amongst ancient political adversaries.   No matter.   We have won a great victory, and others will follow in short order when the other grievances identified by Tom Foster, Colonel Love and the Royal Commission have been addressed.

With my best wishes for a successful harvest,
Your friend
John Frederick Campbell
Earl Cawdor, MP

When I received this letter, I was all alone in the house, for Shemi has decreed that the weather will break tomorrow, and all available hands were required to help with the Brithdir wheat harvest. So off they had all gone immediately after breakfast, including that intrepid harvester Daisy Morgan, leaving me to keep an eye on the animals, and to snooze in the shade of the orchard. On the receipt of the letter I should have felt euphoria, but all I felt was a sort of emptiness and weariness. So I decided to leave the animals to themselves for an hour or so and to take a walk on the mountain. I climbed and climbed, with the blue rocks baking in the heat of the mid-day sun and with the distant peaks of Mynydd Preseli quivering and dancing in the heat haze. There was a mirage away to the west, and I could see the mountains of Ireland standing high and proud of the horizon. Skylarks carolled above my head, and on the summit a yellow wagtail hopped about, quite unconcerned at my presence, gorging himself on flying ants. Down below, in the topmost Brithdir field, I could see maybe thirty people hard at work on the harvest. I could pick out Daisy. She saw me on the summit, and we waved to each other.

Then I needed to retreat from the heat, and I decided on a few minutes of peace in my cave. I clambered down and followed my normal route between crags and along crevices and through little gaps between boulders. I slipped between the ferns which covered the narrow slit entrance, and as I did so I noticed the two ravens, sitting just a few feet away -- the King of the Mountain and his Queen, once more left to themselves now that their brood had moved on to new territories. I thanked them for their devotion and for their protection, and in acknowledgement they bobbed their heads and looked me in the eye, and launched themselves into a warm gust of air rising across the flank of the mountain.

Inside the cool and dark cave I found, as ever, a sort of peace. I settled myself down and breathed as deeply as I could. I cast away the terrors of past months and tried to replace them in my mind with all that was good and beautiful in my life. Truly, I had much to be grateful for. I mulled over the things which my servants and family had been saying to me, over and again, over the past three months. They had said that I must stop this business of saving the world and indulge myself for a change. They had said that I thought too much of others, and too little of myself. Serenity, I thought, is what I have to find, combined with the sort of inner strength that Grandma Jane had, all those years ago when I had been a wild and emotional young woman. Yes, I thought, I will become a recluse and a saint, passing gently through life like a white cloud, thinking beautiful thoughts and spreading peace and light in all directions. I thought I might become a nun, and abandon the Plas and all that it stood for, and write hymns and poetry by which I might be remembered. So I made my contract with God.

I always was a fickle creature, and my contract with God did not last long. As I sat at the back of the cave, I was stirred from my reverie by the sound of the Plas Ingli bell. I do not know if the sound was real or imaginary, but I thought I had better respond to it, and so I climbed gently down the mountainside in the stifling heat of the afternoon. I could see no signs of anything urgent at the Plas, so I did not hurry. I splashed some holy water from Ffynnon Brynach onto my face and arms and legs as I went past. When I got into the yard I saw a horse tethered alongside the drinking trough. The beast looked happy enough, so I went into the kitchen. Who should be there but Master Hugh Williams, snoozing and snoring, with his chin upon his chest.

"Why, Master Williams!" said I. "What a surprise on this fine summer's day!"

He woke with a start, and apologized for taking possession of my kitchen without being invited in. There was nobody around, he said, so he thought he would wait. Then, before I could forgive him, he started to chatter like an excited schoolboy who has just had his first pat of approval from a fierce teacher. "Martha! I have wonderful news for you! I came straight here because I wanted to be the first to tell you! We have won! The Act has just received the Royal Assent, and everything we asked for has been granted............."

I held my hand up and stopped him in full flow. "Enough, Master Williams. You are too late, since I have the news already. No matter. I am bored with politics, and intrigues, and noble causes, and I never want to hear another word about Wales and its problems. I am minded to turn over a new leaf. Just now it is my intention to go upstairs, and lie on my back, and close my eyes, and think beautiful thoughts. In that enterprise, Master Williams, I need your help."

And before he could react, I took him by the hand and led him out of the kitchen and up the staircase.

Martha Morgan

10th Day of August 1844

ΩΩΩΩΩΩΩΩΩΩΩ

Acknowledgements

As ever, I thank my wife Inger for her endless help during the writing of this book, and for encouraging me to press on towards the completion of the *Angel Mountain* Saga. She has acted as referee, editor, reviewer and proof-reader, and specialist adviser on the female psyche! Stephen, Alison and Martin, Heather and Ken, Hilary and Richard have all given huge family support, and many of my friends have given practical help. I thank them all. Those who have become immersed in the ongoing story of my heroine Martha Morgan and who have been kind enough to write to me with their comments have also spurred me on in my tight schedule of writing and publishing one novel per year for five years.

A great deal of research has gone into *Rebecca and the Angels*, and I should like to acknowledge my debt to publications by David Williams, Pat Molloy, Richard Rose, David Howell, Brian Howells and others. Alexander Cordell's fine novel *Hosts of Rebecca* has been invaluable in helping me to recreate "the mood of the times". Many others have provided me with factual information, and I thank them all.

The illustration on page 24 is reputed to be a wood engraving by WJ Linton, who was a personal friend of Hugh Williams. It was first published in the *Illustrated London News* in 1842 and has been reproduced hundreds of times since then in many different formats.

I am grateful to Irene Payne, Ian Richardson, Robert Anthony and Fred Nicholls for refereeing and commenting upon versions of the text. Irene's generous and detailed editorial input over many months is especially appreciated. Finally, a word of thanks to the Welsh Books Council and Yr Academi Gymraeg for their ongoing support for the writing of Welsh fiction in English.

Brian John

Publisher's Note: Readers should note that this is a work of fiction which should not be used as a historical guide to the Rebecca Riots. While many of the episodes portrayed in the story did happen, and while many of the characters in the story did exist, the author has taken considerable liberties with history in the interests of telling a good story. In particular, the map on pages 274-275 should **not** be taken as a true representation of the turnpike trust roads of West Wales.

Some Published Reviews of
ON ANGEL MOUNTAIN

Welsh Living: Need a book to snuggle up with by the fire? This is it -- a stirring tale of the rebuilding of the fortunes of a Pembrokeshire farming family in the 18th century told through the diary of the young mistress of the house. It's got the lot --love, nature, mystery, mysticism and a lot of charm -- a bit Wilkie Collins. The period detail is so authentic you forget it's recently written.

Keith Johnson, Pembrokeshire Life: There's a lot of colourful period detail woven into the story.......The author shows life as it was for the poor tenants as well as the rich landowners, with no attempt to romanticize the past........... It's a well-paced and well-plotted tale with a gripping finale and a strong sense of place.

Dean Powell, Western Mail Magazine: Few 60-year-old men write their first novel through the eyes of a suicidal 18-year-old woman living in 18th Century Wales. But that's precisely what Brian John has done.. The concept was imaginative and enjoyable......

Margaret Jenkins, Gwales.com (with the permission of Welsh Books Council): The diary gives a colourful account of the life, beliefs, traditions, and working practices in a country estate belonging to a family of the minor gentry. The author's intimate knowledge of the subject is apparent on every page. It is soundly based on historical fact, and allusions to genuine historical people and events give it a feeling of authenticity. But this is more than just a diary of a country lady. Cleverly woven into the text runs a dark and sinister tale.

Fred Nicholls, County Echo newspaper: *On Angel Mountain* is well titled indeed, since its main location is the small mansion of Plas Ingli, under the south-eastern slopes of the beautiful Carningli, and in many ways the mountain itself is not merely a location but almost a character in the dramatic story. It is a sign of the writer's skill and imagination that we enter fully into Martha's vivid world......... If you enjoy a lively, skillful and exciting portrayal of real life in eighteenth-century Pembrokeshire, you will have to buy *On Angel Mountain*.

Some published reviews of
HOUSE OF ANGELS

Catherine Collins, County Echo: Readers are swept along on a roller-coaster of emotion, experiencing Martha's passionate love for her family and their mountainside home to her desire for truth and justice. The plot twists and turns with murder, hidden treasure and romance all preventing the reader from putting the book down until finished.

Robert Anthony, Western Telegraph: This is a splendidly-imagined and well-told tale of good triumphing over evil. The local colour is brilliantly imagined and the incidental historical detail, unobtrusively woven into the fabric of the narrative, is fascinating. Here is an adventure story in which the narrative never flags. The delineation of the main characters, especially the headstrong and irresistible Mistress Martha, by turns spiritual and earthy, is vivid and true.

Dean Powell, Western Mail: This time the beauty (Martha Morgan) is swept through a complex tale of murder, intrigue and romance. Mixing grief and pathos, exuberance and humour in equal measure, the whole narrative has a strong sense of place.

Welsh Living: The beauty of the country and the day to day business of farm life is set amidst intrigue and a collection of compelling characters to make a wonderful winter read.

Derek Rees, Western Telegraph: Martha Morgan becomes a very real person and the books are a compulsive read, with shades of Cordell and Cookson, although the author refutes outside influences apart from the brooding presence of Carningli itself.

Richard Jones, Planet: Martha Morgan, who is young and beautiful, tells the story through entries in her journal, with many descriptions of local characters and customs and so lyrical a response to the beauty of the landscape that she might have been influenced by Dorothy Wordsworth..... All this is satisfying and well told...... In terms of presentation other publishers might learn a few tricks.

Jo Barnes, One Wales magazine: Based on her diary, this novel, like its predecessor, reaches out and pulls you into Martha's small world..... Beautifully written, this book takes you on a journey which you will never forget. If it is not made into a lavish period drama for the television there is no justice!

Some published reviews of
DARK ANGEL

Richard Cluroe, Gwales.com, with the permission of the Welsh Books Council: The third of Brian John's five part Celtic Saga is a fast moving tale of mystery, romance and the supernatural set in the rugged landscape of North Pembrokeshire where the bluestone peak of Carningli -- Angel Mountain -- plays a crucial part.

Ceri Gould, Western Mail: This is the third volume of Brian John's highly popular Angel Mountain series. Many readers are already caught up in the dramatic events and in the heroine's emotional complexity......... Note also the richly textured background against which the drama is played out; the deep, underlying sense of place; the wisdom and humour of ordinary (and sometimes extraordinary) folk; and the keenly researched and observed cameos of domestic and rural life.

Irene Payne, Western Telegraph: The twists come thick and fast in the final few pages as we discover that nothing is quite as it seems. Brian John has again woven a colourful tale full of tension and authentic period detail and with a large supporting cast of characters both imaginary and drawn from history.   But the author's greatest creation is Martha Morgan herself, a flawed heroine who recognizes her own mistakes but is powerless to stop making them.

Keith Johnson, Pembrokeshire Life: The author has woven timelessness into the character of Martha Morgan. This is a love story, a tale of a complex, compelling creature on a voyage of discovery that veers between elation and despair and of a love lost and found. Martha reveals through her diary entries every innermost secret of her being. She is complex and mysterious, at times ruthless, yet it would appear that she is insecure, in spite of the warmth and advice of the people around her. This book is filled with goodness; it is filled with caring, compassionate people. It is a timeless and compelling tale.

Catherine Collins, Pembrokeshire Times: One of the country's most successful series of historical fiction. The author's interest in local history has allowed him to use his knowledge to best effect in a fictional format....... While *Pride and Prejudice* has the female character swooning over a man in wet clothing, Mistress Martha not only gets to see her men completely naked, but the reader shares in her delights and pleasures.

About the Author

Brian John was born in Carmarthen in 1940 and brought up in Pembrokeshire. He is married and has two grown up sons and two grandsons. He studied at Haverfordwest Grammar School and at Jesus College Oxford, where he read Geography and obtained his D Phil degree for a pioneering study of the Ice Age in Pembrokeshire. He then worked as a field scientist in Antarctica and spent eleven years as a Geography Lecturer in Durham University. He has travelled widely in the Arctic, Antarctic and Scandinavia. In 1977 he and his family moved to a smallholding near Newport in Pembrokeshire, and for the last 27 years he has made his living as a full-time writer and publisher. He is also actively involved in a number of environmental and community organizations. He has published hundreds of articles and over 50 books, and among his publishers are Collins, Pan, Orbis, Aurum Press/HMSO, Longman, David and Charles, Wiley and Edward Arnold. His published output includes university texts, walking guides, coffee table glossies, and books of popular science. Many of his titles have been published by Greencroft Books, and have covered topics of particular interest to readers in Wales -- for example tourist guides, books of local jokes, walkers' handbooks, and a series of books on local folklore and traditions. *Rebecca and the Angels* is the fourth novel in the Angel Mountain Saga. The three previous books have received wide acclaim for their narrative skill, their strong sense of place, and their historical authenticity. The Saga has been a runaway success, and the heroine, Mistress Martha Morgan, now has a cult following of readers from all over the world.